The Venerable
Vincent Beattie

The Venerable Vincent Beattie

A Novel by

Wil Glavin

First paperback edition August 2020

Book design by BuzBooks

ISBN: 978-0-578-71215-4 (paperback)
ISBN: 978-0-578-71216-1 (eBook)
Published by IngramSpark

To Wendy, Jim, Kyle, Oliver, Bill, Bill, RoseMary, Carl, Cath, Meghann, and Espy. Thank you for always inspiring me and molding me into the person I am today.

Table of Contents

Book 1

CHAPTER 1

THE INTIMIDATING HALLWAY WAS PROPPED up by a series of lengthy, gold columns and decorated with genuine Baroque vases and furniture. A collection of neatly trimmed orchids adorned the diminutive, eggshell marble tables that separated the east and west sides of the hall. The combination of the floor's recently shined tiles and the bright, overhead lights made the entire area shimmer. Several windows lined the symmetrical hallway and let in an adequate amount of sunlight for an autumn afternoon.

I attempted to hide my trepidation and focus on my sprightly companions, but once I became anxious, there was rarely a positive outcome.

I'd always found comfort in emulating those nearby, so I had ample practice mimicking the gait of those in front of me. Although the accompanying, reverberant sound of 160 shoes clacking against antique tiles was unfamiliar.

There were approximately 40 people lined up along the east side of the hallway, each with khaki pants, a navy blazer with gold buttons, and an air of atavistic smugness that couldn't be purchased nor emulated.

Twenty of my compatriots wore brown penny loafers and belts, while 19 of my peers and I wore black penny loafers and belts. There was no rhyme or reason as to why I wore black, nor was there any explanation as to how the colors were so evenly distributed. It was just one of the many, seemingly insignificant details that went overlooked.

The tie was the one area where creativity was commended. The color, design, and knot were all carefully examined by peers and superiors alike. My father once told me the best way to get to know a man is to look at his tie. Was it loosened with the top button undone? Was it a perfectly constructed Windsor knot? Did the tie have polka dots or animals or stripes? Were the stripes thin or thick? Was the tie checked? Was it wide or narrow? What was the tie's base color, and what were the undertones? The answer to each question painted an alluring portrait.

For example, according to my father's system, a thick, lime green tie with peach polka dots meant the person was boisterous, vain, and possibly lazy. Whereas, a medium, hunter green tie with minuscule scarlet stripes was worn by a deep thinker who preferred to listen before passing judgment. I never believed the system was foolproof, nor even particularly useful, but at the time, I found it fascinating. My father was a cornucopia of riveting opinions.

My mother, on the other hand, always believed in focusing on yourself and ignoring what everyone else thought or did. This line of thinking led me to utilize the Beattie family's endless string of recessive alleles whenever possible. In this case, that meant blue ties. And on this particular occasion, a thin, navy blue tie with two tiny stripes: one royal blue and the other gold. I was proud of the way I dressed, even if no one cared to notice.

All of a sudden, the clattering of shoes stopped, and the previously bustling hall lost its lively song. I was one of 40 young men with their backs against the east wall. I tried to look straight ahead at the west wall eight feet in front of me, but my line of sight was impeded by 40 interminably lurid dresses draped across 40 inscrutable, young women.

Unlike the men, each one of them had a unique style that allowed for improvisation. Gold earrings, silver bracelets, pearls, emerald and ruby rings, one-inch heels, three and a half-inch heels, bows, barrettes, and headbands all accompanied the vast array of kaleidoscopic dresses that brightened the already magnificent hallway. The only similarity between the flock was the mandatory white gloves that were never to be removed.

I scanned the area in front of me, trying to find my favorite person, someone to fawn over and pine for, but was interrupted by the program's director. If memory serves, he said:

"Everyone, thank you very much for coming." He spoke with a thick French accent, likely from the Lyon region. "If you'll please follow me into the ballroom and take your seats, we can get started. No talking, please."

The garrulous group of girls was now silent as we marched ahead into the ballroom. The boys followed along on the other side, entering the daunting hall and making an immediate left, while the girls turned right. Everyone took their seats and stared at the director in the middle of the floor. He started to speak, but I didn't listen. I was awestruck by the sheer grandeur of the ballroom. There were no walls, but rather endless mirrors acting as wallpaper, and the room was lit by the grandest chandelier I'd ever seen.

The director stood in the middle of the room and made grand gestures with his hands and occasionally broke out a three-second version of what I'd later come to know as the foxtrot. He had white hair, rugged skin, and a prim and strict demeanor. His clothes were small, taut, and perfectly ironed, and he was the only one in the room wearing a pocket square.

Then he stopped speaking, and everyone from my side of the room leaped up and strutted across the room like peacocks brandishing their plumage. The girls adjusted their posture, crossed their ankles, and caressed their hair. Half of them wielded brace-faced smiles, and several secretly removed their gloves to wipe off the irrepressible moisture before quickly covering their hands in white once again. I was startled at how quickly and confidently my peers became men. Before I could even develop the temerity to stand up, several of my vainglorious compatriots had what seemed like pretty little trophies attached to their left arms. Eventually, I stood up.

There I was, in the center of the ballroom, a pusillanimous pre-teen who would rather be at home playing *Madden '07* by himself or reading

Mark Haddon's The *Curious Incident of the Dog in the Night-Time.* This was the exact situation I needed to tackle to continue my progression towards the adult world, but instead, I cowered in trepidation. Also, my 40 boys and 40 girls' approximation turned out to be slightly off. There were only 39 of the latter. Therefore, my first ever foxtrot was with the program's white-haired director.

The first dance was uneventful, aside from a few snickers in my direction and several whispers of people calling me gay. My classmates didn't bother me, though. I was more concerned with my lack of confidence. Who was going to want to dance with and in 20 years or so marry, the short, taciturn young man with bangs, braces, and a few extra pounds of fat?

While I wasn't able to solve that question in one afternoon, my time at the Boxington Dance Club improved over the next few weeks. Every Wednesday, I'd quarrel with my mother about how I didn't want to go and wouldn't have any fun. And yet, every Wednesday, I found myself in that same glorious hallway facing the same giggly 13-year-olds to which I'd become accustomed. In time, I was no longer the one boy not dancing with a girl. I gradually went from the most reserved student in the class to maybe the 36th. The best days were the Sadie Hawkins' days. I could sit back quietly in my chair and wait for an equally craven character to approach and mutter those faithful words: "Would you like to dance?" One of these dances surprisingly led to a conversation, which was more than I ever thought possible. It was something like:

"So, um, I was wondering..."

"Sorry, I, uh...um." My impressive lexicon refused to come out in front of her.

"Oh, um, I was just..."

"Heel, toe, heel, toe," I whispered.

"Sorry. What were you saying?"

"Oh, I'm just counting out the steps. It helps me."

She wore a simple, peach dress with a black belt and heels to accompany her mandatory white gloves. Her auburn hair was tied in a ponytail, and she had braces with alternating blue and white bands.

"Yeah. Right. Sorry. So anyway..."

"You were saying something?" I spent most of this conversation look-ing at our feet.

"My best friend, Allie, she's over there." The girl motioned to what could've been seven different people and then continued: "Her Bat Mitzvah is on December 16th, and she doesn't have any guy friends, and she thinks her party will be like, lame if guys don't come."

The more we spoke, the sloppier our waltz became.

"Well, Mazel Tov, right?"

"Sure, whatever. I mean, like, do you want to come?"

"To what? Her Bat Mitzvah?"

She rolled her eyes and smiled.

"Yes, dummy."

"Well, I don't know. I'll ask my mother later."

She looked frustrated, although I wasn't sure what I did wrong.

"Do you have a phone yet? I'll put my number in your phone."

"No, I don't. My mom says I don't need one."

The song continued in the background, and I resumed my eight-count. Although, it may have necessitated a four-count. I wasn't sure. Several of my classmates then realized I was talking to a girl, which led to several grins, winks, and smiles from the other dancing Hollandsworth boys in the room, while I stared blankly back at them.

My friends from school would tease me occasionally, but deep down, I knew they were always rooting for me. At the time, I was far from the most popular child in my all-boys school but was reasonably well-liked. I was voted class president in fourth grade and intramural baseball captain in sixth. I wasn't a natural-born leader, but had a quiet charisma and never annoyed anyone. At that time, my defining feature was a trademark, oversized dimpled smile. Over the years, this gradually devolved into one of the Cheshire Cat variety, but for now, males my age enjoyed my company.

At the end of the dance, the impudent, auburn-haired minx curt-sied in front of me, as was customary, and then said:

"Before you leave today, I'm going to write down the information for the Bat Mitzvah party. December 16th at the Yale Club, got it?"

"Yes. Thank you for the dance."

Later that evening, our housekeeper Nara was waiting outside to pick me up. My mother used to drop me off and wait, but she had seemed particularly lethargic over the preceding month or two, so Nara accompanied me more frequently.

Narantsetseg, or Nara as we called her, was a pudgy, Mongolian Buddhist whom my father had hired to help my mother with the childcare and housework. She was in her late forties and was a soothing presence to have around the house. Nara would hum, sing, and meditate throughout the day and occasionally cooked dinners for my older brother Charleston and me. She made Mongolian dishes, whose names I could never pronounce, but they generally consisted of dumplings, noodles, and rice dishes with beef or pork. Nara moved to the United States a year before working with us, and my father was referred to her by someone at work. She spoke minimal English and only piped up when addressed, but everyone in the family was always glad when she was around.

Nara and I walked to Park Avenue and took a taxi to the townhouse on 95th between Lex and Park. I wanted to tell my mother Phyllis about this exciting new Bat Mitzvah development, but Nara informed me that she was sleeping. I used to believe my mother's 4 pm naps and occasional 7:30 pm bedtimes were natural, but when driblets of alcohol or pieces of drug residue were visible in the kitchen or bathrooms at odd hours, I knew there was a problem.

Today, we walked through the townhouse door, and Nara immediately went upstairs to my mother's bedroom and returned with three empty bottles of Mike's Hard Lemonade in her arms. Nara muttered the word "shower," and so I went to the third floor and washed the intoxicating smell of flowery perfume I believed I was exuding.

The townhouse was massive. It didn't have the same expensive furniture and paintings that my friends' houses had, and the location wasn't as pricey as places on Park, Madison or Fifth, but it was more space than I needed. There was a basement playroom for my brother and me with a six-foot-tall basketball hoop, large TV, Xbox, and Legos, K'NEX, Tinker Toys and action figures from our younger days. The first floor consisted of the kitchen, living, and dining rooms, which were decorated by my mother with only imported French goods. As I grew older, I realized she was the world's biggest Francophile who didn't actually speak the language.

Then, the second floor had my parents' bedroom on the left and the study on the right, while the third and final housed my older brother and me in separate bedrooms. All of this was made more impressive by the fact that my mother hadn't worked in over a decade.

My father Morgan, on the other hand, went through a 15-year period where he never missed a day of work, except for a few funerals. He grew up in the small town of Hamden, Connecticut, where he was raised by a deceased alcoholic father and a recently deceased, possibly closeted lesbian mother. And both were devoutly Irish-Catholic. He and his two siblings lived a shade above squalor and frequently dealt with definite emotional and possible physical abuse from their father. Morgan's favorite story to tell from his childhood involved his father driving him to his junior prom at Hamden High.

Morgan Beattie sat in the front seat of his father's station wagon. He had no date but put on the best tuxedo he could afford with the money he had made as a local lifeguard. My dorky father wore thick-rimmed glasses and loafers his mother bought at a local yard sale the week before. Morgan was in an optimistic mood as he looked forward to a night with interminable possibilities. Unfortunately, now over 30 years later, there was only one moment that stuck with him. It was a quote from his father. The two of them were sitting in the parking lot of the high school when Morgan reached for the door handle to leave for the evening. His father, who always started and ended his workdays with a glass of straight gin off the rocks, had been silent the entire ride. Then, just as Morgan was about to leave, his father, filled with maudlin sentimentality, uttered, "Morgan, I always thought you'd be the best of my kids..."

My father told me there was a long pause after the word "kids," and then my grandfather continued, "well, good night." It was a malevolent blow from a man my father had no choice but to respect over his first

17 years. He spent his junior prom alone by the punch bowl in a plaintive, introspective daze. And then, unbeknownst to his frequently intoxicated father, Morgan spent the entire summer reading, studying, and practicing for the SATs. He applied to four schools without any help from his parents and wound up attending the University of Pennsylvania, followed by the Wharton School of Business.

Sometime in the 80s, his father died alone in a New Milford motel room due to liver failure. This ending was inevitable, my father told me, but my grandfather and grandmother's divorce sped up the process.

Morgan graduated in the top 20th percentile of his class at Wharton and worked his way up at a mid-tier brokerage firm near City Hall called Sabbaday Capital. To this day, he sits in the same seat he sat in when he started there a quarter-century ago. Despite receiving offers from Credit Suisse and Deutsche Bank, my father's always been a loyal man and never desired a corner office. He preferred to be out in the middle of the floor, chatting and getting acquainted with everyone at the company. He never rose past VP there and was rarely the wealthiest man in the room of the Manhattan circles he frequented. However, compared to everyone else at Hamden High School, he was a man that deserved the utmost adulation for his career and financial accomplishments. Unfortunately for my brother and me, his eight to six job, and proving his omniscient father wrong, trumped the illusory awards he could receive in fatherhood.

After a lengthy shower, I walked down two flights of stairs to find him sitting at the dining room table with my older brother Charleston, eating Nara's cooking in silence.

"Hi, Dad," I said.

"You got some good news for me?" He paused and then looked at my brother. "You know, Charleston got an 82 on his biology test?"

Charleston was in his freshman year at Verity Prep, a co-ed high school on 87th and 5th, while I was busy finishing my final two years at the all-boys school, Hollandsworth, on 69th between Lex and Park.

"Well, I, uh, got invited to this girl's Bat Mitzvah in a few weeks?"

"Grades still good?"

"I think so, sir."

"You tell your mother?"

"She's, uh...like"

"She's like? Or she is?" There was no worse word in the English language than a misused "like," according to my father.

"She's asleep."

My father rolled his eyes and took a sip of one of his two nightly beers. He was partial to Pilsner Urquell back then.

"Nara, get in here."

Our housekeeper nervously scurried from the kitchen to the dining room.

"Yes, sir? Home now?"

"What? Yeah. Yes. Money's in the drawer next to the sink. 7:30 am tomorrow? Phyllis will need you to take the kids to school."

"Thanks."

Nara was always frightened of my father and generally preferred to leave before he arrived home from work, but my mother's recent issues precluded an earlier departure. Nara had a 90-minute commute to somewhere deep in Queens. It was a trek that always included two subway transfers and a bus ride. I would've felt bad for her, but she always seemed so at peace. Additionally, and much to my father's chagrin, her $20 an hour for 50-60 hours a week made her the envy of many Upper East Side babysitters and cleaning ladies.

"Well, Vincent, grab some noodles and take a seat. You don't need an invitation." My father said.

I scooped some food into a bowl, poured myself a glass of milk, and sat down next to my father. He had the New York Post in front of him and spent his meal scoffing at the Orioles' two most recent offseason transactions. Despite all the confusion and hatred he had towards his deceased father, my dad still rooted for the same teams his Baltimorean sire once did.

After dinner, my father excused Charleston and me. We then went downstairs, finished our homework, and played video games until my immutable 9:30 pm bedtime.

CHAPTER 2

MY FATHER DROVE ME TO the Bat Mitzvah at the Yale Club. He didn't leave me with any words of wisdom, but rather a simple: "Have fun. Don't get a girl pregnant. I'm extending your bedtime tonight, but don't get used to it. I'll be back at 11:04 pm. Don't make me wait."

A valet directed me to a ballroom where I heard an Akon song playing. What was typically known to be an illustrious club was turned into a rambunctious mess. We were a garish group of haughty 13-year-olds wandering around a variety of booths trying to cure our ennui and ADHD prior to the smartphone era.

In the one singular ballroom, there was a dance floor, photo booth, karaoke section, pop-a-shot area, miniature bouncy house, and a set of beaded jewelry-making stations. The dance floor not only consisted of awkward, mostly Caucasian children in designer clothing, but also three hired professional dancers whose sole purpose was to demonstrate the correct way to sway to the current Justin Timberlake or Lil Jon songs. Their other, and more critical duty, was to convince the most taciturn teens that dancing in the middle of the floor surrounded by judgmental, popular people was a grand idea.

Naturally, I stood off to the side near the restrooms and observed. I saw some of my glibber Hollandsworth friends attempting to seduce the innocent Cordelia and Nightingale girls I had seen or danced with at Boxington. My cohorts' odds of success ameliorated with each attempt. I picked out my auburn-haired dance partner from a few weeks ago. She wore a fetching royal blue knee-length dress and was cute, but no more so than the 50 other young ladies there. It was my first party of this magnitude, and it didn't disappoint. All the girls looked like TV and movie stars to me. It was like watching my own version of a Nickelodeon show filled with Jamie Lynn Spears, Victoria Justice, and Alison Stoner look-a-likes. However, these girls had designer handbags and heels in addition to the best educations money could buy. I would've loved to approach any of these fluorescent tweens, but there was something about them that seemed unattainable. I was too nervous to speak, and yet I knew I needed to practice talking to members of the opposite sex.

As I stood scanning the room for what could've been 15 minutes, a thought dawned on me; I'd much rather be at home. What was I doing here? What was the point? What happens when I talk to a girl? Then I thought about my mother and what she was doing at this moment. The languid woman was stuck in an interminable stupor that even a son's love couldn't cure.

My heart was racing, and I wanted to leave. I thought about exiting and walking home, but it was over 40 blocks, and it was a frigid December night. Unfortunately, I was left without a cell phone, money, or a MetroCard, so I was stuck until 11:04 pm. A few of my Hollandsworth acquaintances raced by me and motioned for me to follow them. They were going to play pop-a-shot, so I dawdled behind.

We alternated turns, and I finished with 48, the second-best of my crew. The key to my modicum of success was to ignore the "in-game" form I was used to. The name of the game is to shoot as my shots as possible. What's more fruitful, making 15 out of 25 shots in 60 seconds or 20 out of 50 shots in 60 seconds? In a typical game, you'd prefer the former's higher percentage, but in the more casual pop-a-shot with no statistician present, the latter's optimal.

I left my friends to use the bathroom. I didn't need to go but found that locking myself in a stall where no one could find or converse with me provided much-needed solace. Instead of sitting, I stood with my feet facing outward, so any incoming passerby would believe I was actually using the facility. I took several deep breaths, closed my eyes, and pondered my future. Is this what high school was going to be like? What about college? How was I supposed to get married if I couldn't even carry out a conversation with benignant 13-year-olds?

One of my rambunctious classmates burst into the bathroom and shouted:

"Ciara's here!"

I escaped from my trance and remembered eavesdropping on someone saying that Ciara, the famed pop star, was performing at Allie's Bat Mitzvah. I couldn't name any of Ciara's songs off the top of my head, but I knew I had heard her on the radio, and from the screams down the hall, I could tell she was well-liked. And an appearance from a superstar at a Bat Mitzvah wasn't unusual in my childhood.

Ciara was walking through the mosh pit of pre-teens when I returned from my excursion. She was smiling and taking pictures with all the screeching boys and girls. To get her to the stage, however, the DJ needed to distract all of Ciara's fans. He shouted into his microphone and put on the Electric Slide. I was unfamiliar, but the tune was catchy, and the dance moves were simple enough to practice, so I strutted onto the floor.

I never quite had the steps, but I had a smile on my face for the first time that evening. After the song, Ciara took the stage and proved to be adroit at working a crowd. She was gyrating and sweating to the point where Allie's parents seemed borderline uncomfortable. I couldn't blame them. Her outfit was revealing, and her midriff was clearly showing, which under normal circumstances would be fine, but in this setting, somehow seemed inappropriate. However, no one, including me, could critique her performance of "1, 2 Step."

I did wind up leaving the party at about 10:45 pm and walked up and down Vanderbilt Avenue while I awaited my father's navy BMW 3 series' arrival.

"Hey, sit up here with me."

I closed the backdoor, opened the front, and sat with a noticeable glower on my face.

"So, how'd it go, big guy?"

I could smell the faint tang of Pilsner Urquell on his breath.

"Fine."

"Glad you went?"

"Sure, I guess."

"When am I going to meet your first girlfriend?"

"I don't know. I don't want to talk about it."

"Jesus. Such a sad sack."

The subsequent months of my penultimate year at Hollandsworth were unmemorable. I wrestled in the winter and played baseball in the spring while continuing to attend my weekly Boxington classes. I was slowly becoming a deft ballroom dancer, even as I avoided talking to my white-gloved partners. My only real academic highlight was being a finalist in Hollandsworth's annual public speaking contest, but I lost. It was an especially heartbreaking defeat for me because my mother had dragged herself out of bed and sat in the 300-person auditorium to watch her typically timid son wow such a massive audience. My mother looked so proud as she sat in the balcony. Unfortunately, in her current sedated state, she forgot to turn the flash off of her camera. This meant that during my speech, where I argued the popular vote should replace the Electoral College for presidential elections, a bright light went off. That one flash dissuaded me from pursuing anything involving public speaking or broadcasting, despite showing a relative knack.

Seventh grade ended, and eighth grade began without much fanfare. My dad worked a lot; my brother was occupied with high school friends, homework, and social pressures, and my mother continued to spend 18 hours a day in her bedroom. It became such a quotidian practice that none of us batted an eye when walking by the master bed-room and seeing the lights off and empty pill bottles on the floor. On the occasions my mother was conscious, her behavior was erratic at best and lobotomized at worst. My brother and I would receive the occasional somnolent "I love you" from her, but it had been a long time since we all fraternized as a family. Nara gradually took on more cooking, cleaning, shopping, and babysitting to the point where she did 100% of the work around the house.

It was September 24th, 2007. Morgan Beattie had had enough. There was no straw that broke the camel's back. There was no shouting match, nor was there a sudden rock bottom. My father came home from work that night while Nara was preparing pork dumplings in the kitchen, and Charleston and I did our homework at the dining room table. My mother was snoring upstairs when our father burst through the front door.

"Hi, Dad." My brother and I instinctively shouted.

He marched by us and stomped up the stairs, with his shoes still on; this would've been a significant argument had my mother been her typical self. My father barged into the master bedroom, which he chose to sleep in less and less these days, and yanked the drawers of the bedside table onto the floor. Charleston and I left our designated spots and slowly crept up the stairs trying to zoom in on the unusual commotion.

"Morgan is that..." her voice trailed off as her head fell back on her threadbare pillow.

My father, still not having uttered a word, stripped the bed of its duvet and sheets.

"Morgan, what's? I don—" My mother's muddled thought process couldn't grasp the sudden alterations being made to her previously con-genial cache.

He snatched the pillow beside my mother and, finally, the one hold-ing her frail head up from the Tempur-Pedic mattress. My brother and I kept inching closer to the door until our father spotted us out of the corner of his eye. He snapped his fingers, pointed at us, then down-stairs, and we immediately obliged. Before sprinting to the first floor, though, I glimpsed at my mother's emaciated body being covered only by an extra-large, mangy white t-shirt that contained what appeared to be drool and dried mucus.

We stood at the bottom of the carpeted staircase listening to the plaintive palaver that reverberated throughout the townhouse. We heard my father's faint shouts as he tossed pill bottles to the floor. There was a clatter of glass and then muffled crying. I began to shiver, while Charleston stood motionless. His pallid cheeks and sempiternal look of consternation made me worry even more. For the next three minutes, the entire apartment was silent. The ever-halcyon Nara finally left her post by the stove to comfort us. She brought us in the kitchen and had us smell and taste the dinner she was preparing while softly cooing in her native language.

The silence was broken by my father's wingtips gliding down the stairs with my mother being yanked behind him. She was now dressed in grey sweatpants, a clean white t-shirt, and my father's brown Crocs. My mother's unkempt hair covered her eyebrows, and it looked as if she hadn't put on makeup or lipstick in months.

"Morgan, don't w—"

"What?" My father stopped in the middle of the staircase, carefully balancing my mother's weight and his own against the banister.

"Morgan, don't wear shoes on the carpeting."

"What?"

"I've told you..."

My father continued walking down the stairs with my mother in tow.

"I've told you a million times. Shoes off at the door."

"Boys, I'll be back later tonight. Nara, it'll be a few hours. I'll pay you overtime."

Nara nodded.

"You just—you never list..." My mother's voice trailed off as they exited the townhouse.

"Boys. Plates. Glasses. Napkins." Nara whispered in her most tranquil tone.

My brother followed orders, but I quickly sprinted up the stairs to view the carnage in the master bedroom. There were three empty bottles of Mike's Hard Lemonade under the bedside table and then a slew of pill bottles strewn across the carpet. I picked up each one, hoping to find some kind of solace in the long, impossible to pronounce names. Zolpidem, Avodart, Effexor, Spironolactone, Oxycodone, Quetiapine, Rosuvastatin, Diethylpropion, and Ambien littered the room where I used to joyfully enter to snuggle up next to my mother and watch American Idol. She'd tell me that on my 16th birthday, we'd drive to an audition. We'd journey to Pittsburgh or Charlotte or Louisville, and with my emergent vocals and her unwavering persistence, I'd get on TV one day. My mother's only rule was when I finally arrived on stage in front of a live audience, I had to thank her, tell her I love her and blow her a kiss. I always considered it a silly pipe dream, but at that moment, the thought brought tears to my eyes.

CHAPTER 3

THE NEXT MORNING OUR FATHER clued us in on the situation. Our previously fastidious, doting, and elegant mother had transformed into a person with deep depression and addictions to Ambien, alcohol, and several other drugs. Morgan drove her to a facility in White Plains where she could get treatment. He assured us this was a minor speed bump, and everything would return to normalcy in maybe three months. Despite my immense curiosity, I never dared ask what drove him to commit her involuntarily. From where did the emanating thought come? Or why did he wait almost a year to take action? Asking these questions would go against the way I was raised by both my parents and teachers, who inculcated a certain code in me at a young age. Throughout my formative years, when someone was having a significant problem, a momentous life event, or even a conflicting thought, it was best to mind your own business. Keep your mouth shut. Be kind and courteous, but don't intrude on a person's issues. Don't try to fix the unfixable. Mind your own business. These were the tenets of the Upper East Side philosophy. If a classmate's parents divorced, you didn't bring it up. You maintained the status quo. If a friend's grandfather died, say "sorry," but don't dig too deep. If a parent was arrested for a white-collar crime, you ask the child if they caught the Yankee game last night. This was an atavistic trait possessed by a particular crowd, and there was never a reason to delineate from this unique philosophy. On that basis, no one ever asked me how my mother was doing. Not teachers, not parents and not friends, because it was none of their business.

The Beattie family soldiered on with minimal difficulty. Given how little my mother had been involved in the previous season or two, there were no real changes to my daily life. Nara handled all the housework, shopping and meals, while my brother and I attended classes and played sports at our respective schools. Morgan continued to toil away as if nothing happened. I'd receive occasional reminders of my mother, though. The most notable moments were when I was singing in Glee Club, picking out my clothes in the morning, listening to my father saunter up and down the stairs in his wingtips, and driving in the car with Charleston now occupying the front seat. The only instances that truly exacerbated my dispirited condition were when I noticed a change in my father and brother. They gradually acquired a new way of talking to me that was rife with acerbity. By December, it was rare for anyone in my family to speak more than a sentence to one another. My father was naturally tight-lipped and avoided discussing his feelings, while my older brother seemed to emulate our father's increasingly icy demeanor. Morgan's tone wasn't naturally quarrelsome but was influenced by a change in his nightly drinking habits. Two or three years ago, he'd share a glass of white wine with my mother on a nightly basis; they were partial to Grgich Hills Chardonnay. However, due to our family's tribulations, his one glass turned into one glass with an accompanying Pilsner Urquell. Then, as my mother stopped eating dinner with us, he no longer bought Grgich Hills because "I'm not gonna throw $350 in the trash every week." These days, my father would come home and open a beer before his greeting. Then he had a second with dinner, and a third while he watched the Yankees or Giants game alone in the master bedroom. And due to his love for the Baltimore Orioles and Indianapolis Colts, née Baltimore, he always rooted for New York to lose, even if his favorite teams weren't involved. My father would watch a New York Yankees-Oakland A's game, for example, and we could hear boos from his bedroom. He never cheered. My father watched solely to boo the teams his father had taught him to despise.

The cold, emotionally empty townhouse would eventually receive a brief respite of our interminable wallowing when our father decided to have the three of us visit our mother in White Plains on the final night of Hanukkah.

My father picked us up outside the house in his navy BMW. Charleston sat in front while I was perched next to a pile of bric-a-brac that was topped off with out-of-season sunflowers, although they were always my mother's favorite in the summertime. We sat in silence until we reached I-87.

"I'm sorry you guys have to deal with all of this," Morgan said.

"When do you think she's getting out?" I asked.

"I don't know. I'm no doctor. They've got her on Lithium, which is supposed to help something. But what do I know?"

"What are we gonna do when we get there?" Charleston added.

"Boys, I don't have the answers to any of your questions. We'll see how she's doing. Smile. Give her hugs and kisses. Tell her you love and miss her. That's all I got."

"Wake me up when we get there."

Charleston closed his eyes, while my father put on the James Blunt *Back to Bedlam* CD he had been listening to nonstop ever since my mother was committed.

"Dad," I asked. "Do you think there's a chance she never comes back?"

"Nah, come on. You know your mother. She's indestructible."

We arrived at the facility past sundown with the menorah, yarmulkes, and electronic candles. My father checked us in, and we were given a private visiting room for our meeting.

The hospital was cheaper and less well-known than other facilities in the tri-state region. Perhaps the doctors and nurses went to the top state schools in the country as opposed to Ivies. And the décor consisted of stained white walls and uncaulked bathrooms. However, it wasn't decrepit. Simply put, it was an unspectacular lodging area for someone of my mother's background.

While awaiting Phyllis' arrival, my father found a large pitcher of water in which to place the wilting sunflowers. I sorted out Scattergories trinkets, and our family's dreidels and Charleston put everyone's yarmulkes on their heads and arranged the room's furniture in an aesthetically pleasing manner.

A nurse brought my mother to the room and sat her in one of the empty chairs. The men of the family exchanged abhorrent glances as we saw our once ferocious fighter reduced to the gaunt stranger sitting before us. No one knew what to say until my father interrupted with the obvious.

"Go hug your mother, boys."

We hustled over and embraced our mother. She smiled at first but was clearly groggy.

"Phyllis, how are you? We brought you some flowers."

She frowned.

"Oh. Sunflowers in the winter. How...thoughtful."

The nurse nodded at my father and left the room.

"Mom, we brought Scattergories. Do you want to play?" I said.

"No. I don't like that game."

My dad and Charleston looked at each other.

"Well," started Charleston. "Happy Hanukkah. We brought everything for the final night."

"Have you been lighting the candles while I've been gone?"

"Well, um, no, Mom. We were sav—"

"Nice, Morgan. Really nice," my mother said.

My father placed the menorah on the table and put the nine electronic candles in their appropriate places.

"No, Morgan. You have to start from the other side. You place the candles on the far right first." My mother scolded. "And where's the zebra menorah? Where'd you buy this cheap thing?"

"Come on, Phyllis, be nice. We can't light real candles in here. And we're all very happy to see you."

"Well, you could've put in a little more effort. Maybe Vincent could've worn something a little nicer than a Hollandsworth sweatshirt."

My father placed the candles in the menorah the proper way and adjusted the miniature light switches on the backs. My mother then led us in the Hanukkah prayers we had all memorized after hearing the same verses for nearly a decade and a half.

"You know Morgan, just because you don't like my religion, doesn't mean you can turn my kids off it."

"Phyllis, who said I don't like your religion? It's fine with me. I just never saw the point in religion. Spouting a bunch of nonsense in a language our kids don't speak, but whatever."

"Well, you know what?" My mother began raising her voice. "You can just leave then."

Charleston and I stared at each other in disbelief.

"Boys, can you give us a second?"

Charleston nodded and escorted me out of the room. We peered through the glass windows of the dull, white space. The fluorescent lighting reflecting off the newly-painted walls hurt my eyes. Our parents fought as my brother and I stood in silence watching, unable to hear what was being said. The poorly decorated room was adorned with the two beige chairs my parents were sitting in and the cheap lime green couch in which I previously sat.

"You okay, Vincent?"

"Not really. You?"

"We'll get through this. We always do. We're Beatties. Remember, we're smart, tough as nails, and can't do pull-ups."

My brother was quoting my father's oft-used adage from our childhood. I chuckled, and he put his arm around my shoulder. At that moment, our mother started to cry. My father tapped her leg, but she wouldn't stop. He glanced at us and mouthed that we should come back in the room.

We returned and immediately gave our mother hugs and kisses, then sat on the couch in the room with the blinding overhead lights.

"Mom, what's wrong?" I asked.

"It's just that," she struggled to get through her thoughts without bawling. "You all could've made a bit more of an effort. Vincent, you're in a sweatshirt, and Morgan hasn't been lighting the candles, and I feel like I'm losing my boys."

"Mom, you're not losing us." We demanded.

"You're just becoming more like your father, and I don't want to play board games or get dirty flowers or..." Then she started weeping.

She tried to wipe away her tears and then looked at the menorah and stared off into the distance. I briefly thought about what I'd be doing if we'd never drove out here. Would I be having more fun if I were at home under my covers reading Yann Martel's *Life of Pi*? Or maybe I would've wanted to relax and play video games in the basement? Or practice playing Louie Armstrong's "When the Saints Go Marching In" on the piano? I wanted to be anywhere but here.

"You gotta get me out of here." My mother said, her mood shifting in a split second. "I don't belong here. Everyone's nuts, and these doctors are all quacks."

"Phyllis, why don't we talk about something else?"

"What's wrong, Morgan? Don't you believe me? I'm perfectly fine. I don't need to be here."

"Boys, why don't you give your mother a hug and wait in the car?"

Charleston and I stood and went over to embrace our flustered mother, but she pushed us away and crossed her arms.

"I need some alcohol. Can you maybe go across the street and sneak me in some Ketel One?"

"No, I'm not going to do that. Come on, listen to yourself...let me get the nurse. We should be going."

"Don't leave me here. Morgan, please."

"Boys, get your coats, and give your mother a hug."

"Don't leave me here. Take me back with you. I need to get out of here. The other patients are insane. They're making me go crazy. Please. I'm not depressed."

We stood and walked out the door. Charleston muttered an "I love you, Mom," as we exited. The three of us then walked out to the car with my dad muttering:

"I'm so sorry, guys."

Then we drove home through the dreary December night devoid of stars. No one said a word as the voice of James Blunt crooned throughout the navy BMW.

My final semester at Hollandsworth began with some much-needed positive news. I was accepted into Verity Prep, the same high school as Charleston. I spent the plurality of my second semester daydreaming about what life at my new school would be like. The most significant development would be transitioning from an all-boys school to a co-ed one. I thought about my future amatory exploits. In six to nine months, I could be kissing my first girl or be in a steady relationship with my new girlfriend. I thought my ideal girl would like baseball and video games and bacon burgers with no cheese. I also dreamed that phantasmal female would have long hair and be kind and smiley. I didn't feel I was too picky. I would've gone out with any of the girls from Boxington, but it never felt like the right environment for chatting. It didn't help that I stopped going to dance classes after my mother left. There was no one to motivate me, and I didn't have any fun, so I quit and continued my descent into interminable apathy.

There also wasn't much to miss about Hollandsworth. It had been a great school and helped me develop into a wise beyond my years student, but I didn't gain much regular enjoyment. Classes became boring and unimportant now that I was already accepted into a high school. Wrestling and playing baseball were amusing but seemed childish with high school sports on the horizon. The worst part of my days, though, happened to be pick-up time. Even though Phyllis hadn't come to school in over nine months, watching my friends walk hand-in-hand with their mothers or calling their parents on their new cell phones, made me wish my mother was back home and more involved. It's hard to explain to a 14-year-old why a depressed person can't just be happy and get lost in hobbies, activities, and friendships. If I were ever sad, I'd spend time with family or friends or play sports or video games. There was always a solution. In my mother's case, no one could find a way to make her happy. It may have helped if my father sat me down and explained that no one was at fault, but those saccharine discussions were "for chicks" as he once not-so-eloquently put it.

My father did come home from work one day in March with some potentially cheery news. One of my best friends from Hollandsworth was also accepted to Verity Prep. My father sat across from me at the dining room table to tell me the news. He had a goofy smirk that disappeared each time his bottle of Pilsner Urquell grazed his lips.

"Vincent, Albert's mother just called me and told me the news. Albert was rejected from his first-choice. The only school he got into was Verity."

"Really? That would be sick. We could help each other make friends and study together and play sports."

Albert and I had known each other since we were two. We both went to the same preschool and then spent the previous nine years together at Hollandsworth. We used to be best friends, but every few years, he'd add a new best friend to his arsenal, and I gradually dropped from number one on his list to maybe four or five. This was still a huge boon for me. Having someone I'd known my whole life accompanying me to high school? It sounded like an ideal scenario.

"His mother sent me an email at work today. She asked me to call her when I got home. She knows Charleston has spent the past year and a half there, and she wanted to get my input as a Verity parent."

"I thought it was the only school he got into? So, doesn't he have no choice but to go?"

"I don't know."

"Well, like, why is she calling you?"

"'Cause it'll make her more comfortable about sending her kid somewhere. I have no idea...Nara," My father called. "Bring me another beer, and is dinner ready?"

Nara dashed out to the living room with a beer.

"Five minutes." She then retreated to her sanctum, humming softly.

My father drank a sip of his beer and took out his black Razr cell phone.

"I'm going to call her now. I'll put her on speaker, but don't say anything. I don't want her to know you're listening."

I nodded and zipped my lips.

"Hello?" We heard a woman's voice on the other line.

"Hey, it's Morgan Beattie. How are you?"

"Oh, hi there. I'm fine. Having mixed feelings about Albert's lack of options, but perhaps you can assuage my doubts."

"I'll certainly do my best."

My jovial father winked at me, softly belched, and kept up our charade.

"So, Morgan, can you give me a brief overview of your thoughts? What does Charleston like and dislike?"

"Of course. So, Verity's main draw is probably its arts. Charleston has developed into a sculptor or some ceramic guy. There are big art and music departments. They have computers and other techy stuff everywhere. Definitely hipper and more modern than Hollandsworth."

"Well, I suppose there are pros and cons to modernity."

"Athletically," my father continued. "They're a weaker school. They don't have any contact sports, but that probably doesn't affect Albert. But Charleston and Vincent had, or should I say, have, to give up on football and wrestling. It kind of blows."

"Right. Well, what are the students like?"

"Oh, it's much more diverse than Hollandsworth."

"Hmm, is that so? How do you mean?"

"Yeah, you notice it right when you open the school directory. It has a much higher Jewish population, which makes Phyllis happy, so that's a good thing."

There was a pause. Albert's mother softly squealed.

"Oh...um...well, my husband's not going to like that."

My dad and I exchanged glances.

"Um...well, you know we're devout Lutherans." She added.

"Right. So?"

"I'm going to need to talk to my husband about this. But thank you for bringing this to our attention. We had no idea."

Albert's mother hung up.

"Dad, why would you tell her that?"

saying goodnight to my brother and me, he reminded us we still needed to pick up Mother's Day cards and flowers the next morning. My father would be setting an 8 am alarm so we could stop at CVS and the corner grocery store and continue our mawkish annual traditions.

"Boys," my father whispered the next day. "Get dressed. It's eight o'clock. Got any flower recommendations? Is it sunflower season yet?"

We quickly put on our outfits, which consisted of Nike and Hollandsworth paraphernalia. However, before we could walk down the stairs, our suddenly perceptive father told us our clothes were grossly inappropriate for a holiday celebration. We nodded, turned back upstairs, and clothed ourselves in khakis and lurid button-downs with shades of magenta, tangerine, and crimson. These garments waited patiently on our pubescent torsos to brighten our salubrious mother's day.

"Charleston, you take Vincent to get Hallmark cards at CVS," my father said as we left the townhouse. "I'm going to buy flowers. I'll meet you right here in 15 minutes."

"But, Dad," my brother yawned. "What about presents?"

"Come on, who do you think you're talking to? Got a gift and chocolates yesterday before I picked her up."

"Wow, what a husband," I said. "What'd you get her?"

"Well, you know how she's been complaining about her herniated disks for years?"

We nodded.

"Got her a back massager from Sharper Image. It's portable. She can use it during long drives."

"Oh, she'll love that," Charleston said.

"No, she won't."

They both stared at the Beattie family runt.

"She wants, like—"

"Don't say like."

"She wants jewelry and clothes. We have to get her girly things," I demanded.

"We get her that stuff every year," Charleston said.

"Whatever, I bought her chocolate truffles from Maison du Chocolat too. Between the gift, chocolates, flowers, and cards, she's bound to like something."

We arrived at home, checked to see that Phyllis was still sleeping, and then sat at the dining room table to fill out our cards. Charleston chose a comical one, while I picked a more heartfelt one with a kitten on the front. I wrote:

Dear Mom,

Happy Mother's Day! We're all so glad to have you home again. I can't wait to watch movies and TV with you and taste your chicken fajitas. They're great. I also want to go shopping for new clothes with you since I'm starting at Verity in the Fall and no dress code! I hope this is your best Mother's Day yet!

Love,

Vincent

It was 11 am, and my somnolent mother was still snoring in her bedroom. By now, we had all finished breakfast and organized all of her gifts in an aesthetically pleasing manner on the dining room table.

"Boys, why don't you run out and get your mother two croissants from Corrado and grab her a venti black coffee."

My father hoped the fresh air would alleviate our perturbation, but it didn't help. Charleston and I went out to grabbed her victuals and returned to find the first floor empty. We both timidly climbed the carpeted staircase and made a left to our parents' bedroom. We peered through the door furtively.

"Boys, get in here." My father said.

Our mother was half-asleep and looked as bewildered as ever. Three pill bottles sat menacingly on her bedside table.

"Happy Mother's Day," I whispered.

"Boys, thank you."

She slowly rose to a seated position.

"Phyllis, what are you doing with the pills?"

"They're prescribed. The doctor and I agreed that I can't quit every-thing because then I can't get any sleep. I only take like a half...or one Ambien and then some hair loss medication, weight loss pills, and a small dose of Lithium."

"Phyllis, come on. What's going on?"

Our mother stood and placed a robe over her shoulders.

"Call my doctor, Morgan. You're so smart and sure of everything, right? Call my doctor. Here's the number."

"It's a Sunday."

"So, what are you going to do? Dump out all the pills that I need to survive?"

I was my typical taciturn self, but this sight left me dispirited. Nothing seemed to have changed. My mother still took pills, fought with my father, slept late, and was querulous whenever conscious.

"Phyllis, just come downstairs. We have some surprises for you."

Everyone cautiously exited the bedroom and made their way to the dining area. She glanced at the in-season sunflowers, the perfectly arranged truffles, and the cheery cards. My mother beamed. I actually couldn't remember the last time I saw her smile like that. Every skirmish was forgotten. Her time in the facility seemed trivial, and we felt like a real family again. The moment may have seemed platitudinous from an outside observer's perspective, but in a year where so little had gone right, any semblance of gaiety was greeted with open arms.

"Wow, thank you all so much. This is just wonderful. What an amaz-ing start to the day." She hugged and kissed each of us before continu-ing. "And where's my present?"

My father went into the foyer and lifted the box, which in hindsight should've at least been wrapped. My mother's contagious smile gradu-ally vanished as she squinted at the "gift" my father was carrying.

"What's this?"

"It's a back massager, Phyllis."

"A what?"

"Mom, we all thought 'cause of your bad back, this would be a perfect idea," Charleston was silently begging her to like it.

"My gift on Mother's Day is...a...back massager?"

On the positive side, she no longer appeared her weary self. However, I would've gladly taken a docile sloth over a stampeding rhino.

"Is this a joke? I...I...don't understand. Why would I want this?"

"To help you feel better, Mom. It's a kind gesture. Maybe your back hurts from those unforgiving hospital beds?" My older brother just wanted her to be happy. He almost pleaded it into existence.

"I just don't understand how you can all be so selfish. I sit alone for months. No calls—"

"Mom, we did call—"

"Shush." She snapped at my brother. "No calls. No visits. You wanted me to rot in there while you all had fun in your frat house. No need for Mom anymore. Oh, let's just get her the first cheap thing we see in a store window," she started to cry.

"Phyllis, can you please cheer up? I don't want to put the boys through any more pain."

"Oh, the boys, Morgan? What about the pain I've gone through? God, you're all just so selfish." Our mother started mewling loudly as she stormed up the stairs and locked herself in her bedroom.

"Guys, I'm sorry. I don't know what to say," my downtrodden father shook his head.

Charleston and I hugged him as the scent of freshly baked croissants shrouded the dining room.

A month had passed, and my mother's condition deteriorated. She was back to sleeping the majority of the days and nights and had likely increased her pill dosage without telling anyone. My mother also began drinking her favorite Mike's Hard Lemonade in the late mornings and

occasionally had Nara mix her an afternoon triple Ketel One on the rocks with diet tonic. Nara would decline at first, but when my mother snapped or screamed or cried, there was no defense against it. I heard my father call her doctor one night and spoke about having her committed again, but the doctor disagreed. After hearing this call, I pressed my father about getting Phyllis the help she needed, but he said,

"The doctor told me 'the best thing for Phyllis is to be with her loving family. You definitely can't let her drink and self-medicate, but other than that, there isn't much more we can do at a facility. She needs to show a desire to improve, and after speaking with her, the only motivation she has is her two boys.'"

The next week, she missed my Hollandsworth graduation. To no one's surprise, she overslept. At first I was distraught, but then I figured she would've snored in the auditorium or done something to embarrass me in front of my classmates. My father and Charleston were in the audience, and that was enough. However, moving forward, we all wanted Phyllis back to her old self. Our father decided to make one last-ditch Hail Mary to halt our family's screeching, seemingly inevitable collapse.

For weeks, he couldn't figure out a way to alter the townhouse's plaintive mood. The whole family was in an interminable rut until one day, he came home and called us all into the master bedroom.

"Listen, everyone, I know our lives haven't been easy."

My mother's eyelids fluttered, but she was curious as to where this was going.

"I decided that we need to leave the city for a while, so I rented a house in Bridgehampton."

"What?" My agitated mother murmured.

"I don't want the boys sitting inside all summer with nothing to do, and I don't want you lying in bed all day. I know you're concerned about the sun, but I'll buy dozens of bottles of sun-tan lotion. SPF 60."

Charleston and I were both excited at the prospect of spending two months in a relaxing, other-worldly setting with beaches, Wiffle Ball,

golf, plenty of room to run around, and great food. However, our mother wasn't as ebullient.

"I'd prefer to stay here," she said calmly.

"You know what, Phyllis, I'm putting my foot down. You're going. I'll take the train out on Friday nights after work. It may be healthy for you to spend some time away from me. You'll have five days a week to entertain the boys, drive them around, relax by the ocean, and see some old friends. Then, I'll come out and cook and clean and watch the boys with you on the weekends. It'll be great."

"Is there a pool at least?" She asked.

"Well...no. I got the house on such short notice, and it was pricey enough already."

"I should've known. I know you too well, Morgan."

"Boys, pack your bags. We leave on the 29th...Phyllis, you're going. You need fresh air and a change of scenery in the worst way."

"I'll think about it."

Phyllis groaned and placed her pillow over her head.

"I called your doctors, and they agree with me. We need to get you out of this townhouse."

Charleston and I spent the next few days playing video games, going to the 92nd Street Y to play basketball, and packing our bags for the upcoming trip. I felt my father had made an informed decision. Charleston and I were downright sprightly. We used to have the beloved Southampton house when we were younger. We played sports in the backyard, swam, hung out with friends, played tennis and golf at nearby clubs with Hollandsworth friends, and had family dinners at the elegant restaurants that lined Main Street and Jobs Lane. It was pure, idyllic bliss for adults and children alike.

On Thursday the 26th, Charleston and I had nothing on our schedules. We woke up, had our bowls of Kix, and continued to pack our bags.

"Hey, how many bathing suits do you have...that fit?" Charleston shouted from his room.

"Maybe one. It's navy with baby blue turtles. It's Vilebrequin."

"I only have two. I have two others that don't fit me anymore. Do you want to try them on?"

"Gross," I shouted back.

"They've been washed."

"I don't know. It makes me feel uncomfortable. Like, your private parts have touched the suit's lining. I don't want to think about that."

"How about bathroom towels then, genius?"

Charleston walked into my room wearing shorts, a t-shirt, and flip-flops.

"Where are you going?"

"Get dressed. We'll head to the Vilebrequin on Madison and buy both of us another pair."

"Do you have the money for that?" I asked.

"Yeah, Dad just put money in the drawer last night."

Ever since Charleston went to high school, and my mother became ill, my father started putting large wads of cash in our family's communal "money drawer." It was in the kitchen to the right of the sink and was refilled every few days. My father knew he could be indolent at times and felt this was an acceptable solution for two children seemingly raising themselves. It spoke to the trust he had in Nara as he'd leave hundreds of dollars in the drawer and explained to our beloved housekeeper that she could take whatever she needed for groceries and toiletries. As far as we were concerned, no one ever dared take more than necessary.

Charleston and I walked down the stairs and peered into our mother's room. It was 10 am, but she was clearly in a deep slumber. We chose not to wake her. My brother and I then sprinted down to the first floor, told Nara where we were going, and began our excursion towards Madison.

We stayed out for about an hour and a half, stopping to grab food at Yura on our way home. Charleston and I walked into the townhouse to find Nara dusting the living room vases.

"Nara, is Mom still sleeping?" Charleston asked.

"Yes. Sleeping. I check."

"Jesus. 11:30."

Nara scampered up the stairs, and we followed close behind; after removing our flip-flops. She opened the door, and our mother was still silent.

"Phyllis, wake up."

Nara turned on the bedside light. My mother's face had shifted from its sickly white to a slate grey.

"Mom...wake up," I shivered, sensing something was wrong.

Charleston went over and shook her shoulders.

"Vincent, call 9-1-1. Now."

I sprinted downstairs, dialed the cordless phone, and told the woman our address. I then explained the urgency and my mother's prolonged issues. Right after I hung up, I started to cry. I darted upstairs and found Nara attempting to give CPR to my mother. Charleston sat in the corner of the room with his head in his hands, rocking back and forth.

"Vincent, tell Dad to get home right now."

I dialed his work number, while a driblet of water landed on the phone's screen.

"Dad," I left the bedroom. I didn't want to look at her anymore.

"Hey, buddy. What's going on? All ready for—"

"Stop." My voice shook.

"What's up?"

"Come home right now."

"I can't just leave the office. I'm in the process of making a trade. Can't Nara handle it?"

"Dad, Mom's in big trouble."

"Well, son, she's always in big trouble. Can I call you back in 5?"

"No, Dad. Just listen." I started bawling through the phone.

"Christ. I'll leave right now."

The ambulance arrived a few minutes later. I answered the door and directed the two paramedics upstairs. Nara and Charleston exited the room, both in tears. Our housekeeper pulled us into the study across the hall and held us against her bosom. She cooed a Mongolian lullaby, pausing to sob every so often. We heard the paramedics bring our mother down the stairs and out the door.

"Excuse me," a paramedic interrupted us. "We're driving to Lenox Hill now."

"Is...she...breathing, sir?" I asked.

"We're working on it."

Unfortunately, the paramedics never had a chance. My mother was pronounced dead on arrival. She died in her sleep, they said. Her official cause of death, as we later found out, was an accidental overdose of Ambien. Charleston and I were inconsolable. Nara hugged us as tightly as she could for as long as she could in the Lenox Hill waiting room. And after an indiscernible amount of time, she released us and took action.

"Must call Morgan," she said as she wiped tears from both of her eyes.

As I later found out, my father was sitting alone at the dining room table of the townhouse, drinking his favorite imported beer from a green bottle. No one had a cell phone to reach him, so when he arrived and found no one at home, he assumed the worse. My father eventually received Nara's jumbled call from a hospital phone and begrudgingly exited the townhouse, filled with trepidation and indignation.

My mother had no last will and testament, was an only child, and had previously suffered through the death of both of her parents. My father, Charleston, and I were the only family she had. We each spent the next 24 hours sleeping, crying, and not eating, while her widowed husband drank and attempted to arrange a funeral.

Her service was held at Temple Emanu-El, which we all felt was appropriate. My father had the Hollandsworth headmaster send out an email to the parents of children in mine and Charleston's grades. My father also called a few of Phyllis' friends he remembered from various phone calls, weddings, funerals, and holidays over the previous decade. My mother kept a neat, red Moleskine notebook with phone numbers and email addresses, a boon for planning the service.

Her funeral was held on Monday the 30th. My plaintive father hugged Charleston and me before we trudged into the colossal synagogue in our ill-fitting, day-old tuxedos. Nineteen people were in attendance. My only other memory from that day came from Phyllis Beattie's only eulogist—my father.

"Phyllis Beattie," he began. "you were and always will be the love of my life. Ever since I laid eyes on you in that bar in Center City Philadelphia, I knew I loved you. Your beautiful smile is what first drew me to you, but as I soon found out, that was just the tip of the iceberg. I love...loved your cheerfulness, passion, kindness, elegance, and pugnacity. You never backed down from anyone or anything. You also happened to be the ideal mother to our perfect children...I'm sorry...I need a moment..."

It was the first time I had ever seen my stubborn father cry. He turned around, wiped his eyes, and cleared his throat. His hands gently shook as he continued:

"You loved our children more than anything else in the world, and I promise you I will make sure to raise them in your image. They'll be kind and courteous. They'll choose their passions over money. They won't do drugs. They'll learn to be well-rounded and fashionable young men. I promise you your boys will always carry on your legacy...they won't be getting tattoos either, Rabbi...But in all seriousness, for the rest of my life, our family will only be three-quarters full. There will forever be a gaping hole left behind by the finest woman I have ever and will ever meet...Before I finish, I want to tell you all about a memory that keeps popping up in my head. Phyllis and I were on our third date. This would've been '86, maybe '87. She asked me to go dancing with her at her family's country club in Bala Cynwyd. I obliged because I learned early on, I'd get yelled at if I said no to her. Anyway, I wore my father's old tan suit and a tie I bought from the Wharton bookstore. She wore a beautiful pink gown with her hair tied up. Right when I saw her, she adjusted my tie and buttoned the top button. Then said hello and kissed me on the cheek. That's the kind of woman she was. Well, so, we wound up going on the dance floor, and the DJ played slow songs, waltzes, and shi—err I mean stuff. I was tight and wanted a drink in the worst way. She was bored of me. I could tell. Then the DJ put on "Shout" by The Isley Brothers, and it took me back to my fraternity days. I instinctively became the loudest, most obnoxious person in the room. Then, midway through the song as it started to get a little bit louder, I shouted "Gator" like I'd seen in *Animal House,* and I dropped down on my back and began flailing around. Looking back on it, I'm surprised she didn't dump me right then and there, given her family and upbringing. Instead, Phyllis laughed hysterically and then joined me on the floor, flailing her arms around while lying on her back. I fell in love with her right then and there...uh...well...I better leave before I embarrass myself by crying again."

I'm not sure how Charleston felt, but I was genuinely proud of my father. He showed tremendous temerity and vulnerability. I had never seen him like that before, and any bitterness I felt towards him at that time had dissipated.

CHAPTER 5

TWO DAYS LATER, WE WERE driving out to the rented house in Bridgehampton. My father said we needed a change of scenery from the ostensibly haunted townhouse. Charleston and I weren't in a garrulous mood, so we simply obliged. My father said he'd take a few days off from work to keep us entertained. On July 6th, he'd take the train back to the city, and Nara would take the Hampton Jitney and stay with us on weekdays. The two of them would rotate all summer, and then I'd start at Verity Prep in September, and Charleston would begin 11th grade.

The three of us were aloof for the first quarter of the ride, but then my father became uncomfortable and put on a new CD he had burned. "Cross Eyed Mary" led off, followed by a bunch of songs from The Doors and The Allman Brothers.

My father continued driving along the Southern State Parkway, while he hummed to himself. The road was heavily congested due to the throng of people hoping to celebrate our country's birthday by sipping mimosas and Bellinis on private beaches overlooking the hypnotic undulations of the Atlantic. Nantucket red pants, navy Sperry's, and bone-colored Irish linen shirts would be adorned by men and boys all up and down Route 27. Seersucker pants and blazers would cling to the more voguish male bodies, while jonquil and amber floral sundresses prettified the ladies of the South Fork. I was typically ebullient to join my spoiled teenage compatriots, but after our family's recent tribulation, I was overrun by passivity.

"Boys," my father turned around briefly to make sure I was listening too. "Do you believe in God...er...I mean, I know we rarely took you to church or synagogue, and I didn't know what your thoughts were."

"I don't know, Dad." Charleston's lugubrious voice was discouraging.

"You know what I think," my father continued. "God doesn't exist. Never has. Never will. You know why? Two numbers."

"What?" My brother and I feigned quizzicality.

"9/11."

I wasn't emotionally salubrious enough for this type of conversation, but he continued regardless.

"That's it. 9/11. How can a God allow that to happen? Three thousand innocent lives lost for no reason. Senseless terrorism with no deeper meaning. No God would allow that many people to lose their families and friends. I was 20 blocks away, you know? Then you have children being raped and murdered throughout this country on a daily basis. Kids being kidnapped. If there were a God, He wouldn't let those things happen. Your mother too. No God would take away a mother of two young boys. There can't be a God. Just can't. Drunk drivers plowing into innocent people...Jesus Christ. Deeper meaning? God's plan? Disgusting. I'm so sick of it."

I didn't know how to respond. Part of me wished he'd just stop talking, but I wanted him to grieve.

"You know, I used to yell at Phyllis about the Equal packets. Ever since we started living together some 25 years ago, every morning, she'd make her coffee and pour Equal in her mug. Then she'd leave the empty packets next to the coffeemaker. There were always white grains and spilled coffee staining the marble. I must've told her 300 times throughout our lives, 'Phyllis, please put the goddamn Equal packets in the trash. How can you just leave them out?' She usually ignored me, but every so often would say something like 'they always wind up in the garbage. It doesn't really matter who puts them there.' Friggin' Equal packets."

No one spoke for a while. I just thought about our mother being lowered into that empty hole. Soil and worms everywhere. Maybe a mole would chew through her coffin. I didn't want to be alone with my thoughts. I didn't like where my brain was headed, and I'd never felt such a lack of enthusiasm. I tried to get out of my own head I began to watch the other cars that drove past us. I softly bit my tongue every time we zoomed by a green highway sign. I then heard "Fire on the Mountain," that depressing old song from The Marshall Tucker Band.

We eventually arrived in Bridgehampton and made a brief stop at the King Kullen before driving to our new summer home on Pauls Lane. It was a two-story house with chestnut shaker siding, just like my mother preferred. It paled in comparison to the vast majority of Hamptons houses, both in sheer magnitude and ostentatiousness. With the size of our Manhattan townhouse, I'm sure my father could've rented something nicer, especially considering this was supposed to raise my mother from her hopeless funk. Honestly though, she would've liked the gazebo sitting right in the center of the half-acre backyard. A pool would've looked better in there, but we made do with the ivory-colored pillars and beige hammock.

Charleston and I took our bikes off the back of the car and rode them into the garage, while our father unloaded groceries. We joined him inside our winsome new abode, each of us touring the rooms separately. Charleston and I took the two downstairs bedrooms with twin beds, while my father would sleep upstairs in the master. I appreciated the house's nautical decorations, as seashells, conches, and sea glass garnished the shelves and drawers. I picked up a piece of sea glass and gently poked it into my thumb. I didn't say a word for the first 15 minutes, nor did my mourning family members. We each brought in our bags, folded our clothes, and decorated the bathrooms with toothbrushes, toothpaste, shampoo, and other toiletries.

"Let's bike down to the beach." My father announced. "See if we can bodysurf some waves. And you know what? Tomorrow, I'm gonna ask around. Sailing lessons for the two of you. Need to keep you occupied when I head back to the city."

That Friday, my father drove us to our first sailing lesson in one of the duller areas of the Hamptons, Noyack. We were going to practice in a little alcove along Noyack Bay. For the time being, we were barricaded by Shelter Island and the North Fork, but if we ameliorated enough, maybe we could sail out towards Gardiners Bay.

My father parked the car in the dingy niche overlooking the less than glamorous Peconic Bay. It was a far cry from the resplendent beaches south of the highway. The three of us then approached a gangly-looking Australian man in his mid-30s with stringy blonde hair, leathery skin, and blue-lensed Aviators that never left his face. I, on the other hand, wore my navy Vilebrequin bathing suit with the baby blue turtles, and Charleston was clad in a carrot-colored pair with brown orcas. We both had on matching white t-shirts and flip-flops.

My father gave us firm handshakes before retreating to the BMW while Charleston and I silently looked on at our inscrutable instructor, Bobby. The Australian clapped and had us follow him down to the water.

"Waitin' on one more, mates."

We saw a 2008 jet black Porsche Cayenne pull up to the tiny, dirt parking lot. It let out a beautiful young girl in a shin-length blue and white striped jumpsuit, an off-white sun hat, and open-toed caramel-colored sandals. She had long hair that appeared to be light brown under the straw, but the tips were dyed a dirty blonde. The ingenue removed her hat, transferred it to a hand sticking out from the car, and ran towards us.

"That's gotta be her now."

The girl in the jumpsuit approached Bobby and held out her tanned hand with her palm facing the ground. Bobby reached down and kissed it for some reason.

"Melissa, I presume?"

"Missy. M-i-s-s-y."

She grinned and showed off her bright, white teeth. It was a uniquely toothy smile. A large, peculiar grin that I remembered being able to count every single white stub protruding from her gums.

"Well, Missy, I want you to meet my two mates...uh..." Bobby pointed at us.

"Charleston."

"Vincent."

"Right, gotcha," Bobby nodded. "Let's get to work. Hop in the boat, toss on a life jacket, and you all need to bring better shoes next time. For now, take off the sandals."

Sixty seconds later, we were sailing. There was no classroom teaching period. With Bobby, it was life jackets on, and let's learn by practicing. The Australian steered us out into the open water, quickly spitting out the meanings of starboard, stern, bow, and port. I wasn't a sailor nor mathematician, but the boat was around 20 feet long and 10 feet wide with benches along the port and starboard sides.

Missy sat on the starboard side while Charleston and I sat across from her. Bobby was stern side steering us and shouting instructions in what sounded like a fake Australian TV accent.

"Wait, Charleston, right? I know you," the cheerful Missy crowed.

"Really," my brother perked up." From where?

"Did you go to Hollandsworth?"

"Yes, why?"

"You've been over to my house."

"What do you mean? How?"

"Vincent, step back here. I'm going to show you how to tie a few basic knots."

I followed Bobby to the stern of the boat but listened intently to my brother's conversation. The wind howled, but I faintly heard:

"My brother Christopher was in your grade."

"Oh, really?" Charleston smiled. He seemed fascinated by her. "He's great. We had some good times together on the wrestling team. How's he doing?"

"He's fine. He can be a pain sometimes, but like all siblings can. You guys are brothers, right?"

"Yeah, Vincent's going into his freshman year at Verity, and I'm going into 11th grade. What about you?"

I was struggling immensely with the overhand knot. This was to be expected considering I never learned how to tie my shoes in the "correct" manner. I simply made the "x," looped the right lace under the left one, then created two bunny ears, swooped them together and pulled. Then I did two bunny ears again and looped them together to double knot. My father spent years trying to teach me the "normal" way, but some psychological block prevented me from learning. Now my childhood foibles were catching up to me out on the docile bay.

"Wow, you look younger than my brother," she said. "And I'm going into my freshman year at Hewitt."

"Oh, congrats. I hear great things about Hewitt. It's not co-ed, though. That must suck."

My brother had such an easy time talking to her. He wasn't dealing with introspective anxiety and didn't seem to be reminded of our mother as much as I was. Instead, he was suave, well-spoken, and a blatant extrovert. I knew next to nothing about girls, but Missy appeared to be smitten.

"Missy, why don't you come back and take a turn with the knots. My mate here's having some issues."

I glared at Bobby for a second, but couldn't pierce his Aviators. Missy sat down and tied the overhand knot with ease. Bobby then let her steer the boat around the bay while he went to check on the sails.

"One second now. We're tacking. I'll fix this in a jiffy."

I had no idea what that meant, and as an instructor, Bobby should've asked if we knew the term "tacking," but I suppose I was also at fault for not asking him to explain. He handled the submissive Peconic Bay with ease, but at no point during the first day did I feel I learned anything of value. Although, I have this permanent image etched in my mind of Missy steering the sailboat with her blonde tips blowing behind her and all 32 teeth displaying how happy she was with the zephyrs and splashes of water grazing her smooth, tan skin.

On Sunday night, my father drove into Bridgehampton to pick Nara up from the bus station, who then dropped him off at the nearby train station. We had a weekend filled with Wiffle Ball, golf at the local Poxabogue Course, and two trips to Mecox Beach. We chose not to do anything exciting for Independence Day because there was really nothing to celebrate. Every day was equally painful at first, and my father's constant "you doing okay boys?" didn't help. Nara's arrival would be a blessing to my brother and me. Her tranquil mien would be a welcome addition to a house filled with three, soon to be two, brooding males. I hugged my father before he left and then prepared myself two peanut butter sandwiches for dinner. I was actually looking forward to Monday because our sailing lessons were held on Mondays, Wednesdays, and Fridays.

The next day, Nara drove us to Noyack in silence, and we met Bobby by the boat. Missy was late again, but I didn't mind. She walked towards us, and I couldn't help but stare at her more easygoing outfit. Missy wore a canary yellow bikini bottom with black polka dots and a long, white translucent tank top. Her bare legs displayed a symmetrical color change due to a weekend sunburn she must've sustained while wearing short shorts. I just had to build up the intrepidity to talk to her today. I wanted this girl to be my first kiss. Not just this type of girl, but Missy herself. This vivacious, infallible beauty who was my age and came from the same background as me. I didn't deserve her, but what a summer-altering moment that could've been.

"Hi guys. Sorry I'm late."

"No worries, Sheila. Wind's blowing 12 miles an hour from the west. Maybe we'll try to make landfall at the atoll in the distance."

Today, Charleston sat on the port side first, and Missy climbed onto the boat and sat right beside him, while I had no choice but to man the starboard side. Bobby adjusted the sails while Charleston and Missy started chatting like decades-long comrades.

"So, what's high school like? What should I be prepared for?" The perky vixen asked my unassuming brother.

"Oh, you're gonna love it. For me, ninth grade was looser and more relaxing. The free periods in the lounge...uh, do you have a lounge?"

"Mmhmm."

"Cool, well, the free periods are great for making new friends, and depending on the school, you can go out to lunch or breakfast or whatever."

"That sounds super awesome."

"Yeah, and I actually had less homework in ninth grade at Verity than in my final year at Hollandsworth. You're gonna love it. You have nothing to stress about."

"It sucks there won't be boys, though," Missy said, oozing with subtlety.

Bobby sailed onward with his Aviators staring directly into the sun. He was clearly in his element. I, while firmly outside my element, couldn't stop looking at Missy. Her long, trim sunburnt legs leading to that diminutive, yellow bikini bottom; her dirty blonde hair blowing unceremoniously across her habitually smiling face; her tiny bikini top, barely noticeable through the white tank; every movement she made was mesmerizing.

My thought process was quite peculiar because several months prior, girls were simply an afterthought. They were just dance partners and exotic creatures to look at from afar. But seeing Missy while firmly entrenched in a pubescent stage, changed my entire view of the gender.

"Charleston, come on back here. Steer us into the isle due northwest. We're gonna get out by the sandbar."

Charleston leaped to his feet, walked to the stern, and held the rudder. Missy placed her dainty fist beneath her chin and gawked at him.

"So, um...Missy. Do you—" I attempted.

She was caught in a deep trance.

"What do you like, what do you do for like, fun?"

"Were you talking to me?" She said in what I felt was a sweet tone, but everything she did seemed sweet to me.

"Yeah, uh, what do you...what are your hobbies?"

"I don't know like I don't play on any teams or do any clubs. I just like hanging out with my friends."

"That's not really a hobby, though," I said.

She either didn't hear me or intentionally ignored me and looked towards the approaching island.

"Perfect, Charleston. We're aground now. Everyone hop off the boat and follow me. There'll be fiddler crabs, come on now...oh and the water's gonna be up to your stomach or shoulders so dress accordingly."

Bobby leaped into the bay and steered the boat closer to shore. Meanwhile, my older brother instantly took off his shirt. He didn't lift weights and wasn't naturally sinewy, but he was skinny and four inches taller than me. Charleston had curly brown hair that was neither light nor dark. At a younger age, some of the less clever and more nefarious boys would tease him for having a "Jewfro." The hair in its current form could probably fit snugly into that colloquial categorization. Charleston also had some light chest hair that plenty of girls our age with Electra complexes would find attractive and manly. He had never brought a girl-friend home before, but Charleston had his braces taken off about six months prior, and very few would have just cause for calling him ugly.

He dove into the water headfirst and emerged with one loud breath while Missy was about to follow. She took off her shirt, but I was behind her and couldn't achieve the ideal view of her front. All I saw was one small string tied across the middle of her back, doing a poor job of covering her tan lines. I thought about what seeing my first pair of breasts would be like. The mesmerizing power a body part could hold. However, an image of my mother wearing a one-piece at a beach in France suddenly popped into my head. I pictured her scolding me and immediately regretted my dirty thoughts. Then Missy jumped into the water.

I hesitated for a few seconds and elected to leave my shirt on as I leaped in to join my fellow sailors. Compared to my shirtless brother, I was unattractive. I was carrying five to seven pounds of baby fat and was considered short for a 14-year-old. In my 40-person grade at Hollandsworth, I was outside the top 30 in height. Naturally, acne began to appear on my face and back, and I still had a year left of braces. I wrestled and played football and baseball during the school year, but never did any weight training and relied on pure genetics and repetition to be a team leader. I learned a short time prior that my father didn't find me to be a handsome child.

I know this because about two months ago, I bravely entered the master bedroom to see if I could watch the Yankee game with him. He nodded as he took a sip from his beer. We didn't say a word to each other, but occasionally my father would let out an audible snipe at the umpires who were clearly listening intently to his intelligent and well-thought-out critiques. As the game progressed, I became uncomfortable and chose to lay on my stomach at the foot of the bed. By the eighth inning, through the natural contorting of my body's position, my stomach became visible. I noticed my father looking at me and at the end of the half-inning, he said:

"Vincent, stand up."

I stood.

"Lift up your shirt." He demanded.

"Dad, what are you doing? This is weird."

"Lift up your goddamn shirt," he said, and I obliged.

My father looked at me in disgust.

"No dessert for a week."

I left the room and didn't bother to watch the rest of the game.

Anyway, my point is, if my own father didn't find me attractive, why would some random, pretty girl?

I attempted to hide my feelings of insecurity as the four of us swam towards the shore. I felt my t-shirt increasing in mass the farther I swam while the three of them seemed to glide through the shallow water like porpoises.

"Let's race to the shore," Charleston shouted to Missy and me.

Everyone immediately took off, and my brazen brother had the early lead. I splashed around sluggishly as I shifted between the crawl and breaststroke, quickly learning my efforts were futile. Missy's feet kicked right in front of my face, and I ruminated about how much more aesthetically pleasing her feet were than mine. Hers appeared silky with recently-applied teal nail polish, while I had rugged soles from a decade of athletics and the occasional wart removal.

Bobby guided the boat ashore while Charleston ran out of the water onto the beach with his arms in the air. Missy followed behind him. I was a few strokes away from standing distance but paused when I witnessed Missy turn around for the first time. Her svelte figure left me in a watery stupor. At that time, she was the definition of beauty from head to toe.

Her wondrous hair and face couldn't bear to match the flawlessness of her body. Her flat stomach and trim waist created a seemingly illusory image that, to me, became the quintessence of what a 14-year-old girl should look like. I paused my stroke and remained in the water as any pubescent boy would need to.

"Come on, Vincent, check out these fiddler crabs," Bobby shouted.

"One second, I'm just dealing with a leg cramp."

I eventually joined the group onshore, and we watched as a cast of crabs sidestepped with no real direction in mind. This sandbar-island hybrid was only about 40 feet long and 15 feet wide, with reeds growing out of the western half. It was dull, but the crabs' roguish strut was enjoyable enough to watch.

"They're so cute," Missy said, breaking the silence.

"We used to have to take care of these at Hollandsworth, remember Vincent?"

"Yeah, in science class."

"Right, it was fiddler crabs and anole lizards, and kids would have to take home the pet for a week to look after. That was a fun assignment."

"I wonder why one claw is bigger than the other?" Missy asked rhetorically.

"They're evolutionary traits," my brother added smugly. "The bigger claw is for combat and mating, while the smaller one helps with food consumption."

Charleston's primary hobby throughout childhood, if you can classify it as such, was "animals." He seemed to know everything about any genus we encountered. Growing up, he'd continuously watch Animal Planet; specifically, his favorite show, *The Most Extreme.* Each episode ranked the 10 best animals in a specific category, like speed, for example. Charleston was glued to the TV and memorized thousands of meaningless facts. My parents would heap praise upon him anytime we went on a hike or swim, and he pointed out some obscure note about bat guano or tropical fish lifespan. He interned at the Central Park Zoo the summer before my mother became sick. Presently, it was a declining passion, but that didn't stop him from spouting supercilious comments whenever possible.

"Wow, you know a lot about animals," Missy said, while she punched his upper arm.

"Thanks," he looked at her but with unmatched enthusiasm.

Bobby had wandered off back to the boat, leaving us unsupervised. No one else seemed to notice or care, but it was unprofessional.

"Come on, fellas," Bobby eventually shouted. "Back to the boat."

My heavy shirt latched on to my amorphous torso as I ran towards the boat, while Missy's sun-kissed skin gleamed in front of me. She laughed as we swam back to the water. I thought about how it must've been nice to be able to laugh and have two parents and a beautiful body.

Back aboard the boat, Bobby adjusted the sails, without explaining what he was doing, and handed the rudder to me. I steered for 20 minutes and then rotated with Charleston and Missy. After an hour or two, we arrived back to the Noyack alcove, where Nara was patiently waiting for us beside my father's car.

Truthfully, I was shocked my father allowed her to drive it, but I guess it was better than the alternatives of: spending money to rent a second car, forcing us to bike 5-10 miles everywhere, or making us stay in Manhattan on weekdays. Nara was a safe, passive driver who sang quietly while she cruised past multi-million-dollar houses in her new, navy BMW. I wondered what she would've thought if five years ago someone allowed her to see into the future. She went from an Ulaanbaatar native struggling to make ends meet to this peculiar role.

Nara continued to drive us to and from our thrice-weekly sailing lessons for the rest of the summer. On the first day of the class, the three of us all seemed genuinely excited to learn and be out on the open water, but by our final one, we were each disappointed in some way. I never had a lengthy conversation with Missy, nor did I build up the temerity to kiss her, let alone ask for her phone number. She also could never breakthrough Charleston's aching heart. Missy tried every flirtation device a 14-year-old girl had at her disposable, but he just didn't seem interested. He enjoyed talking to her; they spent countless hours chatting about school, animals, their futures, TV shows, movies, and even sailing, but they never advanced past meaningless summer friendship. I wasn't sure what Charleston's issue was. Maybe Missy was too young for him? Perhaps she wasn't attractive enough? Was he too distraught over our mother? Was he holding back his feelings because I was so blatant about my infatuation? I never asked him. We didn't have that kind of relationship. Charleston himself had a disappointing summer simply because he didn't learn how to sail. He was the most interested of the three of us and actually chose to ask questions when our valiant captain neglected to explain something. In the end, it was a wasted summer that started as dreadfully as possible and only improved because each passing week was another further from our mother's passing.

I typically loved the Hamptons, but it was challenging to get excessively excited about anything at that time. Our days livened when our father came out on the weekends, but only because it meant spending less time cooped up in the house. We didn't have our mother there to help us experience the more haute side of the Hamptons. There were no more expensive dinners, shopping trips, or visits to friends' magnificent homes. It was a lonely summer filled with contemplation about the horrid past few months and the nerve-racking near future.

My first day at the co-ed Verity Prep was fast approaching, and that meant I needed to figure out ways to make friends, talk to girls, join sports teams, and make teachers like me. It was daunting to think about, and I would've loved to discuss these emotionally strenuous thoughts with my mother, but I was now left to fend for myself as a fearful freshman with no social skills.

Book 2

CHAPTER 1

I OPENED THE LOBBY DOORS to Verity Prep and found girls everywhere. Some were my age; some were seventh-graders; some were 12th graders; each one was stunning in her own way. They each represented limitless storylines. These would be my friends, girlfriends, crushes, and potential loves of my life. My heart was throbbing, but everyone else seemed stress-free as they strolled through the student lounge on such a momentous day.

I thought the main area was similar to that of Grand Central Terminal on a weekday morning, filled with congested air and the bustling, cacophonous sounds of rowdy fast-walking New Yorkers. As I continued through the main hallway, which was adorned with ceramic sculptures and abstract paintings, I felt oddly content. The bright colors, combined with the laid-back students taking advantage of the "no dress code" policy, was the polar opposite of anything I was accustomed to. There were no ties and blazers, and no one was shushing the students and telling them to show some decorum. It was a fascinating, welcome change.

The school's receptionist directed me to my homeroom on the 3rd floor, where I'd receive my schedule. After trekking up a couple of flights of stairs with my soon-to-be filled black North Face, I entered a classroom and took a seat by myself in the back row.

"What's your name," the homeroom teacher asked.

"Vincent Beattie."

"Here's your schedule. Let me know if you have any questions."

I'd spent a few hours on my computer in August choosing electives and clubs and was admitted to every class I wanted. This was a welcome change to Hollandsworth's rigid schedule structure. Instead of taking Latin and other similarly tedious courses, I was now enrolled in Digital Photography, Sports Debate, and Acting Improv. I was still required to take English, American History, Geometry, and Biology, but just to have some semblance of freedom was invigorating, as was my newfound ability to dress myself.

On my first day of school, I came dressed in Nike sneakers, blue jeans, a green American Eagle t-shirt, and a charcoal hoodie with the sleeves rolled to my elbows. It was sincere and straightforward. The last thing I wanted to do was stand out.

I elected not to speak to any of the teenagers that filed into my homeroom. I sat still, quietly observing their mannerisms like I was on a riveting safari. The diversity my father once spoke of was apparent. And, my old friend Albert's parents would've been disappointed at a classroom that could've been at least 50 percent Jewish. This was a far cry from the Hollandsworth population. I also found it thrilling to try to figure out which boys and girls were new to Verity and which had been there since Kindergarten. I used the terms "lifer" and "newbie" to differentiate between the two. Verity was a K-12 school, but the majority of Upper East Side same-sex schools ended after eighth or ninth grade, so there was a flood of newbies on the first day. My incoming class had around 100 teens, and the ratio was roughly 70 lifers to 30 newbies. This was a beneficial system because I didn't have to feel like the only one going through the tough acclimation period.

I still remember my first class of high school being Digital Photography with Mr. Edwards. He was a 45-year-old Jamaican man with long dreadlocks tied in a ponytail. He spoke in a slow, dulcet manner and would frequently arrive late to class. His idiosyncratic style made for an atypical 40 minutes. However, he was only the second most memorable person I met on that first day.

When Raven Jimenez entered the compact, eight-seat classroom, I gawked. This wasn't a brief, half-second stare, mind you. This was a wide-eyed, mouth open, one eyebrow raised, grasping my keyboard as if I'd been thrown backward, type of stare. Any memories of Missy immediately vanished from my mind forever the moment Raven took her seat next to me. My eyes were immediately drawn to her perfectly straightened golden blonde hair. It hugged her neck and upper back before it naturally fell towards her behind. How did one get their hair to be that color? It deserved not just compliments but veneration.

Raven turned towards me, and I saw her face for the first time. Her hair was parted perfectly down the middle and trickled past her cheeks, framing a petite, symmetrical visage. Next came her thin brown eyebrows that gave way to prominent sea-green eyes. Raven's closed eyelids helped display her cat-eye makeup that would've made Cleopatra jealous. The blonde's delicate nose and thin, rose-colored, succulent lips rounded out her diamond-shaped face. I quickly found she typically leaned her head inward and to the right as if to show the world that her left side was especially praiseworthy.

Raven looked over at me for the first time and smirked, showing off her extensive dimples. At that moment, I would've chosen her over any girl in the world. I glanced up and down her body with the subtlety of a first-time birdwatcher. Raven was on the shorter side, perhaps five-foot-three, but she had these long, olive-colored legs that made her seem four inches taller. That, combined with her natural swagger and atavistic aplomb, deserved my highest exaltation.

Even her fashion sense was fastidiously surreal. It was the first day of high school, and she was wearing black knee-high boots to match her dark shorts that seemed to fall many miles away from her knees. Then there was the hunter green hoodie. This was no ordinary Gap purchase. The piece was likely a Barney's accoutrement Raven stylized herself. It was formfitting but also had a noticeable fringe, proving she was quite handy with a pair of scissors. The hunter green fabric laid just an inch past her waist with frilly strands creating a makeshift border. The sleeves then cruised beyond her wrists and landed safely along her knuckles. Finally, came the zipper.

I specifically remember thinking about Raven looking at herself in the mirror before school. My idiotic one-track mind pictured her topless with just the enigmatic hoodie draped over her lissome body. She was grasping the silver zipper and figuring out the perfect place for it to live. Raven clearly felt the need to be a sexy provocateur, but also didn't want the reputation as someone who was licentious. Where did that pesky zipper belong? Raven would've zipped it too high at first so no cleavage was visible. Then, she would've seen her cat-eye, golden blonde hair, and short shorts and felt the zipper belonged lower. Raven would then realize it was too low, and certain parts would be visible if she made some kind of elephantine turn or gesture. The priggish zipper eventually rose to its final resting place. It had now achieved the moment of success Goldilocks had on her third and final attempt. The hoodie was school-appropriate but left enough for the imagination of the incoming boys who had never been in the presence of a teenage deity.

Mr. Edwards started by demonstrating how to use the software on the school-supplied Macs and gave a few before and after examples to teach the importance of particular techniques. Unfortunately, I never learned these seemingly helpful methods. I was ogling Raven while she stared intently at the teacher. Raven was intelligent and inquisitive, too. In our eight-person class, she was the only one to raise her hand and ask a question following the predictable "any questions?" from Mr. Edwards.

"In what instances would one like, use the lowest and highest saturation settings?"

While Mr. Edwards answered, I thought about Raven's ambrosial voice. It was high-pitched like a meadowlark, but had a hidden ferocity I'm sure could spring out at any time. Her tender tone reverberated throughout the 200 square foot room. I couldn't believe she *chose* to sit next to me.

I didn't speak to anyone for the entirety of Digital Photography, nor did I break my conversational virginity in my second-period Geometry or third-period English classes. I did say my name when we went around the room and introduced ourselves, though. People now knew the nasally, atonal voice-cracking squeaks were coming from my braces-filled mouth. That was a minor victory. The next positive was that my pusillanimous strategy to the first day of school would be challenged by the one class where speaking was required—fourth-period Acting Improv.

I was the first one to arrive at the school's noteworthy auditorium, and once there, I introduced myself to the pudgy, middle-aged teacher, Ms. Cuzano, and then the students began to irrupt. As luck would have it, there were nine girls in the class, and I was one of just two boys. It was a serendipitous and necessary moment as I was being thrown into the deep end of a pool surrounded by well-dressed, long-haired barracudas.

Ms. Cuzano began describing the weekly elective, but then I heard Rihanna singing softly in the hallway. She was approaching the theater while singing "Umbrella."

I remembered thinking what would Rihanna be doing at Verity Prep on the Tuesday after Labor Day? But then Raven, that commendable seductress, skipped into the theater. She had a flawless singing voice that mimicked Rihanna's to perfection.

"Raven? You're joining us again this year?"

"Yes, Ms. C." She sat in the third row, where I was the only occupant.

"Well, we're all delighted. Maybe arrive on time next week?"

"It's difficult to make an entrance when you enter the room first."

"I suppose every troupe needs its diva."

I heard a very soft "cunt" muttered under the breath of this Aphrodite.

Ms. Cuzano described the mundane activities of Acting Improv, before telling us to join her on stage for a rousing game of "Freeze." I rose to my feet and realized I'd have no choice but to cross paths with the now-texting Raven. She was seated in the aisle with her BlackBerry in hand when I stood over her. I remained silent, hoping she'd notice and stand or move her olive shins closer to her body, but to no avail. After four seconds, she looked at me and said something along the lines of:

"You need something?" Raven's angelic voice made every sentence sound like a lullaby.

"I...uh...I'm just—" She interrupted me and said:

"Wait, you're into DP too?"

"Um, what?" I stood dumbfounded and instinctively looked at her breasts.

"Digital Photography, perv."

"Yeah, I...uh...of course."

"I'm just messing with you. Loosen up, man. We sat next to each other. You're the guy who didn't speak and seemed incredibly anxious and uptight."

"That sounds like me," I chuckled.

"I'm Raven."

She held out her hand with the palm facing down. What was I supposed to do with that? Should I emulate her? Give her a firm handshake? Kiss her hand? Second-period Geometry was simple compared to this.

I grabbed her hand and gave it a firm shake as I'd frequently done throughout my life.

"Don't break my hand, killer," she smiled.

"Raven, you're holding up my class again," Ms. Cuzano said.

"One second dearest," my sardonic companion replied.

"Vincent, a word of advice, don't let sirens draw you into the rocks."

Raven and I were the last two students to take the stage. We played this game called "Freeze," where two people began acting out a scene, and one of the other students off to the side would yell "freeze." The actors would stay still, and the interrupting member would jump into the scene in place of one of the two initial students. It was quite chaotic at first. We went from 13th century jousters to toddlers in a sandbox to two girls on a date. The game moved at a blistering pace, and I wanted no part of it. I sat on the sidelines quietly observing my fellow thespians. It was my own version of assimilation.

"Freeze," Raven yelled as she took the place of an older looking girl.

Raven and her partner seamlessly shifted from sawing a log in half to sunbathing on a beach.

"I've been so stressed recently," Raven said in character. "Will you put this lotion on my back."

Raven turned over, and her younger partner hesitated for a few seconds before gently touching the meritorious hunter green hoodie. Had I been more seasoned in the art of seduction, I would've yelled "freeze" right then and there and began the next scene with my hands on her back. However, my only other male peer and I were too terrified.

"Oh, yeah. Now lower," Raven moaned.

"Hey, are you looking to avoid the sun or get a free massage?" her partner retorted and climbed off of her.

"Isn't it beautiful out here? I love watching the waves. Ibiza has always been my favorite," Raven rolled the "th" sound in Ibiza like a true Spaniard.

"Yeah, but it's a little too hot today. I'd like to go back to our air-conditioned room."

The scene didn't grab the viewer, but Raven certainly wasn't to blame. I think if I had been there with her, the whole audience would've seen genuine chemistry at work.

Someone eventually yelled the magic word and joined the next scene in a doctor's office before Raven finally exited center stage. We continued playing that same game before shifting to some other improv favorites like "Pass the Invisible Ball," and ending the class with "Park Bench."

The latter was a simple enough concept. Two strangers sat on a park bench, and through conversation, their identities were eventually revealed. It soon became my favorite because it allowed more creativity and less training.

"How about someone we haven't heard from yet?" Ms. Cuzano said. "My only two members with Y chromosomes, sit on the bench please."

I exhaled deeply and convinced myself that even a mediocre scene would be acceptable. I remember telling myself not to be the one ignominious memory Raven and the rest of the girls would have from the first day.

"Hey, dude. I'm Frankie McDaniel," my presumptuous partner whispered.

"Vincent." We shook hands as we walked behind the bench.

"And...scene," Ms. Cuzano yelled.

I chose to play it conservatively. I'd act as a senior citizen feeding pigeons. That was simple enough. I'd slow my speech pattern and speak with an achy voice. I just couldn't humiliate myself.

"Wow man. You're looking swole," the sinewy Frankie said to my character.

"What's that now?"

He started touching my calf.

"What do you think you're doing, mister?"

"Yo, who's your trainer? Whoever he is, I could make you 10 times bigger."

"That's alright young man. I'm just here to feed the birds."

"Birds? That's lame. Let's go work out and chase some tail, bro."

We chose two polar opposite characters, and he clearly wasn't going to adapt, so I had to lead the scene. I saw Raven watching us intently. The BlackBerry remained on her slender thighs as I gave the pigeons another fistful of imaginary feed.

"Well, I suppose I could go for a light jog. Keep my heart healthy."

"Fu—I mean, screw that. Let's get a pump in."

"Now, sonny, you're going to have to meet me halfway here."

"Finish feeding your rats or whatever, and then we'll work out and get smoothies."

"Alrighty, but I won't pay you a dime."

"And scene," Ms. Cuzano yelled. "Nice job, gentleman. Vincent, way to think on your feet. Nicely developed characters."

The bell rang shortly thereafter, and I encountered the same precarious position where I stood over a texting Raven in the third row.

"Excuse me," I said with a brazen tone I didn't know I possessed.

"Oh, what was your name again? You did a nice job."

"Vincent from Digital Photography."

"That's right. Vincent."

She stood, picked up her black Givenchy bag with a gold chain that seemed too formal for school, and followed me out of the classroom to the staircase.

"First day here, right?" She said.

"Um, sorry," I turned, startled. "Were you talking to me?"

"Yeah."

"Yeah, it is."

"Don't sweat it. You're doing fine."

"Thanks," I stared at her delightful dimples. "It's not your first day, right?"

"No, I'm actually a sophomore. Been here forever."

"Oh, you're a lifer?"

"Lifer?" She smiled her trademark grin that never included teeth. "I like that."

Raven exited the staircase while I stood on the landing in my irrepressible stupor.

The rest of my first week was uneventful. My core courses seemed surprisingly easy, particularly American History, where my fellow acting enthusiast Frankie also resided. I didn't make any friends but was enjoying the French-Indian War, Geometry, and even my first foray into the mind of fellow New Yorker, Holden Caulfield. After school, I chose not to play any sports in the fall, so I was typically home by 3:30 pm and finished my homework by dinnertime. My indifferent brother was decent to me at home but never made an effort to show me around or introduce me to people at school. He was too preoccupied with navigating the inscrutable world of the upperclassmen. I occasionally saw him from afar in the student lounge, and he seemed frequently stressed with the pressures of Verity's social hierarchy. Charleston wasn't Prom King material, although the Manhattan private schools had a strict no Prom King and Queen rule, but he wasn't a dunce either. Charleston was a bit of a goofball when he was surrounded by his seven to 10 male friends, but at home or by himself, Charleston was typically morose. Had he been cheerier, I would've asked him for help on my first digital photography assignment.

By week two, Mr. Edwards told his students they needed to travel to a significant New York City landmark and take pictures of the exterior, interior, and any other defining features. I didn't put a lot of thought into the task because, while I wanted to impress Raven, it was still Digital Photography. That was the mindset I'd acquired from my meddlesome father.

Prior to Charleston's first day of ninth grade, he had to pick his clubs and electives online. He requested my parents' aid, and they guided him towards two antonymic course loads. My father suggested classes that would aid in his academic development in core courses: Finance Club and SAT Prep Club. Morgan believed it was never too early to focus on college and beyond. There was no reason to fritter away with trivial, time-wasting classes. Phyllis, on the other hand, believed Charleston should further his budding passions. She recommended Ceramics, Sports Debate, and Drawing. I saw the merit in both strategies, but Charleston sided with my mother without much hesitation, and the latter grouping made up a quarter of his weekly schedule.

Each time my brother's report card arrived, my mother would applaud him for his A's in his clubs and electives and glossed over his B's in Geometry and French. My father would say:

"You don't get an A in Ceramics; you should be riding the short bus."

Morgan continued to remind everyone, "well, that's not a core subject" or "you're not focusing enough on the core subjects: English, History, Math, Science, and Language."

Since I no longer had my mother's powerful perspective, I garnered my father's avowedly outdated thought process. I'd still try to get an A in Digital Photography and my other non-core courses, but there was no need to spend more than 15-30 minutes on an assignment. Given that line of reasoning, after school on Friday, I walked two blocks to the Guggenheim Museum.

I stood across the street from the famed spiraled exterior and took a few tenebrous pictures. I started with my camera facing vertically and then tried horizontally. I then walked south of the architectural marvel and took a few more photos before heading north of the building and doing the same. I finished my 10-minute assignment by standing right underneath the first "G" in Guggenheim and panning my camera upwards. I never even went inside the building. It was an indolent way to accomplish a captivating assignment, but I didn't care. It was only Digital Photography.

On Monday, I walked into that dorm-room-sized class and uploaded my photos onto my Mac, while Raven sat to my right, seeping intensity.

She wore a white t-shirt that had holes on the shoulder areas and bared the ideal amount of midriff. Raven's tawny skirt was the focal point of the outfit, and it had an off-white design that looked like a large grouping of neurons or spider-webs. Raven's matching tawny sandals went well with the band at the bottom of her golden blonde hair that was braided and tied at elbow length. The beauty's sea-green eyes were fixated on a picture of a bridge with the sun fading behind it.

"Raven," Mr. Edwards said. "The contrast here is exquisite. Everyone, slide your chairs over here."

Eight people crowded around the wunderkind.

"So, Raven, as we can see, went to DUMBO. Notice the darker buildings in the foreground and then the vivid oranges and blues in the background. She caught the sun setting just beneath the bridge, and I think the lack of people in the image is a great choice. Really solid start."

"Thanks. It took me forever to get this shot. Like, 300 pictures."

"Everyone, back to your computers. I'll be coming around individually to review your work," Mr. Edwards announced.

Naturally, I had to follow the class's virtuoso.

"Now, Vincent. Is this your first time dabbling in photography?"

"Yeah, well...I mean...yeah, I haven't really..."

"So, this is a standard picture of the Guggenheim. Beautiful building. Frank Lloyd Wright. I need to get *your* take on this. Any tourist could've taken this picture."

"Mmhmm."

"What does this image say to you? Focus on something unique. This can be done by zooming in or out, visualizing each end of that spectrum. Or, you could focus on the lettering. Possibly experiment with black-and-white features. Highlight your whites and dim your blacks, for example. I want you to have fun with this."

"Gotcha, that's very helpful."

This wasn't the Sistine Chapel. This was Digital Photography for underclassmen. Then again, I was always well-liked by teachers, and I wasn't going to argue or start off on the wrong foot.

Raven shifted her attention to my screen as Mr. Edwards walked to another computer.

"Sorry about that," she whispered. "I think he was a little too hard on you. Some of these are really cool angles. I like...wait go back."

My hand nervously clutched the mouse. I was perfectly content being subservient to her.

"Yeah, this one. The shot directly beneath the exterior. Here...let's, if you don't mind."

Raven then placed her hand on top of mine and guided the mouse along my screen. I let out an uncontrollable, but nearly silent whimper.

"You good?" She asked.

I nodded and then honed in on the orgastic feeling of her warm, soft hands rubbing the tips of my fingers. I closed my eyes for a moment and felt the tickle of her leather bracelet against my wrist.

"There. See. If we just center the subject and maybe introduce some rack focus...looks better already."

"Thank...you," I said as my lip quivered.

At that time, I knew next to nothing, but that felt flirtatious to me. There's no way she would've placed her hand on top of mine had she zero romantic interest. I needed advice. My heart raced as I contemplated potential next steps.

After the bell rang, I checked my schedule and saw I had a free period, so I dashed to the student lounge and took a seat at an empty freshmen table.

The way our lounge worked was each grade had a specific section of tables and chairs. I didn't know the punishment of sitting at an older grade's table without an invite, but I wasn't going to ask.

The bell rang a second time, and a few people sat at my table. To my right was Frankie McDaniel, while two lifers sat on my left and a boy I faintly recognized, sat directly across from me.

"What's going on, dude?" Frankie said to me.

"Not much. Just got back from Digital Photography. I've got French next."

"By the way, we were right about Acting Improv."

"How so?" I responded.

"So many hot girls. I mean, dude, are you serious?"

He was clearly a newbie.

"That girl you—" he was interrupted by the innominate stranger in front of us.

"Vincent, right?"

"Yeah, where do I know you from?"

"Digital Photography. I sit in the back corner. Dexter."

"Oh, gotcha. Nice to officially meet you."

Dexter was a scrawny newbie but had the extroverted personality of a lifer. He had two big buck teeth, and if you squinted your eyes, he looked like an oversized rat. I wasn't going to judge a book by its cover, though.

"What did you do for your first assignment?"

Frankie took out his phone and started texting while my conversation with Dexter continued.

"I went to the Intrepid and took some shots of the boat's exterior with the Hudson River in the background."

"Oh, that's a neat idea."

"So, what's the deal with you and that Raven? She's a sophomore, right?"

I innately looked over at the two girls at our table who didn't appear to be listening. They were immersed in their own in-depth conversation about what I had no idea.

"Yeah, she's a sophomore."

"Are you guys like, a thing?"

"What...us? God no," I found the assumption quite flattering.

"But you'd like to be?"

"I mean...uh...like, of course. She's really something."

"You guys talkin' about Raven from Improv," Frankie suddenly looked up. "Such a smoke."

I looked over at the girls next to us, and they were staring off in the other direction, but there was something disingenuous about them. I had a strong notion they were hanging on every word we said, ready to unleash the gossip around the school like artillery at a firing range. I had a brief bout of queasiness before I closed my eyes, inhaled deeply, and took out my geometry textbook.

Later in the week, while walking to Sports Debate, I saw Raven turn the corner in front of me. She was 10 feet away and inching closer. The whole lounge slowed as I thought of what our in-the-halls interaction would look like. Her sea-green eyes spotted me and honed in on their target. She raised her right hand in the air, where it stood motionless. Her fingers pointed upwards at a 45-degree angle. Raven's elbow was tucked in against her right rib cage. The two bracelets on her wrist twisted. The fetching dimples protruded from her cheeks. I was in a state of unmitigated panic. Given the angle of her arm and hand, how should I react? Was this a high five? A wave? An incoming brush upon my shoulder? If I think it's a wave and she meant for it to be a high five, would she be offended by my lack of enthusiasm? How many awkward predicaments could I have possibly encountered in just the first two weeks of my high school career?

I high fived her. It was flagrantly awkward. Raven seemed to grimace at my unbelievably poor taste in judgment. I made it quite evident I went to an all-boys school and had no experience with confident, strikingly beautiful women.

I trudged on to Sports Debate with my head hung low. I swirled my tongue around in my mouth, wondering if I had blown my shot with the enigmatic deity. Then I saw my older brother in the classroom, and it made me think about my mother. She would've been able to offer advice at a time like this. Phyllis was hip. She understood how stylish, sprightly sirens' senses worked. My mother would've told me to be myself and find common ground with the taut temptress. I needed to stop wallowing in self-pity and start demonstrating my worth.

"You're gonna love this class," Charleston smiled at me. "It's pass/fail. Four people debate about sports each week, and everyone else watches and picks a winner."

"Sounds perfect."

"Yeah, it's ninth through 12th graders, but age doesn't seem to matter. It's all about charisma, poise, and knowledge. I'm arguing that baseball is the hardest sport to play, and my opponent thinks hockey is."

"Can't wait. Good luck," I said.

"One day, you and I will partner up. We'll unleash a Beattie family smackdown."

After the bell rang, my brother gave a rousing argument about how baseball is three sports in one. Not only must one learn how to hit a tiny, white ball curving and sliding towards them, but a player also must learn how to field grounders and catch fly balls. If that weren't enough, you need to be able to throw hard and accurately from every position and ideally run quickly. It was a sound argument.

Charleston seemed calm throughout and handled the debate with impressive equanimity, earning the victory. I was proud of the way he put our family troubles behind him and became a well-regarded student and classmate. While we didn't talk much outside of school, watching him in something as simple and unimportant as Sports Debate made him an adequate role model. He hid our family's baggage and showed no signs of odium.

Next week in Digital Photography, I saw Raven walk in and sit next to me as she always did. Yet, in this specific class, I realized I felt less frightened and threatened. Raven was still her cool and laid-back self. Her midriff was showing; her legs long and thin underneath her skirt; and the golden blonde hair sizzled in the bright, white classroom. However, I felt a strange confidence that I attributed to my thoughts about my mother and brother and how they'd handle such a tempestuous young filly.

"Hey Raven," this was the first time I began an interaction. "Can you show me how to utilize shadows more? I'd ask Mr. Edwards, but—"

"I know. I hate how he leaves class every 10 minutes. It's like, some of us need help here."

"Well, not you. I mean, uh, your images of the Williamsburg club scene are awe-inspiring."

"Come on. Stop. Don't make me blush," she flashed her infectious dimples.

While Raven started to show me the tenets of shooting with shadows, I noticed Dexter looking over at us. It was more of a vindictive glare than a harmless, misplaced glance. He seemed like an oddball.

"You're like, I mean, like an expert at this," I tried to find the mix between fulsome and flirtatious.

Raven was wearing a striped skirt, an opalescent summery outfit with peach, turquoise, bubblegum pink, and bone-colored lines. She was the first person I'd ever met who could look smolderingly attractive in absolutely any outfit. It didn't matter if it was a parka, a skirt, leggings or a jersey; Raven made it all work. Her eccentric style matched her witty, lascivious personality to perfection. I would've given anything to have made her like me.

"Are there any other classes you're, uh, passionate about?" I asked.

"Hmm, well, I've always loved to sing and play guitar. I'm in the glee club and sometimes perform at school functions with my father's retro, acoustic guitar. Music and photography are the two things that keep me at peace."

"That's really cool that you have such strong passions at a young age."

Raven turned to me, tilted her head and squinted her piercing, sea-green eyes. She then shifted her focus back to her screen, adjusting the yellows and reds of her Williamsburg club. Her kaleidoscopic wonders could've hung in our townhouse any day.

CHAPTER 2

A S THE CALENDAR FLIPPED TO October, I became more jocose when I was around Raven. Anytime I saw her in the hallway, my ebullience was palpable. The beautiful deity continued to raise her arm in the air in that precarious position whenever she saw me. Sometimes I'd let her hand graze my shoulder while other times I'd wave to her from afar. An "A" on an American History test meant far less to me than a Raven Jimenez smile or even just hearing her pitch-perfect voice call my name in class.

On a Friday evening after school, the Glee Club was performing an autumn concert in the auditorium, and I went for the sole purpose of watching my frisky friend show off one of her interminable talents. I chose to sit in a particularly umbrageous spot against the wall on the left side of the theater. I was off to the side and by myself because I often felt apprehension when I was the centerpiece of a large crowd.

Raven came out on stage in a skin-tight black, sleeveless gown with her golden blonde hair falling symmetrically over her bosom. She was also wearing a gold necklace with a heart-shaped talisman sitting comfortably above her cleavage. Her hair, parted perfectly down the middle, created a triangular-shaped forehead framed by her neatly plucked brown eyebrows. I was besotted with this glowing goddess.

The various tenors, baritones and basses belted out The Beatles' "Let It Be," Billy Joel's "For the Longest Time" and Elton John's "Your Song" before the group separated into solos. The star of the show was unsurprisingly, Raven. She brought out her vintage Fender acoustic and played Heart's "Crazy on You." It was the perfect amalgamation of ferocity and frightening beauty.

I remember closing my eyes and imagining Raven serenading me with this song in a Caribbean villa. The doors and windows let in a light breeze, and wisps of Raven's hair straddled her flawless face. She touched my cheek softly, and I felt her breath in my ear. I heard "Vincent" uttered at a nearly indiscernible volume. I felt Raven's thin, rose-colored succulent lips gently graze my neck and chin. Her orgastic voice and perfunctory movements placed me firmly inside my idyll.

My pupils peeped onstage and watched as the girl of my dreams seemed to be staring in my direction and singing to me. Each high note reverberated throughout the fixated crowd. Raven's preternatural ability left a look of shock on the faces of those who'd never heard her sing before. She was a magnificent wonder, and I showered her with rapturous applause.

I chose not to stick around after the show to embarrass myself by gawking at this virtuoso. I went home, greeted my brother, and went into my room to do homework. However, I couldn't get Raven out of my mind. I went on her Facebook and immediately added her as a friend. Then I went back to my homework before hearing that glorious notification sound. Raven had accepted my request.

I went on her profile and found her AIM account. I wasn't going to message her immediately but wanted to have the option in my back pocket. Her instant messaging screen name was the very fitting: "Ralove414." I then continued to scroll through her Facebook wall and found a video she sent to her friend. It was of Raven rapping the "Lollipop Remix" by Lil Wayne.

It was sleek and intoxicating, as was the video of her dancing to Pitbull's "Go Girl." I remembered thinking about how amazing it would be if my feelings were reciprocated.

I thought about asking Charleston for advice, but figured he might just laugh at me or feel an ignominious shame at his pathetic, lovesick younger brother. Instead, I chose to talk to Frankie and Dexter in one of my free periods the next day. Who better to give advice then teenagers who were presumably having the same restless feelings towards other girls?

"You guys, I need help," I said matter-of-factly.

"What's going on, man?" Frankie responded.

"I think Raven is like, really hot and perfect, and she might even like me."

"I doubt it," Dexter said. "She's kind of a slut I hear. She's a real man's lady. Always flirting with everyone she sees."

"That's not true," I raised my voice in defense of my gorgeous friend.

"Look, I guarantee you. She's not interested."

"She accepted my Facebook friend request," I said proudly.

"Yeah, along with 500 others." Dexter seemed to have an answer for everything.

"I have evidence."

"You guys hook up already?" Frankie asked, trying to get a word in.

"No, but she chooses to sit next to me every class. Um, and she's touched my hand. Plus, she waves at me and jokes around with me. No other girl here talks to me. There's something here. I can feel it."

I was getting frustrated by Dexter's lack of faith. No one understood the intricacies of my relationship with Raven. I'd been living through it. I didn't know anything about women, but this girl definitely liked me. The way she flashed her dimples and fluttered her eyelashes. I wasn't 100 percent sure. Maybe she didn't like me. It was so difficult. I had to find out Raven's true feelings.

"I hear she blew some eighth-grader over the summer," Dexter added.

"That's not true. She wouldn't do that. She's prim and moralistic...I think."

"Yo, are you guys trying out for basketball next week?" Frankie interrupted our philosophical discussion.

"Yes," we both agreed.

My powwow with the two of them concluded with mixed results, but a chance happening after school led me to the deduction that I was right, and everyone else was wrong. It reminded me of a phrase my mother used to say:

"Be a Fruit Loop in a bowl full of Cheerios."

She had wanted her boys to be unique, free-thinking young men who didn't fold to peer pressure. I felt my ameliorating relationship with Raven would've made my loving mother proud.

Instead of going straight home that day, I decided I'd take a taxi to the Wagner Middle School Gym. It was where some Hollandsworth friends and I used to practice and play 3-on-3 games. They had an open gym on Wednesday afternoons, and I decided to take advantage prior to next week's tryouts. However, when I walked out onto Fifth Avenue to hail a cab, I saw Raven sitting with a friend on a bench outside of Central Park. I chose to cross the street with my head down, pretending I didn't see her. Then, without making eye contact, I turned and raised my arm to call a taxi. I expected Raven would see me and perk up, and my feminine instincts were surprisingly correct.

"Vincent? Hey," Raven's voice shook.

I put my hand down, turned around, and looked to see from where the voice was coming. It wasn't my best acting performance, but eventually, I was able to spot her sitting no more than 10 feet away. I strutted towards the beauty. Raven was wearing that hunter green hoodie I loved so much.

"How are you?" She asked.

"I'm good, um, I, uh, am just heading to the gym to play basketball."

"Cool."

"Are you cold? You seem...uh, freezing."

"Oh, I am." Her teeth clacked together. "Can you hold my hands. They're practically blue."

Raven extended both of her arms out like a 21st century mummy. Her cerulean-tinted hands shook. I was startled at the request but attempted to hide my libidinous notions.

"Of course. I'm, uh, happy to do anything to help."

I moved in slow-motion as my palms crept closer. I thought about how I'd had a nice three-inch growth spurt over the previous six months, and perhaps my fingers had elongated during that time as well. I clenched her frigid, silky hands with my nervously shaking ones. Raven tilted her head, blew some strands of hair away from her mouth, and smiled delicately, continuing to never show her presumably bright, white teeth. I began to rub the tops of her hands with my thumbs. My digits rotated clockwise atop her blue knuckles.

"Mmm, that feels nice," she said, dripping with éclat.

I nodded at her, completely unsure of what to say or when to let go.

"You seem like a really kind guy."

Her lurid, green eyes penetrated my doughy face. I felt the need to say something but was lost in her effervescent beauty. Raven wanted me to speak, to mutter anything. Instead, we both just remained in our spots; her seated and me standing. The ever-garrulous Raven wouldn't say a word. She was thinking about something, but I had no idea what. All I knew was she liked me.

Raven eventually let go of my hands, stood up, and gave me a warm embrace.

"Wow, you feel hot," she said, trying to perforate the blatant awkwardness.

I smirked, released her, and walked towards the street without saying a word.

"I feel much better now. Have a good practice, Vincent."

I was walking to Digital Photography class with a sheepish grin. How would Raven treat me after our first, ardent embrace? I decided I'd play it cool and just pretend like nothing had changed. However, when I spotted Dexter on my way to class, he told me he had an idea.

"If Mr. Edwards leaves the room, I know just what to do. Follow my lead."

I had no reason not to trust him. This moment reminded me of my early Boxington days. My Hollandsworth peers would cheer me on or give me a thumbs-up whenever I was dancing with a cute girl. Throughout my life, my friends had always rooted for me to succeed with women. My compatriots knew about my prudish personality and were always glad to see me succeed outside of my comfort zone. Dexter seemed to have my best interests in mind. He was a friend helping out a friend.

We entered the classroom and took our usual seats. Raven walked in, and I proceeded with my daily routine of staring at her immeasurable beauty until she looked in my direction. Today, Raven was wearing a short-sleeve turtleneck that bared ample midriff. It was mid-Fall by now, and she'd been known to complain about the cold, but I suppose Raven was one of those people who chose fashion over comfort. I certainly wasn't going to talk her into displaying less of her alluring, toned abs. The turtleneck was violet with light blue and beige horizontal stripes, and Raven also wore a black scarf draped around her neck and past her waist. The scarf's prominent feature was the lengthy fringe that made up a solid third of the garment. She was wearing skin-tight black leather leggings to match her thigh-high black boots. This modern-day Venus was also adorned with a new royal blue Hermès bracelet and a silver watch. It was a more daring, less colorful look, but Raven nailed it as always.

Anyway, after my daily, moronic objectification finished and class began, I started editing a series of pictures I took at the Central Park Zoo. My favorite of the sequence was a zoomed-in image of the famed clock tower. Metal hippos, bears, and elephants danced around counterclockwise while two monkeys rang a bell. It was an iconic sight for New Yorkers and tourists alike. I chose to zoom in on the clock itself and have the animals dance their repetitive jig in the background. Raven peered over at my screen and offered some advice:

"I think you should highlight the leaves in the background. They've got this cool yellow-green tint that could be utilized."

"Oh, um. Thanks."

"Yeah, raise the saturation here and lower it on the metal clock pieces."

"Cool."

At the time, I was always so focused on Raven's outer beauty that I tended to ignore her intelligence. She was an unquestionable expert at photography, and I was her malleable pupil. Raven also had such a memorable singing voice and always seemed so passionate about her loves. I envied the euphoria Raven experienced any time she was cocooned in her worlds of pictures and melodies. I didn't have anything like that. I was above average at several sports, but as a ninth-grader, there was no area where I was easily superior to my classmates. Raven had two of those, maybe more. She could've received a record deal, modeling contract, or art gallery showing all by age 16. I was always impressed by her.

"Your pictures keep getting better, by the way," she added.

I looked at her cat-eye makeup and smiled my goofy, brace-faced grin. I then gave a calculated glance in Dexter's direction, but he wasn't paying attention.

"Class, I need to check on my black-and-white photography students. I'll be back in 10 minutes. Sophomores, you're in charge while I'm gone."

Mr. Edwards left the room, and no one batted an eye at this common occurrence. However, I was particularly interested today, given Dexter's supposed plan. I made another cursory nod in his direction, but he didn't notice. I thought maybe he'd forgotten, so I went back to editing my rambunctious, bronze animals. After a few minutes, my accomplice rolled his chair between Raven and me and said:

"You guys, let's play a game."

I didn't think Raven knew Dexter well, but her adventurousness knew no bounds. She always appeared ready for whatever life tossed at her.

"Let's test our pressure points," Dexter said.

Several other members of the class looked over at him curiously, before ignoring the clamor and returning to their unexceptional works of art.

"Okay, how do we do that?" Raven's interest was piqued.

"It's simple. Let's form a triangle between our chairs." Dexter's rat-like face lit up as if a small slice of odiferous Brie was within his grasp.

We turned our chairs inward as the rest of the class continued to disregard our antics. I was admittedly excited to see how this game would help me.

"So, my physical therapist taught me everyone has a ton of pressure points on their bodies. Shoulders, arms, stomach, legs, wherever. It feels like, good or weird. You'll see. Watch."

Dexter reached over to Raven and squeezed her shoulder. She instinctively twitched and wriggled her delicate nose.

"Whoa. That feels...strange."

"Vincent," Dexter said, practically frothing at the mouth. "Try my sternum."

I poked him, and he reacted with a mild flinch.

"This is fun," Raven said. "Let me try one."

"Poke Vincent's stomach."

"Wait, I don't think—" but I was too late.

Raven's finger prodded my stomach, but instead of injuring it on my chiseled abs, Raven's infallible index became engulfed in a bottomless abyss, surrounded by blubber. My two or three rolls of fat swallowed her dainty finger whole. Raven's typically cheery disposition switched to one of repulsion and disappointment. She yanked her finger out of my protruding paunch and placed it on her lap. I cringed and could feel tears welling up in my eyes. I had always worn looser fitting American Eagle and Urban Outfitters t-shirts, so maybe Raven thought I had a fitter physique. She knew I played basketball, so it was in the realm of possibilities that I had washboard abs.

"Try my stomach Raven," Dexter grinned.

The notorious cross-country star knew that one prick and Raven would be hooked. She pressed her finger into his supposed pressure point, which elicited the desired response.

"Wow, you must work out," she smiled at Dexter.

Mr. Edwards walked back into the classroom, and that seedy rat scampered back to his computer. Raven and I didn't speak for the rest of the class.

That afternoon, I cried on my walk home from school. Dexter must've planned that. He wanted Raven all to himself. I reached underneath my shirt and grabbed a handful of flab. How did I let this happen? I played sports year-round at Hollandsworth, and while I hadn't done any athletics from this May to October, I had recently started practicing basketball. Well, and my diet certainly became less healthy after Mom left, but I thought it was all about portion size? I ate bacon burgers, pizza, pancakes, plenty of chocolate, and usually had a Coke a day, but I never used to feel so overweight. I thought I was average-sized. Maybe Raven didn't care. She was simply surprised. Everything would be back to normal tomorrow, I thought.

Right when I entered the townhouse, I locked myself in my room, took off my shirt, and started doing crunches. My tears began to mix in with sweat, and my stomach immediately started to burn. I couldn't stop. I kept going up and down. If only I could get to 20 or 40 or 80, maybe then Raven would like me. I couldn't stop sobbing until I heard the door slam from two stories down. My father was home.

I sprinted into the bathroom, washed my face, and put on my unclean shirt.

"Dad," I shouted as I marched down the stairs. "Dad."

"Jesus. What?"

I stood in front of him in the foyer. His hair contained a few more grey strands then I remembered, but he was in tip-top shape for someone his age. My father was now only two inches taller than me, but his arms and legs were defined, and his pectorals jutted out further than his stomach.

"Vincent, what's wrong? Are you okay?"

"Um, Dad. I want to get a chin-up bar."

"Okay, sure. Whatever. Don't scare me like that."

"Well, can we go now? I want to go to Modell's right now. Will you come with me?"

"Come on. I just got home. Can't it wait?"

"No, I want to get in shape. Um, basketball tryouts are in a few days, and I want to make the team."

"Oh, I got it now. Yeah, of course. Let's go."

I dragged my father to Modell's, and we bought a silver and black bar to be hung on the third-floor bathroom door. We then went to Roma Pizza on our way home to pick-up slices, but I declined my usual two Meat Lovers. I told my father I wasn't hungry and just wanted half a peanut butter sandwich at home. Before we re-entered the townhouse, I had one more thought.

"Dad, can I get a gym membership at the 92nd Street Y?"

"What? We just bought you a chin-up bar."

I decided to ride the basketball angle. Sports were the easiest way to my father's heart.

"Well, yeah...but if I want to get good and start for the JV team as a freshman, I need to practice more."

"You know what, okay. I like how motivated you are. Maybe I'm looking at the next white Gilbert Arenas," my father tousled my unkempt, dark brown hair.

I spent the rest of my night figuring out how to alter my frame as quickly as possible. I did 128 crunches, 84 push-ups, and six and a half chin-ups over the next several hours. After that barrage of exercises, I had no feeling left in my arms. I then googled "movies with abs" and stumbled upon David Fincher's *Fight Club*. Not only did the film instantly become one of my favorites, but I also looked at Brad Pitt's body for inspiration. Every girl found him attractive. If I could just make my body look half as good as his, I could get any girl in the school to like me.

CHAPTER 3

THREE SIGNIFICANT EVENTS TRANSPIRED OVER the next three days. First was the subsequent class of Digital Photography, followed by the much-discussed basketball tryouts, and finally, a new form of edification to improve my daily well-being.

I arrived first to Digital Photography and took my same seat. Mr. Edwards, Raven, Dexter and the rest of the group filed in as if nothing had happened. Everyone sat in their usual swivel chair, and the conversation was kept to a minimum. Raven wore a virginal white dress with a mint-green headband that matched her boots. I opened one of my Central Park Zoo pictures, and Raven eventually peered over and said:

"I'd try that one in black-and-white. The image will be much more striking."

I looked over and nodded at her silently. For some reason, I felt a prolonged embarrassment when I looked at her. Prior to this week, I was finally able to be somewhat comfortable around Raven, but after the humiliatingly rotund affair, I was back to square one. I could no longer speak to her. Raven became an unattainable woman once again, and I was a mere pudgy mute. She made another comment that class and two more the following week, but I never uttered another word to her. Our interactions soon consisted of nods and waves, before even that ceased. A month later, I saw her holding hands with Dexter in the student lounge, and they became affable companions. They never sat next to each other nor dated, to my knowledge, but I never forgot that October morning.

In the following weeks, I convinced myself if only I worked harder in the gym and my classes, I could be worthy of the ebullient, effervescent beauty who brightened my every day. My mother had gone away a few months ago, and I was in a perpetual state of languor. Raven's face, body, voice, words, and actions all gave me a succulent taste of euphoria, even if only temporary. At that time, I didn't consider her a crush, but rather a great love that would resurface when I was worthy. All that was left to do was to traipse forward with the nugatory events of ninth grade.

I arrived at basketball tryouts and immediately noticed a difference in attire. There were the sleeveless, sinewy six-foot upperclassmen, and then the ninth-grade newbies who looked tense and out of place. Not only was I in the latter group, but I was also one of the only people wearing a t-shirt underneath their jersey. In the NBA and college, this look was reserved for the pudgy, 3-point specialists who didn't want to display their undefined arms. And I fit safely into that categorization. I wasn't looking to be a team's star player. In fact, I'd spent the previous two winters wrestling at Hollandsworth and finished with a career record of 21-7. It was definitely a skill of mine. I wasn't a physical specimen, but rather was a tactician on the mat. If Verity had a wrestling program, I'd undoubtedly be a vital cog, but unfortunately, their "no contact sports" mantra was immutable. I still wanted to play on some kind of team and felt it would be an effective way to make friends. Plus, I wasn't just a space-eater on the floor. I was a useful point guard in the Yorkville weekend basketball league, where I played for six years. That being said, no coach would've been drooling over my talents.

Tryouts began with stretching and sprints before we broke off into two gyms: The North was reserved for players who were locks to make varsity and people whom the coaches had tried out in the past. The South was meant for new students at the school as well as the few 11th- and 12th-grade stragglers who figured now was the perfect time to join the team with college applications fast-approaching.

Twenty-five players occupied the North Gym, although every 15 minutes or so, an unlucky one or two would be relegated to our smaller confines. We did layup lines, shooting drills, and 3-on-2 fast break situations. I felt comfortable placing myself in the top 8 players in the South Gym but was still out of practice and short. The six-foot-tall Frankie and the rat-faced Dexter were also in my gym trying to make their mark.

Frankie had a hulking physique that was continually improving due to his strict diet and workout regimen. He was a fierce defender and excellent ball handler but lacked the shooting touch for varsity. Dexter, who was my height, could be best described as scrappy. He was a little gnat on the floor, getting steals on defense and lobbing floaters from the free-throw line.

When the results were posted at the end of the day, I wasn't surprised to find myself as one of the 13 players selected to the JV team. The roster consisted of seven freshmen, four sophomores, and two juniors. Two freshmen, whose names I didn't recognize, surprisingly made varsity. I actually felt satisfied with myself. Out of 50 males in the Verity Prep ninth grade, I was one of the nine best basketball players. It wasn't a Raven-esque skill, but it was something that made me, and I'm sure my father, proud. Besides, baseball was always my best sport and occupied most of my athletic practice time, so even making the JV basketball team was an accomplishment. Following tryouts, I began going to the Y every day after our two-hour basketball practices at school.

This leads me to my final pivotal moment from the first semester. I had quickly convinced myself that if I wanted to be a boy Raven could love, I needed to get in spectacular shape. It wasn't just for her, though. My father effectively called me fat, and a workout regimen could only improve my athletic ability and looks. All I had to do was figure out a routine to which I could stick. My father wouldn't pay for a trainer, so I decided, against any weightlifter's advice, to make my own workouts. I felt the "glamour" muscles were vital for someone with my goals. I didn't need to be able to lift a truck; I simply wanted to look jacked in my everyday clothes and with my shirt off.

Leg workouts seemed to be a colossal time-waster given that in Manhattan, people wore long pants nine months a year. I started off with 15-pound bicep curls and then shifted to the shoulder press, lat pull-down machines, and 10 minutes for ab exercises. I'd occasionally add in new exercises I heard about on TV shows or from eavesdropping on my similarly ambitious peers at Verity. Towards the end of October 2008, I made an oath to myself: from this moment forward, I'd work out four days a week for 45 minutes each day. If I did that, even without any professional training, I was sure I'd continue to look better every month. That vow, my unmatched will-power, and a few final dietary adjustments helped to transform my body over the next few years.

Since my mother's passing, my diet had become repulsive. Eliminating Nara's greasy noodles, dumplings, and pork wasn't even enough. At this point in my life, I decided to cut out soda, fast food, and breakfast. Most dietitians would have no issue with the previous two omissions, but the latter could've been problematic. Everyone always rehearsed the cliched "most important meal of the day" line. It didn't make sense to me. I was never hungry upon waking and only ate my cereal because that's what I'd been programmed to do. One day, I stopped eating before lunch, and my father and brother didn't seem to care, so I never ate breakfast again. After a week or so of forced fasting, my robotic brain and stomach coalesced.

When lunchtime approached, I decided to pass up trips to McDonald's and Famiglia and instead became a daily visitor to Subway. If I just ate six-inch Subway sandwiches every day, I could experience a weight loss. I only had one final issue to solve: my picky eating habits.

As a young child, I was decisive. This was the case with school, sports, hobbies, and, most notably, food. When I was six or seven, my mother would make salmon or flounder, and I'd take one bite, calmly spit it out into my napkin and announce:

"I don't like this. No need to get up, mother. I'll make myself a bowl of cereal."

This became common, and by age eight or nine, my parents stopped making me new and exciting foods. If I didn't like something once, there was no reason for me to try it again. Therefore, the following victuals, in no particular order, were permanently off-limits:

- all Mediterranean food
- cheese (Stipulation: I'd eat it on pizza) (Stipulation: pita)
- turkey
- fish/seafood (Stipulation: I loved
- stuffing
  all kinds of shrimp)
- potatoes (Stipulation: Everyone -eggs
  eats French fries)
- pumpkin
- tomatoes (Stipulation: I'd eat -açai
  ketchup and salsa)
- grapefruit
- lettuce
- all cream sauces
- onions
- mayonnaise
- bananas
- any chipotle-based sauce or aioli
- cherries
- coffee
- berries (Stipulation: Strawberries -wine
  were edible)
- beer
- lamb
- pomegranate
- duck
- escargot
- venison
- eggplant
- squab
- squash
- foie gras
- zucchini
- caviar
- mushrooms
- all Indian food
- avocado

When I went to Subway, I'd create my own sandwich consisting of steak, grilled chicken, bacon, and barbecue sauce on wheat bread. The triple meat was pricey, but my father continued to leave cash in the money drawer for Charleston and me to use. Plus, my father never complained nor asked for receipts.

My new diet, workout routine, and lack of girl to obsess over made the rest of 2008 relatively dull. I played on the basketball team and spent my free periods studying, doing homework, and observing those seated around me. I had no friends and lacked the temerity to make them at the moment, but at least my classes were going quite well.

One November day, while studying for a biology test in the student lounge, I created what I felt to be a fascinating hypothesis. It wasn't a Harvard-level theorem, but my interminably racing mind exploded with giddiness once I had made my earth-shattering discovery.

Several girls were chatting at one of the two adjacent, circular freshmen tables in the lounge. The three teens spoke in a tone I'd heard thousands of times before but had never truly listened to and noticed their peculiar inflections and intonations. This group's dialect felt very local. There was a sense of mimicry with their tone and pitch. They each spoke swiftly, and something about their voices made me instantly believe they came from money. I don't mean their families had net worths of $500,000, but rather these were the daughters of the uber-wealthy; the multi, multi-millionaires; the heirs to notable fortunes. I could tell just by their voices.

It was a multi-generational, atavistic, Mid-Atlantic accent. No one whose family had immigrated in the past 50 years could emulate this voice without another member of the exclusive group noticing. But that Mid-Atlantic definition was too simplistic. This specific type of speech was its own, unique subset. It was classified by its lightning-quick pace, along with the innate ability to slow down and over-enunciate the most crucial word in a sentence. The inane, misplaced "like" could be heard frequently, but once these women became of age, the "likes" seemingly vanished. These girls specialized in dry, deadpan humor with accompanying eye-rolls. Their vowels were much more pronounced than the fatuous consonants. Despite the rapid and caustic words rolling off their tongues, these girls spoke with perfect punctuation and diction. They also obtained this sempiternal half-laugh that appeared both when they were insulting someone and when slanderous barbs were thrown back in their direction. The girls never seemed to be nervous nor overwhelmed, and no one, under any circumstances, was ever able to witness them crying. If a topic weren't to their liking, the jocose girls would simply switch it with a non-sequitur and refuse to turn back around and face their displeasure. However, their voices were only part one of my comprehensive postulations.

The attire was how one could spot these girls from any distance. The typical November outfit consisted of a fur vest, which was usually Kelli Kouri, Gorski, or Tom Ford. However, I learned early on that girls not belonging to this subsection would buy imitation fur vests at Zara. By the second semester of my freshman year, I could spot the difference between Tom Ford and Zara right when I entered a room. Most of these girls wore black leggings every day to school as they were simple enough to match with and showed off their taut legs and behinds. In the warmer months, short skirts, spaghetti strap shirts, and halter tops were acceptable. While in the winter, Uggs were a necessity, but Chuck Taylors were also a favorite of the group. The girls always made sure to wear minor accessories that showcased their wealth. These included: an Hermès Clic H Bracelet, a silver or gold Van Cleef clover necklace, and an assortment of colorful Chanel bags. However, the item of absolute paramount importance was the prized Moncler jacket.

Prior to the Canada Goose jacket obsession that overtook Manhattan in the subsequent decade, the Moncler jacket reigned supreme amongst the most voguish girls. The piece itself was form-fitting and contained 10 quilted, lightweight conduits that clung to the most attractive girls' skin. The jacket had painted buttons and discreet pockets along with an attachable fur hood. The glorious Moncler jacket was all one color, and its sleek stitch-work made sure no one looked heavier than they were, which is a common issue with bulkier winter coats. The particular Moncler jackets these girls wore never went more than a few inches below their waists, and the group, as a whole, was partial to the black Moncler Armoise short down jacket. Each garment's defining feature was its anomalous white and navy logo with mysterious red and blue etchings that could've been mountain peaks, arrows, or ski poles.

Listening to these girls speak, while wearing their seemingly mandatory uniforms made it necessary for me to coin a term that suited these distinctive, haughty creatures. From that moment on, I referred to them, behind their backs, of course, as "Moncler Girls." These young ladies certainly spoke and dressed in their own way, but the final, most important piece of the puzzle was their personalities.

The Moncler Girl was a WASP/JAP hybrid of sorts. They could be placed under the umbrella of the White Anglo-Saxon Protestant or Jewish American Princess, but this specific form of prestige was reserved for the girls sitting only a few feet from me. Upon further analysis over the next few weeks, I felt Moncler Girls were ultra-high-maintenance, emotionally manipulative bratty teenagers and college students who did an excellent job of hiding their low self-esteem. The girls were always counting calories, even when it came to alcohol. It was strictly cocktails and pre-2000 wine. There were no overweight Moncler Girls. It was as if Moncler refused to sew coats for size 6s and up. I'm not sure whether it was due to devastating bulimic issues or dedicated spin and Pilates classes, but they were always in terrific, enviable shape. The girls were also conceited and obscenely wealthy with a token Hamptons house, spring break trips to various Mediterranean islands, and winter break excursions to Gstaad, Courchevel, Lech-Zürs, or Baqueira Beret. These Moncler Girls never worked before graduating college, instead spending their free time at nightclubs on weeknights or apartment parties on weekends. Even as 15-year-old girls, they had no problem flashing fake IDs or $100 bills that allowed them to skip the lines and unruly members of the New Jersey and Long Island detritus; typically referred to as the "bridge and tunnel crowd." At hot nightclubs such as 1Oak, Lavo and Marquee, these Moncler Girls flashed not just money but status all throughout the school year. In the summertime, they lounged by their Hamptons pools and jacuzzies before dinners at 1770 House, Sunset Beach, 75 Main, Cittanuova, The Crow's Nest, Navy Beach, or the increasingly popular Surf Lodge. Their teenage lives revolved around anonymous approval and online likes before they eventually settled into their family's real estate or finance corporation and married their own Newland Archers. I know this group would've repulsed my mother, but I was weirdly smitten by these magnetic, vainglorious, and verbally abusive women.

"Hi, I don't think we've ever, uh, met," I bravely stuttered as my pubescent voice cracked.

The three Moncler Girls turned to each other, not so subtly rolled their eyes and vacillated between whether to ignore me entirely or dignify me with a curt reply.

"Vincent? Hollandsworth?" One of the femme fatales articulated.

"Yeah, have we met? How'd you know that?"

"No one walks through the doors of Verity without us knowing everything about them."

"Um, alright."

"I usually like Hollandsworth boys," another one chimed in quickly.

"Uh, thank you."

"You're too awkward and short, though. How unfortunate."

"Well, I..."

"You're still young. You could be cute one day."

I turned back to my biology textbook and felt goosebumps emanating from my pallid skin. Their virus infected me on that November day. The black leggings, the fur vests, and the despotic criticism were enough to kindle the sexual and romantic desires of any young man. After our brief conversation, I wanted to be better. I needed to be someone these girls could idolize. Receiving a compliment from a Moncler Girl would be a crowning achievement. I didn't want to be more attractive, smart, and athletic for my own sake; after that moment, I was doing it for the anonymous Moncler Girl who challenged me to be a man she'd love one day. They became my motivation.

Oddly enough, the first time this became apparent was on the basketball court. The JV team played our first game at Dalton, and I'd be coming off the bench. The opposing Tigers appeared faster, taller, and more muscular than us in warmups, but we had an effective defense with a starting lineup consisting of:

PG: Ellington Stevens III, sophomore, 5'5" 145 lbs
SG: Dexter Dugan, freshman, 5'5" 130 lbs
SF: Fallon Zombo, sophomore, 5'7" 160 lbs

PF: Austin Weinberg, freshman, 5'10" 230 lbs
C : Frankie McDaniel, freshman, 6'0 225 lbs

I came into the game in the 2nd quarter but felt overwhelmed immediately. The ball was moving too quickly, and the bigger Dalton bodies were thrashing through the paint. I was only in for five minutes before the coach took me out and put Dexter back in the game. Even in my four second-half minutes, I was too anxious and afraid to shoot. We lost 63-44, and my disappointed father, who arrived at halftime, approached me after the game.

"Jesus, that was embarrassing."

I could smell alcohol on his breath and noticed he had a McDonald's cup in his hand that was likely not Pepsi.

"I don't know what happened. It's been a while since I've played in a live game."

"Looked like a friggin' retard. What's the point in all those trips to the Y if you're gonna stand around, not play any help D and pass the ball the second it touches your hands. Jesus."

The next week, however, we played Trinity in Verity's North Gym. During warmups, I noticed Raven in the crowd, a group of six Moncler Girls, and even Charleston was able to make it; while my father couldn't.

We were down 16-7 after the first six minutes, so the coach decided to put me in for Fallon. I walked over to the scorer's table, and right before checking into the game, I looked at the crowd of around 100 people. The Moncler Girls were undoubtedly staring right at me. Was it because I was the only Verity player wearing an undershirt, or did they want to assess my value? Could the aloof, pusillanimous Vincent show any sort of talent in front of a modest crowd of supercilious students and parents?

I was shockingly electric. Before halftime, I had two steals that concluded with fast-break layups, plus I knocked down a 17-footer and made a contested lefty layup. My eight first-half points energized the crowd, and we took a 30-28 lead. When the 3rd quarter began, Dexter started over me, and we immediately gave up our slim lead. By the time I was finally called back into the game towards the end of the 3rd quarter, I had noticed two Moncler Girls point at me. They *wanted* to watch me play.

Upon entering, I ignited the offense with a behind-the-back pass to the plump power forward Austin Weinberg, who made a three. Then on the next possession, I hit my own rare three-pointer. There was something about playing in front of the home crowd that made me want to perform. We wound up losing the game 59-53, but I finished with 14 points, one rebound, four assists, and three steals.

As I was leaving the gym, I looked over at the departing group of Moncler Girls. I had a waterfall of sweat dripping down my bangs as well as my nonexistent biceps, which were half hidden by my undershirt. I paused in front of them, ran my hand through my hair, and shook my head. The group of girls was fixated on Verity's MVP, but there was no "good game Vincent" nor "you'll get 'em next time." They stared at me and didn't say a word. If only I were a little bit better, the Moncler Girls would've noticed and complimented me.

My season ended on a rather sour note, however. In our third game, one that was on the road, I broke my ankle. It was already a mediocre performance even before I jumped for a rebound and landed on an opposing player's foot. I heard a crack but refused to take myself out of the game.

"Vincent," my coach shouted from the sidelines. "You're limping. You need me to call a timeout?"

I shook my head and stayed in for four more minutes while scoring six points. The team lost, and four more in a row as the calendar flipped to January. Verity's JV basketball team finished the season 3-12.

My cast was removed in February, and by March, I was nearly done with physical therapy. The doctors thankfully said I'd be ready just in time for baseball season. And, the even more cheerful news was I now had two boys who I could safely call friends. Frankie McDaniel was my vexatious, competitive, and scoundrelly companion. We'd talk about which girls we thought were hot, how much money we thought we were going to make in the future and who could get a better grade on upcoming history tests. He was entertaining at best and revolting at worst. He once referred to us as "possibly the two poorest white families in our grade." Frankie was self-conscious about being on financial aid, and I didn't feel comfortable discussing my father's net worth. It was an idiotic comment but was par for the course when speaking with Frankie.

Austin Weinberg, the JV power forward, was my other, newer friend. He was a docile, introverted lifer. Austin was one of the few people who was more fretful in social situations than I. This stemmed from his insecurity about his weight. He wasn't just a few pounds overweight, but rather a cozy 25 pounds past the healthy portion of the BMI scale. However, he excelled at more important matters. Austin was one of the few genuinely kind, good-natured members of the Verity Prep class of 2012. He was an awkward, brown-rimmed glasses-wearing teen who enjoyed playing sports, talking about sports, and unwinding with a video game after a nine-hour school day. Austin was also not one of the wealthier males in our grade, but that wasn't a necessary quality for my friends.

He and I became even closer during the Verity baseball season. We were undoubtedly the best freshmen players at the school and took on significant roles on the JV team. Austin was the portly ace on the mound who unsurprisingly didn't throw hard, but relied on deception and movement. Even as a freshman, his curveball-changeup duo was as good as anyone's at Verity.

Austin and I would sit next to each other on bus rides and chat about in-game strategy. Then we'd jog, stretch, and warm-up together before running out onto the field. Austin was partial to barbecue-flavored DAVID sunflower seeds and always made sure to pack a lip-full when he was on the mound. He had two other noteworthy whimsicalities. The first and less popular was when he faced off against batters who wore jewelry. The high school baseball rule book stated, "batters had to remove jewelry at the pitcher's request." No one generally abided by or was bothered by this, but Austin made it a habit.

"Excuse me, Blue," he'd yell across the field at the umpire. "Can you tell the batter to remove his extremely distracting silver necklace?"

The whole game would stop, and everyone would stare at the typically timid Austin, but he enjoyed the attention in moments like this.

His second unique action occurred only in close games. He became so enthusiastic in the later innings of one-run and tied games that after recording an important inning-ending strikeout, he'd place his black glove right in front of his face and scream into it. It was entirely out-of-character, but I always loved that.

I, on the other hand, started at shortstop from day one. I was an excellent fielder whose promising adroitness stemmed from years of fielding ground balls in Central Park hit by my father. I was also quick on the base-paths and batted lead-off in every game, renowned for my ability to hit the ball to all fields and effectively work a count. My primary foibles were that I wasn't muscular enough to hit for power, and I didn't throw as hard as a coach would've liked. However, I finished as one of the school's standout young players with a bright future for the program.

This, however, didn't translate to popularity. Baseball was Verity's least attended sport for good reason. We were a Manhattan school that couldn't obtain permits for Central Park fields, so we were forced to ride chartered buses to the East River's 2nd most popular islet, Randall's Island. Every day after school, we were driven 20 minutes to a mostly unpopulated island whose sole purpose was to house endless sporting events for Manhattan private school children. Oh, and the island was home to a mental asylum. The point being, aside from a few dedicated parents, we never had any fans. No girl at Verity ever witnessed my diving catches or Austin's devastating curveball. We were unsung heroes of the school. Our team finished the season with an 11-3 record before we lost in the Manhattan Private School tournament to Collegiate.

CHAPTER 4

MY FRESHMAN YEAR ENDED WITHOUT much splendor, although I now had two quality friends and many experiences from which I could learn. I was still searching for that elusive first kiss, but I felt more comfortable around girls with every conversation. And over the summer, my weightlifting routine continued, as I added new exercises to build my budding glamor muscles.

My father didn't bother to rent a Hamptons house for the summer, so Charleston and I were cooped up most days and nights. My brother typically went to hang out with friends, and my father started to work longer hours, so the townhouse's occupants were frequently just Nara and myself.

One night in August, as I was making my way home from the Y, I received a BBM from my father on my new BlackBerry Curve.

"Dinner tonight. You. Me. Charleston. Brother Jimmy's," it read.

I was taken aback, considering how little I spoke with my family members. We always exchanged pleasantries after school and work, and my father attended my sporting events, but there were never any tête-à-têtes. Charleston and I would do our homework in separate rooms, and our father would develop a mild buzz while rooting against the Yankees. Even before my mother's death, my father had always been stuck in an emotional cocoon. No one, not even his wife, knew of his inner thoughts. Talking to him about our daily ethos was a fool's errand. Charleston and I knew he'd turn the conversation into some kind of joke or change topics immediately. Our father had become an even more staid man, and having a candid therapy session with him would be laborious and frankly, pointless. Speaking of therapy, that was out of the question because my father said $300 a week was an obscene amount. So, the three living Beatties beat on with wholly ambivalent, never discussed futures.

We sat in the backroom of Brother Jimmy's on 92nd and 3rd and ordered our burgers and wings. One of the few commonalities my father and I possessed was our mutual hatred of cheese. Our burgers came plain with bacon, while Charleston's was drenched in gooey, mushy American cheese. My father and I instinctively winced at both the mephitic scent and grotesque sight.

"Boys, we're moving," my father announced abruptly.

"I'm sorry, what? Where?" Charleston said.

"The townhouse is too big and expensive. Reminds me of your mother. We need a change of scenery."

"We're staying in the city, right?" I asked.

"Of course. I already found the place. I'd been meaning to tell you."

"Jesus, Dad," Charleston chewed with his mouth open. "You shoulda said something sooner."

"Eh, it's the summertime. You guys got nothing going on. It'll be simple. Ripping off a Band-Aid."

My mother would've likely been appalled. She would've commented on Morgan's elbows on the table, Charleston's chewing habits, and all of our willingness to abandon her capacious dwelling.

"Gotta sell a bunch of the furniture and paintings. It's going to be a two-bedroom on 92nd between Lex and 3rd. Apartment 4D. We passed it on our way here."

"A two-bedroom?" I said. "We're going from a four-story townhouse to a two-bedroom? How'd that happen?"

"Read a newspaper—the whole country's in shambles. I could lose my job. Stocks are plummeting. Goddamn recession."

"This night keeps getting worse," Charleston said. "We must have a ton saved up, right?"

"Nothing I can do about a mortgage crisis. I've put aside enough for high school and college. I'll make some money off the imported

French stuff...um...aside from the much smaller place, your lives will be the same...Vincent, you'll be even closer to the Y."

"Dad, that's not my number one priority."

"You look bigger. Muscles are coming in. You're filling out well. Girls will be all over you this year."

"Is he going to bring them back to our shared bedroom?" Charleston asked.

"Don't be so spoiled. Eat your goddamn burgers. You're both lucky to be alive."

The move was arduous and demoralizing. It felt as if I was losing another piece of my mother. It wasn't just our townhouse that was gone. I watched paintings, couches, and chairs I'd been accustomed to seeing my entire life sold for scraps. It was devastating. My mother spent years and several trips to France decorating and re-decorating the living room, dining room, and bedrooms. Most of her hard work was now in someone else's house or our storage unit.

The despondent furniture that made the cut was crammed into a puny combined dining and living room no larger than the townhouse's kitchen. No one would have any alone time. The only place in the apartment that was truly mine was my mattress. Upon moving in, I made a rule that no one was allowed to touch or sit on my bed. It was my sanctuary. My sheets and blankets were an innocuous space I could meditate and unwind in at the end of the day. I needed this one haven. Nara was permitted to make my bed, but other than that, no one could touch it.

As a 12th grader applying to colleges, Charleston had more of a right to be upset than me, but he was sedated. Charleston must've thought about it as a final nine months before his adulthood and freedom could officially commence. He had the mental fortitude to survive three quarters of a year.

I received my new schedule on the first day of 10th grade. English, European History, Algebra II, Chemistry, and Spanish 1 made up my core courses, while I chose to take Acting Improv, Sports Debate, and Film Appreciation clubs on the side. It was a tedious but expected schedule with the one significant adjustment being Spanish over French.

My mother would've been devastated to learn I was leaving behind the language of which she so desperately wanted me to achieve fluency. However, it was an easy decision due to my freshman year grades in core courses:

English-A
American History-A
Geometry-A-
Biology-A-
French-C+

I gave the maximum effort I was willing to on schoolwork, and the best I could muster was a C+ in French II. It was only going to get harder from there. I asked my father a few weeks before my sophomore year started, and he said:

"Drop it. No question. Don't look back. Spanish 1 will be a breeze, and then you'll figure it out from there. Screw French."

My indecipherable father wound up being correct. From day one, it was clear I'd receive an effortless A in Spanish 1.

My other classes were varying in difficulty, but undoubtedly less enjoyable than my previous year's. My English, History, Algebra II, and Chemistry teachers were all less captivating than my ninth-grade instructors. Austin happened to be in Algebra II, so at least I had a friend in one of my classes, but overall, it was looking like a down year.

Despite my initial perception, there were flashes of enjoyment and optimism in the opening month. The first of which occurred during my English class taught by the veritable Ms. Bissinger. She was a knowledgeable, middle-aged woman with glasses, who spoke softly and expected a tranquil, uninterrupted 40 minutes from a group of passionate students.

My favorite of her strict rules was her forced assigned seating. This was a blessing because it took the awkwardness out of the daily desk selection. Plus, the mythical academic gods presented me with a perplexing opportunity. Bissinger's random selection sandwiched me in between the two most popular males in our grade. They had wildly different personalities and were well-liked by separate crowds for different reasons, but befriending one was of the utmost importance.

Over the course of the semester, I rarely spoke to the boy on my left. He was tall, jovial, goofy, and beloved by all the teenage girls, but I didn't think we had anything in common.

Meanwhile, the scrawnier Caleb Pearl sat on my right every day for the entire semester. His defining feature was his styled and exceptionally well-conditioned flowing, voluminous brown hair. Personality-wise, his textbook bad boy nature entranced countless young women, and it also didn't hurt that he came from the wealthiest family in our grade. Caleb lived in a six-story townhouse overlooking the East River. And despite this fact, Caleb wore purple and green three-striped Adidas sweatpants on most days with a white, deep V-neck t-shirt. His hair, combined with his attitude and perpetual tan, made most girls drool over him. Although, not the members of our grade. Caleb was a certain type of Lothario that many girls in our class found to be annoyingly belligerent. However, the juniors and seniors thought he was a desirable type of villain, both sinful and sexy. And not only did older girls like Caleb, but he was also beloved by the city's night owl socialites. He was a true club rat who was a mainstay at any establishment where Moncler Girls flocked. From a high schooler's perspective, Caleb was wealthy, handsome, and could easily obtain alcohol, drugs, and bottle service wherever he went. He always lived his life at an allegro tempo, and I found that thrilling.

However, while Caleb was the most well-known Verity Prep 10th grader in the city, some viewed him as easy to dislike due to his innate apathetic nature and blatant disregard for which girls already had boyfriends, but I always chose to meet everyone with an open mind rather than rely on rumors and gossip. From what I could tell, Caleb Pearl was the least popular, popular high schooler in history. On Friday and Saturday nights, he was a king, but in class and the student lounge, a leper.

I thought he was a treat to have in class because he regularly defied Ms. Bissinger and his mutinous outbursts frequently elicited near-silent snickers. Befriending him, I thought, could lead to me joining the next tier in popularity. This potential friendship, combined with my still religious workout routine, could only help in my quest towards my first kiss.

In October, Ms. Bissinger gave us our first group project. We were to rewrite a scene from Edith Wharton's *The Age of Innocence* depicting what would've happened if the novel had taken place in 2009. Our teacher allowed us to take three minutes to choose our partner, and before she'd finished her sentence, Caleb turned to me:

"Bro, we're working together."

"Um, okay."

"Can you come to my place after school? Let's knock this out quickly. Don't want it weighing on my mind."

"Yeah, I guess."

My stock was clearly on the rise.

I entered Caleb's townhouse just off of York Avenue and was in disbelief. The massive, ivory pillars, the Rococo-style furniture, the gold picture frames, and the 18th-century paintings made our old townhouse look like a brummagem shelter.

Caleb's mother entered the foyer and kissed me on the cheek. She was 45 going on 25, and her flowery perfume grazed my fortunate nose.

"Welcome to our home. Can I get you boys anything?" She said in her thick accent.

Caleb shook his head and led me to their indoor elevator.

"Gym's on the second floor, parents' room on the third, study and theater on the fourth, maid's room and den on the fifth, my room on top."

"This place is pretty cool," I said in the glibbest tone I possessed.

"You know what you're doing with this book, right?"

We arrived on the sixth floor, and the elevator opened to his bedroom. He slept on a California King with 1,500 thread count gold-colored sheets and the fluffiest pillows I'd ever seen. The room contained a desk, a 50-inch flat-screen, and a walk-in closet.

"Take a seat. I'll grab my book."

We both opened our backpacks.

"I don't know how helpful I'll be bro," he said. "I haven't read any of this thing...do you smoke by the way?"

"No, but feel free. I don't mind, bro."

He cracked open his window and let out a puff of what I believed to be marijuana smoke.

"So, you want me just to get started then?"

"Sure, I trust you, dude. Do you drink at least?"

"No, nothing."

I opened my book and began to jot down an opening paragraph centered on Newland's trip to Paris to visit Ellen Olenska. Caleb picked up an Xbox 360 controller and turned on NBA 2K10. It was at this moment I officially realized he only partnered with me so I'd do all the work. It didn't bother me, though. I took it as laudation. Caleb thought I was intelligent. I gave off the vibe of a well-educated, possibly nerdy 10th grader. That's not necessarily a negative.

"If you could hook up with one girl at Verity, who would it be?" He asked as I tried to focus on our project.

"I don't know. I don't want word to get out."

"Bro, don't be a pussy. Just throw out a name. This is how I get to know you."

"Raven Jimenez."

"That was quick. That must be some crush."

"Yeah, I mean, she's alright."

"You got good taste. Bet she'd be crazy in bed."

"How well do you know her?"

"Her best friend blew me in the bathroom at Nobu Fifty-Seven."

"I think I'm going to have Countess Olenska—"

"Don't change the subject. What's your usual type?"

"I mean, I don't have like, I, there's not really—"

"Come on. Don't be weird, bro."

"Skinny girls. Long hair. Um, shorter than me, so under 5'7"."

"Gotcha. You're not like a black chubby-chaser."

"I don't know. I guess not."

"Big tits are lower on your priority list? I respect that. You're a sailor, not a motorboat guy."

"How about you?"

"Gotta be wealthy first off. Can't have some poor society climber turkey basting me."

"What's that?"

"You don't know? I guess the technical definition is when a girl tries to artificially inseminate herself with the remnants of your condom you just threw out.

"Jesus."

It was too distracting to write with his intermittent sibilating, so I put my pencil down.

"Grab a seat on the floor. I'll quit, and we can start over. I'll be the Heat. Be whoever...you want a snack? Make yourself at home, bro."

A few hours later, I left his house and finished the assignment at my apartment. Before leaving, though, Caleb gave me his number so I could BBM him when the paper was finished. He became kinder to me in school and would always have me sit next to him at the sophomore table whenever we had a free period together. I remember thinking everyone was wrong about him.

CHAPTER 5

WHILE WALKING INTO SCHOOL THE next Monday morning, I saw a flyer for the Fall/Winter school play and decided to try out. I had attended Acting Improv religiously and found it to be useful practice for conversing with my peers. Raven was now only attending the club sparingly, and when she did, we never spoke. However, I always admired her outfits, hair, smile, eyes, and sultry voice. I remember thinking she'd like me again one day. There was no doubt in my mind.

In the meantime, this season's school play was Dickens' *Great Expectations*. Ms. Cuzano was directing, and since I had a unique personality compared to the homogeneous Verity theater troupe, I felt confident she'd cast me. And after the painless three-minute audition, I was selected to play 'Magwitch', the convict. Before officially signing on, however, I made sure Ms. Cuzano was aware of my JV basketball schedule. I could only come to rehearsal twice a week and could never miss a game due to the play. I felt like a less handsome Troy Bolton.

Once the first rehearsal began, I was dismayed to find not a single friend or acquaintance amongst the cast. No Frankie, no Raven, and I happened to be the only sophomore in the play. This led me to behave as my typical wallflower self, memorizing my lines, and not speaking to anyone else. I'd listlessly drift through warmups and then sit in the back of the theater, re-reading the script. I probably had the sixth most lines and felt Ms. Cuzano had done an adequate job of assembling her cast.

My *Great Expectations* compatriots were quintessential theater kids. They wore ill-fitting clothes, frequently sang aloud to no one in particular, frolicked and skipped around the auditorium, and seemed to be wary of any nefarious interlopers who clearly didn't belong in their coterie.

My fellow actors seemed upset that a seemingly benighted student, such as I, was able to play both basketball and do the play. I ostensibly stole a role from someone who had paid his dues in previous productions. Had I been nymph-like, sprouting with exuberance at every turn, I may have been a better fit. Alas, I was the pariah. It took a week and a half before anyone talked to me backstage. And the first brave soul to approach the class's resident stylite was Tessa.

She was an eighth-grader who'd somehow captured the gender-bending lead role of 'Pip'. Her character was innocent and friendly, wearing tight-fitting suits and Windsor-knotted ties throughout the performance. And Tessa's personality mirrored Pip's.

The eighth-grader had long, curly brown hair and a memorable, toothy smile. Tessa had an athletic build, with broad shoulders and toned upper arms and thighs. She was a pretty girl who'd spent many summers of her childhood acting in a prestigious performing arts camp in the Catskills. Tessa undoubtedly had talent as laughter and tears exuded from her face with ease. Every emotion and movement she had was believable. I watched her acting and singing chops from afar with great veneration until one day she brazenly walked over to me off stage right and said something like:

"Why are you always by yourself?" Tessa plopped down next to me against a wall.

"I don't know. I guess I don't really fit in here."

"How would you know that unless you tried talking to people?"

"Honestly, this doesn't seem like a crowd I have stuff in common with."

"You're not supposed to judge a book by its cover."

"Thanks," I smiled. "You're right. I always tell myself that I never judge people until getting to know them, but I often forget my own lessons."

"So, what did you think I was like when you saw me from off-stage, smarty-pants?"

"I don't think that's a good idea…Eh, you know what? Fine. I thought that you're an extrovert most of the time, but develop insecurities around the popular kids in your grade—"

"How do you know I'm not the most popular girl in my grade?" She interrupted. "Do you know a lot of eighth-graders?"

"Fair point. Would you consider yourself among the popular girls in your grade?"

"No. Not particularly."

"Anyway, that's not a dig at you. I'm not popular either. It's just an observation. Theater geeks…sorry, theater kids are rarely popular."

"Everyone in this cast likes me."

"But in high school and college, as I've learned, some people's opinions just seem to matter more than others."

"You're kind of a jerk, right? How's that for an opinion?"

"Sorry. I don't mean to be."

"Are you ha—wait, finish analyzing me, doctor."

"Well, I'd say you're…actually, I'm okay for now."

"Okay, dude. Jeez, you can be infuriating."

Tessa stood up, stuck her tongue out at me, and walked away. I shrugged and picked up my script, whispering my lines aloud.

The next week, Tessa approached me again, asking to run lines out in the hallway.

"You gonna be nice today?"

"I'll just keep my mouth shut and rehearse the scene. I'm sorry."

We stood in the hallway outside the theater and traded Pip and Magwitch's quips while adding our own blocking sequences. I was at ease acting beside her. Tessa had a team captain-type confidence. Whenever someone rehearsed a scene with her, nothing could go wrong. No lines were flubbed. No cues were missed. You never lost faith in her. As long as you did your job, the scene would be splendid.

After a half-dozen run-throughs, Tessa skipped to the water fountain to cleanse her agitated instrument. The end of our final rehearsal for the day seemed to augur well. However, Tessa was now preparing herself for a stentorian quibble.

"You know, you're wrong about me," she sat against the wall.

"Yeah, I'm sorry. I really shouldn't have said that stuff."

"No, don't apologize. I appreciate honesty, but you were wrong."

"I don't want to talk about that anymore. I'm sorry. Can we move on and just do the scene again?"

"No," she said. "I didn't get to discuss my opinions of you."

"Fine. Fair enough."

"You're a sad, lonely person. You don't fit in here or on the sports fields. You're awkward and quiet. You overthink and underact. You come off as hoity-toity and prissy. And you have back acne."

"What? How do you know I have back acne?"

"I've seen you change into your costume."

I was growing tired of her incessant hectoring. I don't mind criticism, especially from someone like her, but I was tired and was regretting my decision to do the play.

"My mom died 16 months ago."

"Dude, are you messing with me?"

"I'm not."

"Well, now I feel terrible. This is why you shouldn't play this game."

Tears began to well in Tessa's unimpeachable eyes.

"You didn't let me finish...my mom died 16 months ago. I went to an all-boys school. My father used to make a lot of money, but now makes maybe a third of what he earned in his prime. And I have back acne because I'm in the tail-end of puberty and work out four days a week."

"I'm so sorry. I...let's talk about something else. So, Pip and Magwitch's relationship is—"

"Nope. Now we're in too deep. Say anything else that's on your mind. No judgment."

At this point, I was wondering why Ms. Cuzano hadn't called us back in the auditorium. Tessa and I exchanged a fraught glance. We'd developed a bizarre dynamic, and our age difference made these conversations even more disconcerting.

"I don't think you've ever kissed a girl," she announced proudly.

"What?"

"You heard me."

"I do perfectly fine in that department."

"I mean, dude, you're in pretty good shape. You're kind of cute, but I can't picture you kissing a girl."

"I'm gonna see if we're needed inside."

I stood up, left Tessa alone, and pondered what to do next. Did she want to kiss me? Should I have said something about kissing her? I know people remember their first kisses forever, would I be proud of reminiscing about a girl two years younger than me? I needed advice from a seasoned vet.

During my next free period, I sought out Frankie for sage wisdom.

"You ever see that girl Tessa around the auditorium?"

"Not sure," he responded.

"She's always skulking around the theater. Tessa's the lead in *Great Expectations*. You've probably seen her before or after Acting Improv classes."

"Oh, the younger girl? She's got the Jewy hair?"

"I mean, I don't think she's Jewish, but yeah, if that's how you want to describe her."

"Why, did you guys bang?"

"Not exactly...you wanna go grab lunch?"

Frankie nodded, and we elected to walk outside in the frigid autumn climate. Two senior Moncler Girls were smoking cigarettes across the street. I looked over in their direction, and they scowled back at me. Frankie and I continued down 87th and made a left onto Madison.

"Is she attractive? Or cute?" I asked.

"Who cares? She's a girl. She likes you. You need practice. I'll even set it up if you're too nervous."

"I don't know. She's got these broad, manly shoulders. Plus, is 14 too young? Are there too many red flags?"

"Stop being a pussy. If you don't bang her, I will."

"Can one even do that as a 16-year-old? What makes you think she'd even like you?"

"How hard can it be to pull an eighth-grader?"

Frankie and I walked into Yura on Madison and ordered chicken tenders.

"So, what do I do?"

"Take her for a walk in Central Park. Girls love that romantic trash."

While blunt, his advice seemed logical at that time. So, two weeks later, after another exhausting rehearsal, I approached Tessa.

"Hey, I know you live on the West Side, and I'm seeing a movie on 68th and Broadway in like an hour. You wanna walk with me?"

"Um, I mean, I have my bike. But I guess I can just walk with my bike. Sure."

Tessa and I entered the park on 84th and 5th, and I couldn't stop thinking about whether tonight would be the night. She wasn't Raven. Tessa had flaws, but so did I. Maybe this was the right moment. I had found a non-threatening adversary. Tessa's figure didn't conjure up the piquant image that Raven's did, but maybe that was for the best. I needed to soldier on at an adagio pace with someone I had ambivalent feelings towards. I had talked myself into the idea. Tessa would be my first kiss. She'd be the one to take this leviathanic weight off my mind.

"I think the play's really coming along," I ended the silence. "You're gonna steal the show."

"Thanks, dude. I appreciate you saying that."

"So, you know how I'm always honest with you?"

"Sure, I've started to like that."

"Do you always call everyone 'dude'?"

"What?" She stopped walking and looked at me, quizzically.

"I dunno. I haven't met another girl who calls me 'dude'."

Tessa was understandably taken aback by my bizarre comment.

"What do you care? I'm sure I could criticize stuff you say, too. Always using big words. Who are you trying to impress?"

"When you say 'dude', it just reminds me of like, guys on my sports teams. But whatever. Not important. Moving on."

"I don't care. I just want to be myself."

"No worries, just something I thought of."

Tessa seemed to be holding back a long soliloquy about independence and not caring what people thought, but she paused and said:

"Okay. Fine."

"Well, don't be sad. You know me, I just happen to say the wrong things at the wrong times."

"You need more conversation practice, dude," my companion said.

I vectored my 14-year-old companion towards the 72nd Street park exit. I couldn't interpret her mood. The typically zestful eighth-grader was now detached and alone with her thoughts.

"Are you going to do the spring play?" I asked.

"Um, maybe. Spring is usually reserved for Shakespeare. I like that, but most people don't."

"I may be a one-and-done actor."

"What do you mean?"

"I think this is the last play I'll do at Verity."

"Well, dude...oops. Sorry. I—"

"Don't worry about it. You can say dude if you want. Don't listen to anything I say. I need a goddamn filter."

"True."

"You're tough, Tessa. And toughness is one of the best traits a girl can have."

"Thanks...but wait, why aren't you doing plays?"

"It's pretty obvious I don't fit in. You're the only one I talk to in the theater. I'd rather be doing other activities that make me happier."

Tessa and I exited the park and paused in front of a bench on Central Park West. She was going to head uptown, and I was walking south. We knew this was our final few minutes alone together, and if I wanted to kiss her, it had to be now. The moon was visible, and there was no one around us. It was a tectonic moment.

"Well, if I'm around, you'll always have a good time," she said. "I promise."

She leaned her bike against the park wall and stood six inches from me. Tessa wanted me to kiss her. But then a squall formed in my heart. My body shook. My teeth clattered in the declining temperature and rising wind chill. I stared at her curly brown hair, her toothy smile, her broad shoulders, and toned arms. I thought about how her lips would feel against mine and at what angle my head should sit. I needed to kiss this pretty girl for so many reasons. And so...I quit. Couldn't do it.

"Well, good night," I hugged her tightly.

I felt her head sink into my chest. I sensed Tessa had so overtly pined for this, and even my deformed conversation topics couldn't dissuade her from coveting her crush's virginal lips. Alas, my craven behavior had burdened me once again. I placed my headphones into my ears and walked south along Central Park West. Train's "Drops of Jupiter" permeated throughout my brooding mind.

A few weeks later, we performed *Great Expectations* in a packed auditorium filled with parents, jocks, nerds, theater geeks, Raven, several Moncler Girls, and my father and brother. I pranced around the stage with Tessa and my other unknown cohorts as we slowly divulged the mystery behind Pip's wealth. Ms. Cuzano was thrilled by our performances. I, personally, was proud I had stepped outside my comfort zone and surprised the few audience members who knew me well. My talent was evident, but make no mistake, this was Tessa's show. Several audience members handed her flowers afterward. The eighth-grader was destined to be a star in the Verity theater department for years. Her next role would be another gender-bending performance as the eponymous *Hamlet* in the Spring.

Meanwhile, I walked offstage and found my small cheering section.

"So, what'd you think?" I asked.

"I dozed off," my father announced. "Weren't you playing a dude? Your lipstick looks darling. I'd always wondered what it would be like to have a daughter."

"Dad, stop," Charleston said. "Everyone wears makeup and lipstick on stage under the lights. Nice job, Vincent."

"Yeah. Thanks."

"It was a weird play choice, though." Charleston continued. "I bet they would've had a more diverse audience if they did, like, *The Producers* or Mom always loved *Fiddler on the Roof.*"

"Oh, *The Producers* would've been great," my father added. "*Jersey Boys* is always a good show, too."

"Gotcha," I said. "You want me to bring that up to the teacher while she's celebrating?"

"Don't be such a sad sack," my father said. "We came, didn't we? My dad always used to say '90% of fatherhood is showing up'."

Following the play's moderate success, I shifted my focus back to basketball. The problem was, I didn't have the same skill set as the previous year. My broken ankle sapped my vertical, and I became a more tentative rebounder. In addition, my game experience was lacking given how much of my freshman year I missed. I slowly found myself spending the majority of the time on the bench. I was humiliated that boys and girls from my grade would come to the North Gym and find me seated. I soon realized my basketball career wasn't going to go any further, so I stopped playing after my sophomore season. Austin followed my lead as incoming freshman newbies pilfered his minutes. We'd both choose to focus solely on our budding baseball careers.

During our first spring practice, though, I was happily interrupted by a monumental BBM. I had put my glove down to sip from my water bottle when I saw the flashing LED light atop my phone. Charleston had been accepted to Northwestern. It was thrilling news, and my brother wasted no time sending in his acceptance along with a Morgan Beattie deposit.

When I arrived home that night, I was prepared to laud my brother and tell him how amazing his accomplishment was. However, I entered the apartment and only found Nara cooking.

"Where's Charleston?"

"Out with friends."

I didn't have a chance to celebrate with him because he arrived at home when I was already asleep, but I told him how proud I was the next morning and hugged him. He really did deserve it, and I knew I'd miss him. It was hard not to feel nostalgic. Charleston was getting on a plane a few months later, and I'd only see him in the summer and perhaps over Christmas break. He had been a true constant in my life, and I was partially to blame for not taking advantage of him as a mentor. Had I asked, he could've led me through the arduous underclassmen years and explained how to deal with the strident personalities of Verity Prep's teachers and students. Charleston and I never developed that relationship. We followed in our father's footsteps of burying the past and eschewing succor no matter the cost. Charleston could've assisted in a myriad of situations, but instead, he was simply a friendly, older acquaintance that slept five feet away from me for years.

My nine months as a sophomore were the least influential along my road to nirvana. However, there were two final notable moments. That Spring, my baseball career was the most important activity on my daily schedule. However, it was my first and only Sweet Sixteen invite that altered my upperclassmen years more than anything.

Regarding the former, it became palpable after our first seven games that I was too strong a player for the JV team. I opened the season with 16 hits in my first 24 at-bats and played gold glove defense at shortstop. Had I been playing for a baseball powerhouse, my numbers would've shot off any screen. However, Verity was filled with private school Manhattan socialites, not future MLB players, so no one cared.

After my record-breaking JV season ended in May and classes ceased shortly thereafter, I had too much time on my hands. I thought about my upcoming summer and was depressed at the thought of nothing but workouts at the Y and perpetual acedia. I could count all of my friends on one hand and was still no closer to obtaining that elusive first kiss. However, one afternoon, Caleb called me while I was walking along Lex.

"June 5th," Caleb said through the phone. "What do you got going on, bro?"

"Nothing, why?"

"You know Aurora, right?

"Yeah, we were in Chem together."

"It's her Sweet Sixteen. Roll with."

"I wasn't invited. She barely knows who I am."

"I wasn't invited either, but that's never stopped me."

"Okay. Sure. I'll go."

"Lit."

That was all it took, and on the night of 5th, I met with Caleb outside an awning on Park Avenue. I was overdressed in a white button-down and navy slacks, while he wore jeans and a deep V-neck. Caleb and I waited for a few minutes until another group of boys arrived, and we casually strolled behind the inconsequential sophomores. The doorman then pointed us to the pre-war elevator after hearing someone mutter, "We're here for Aurora's party."

Caleb and I opened the apartment door to a mesmerizing sight. While my companion was unfazed, I was stupefied at the juxtaposition of the palatial living room and the drunken underaged teens grinding on one another while Young Money's "Bedrock" played.

Centuries-old tapestries and urns encircled the makeshift dance area while floor to ceiling windows let in all the dazzle and glory of the most luxurious avenue in the country. In the center of the room stood a magnificent, white Italian-imported sofa that appeared ill-equipped to handle the dangers of the two lustful teenagers who were dripping both saliva and brown liquor from their lips.

As I separated from Caleb and began wandering aimlessly between rooms, I found two girls puffing on a joint while neglecting to ensure all the putrid smoke exited through the cracked window. And as I peeked into what seemed like a bedroom door, I found two Moncler Girls aggressively kissing in what appeared to be a toddler's domicile.

However, the most shocking sight during my jaunt wasn't the lubricious make-out sessions nor the illegal drug paraphernalia nor even the poor ebony wood table being used for beer pong. But rather, I was most surprised to find Aurora's father sitting alone in his study with a green-shaded desk lamp illuminating his paperwork as Lil Wayne's "She Will" could be faintly heard from several rooms away.

"Oh, I'm sorry. I was looking for the bathroom."

"One door too far," the nasally voice responded from behind a colossal marble desk.

I closed his door and turned to find Caleb looking for me.

"Yo, bro. This place is sick, right?" He said.

"Sure is."

"See, told you no one would care we're here."

"I guess."

"Where you been?"

"Just taking it all in."

"You wanna try some coke? I've got enough for four lines. Where's the bathroom around here?"

"No, thanks."

"What do you mean?"

"I don't do that stuff."

"Bro, it's just coke. It's not like I'm offering you crystal."

"No. I'm good."

"I only got the best stuff."

"No, really. I'm fine. I'm not interested."

Caleb then positioned himself directly in front of my face and placed his hand on my shoulder.

"I invited you out to have fun with me. What do you want to do for fun?"

"I dunno."

"Bro, I'm your friend, and I've gotta be honest with you. If you don't drink, and you don't smoke, people aren't gonna invite you to stuff. It sucks. I get it. But that's the way it is, man."

"Not sure why drinking, drugs, and fun have to be mutually exclusive."

"I'm not going to get in an argument with you, bro. That's how all this works. If you want to make friends and be popular, I can help, but you've gotta let me help you. I'll wingman you, and we'll both get laid. We can go to Lavo next weekend and do this all over again."

"I think I should just leave then."

"Bro, it's gonna be a lonely final two years for you. If you change your mind, text me whenever you want a mulligan."

I began making my way towards the exit and, on my way out, spotted Frankie joining Verity's local club rat in the bathroom.

My mother would've killed me if she found out I was involved in these kinds of iniquitous activities. I mean, was I the only one who paid attention in health class? I wasn't going to experiment with gateway drugs and find myself in rehab before I reached college. Unfortunately, it didn't seem like anyone else at that time saw life from my point of view.

Following that night, Caleb stopped talking to me, and word spread throughout the rising junior class that I didn't drink or do drugs. And after his failed conversion of me, Caleb took Frankie under his wing, which in turn led to the latter moving beyond our friendship.

I committed social suicide that night with my self-esteem taking a massive hit. It was a strange situation because I didn't regret my choice. I was destined to be a Sir Thomas More-esque martyr. Looking back, that night should've been viewed as a triumph. My proud superego had defeated my diminutive id. It would've been most parents' dream. Though, I decided not to tell my father about this. He may have tried to force me to drink as he always wanted me to be popular and social. My father wished I was more like Charleston, who was destined for fraternity life and interminable ragers for the next four years. The churlish Morgan Beattie never explicitly told me this, but his disapproving facial expressions and unenlightened opinions of 2010 social situations, made me believe he was always disappointed in how I was developing.

That's how I remember my underclassmen years at Verity. Definitely more negatives than positives, but it was another nine months removed from my mother's passing so that automatically made it easier. In addition, despite the social issues, I was confident 11th grade would see to the inevitable ending of my embarrassing slump with the opposite sex.

Book 3

CHAPTER 1

BY THE TIME 11ᵀᴴ GRADE began, I had reached my adult height of five-foot-eight inches. My baby fat had finally evaporated, and my quad-weekly trips to the gym had left me in enviable shape. By the end of the summer, even my sense of style had changed; as I proceeded to throw out all of my old hand-me-downs and replace them with an assortment of plain, snug-fitting J. Crew long-sleeve shirts.

I had also had both my braces and insufferable bangs removed. If only I hadn't been so introverted and married to my Mormon-like moral code, I could've had a shot at popularity. On the negative side, though, was my core courses continued on a stale trajectory. At that time, I was stuck in a cavernous valley patiently waiting for my life to creep towards its pinnacle.

As it turned out, Tessa was my lone harbinger depicting brighter days ahead. On her first day of freshman year, she'd decided to join Acting Improv. I considered her a friend and was happy to see her after many months; however, I was more concerned with how Raven would react to seeing the new, fitter me. I was seated in the third row, waiting for her to join my section as she had long ago, praying there was a slight chance she had changed her mind about me after nearly two years of Dexter-induced silence.

Instead, much to my chagrin, Tessa and a covert companion chose to sit next to me. I didn't really want Raven to walk in and see me chatting with some freshmen, but I wasn't going to prevent this duo from sharing my row.

"Vincent, how was your summer? You look great."

"Hey, good. Thanks," my restless leg syndrome was flaring up.

"Cool. This is my new friend Devi Kapoor by the way. Today's her first day of high school."

The concealed girl leaned over, smiled brightly, and waved.

"Devi, Vincent is this super cool junior and a great actor. You guys'll get along, I'm sure."

"Tessa," Ms. Cuzano shouted out of the blue. "Come down here. I haven't seen you in forever."

The giddy Tessa leaped from her seat and ran to hug her favorite Verity Prep teacher, leaving me with her anxious friend.

"So," I began, "Where were you before Verity?"

"Oh, it's like a long story. I was at UNIS last year, but my family travels all over the world, and I've, like, spent some time being homeschooled. But I don't want to bore you. How long have you like been here?"

I'd never said a word to her, so I had no idea what Devi's personality was like. However, I could see she was a petite freshman with almond-colored skin and smelled of sandalwood and Argan Oil. The intriguing sprite had long, perfectly straightened black hair that went past her shoulder blades and was parted just left of center. Devi had a perfectly symmetrical face with chunky cheeks and a large lower lip. Her forehead and nose were tiny and thin, though, which made her comically large and cartoon-like chartreuse eyes even more prominent. As I glanced at the rest of her body, I noticed everything appeared dainty like a new-born fawn. Her arms and legs were two or three missed meals away from anorexia. Devi had a small waist and an almost non-existent bust. I came to believe the only weight in her entire figure resided in her pudgy cheeks. I didn't consider her to be strikingly beautiful, but my father had ingrained in me that fat is bad and thin is good, which happened to make this new girl attractive. That, along with her exotic look one rarely sees in Upper East Side schools.

Devi also made no effort to hide her extraordinary wealth. She carried a black Chanel bag with a gold strap around her shoulder and wore a short-sleeve brown and gold sweater I instantly could identify as Gucci. The freshman wore one-inch thick, black heels with matching velvet leggings and was adorned with the classic Moncler Girl talismans I'd grown accustomed to: a navy Hermès Clic H Bracelet and matching gold Van Cleef earrings and clover necklace. Her final bauble was a cheap-looking bracelet with a blue eye on it. At the very least, she piqued my curiosity.

"I said, how long have you been here?" Devi repeated in a high-pitched screech.

"Oh, my bad. Since freshman year. I went to Hollandsworth before this."

Devi stared at me for a second and then shook her head and reached into her bag.

"Do you want a lollipop? I have like this leftover one. It's strawberry-watermelon."

"Uh, sure. Okay."

I took the Blow-Pop as her pointy, witch-like fingers grazed my skin. We made eye contact, but then looked away when Tessa returned.

"You guys having fun?"

I remember asking myself if I had to kiss one of these two girls after class, which would it be? And without hesitation, it was Devi. Although I could see why some boys and girls would prefer a Tessa-type, I was drawn in by a number of Devi's traits, including her evident opulence. Whether she was a true Moncler Girl was beside the point. It was at that moment a frightening thought hit me. I was more attracted to wealthy girls. A penitent look washed over my face. This seemed to be a despicable thought of which I didn't want anyone else to know, but it was undoubtedly true and had been for some time. I quickly buried the hypothesis to the deepest recesses of my brain and focused on the class itself.

Improv began with a rousing game of "Park Bench." I was still distraught Raven never showed up, but I'd have to move past that. I was now one of the senior-most members of the club and had to lead by example. I volunteered to show the underclassmen how to play. Less than a second after raising my hand, I heard Devi shout:

"I'll go."

Her shrill voice was probably her least attractive attribute. It was going to take some getting used to because at the moment, hearing it caused me to wince. She always seemed to speak loudly and off-tune. It was as if I listened to a concerto where every fourth note was an F-sharp instead of a G.

"You're gonna have to help me out here, V," Devi whispered.

Weirdly enough, no one had ever called me "V" before, and I wasn't sure I liked it. Especially not from someone I'd met five minutes ago, but there was no way I'd criticize this girl. I had no interest in hearing the squawks of Moncler Girl-lite.

Ms. Cuzano announced the rules of the exercise, and Devi looked over at me to see if we were in sync.

"And...scene," Ms. Cuzano shouted.

Devi and I took our seats on the bench. I was going to be a tourist who spoke no English and needed directions.

"Hey, boy," Devi yelped. "Get off my bench. I need a footrest."

"Des com pa taysa. Alla posah?"

"Wait. What?"

"Cola patasa," I pointed off in the distance. "Mes com pa lokaba."

"What's happening?"

"Yes and, Devi! Yes and," Ms. Cuzano repeated the two words I'd heard nonstop for two years in that club.

"Get on all fours, boy!" Devi said to me.

I decided to listen to Ms. Cuzano's advice. One of us had to.

"Yesh. An Wol I go?"

Devi grabbed my arm and pushed me off the bench onto the floor. She then proceeded to kick me, so I fell stomach first on the ground.

"Much better."

Devi then placed her heels on top of me and crossed her arms.

"Scene," Ms. Cuzano said disappointedly before pulling Devi aside and whispering something to her.

Devi came to me after class as I was picking up my trusty black North Face.

"That was a lot of fun. I think I like, love this class."

"Yeah, you looked like you were having a good time."

"Hey," she continued. "What's your BBM? I'm just trying to get like as many cool people's BBMs as possible."

I obliged. Using the transitive property, I thought I was bound to like Devi. Tessa liked Devi. I liked Tessa. If a equals b and b equals c, then a must equal c, right? Although Tessa did just meet Devi, so maybe this didn't apply.

As I should've expected, Devi messaged me before the school day ended: "Great meeting you! Can't wait for our next scene together!!!"

At that point, even someone as socially pinheaded as I, was aware Devi liked me. I thought I could grow to enjoy her company. I began to discuss the possibility of her being my first kiss internally. I needed to come at it from a different angle, though. After so many failures, I needed to take on a new persona around this borderline stranger. Now that I was well-built and suaver, perhaps I could play the bad boy? I'd seen this strategy work time and again in film and TV. It wouldn't be difficult for a modest thespian like me to play a more malicious version of myself.

Given the fact we were two grades apart, Devi and I only spoke in person during Acting Improv. Therefore, 90% of our communication over the next four weeks could be found on BlackBerry Messenger after school.

She messaged me first:

September 9th, 2010:
D: Hey!!!
V: What's up?
D: Nm. What r u doing?
V: Nothing.
D: Ur no fun!
V: Sorry.

D: I'm watching Gossip Girl. You know, you look like Penn Badgley.

V: I don't know who that is.

D: You're cuter though!

V: Thanks.

September 10th:

D: I'm eating a blueberry scone right now. U'd love it.

V: Actually, I'm allergic to blueberries.

D: No way. No ur not.

V: You're right. I'm lying (sarcasm).

D: Why'd you type "sarcasm" in parentheses?

V: It's something I started doing 'cause people could never understand when I was being sarcastic over text.

D: Oh, that's really clever!

D: So u r allergic then?

D: V?

V: Yeah, only food I'm allergic to.

D: That sucks. U know, I'm a vegetarian.

V: Wait, really? That sounds like torture.

D: Why?

V: Meat is the best food there is. Beef, pork, chicken? None of it?

D: Nope! Smells gross. I bet it tastes grosser.

V: What would you do if I snuck crumbs of chicken into your salad?

D: When would we be eating together?

September 13th:

D: Hey!! Long time, no speak.

V: Hi.

D: Are you in a bad mood?

D: V?

V: No, why?

D: U didn't put any exclamation marks.

V: I never do.

D: Well, you should. So I know you're happy to hear from me.

V: Hi!! Better?

D: Way better!!

V: So, where are you from originally?

D: So serious all of a sudden!!

D: Jk

D: All over. Rajkot, Luxembourg, Abu Dhabi, a bunch of places.

V: Oh, that's really cool. To get to travel all over the world.

D: I mean, it's like whatever.

D: How bout u?

V: Lived in Manhattan most of my life. Went to an all-boys school until 9th grade. Now I'm here.

D: That's cool too!!

September 15th:

D: Miss me?

V: Sure.

D: Aww.

D: Hey

D: Do u workout a lot?

V: Once in a while.

D: Looks like it. Ur in great shape. I like abs.

V: I have a six-pack.

D: Really??? My favorite!!

D: Maybe I'll see it some time ;)

V: Who knows?

D: Why, do you have a gf?

V: No, I like to keep my options open.

D: Oh good. Me too.

D: Do u think I'm cute?

V: Yeah sure.

D: What's that supposed to mean?

V: You're cute.

D: Why'd u write yeah sure?

D: Are there cuter girls than me?

D: V?

V: Yeah, of course. But there are always gonna be sexier people in the world.

D: What about in my grade at Verity?

V: We shouldn't talk about this.

D: Tell me!!

V: That new freshman girl Chrissy Cavalier. All the guys in my grade think she's smokin' hot.

V: She's got big boobs and long blonde hair and does that duck face thing in her pictures.

V: Devi?

September 23rd:

V: Hey! Haven't heard from you in a while.

D: What do u want?

V: Just thought I'd check-in.

D: How's ur new gf, Chrissy?

V: She's not my girlfriend. Don't be immature. You forced me to name a name.

D: Ur being immature.

V: You looked cute today. I like you in orange.

D: U really think so? Thanks! U always look cute. Or handsome, w/e

V: What's your favorite animal?

D: It'll sound silly, but a gemsbok.

D: They're like these special antelopes that look like unicorns from far away.

V: Yeah, I know what that are. They have stuffed ones at the Natural History Museum.

D: Yes! What about u?

V: Do you know okapis?

D: Yeah, they're super cute.

September 25th:

D: Hey, how many girls have u kissed in ur life?

D: V?

V: Oh. I don't know. Too many to count. How many guys have you kissed?

D: I think, maybe like 4.

V: Maybe you and I should kiss sometime.

D: Yeah, I'd like that. When were u thinking?

V: Right before Improv on Wednesday?

D: I'm so down. We'll be sneaky about it. No one will know. Like ninjas.

D: What's our plan?

V: So, you know how you need a key for the bathroom?

D: Yeah.

V: You get to class five minutes early and get the key from Ms. Cuzano. I'll meet you in the foyer in between the guys and girls' bathrooms.

D: Sounds pretty hot.

September 28th:

V: Still down for tomorrow?

D: Absolutely baby.

The scene for our first kiss was neither mesmeric nor romantic. It was downright cringeworthy, but as a 17-year-old, I knew I had to get it out of the way. There was no more time to freeze or balk. I had to take this next step towards adulthood swiftly. My bubbly new acquaintance was going to be a willing participant in my nascent metamorphosis.

Five minutes before Acting Improv began, I walked to the school basement and stood in the hallway outside the theater. There was a locked door by the stairwell leading to a 40 square-foot foyer with blank grey walls and charcoal tiles on the ground. The men's restroom was immediately on the left and the women's on the right.

I was already shaking by the time Devi met me in the hallway and unlocked the door to the foyer. She was wearing tight, ripped black jeans with a black Helmut Lang long-sleeve cotton slash shirt. Devi had on more makeup than usual along with fire-engine red lipstick. I had only spoken to and seen her a few times in person, but she had the ability to look quite fetching.

Her hands shook as she turned the key to open the door to our woebegone cranny. Devi was silent as the door creaked open. She locked it behind us and positioned herself in the center of the foyer before turning to face me. I was visibly shaking while she nervously twirled her midnight black hair in between her thumb and finger. I crept closer and placed my hands on her smooth, chubby cheeks as I'd seen countless movie stars do. Then Devi hit the light switch behind her and pressed her lips against mine as hard as she could. After about 10 seconds, I remember feeling more comfortable and began alternating between her thin upper lip and thick lower one. Eventually, our tongues scraped against one another, and I could feel her taste buds against mine. It was dynamic and carnal and animalistic. Devi's welcomed assault on my lips left an indelible mark. I knew the class was about to start, but I didn't want this to end. I wasn't going to be the one to pull away, so eventually, Devi found the light switch with her eyes closed while running her hands up and down my torso. We were both awestruck. I was feeling so confident that before I left the now notorious theater bathroom foyer, I lowered my hand down the small of her back and squeezed Devi's behind while whispering "so nice" in her ear.

Once class began, we didn't speak to each other. I had wiped most of the lipstick off my face, but my body wouldn't stop trembling. I wanted to kiss her again. I loved the feeling of being in a dark, soundproof room with this exotic young woman. Devi's soft skin, slim physique, and succulent lips made me crave another moment alone with her.

After class ended, Tessa approached me.

"What's going on with you and Devi?"

"Nothing, uh, not much. Why?"

"You guys kept looking at each other. Do you like her or something?"

"She's fine. Hadn't thought about it."

"Let me know if you want me to set you two up. I think she'd be down."

"I'll keep you posted."

That moment surprisingly had an impact on me. What would happen when everyone in school found out I'd kissed this freshman? Everyone would chastise and tease me. They'd call me a "cradle robber" or a creep. It'd be one thing if I were making out with Chrissy Cavalier. The popular boys in my grade would've applauded me kissing a smoking hot girl who looked like she could be in our grade. However, for the diminutive foreign girl with the chubby cheeks, I'd get bullied mercilessly. I texted Devi during my next free period.

V: That was a lot of fun.

D: OMG. Yes. ;)

V: I'd love to do it again sometime.

D: Same. 1000%.

V: One quick thing, though.

D: What is it? Did I do something wrong?

V: No, nothing like that.

D: Ur sexy, u know that?

V: I think we should keep this between us.

D: Um, okay. I was gonna say the same to u, but what makes u say that?

V: Why do you say that?

D: I asked u first.

V: Well, I don't want people berating us and making us not see each other.

D: Why would they do that?

V: There are a lot of bullies in this school, and I think we'll both have more fun if we keep it secretive. Like ninjas.

D: K.

V: Why did you not want to tell anyone?

D: Well. Cause of my parents.

D: They're very strict and religious and they like don't want me to meet boys until I'm ready to get married. It's like crazy antiquated I know.

V: Jesus.

D: So, if I told a few people and they told a few people, maybe my parents would find out and ground me for like ever.

V: No worries. It'll be our super-hot secret.

V: After school on Friday, you wanna go for a walk in Central Park with me?

D: Duh. Love to babes.

Devi and I met a few blocks away from school and entered the park at 90th and 5th. We held hands as we strolled down the Reservoir's Bridle Path.

"So, what are your five favorite movies?" I asked as we swung our hands up and down.

"Oh. Good one. Like maybe, *Toy Story*, *The Incredibles*, *Beauty and the Beast*, *The Little Mermaid* and then there's like this Bollywood movie *Kabhi Khushi Kabhie Gham*."

"So, you don't like dramas or thrillers? Stuff like that?"

"I don't know. I watch movies to like escape from real life, you know? I don't want to watch sad and scary stuff."

"What's that Indian movie about?"

"It's kind of like this story about unrequited love. It's like really romantic. This guy literally elopes with his girlfriend because his father doesn't approve of their marriage. The father and son need to like, reconcile, or something. You have to watch it. There's a ton of singing and dancing like all Bollywood movies. That's my favorite part about them."

"Here, this way."

I found a hidden large tree off the main path. It had long, willowy wisps that created a partial dome if one stood in the correct spot. The 97th Street transverse blocked people from seeing us from the north, and the tree's leaves blocked the south and parts of the east and west. It became mine and Devi's secluded make-out spot. Over the next few weeks, my smiley companion would practically skip with me towards our tree and then would place her Gucci or Givenchy bag on the brown leaves and grab hold of my face. We stood there and typically practiced on each other for 45 minutes straight. Once we entered our new dwelling, Devi and I would not speak. We'd instantly lock lips and not pause for a single second until our mouths dried. She had this sprite-like nature I became increasingly attracted to. Her previously high-pitched, creaky voice was temporarily transformed into that of a sultry fairy. Devi's pencil-thin legs and small waist now became essential for carrying her and wrapping her around my body. Her annoying textual habits soon metamorphosed into cute phrases and nicknames. She now seemed to have a childish élan that conjured up bouts of nostalgia. Her presence reminded me of the many missed opportunities I had with girls dating back to my Boxington and Bat Mitzvah days. Through Devi, I could undo tween mistakes and redo moments I'd squandered. Her younger age was a definite blessing rather than the negative I'd initially presumed. The more I kissed her, the more beautiful she became. Devi wasn't just a roguish almond-colored freshman; she was jocose and ebullient, an energetic minx who was intoxicated by every word that dripped from my lips. I became hers, and she became mine. To have this seductress following me around, holding my hand and kissing me whenever I pleased was a euphoric sensation I had never felt before.

We met at our tree every week for the next two months. Devi was interminably affectionate and bubbly, while never removing the bright, white smile from her symmetrical face. Her perpetual elation made me always excited to see her. However, it wasn't long before I realized we each wanted to move at different speeds. After living for 17 years without any romantic connection, I now wanted to make up for lost time. My goal was to try everything with Devi as quickly as possible and wanted to learn through practice. Unfortunately, she wasn't comfortable yet, and I never wanted to force her to do something that made her stressed or unhappy. For example, I wanted to see my first pair of breasts, but she'd steer my hands away for weeks. It was frustrating, but understandable once I put myself in her skin. Eventually, Devi would unstrap her bra and become more open with me, but each step would take months.

The other glaring issue was our confines. For all of October, we only ever kissed under our tree in Central Park. She couldn't take me to her home out of a genuine fear her parents would disown her, and I never brought her to my apartment because I didn't have the temerity to introduce Devi to my loutish father. For the time being, I became inured to our less than ideal situation. I soon developed a process for when Devi halted my advancing sexual desires.

If I started to do something that made her uncomfortable during one of our passionate sessions, I'd stop, sit down, and place her on my lap.

"Ask me a question," I opined. "It can be anything you want."

"What are your five favorite fruits?"

"Plums, pears, apricots, peaches, and grapes, in that order."

"I like when we do this. It's like really fun getting to know you better. You're not just like the hottest guy at school; you can also be super sweet."

"Ask another question, Devi."

"No, I'm serious. I appreciate it when you're sensitive."

"Of course. I just want to make you happy."

"I promise one day I'll do everything you've ever dreamed of. I'll literally rock your world. I promise."

"I know you will, Devi."

She tenderly kissed my cheek.

With her puny body still positioned on my lap, I took out my iPod and handed her one of my earbuds. I put on "Mastermind" by Deltron 3030, and the two of us swayed to the funky beat.

For the rest of the calendar year, Devi was the cynosure of my life. I no longer played basketball, Charleston was gone, I elected not to do the school play, and Austin was my only real friend at that time. Therefore, I answered all of Devi's texts and would drop everything to meet her for a date in Central Park. However, by November, we both agreed we wanted to take a step further. This didn't mean telling our parents or the world about our now official relationship, but rather signified the desire to do more couple-related activities. Devi and I wanted to see movies and go to restaurants together and mutually agreed this was more than just two people attracted to one another.

For my 17th birthday, for example, Devi took me to Sarabeth's on the Upper West Side. She and I both lived on the East Side, but we didn't want our friends or families to see us out together, so we ventured to the less convenient 80th and Amsterdam location.

We took our seats in the back of the restaurant and began to scroll through the menus. Devi looked ravishing in a long, skintight plum dress with matching amethyst earrings. Purple had always been her favorite color because it was said to be regal. I was obsessed enough to admit she looked dazzling in whatever she wore.

"I'll have the Wild Mushroom Ravioli," she said to our waiter.

"The Filet Mignon, but no potatoes, no sauce. Medium rare," I added.

Devi made a face after hearing my order. My first thought was she felt embarrassed at my subtractions. Perhaps she was the type who believed food should be served in the way the chef decided. However, once our food arrived, I made the same face.

The waiter offered fresh, disgusting grated Parmesan cheese to my date, which she gladly accepted. Devi waited five full seconds before telling the waiter the mountain of cheese on her plate was sufficient.

"What's with the face, babes?"

"I just despise cheese. I thought you knew that."

"Well, I knew you didn't like it. I didn't know I can't order it."

"You can if you want."

"I don't like the smell of your steak. You know I'm vegan. 'Cause of my religion."

"I don't want to kiss you after you've wolfed down that disgusting parmesan pile. Wait, can vegans eat cheese?"

"I cheat sometimes. Like a vegetarian-vegan mix. But whatever, like, I don't want to kiss someone who smells like a dead cow."

I chuckled.

"I have an idea."

"Yes, darling?" Devi replied.

"After dinner, let's go to Duane Reade and pick up those Colgate Wisp things. We'll each do a firm brushing, and then we can make out for hours."

"That sounds great."

It was a simple resolution to what could've been an evening-ruining contretemps. Moving forward, Devi and I would always brush our teeth or chew two sticks of gum following a meat or cheese meal. This ability to efficiently negotiate or compromise was passed down from my lovely mother.

I began grasping the concept during my toilet-training days. While it wasn't quite a compromise, my mother would bribe me with M&Ms for each effective bowel movement. I was given 10 for every success. And this soon graduated into a sleep for dessert trade. If I allowed her to sleep 30 minutes later on weekends, she'd give me Snackwells Devil's Food Cakes. If I received an A on an upcoming book report, she'd take me to a Mets game. My mother preached there was always a way to motivate someone to do what you wanted. The more you communicated, the more constructive the compromise.

After our mutually acrid meals, the check arrived, and I instantly grabbed it and placed my credit card inside the server book.

"What are you doing?"

"What? I'm paying."

"Are you joking? No way. It's your birthday. Of course, I'm paying."

"Devi, that's sweet to offer, but I want to do the chivalrous thing here."

Before I could argue another word, she swiped my credit card off of the check and placed it inside her wallet.

"How are you going to pay without your credit card?"

I smirked at my wily companion, who paid the bill. Although, I should specify neither Devi nor I were responsible adults paying their credit card bills each month. Those pieces of plastic had our names on them, but our respective parents' financial backing. The payer of the bill was symbolic.

"Let's get froyo. We'll go to 16 Handles on 2nd...oh, then I guess we'll go to Duane Reade after. If you can like stand 20 minutes without kissing your flawless girlfriend."

"It'll be tough, but I'll try."

We hailed a taxi and directed it to 82nd and 2nd, both agreeing to accept the dangers of wandering around in our families' neighborhood. Devi leaned her head on my shoulder and kissed my hand.

"I'm having a great time, babes. I'm so happy we're together."

"Same here. I think you look so beautiful tonight."

I kissed the top of her head as a goofy smile appeared on my face. Devi didn't lift her neck until the cab stopped in front of 16 Handles.

"Can I get my credit card back?"

Devi started digging through her purse.

"Devi, I can at least pay for the taxi. Can I get my card back, please?"

She found two loose five-dollar bills and paid the driver before we exited.

"Did you lose my credit card?"

The taxi drove off, and Devi started walking away from me. She was holding her left arm in front of her face, blocking any view of her cartoonish, chartreuse eyes.

"Devi, are you crying? Come here."

I tracked down my shivering girlfriend and hugged her tightly.

"Everything's fine."

"Don't...be...mad at me," she sniveled.

"Do I seem mad? This is more comedic than tragic. You took my card and then lost it immediately? That's funny."

"Stop it."

"I'm serious. I've never lost any card or phone in my life, and you lose it in seconds. That's funny to me."

"You're not mad?"

"At you? Never." I kissed her forehead.

"I'm so sorry."

"Don't worry. We'll hail a cab and go back to Sarabeth's."

"Let me call the restaurant first."

Devi spoke to the maitre'd, who was unable to find her wallet, which caused my diminutive girlfriend to continue to hide her teary eyes from me.

"I don't care what the maitre'd says. We've got to retrace our steps. I'll call a cab...do you have a few more bucks lying around?"

"Like 10."

I hailed a taxi, and we traveled back to Sarabeth's. I found her wallet immediately. It was the same color as the chair Devi sat in, so there was an element of camouflage.

"See, problem solved. Let's go to Duane Reade now. I need to kiss you."

"Thank you so much."

"Don't worry. I can solve any problem."

CHAPTER 2

A MONTH AND A HALF later, Devi and I had two reasons to celebrate. First, we'd both finished our semesters, and second, it was her 16th birthday on December 18th. The latter fact confused me at the time because I always thought Devi was two years younger than me. Apparently, though, due to some home and international schooling, she was a year older than most students in her grade in America. And even if Devi was bony for her age, nothing could alter my incipient feelings towards her. I was sure she'd grow into her body shortly.

Devi's birthday was on a Saturday and began with us meeting in Central Park for our tree hangout routine. After an exhaustive hour, we dropped to the ground and leaned against the hundred-year-old trunk. It was the first time I had seen her wear a Moncler jacket. Unlike the typical Moncler Girls' black and white, Devi's was military green. It was a skintight, Armoise design that fit snugly around her size 0 waist.

"What are your plans for tonight?"

"Nothing much. Dinner with my parents and sister, then like nothing, I think."

"Cool, can I see you at some point? I want to spend time with the birthday girl."

She kissed me and bit my lower lip.

"I don't know what you do to me, Vincent Beattie."

"Happy to meet you anywhere or do anything you want."

"You know what? Are you feeling dangerous?"

"Around you? Always."

"Come over to my house tonight."

"Won't your parents be there?" I asked.

"I don't care. I need you."

"What's the plan?"

"After they go to sleep, I'll like call down to my doorman and have him let you up. Then, you'll punch in the key to unlock the elevator door: 698140. I'll meet you in the foyer and sneak you back to my room."

"Wait, why does the elevator have a code?"

"I live on the penthouse, sweets. The elevator opens to our apartment."

"Okay, I'm ready for anything. This'll be exciting."

"You better bring me a present, though."

After receiving Devi's BBM, I walked to 79th and York and entered the lobby just after 11 pm. Devi's doorman directed me to the elevator and told me to go straight to the penthouse. After 36 floors, I arrived and had to swiftly punch in the 698140 code before the elevator doors closed on me. Devi leaped on top of me and wrapped her scrawny legs around my waist.

"Take me to my bedroom," she whispered. "I'll direct you...oh, but take your shoes off first. I'll carry them with this hand."

All of the lights in the apartment were off, but the Bow windows allowed the moon's reflection to coruscate off the East River and shimmer into the top floor living room. Anyone's initial thought when entering the foyer had to be the sheer magnitude of this penthouse.

"Go left down this hallway."

The corridor felt lengthier than an entire city block. As I continued to carry Devi, we passed what seemed like 15 doors on the way to her bedroom.

"Open this one."

We entered the room as the household remained silent and dark. I threw Devi onto her California King-sized bed and stared at her, still fully clad in her evening outfit.

"Go lock the door we came in...and also lock the door in my closet. My sister can walk in through there at any time if it's open. I'll turn on my lamp."

I twisted the latch to the front door of her room and then entered her walk-in closet, which seemed to be its own miniature hallway with a bathroom on the right. The penthouse was as if a four-story townhouse was laid horizontally. The Kapoor apartment was nothing short of a prodigious, architectural marvel.

I glanced around the dimly lit area and immediately thought of her parents as posh aesthetes with a predilection for modern art. Devi's room featured a panoply of colorful tableaus and 21st-century sculptures all in the purple, magenta, or cornsilk families. My mother would've appreciated the decorations and also would've loved seeing me this blithesome. Right after my mother's death, I'd reached my nadir. Now, more than halfway through my high school career, I was at my apex.

"What are you waiting for?" Devi's high-pitch whisper creaked.

I leaped onto the bed, straddled her petite body, and removed her dress.

"You're like so hot," she whispered.

My cumbersome button-down temporarily impeded Devi's voracious appetite. But with a few expeditious movements, my shirt had fallen to the floor, and my girlfriend began kissing and licking my torso.

"Babes, I want you to touch my boobs."

"Are you sure? Your parents are home."

Devi grabbed my hands and placed them atop her hot pink bra.

"Unstrap me now," she whispered right next to my ear.

I fumbled with the clasp for several seconds before her undergarment fell to the side, and I was now staring at my first pair of breasts. After years of ensorcelling my teenage mind, I finally understood the reason for my years-long fixation. I immediately kissed and licked her mocha-colored nipples while her sonorous moans reverberated throughout the room. Devi sounded angelic for a brief moment before I heard a harrowing noise in the distance.

"What was that?"

"Nothing. Keep doing that...It feels so good."

Another clearer sound resonated from somewhere down the interminable hallway.

"Wait, shush. It's my dad," Devi said frantically. "Get in the closet. Take your shirt and shoes. Pass me my bra."

I hid in the closet that conjoined two bedrooms and then closed the door as softly as possible while the desperate Devi made sure to cover up any sign of debauchery. I heard the handle on her front door twist.

"Don't lock the door." I heard an accented voice yell.

"Oh, I must've locked it by accident," Devi said as she scurried to open it.

Meanwhile, I realized if her presumed father felt misbegotten activities were occurring in his daughter's bedroom, he'd surely check the closet. I opened the door to Devi's younger sister's room. That would be the perfect place to hide. I entered with the daintiness of a Russian ballerina.

However, when I saw Devi's slightly younger sister peacefully snoring, I panicked. I was in way over my head and began shaking before opening a mysterious door on my right. Luckily, it led to Devi's sister's bathroom, where I must've been safe from Devi's father's ill-conceived wrath. I took a deep breath before a new thought crept into my inquisitive head. What if Devi's sister woke up and had to use the bathroom? If I locked the door and she tried to enter, she'd undoubtedly yell for her parents' aid. I thought about hiding in the shower, but if the sister saw me, she'd immediately yelp. Finally, I considered hiding behind the door and putting my hand over her mouth if she entered, but that would be way too traumatic. In the end, I stood there and awaited the doom I'd undoubtedly face upon seeing her nonplussed father for the first time.

"Don't go in my closet," I heard Devi shout as that door opened.

Fortunately, I thought one step ahead and had long disappeared from that obvious hiding place. At that moment, it also hit me that I never brought Devi a gift as she'd requested. Luckily, my lovely girlfriend hadn't remembered.

"You're just like hearing things. I was listening to music. Don't bother me again you..." Devi trailed off in another language.

The bathroom door never opened. Devi texted me five minutes later, asking where I was and then quickly crept into her sister's bathroom and jumped into my arms. My girlfriend gave me a long kiss before apologizing for the stressful rabblement.

"You should go now, but that was so much fun, babes. I literally had a heart attack. I'll text you."

Over winter break, Devi elected to take a weeklong acting class at the New York Film Academy's South Beach, Florida location. After our ineffaceable evening, I was more attracted to her than ever. The day after Devi departed with our Acting Improv compatriot Tessa, I instantly craved my girlfriend's luscious lips and beautiful body. Less than 48 hours went by before I texted her:

V: You're so hot. I can't stop thinking about you.
D: Babes, I miss u like anything.
V: Come home soon please. I need you.
D: I love how passionate u r.
V: Always for you...how's acting?
D: It's fine. Pretty quiet. I prefer watching u in Improv.
V: Thanks!
D: Ur just so strong. Like your voice and body and emotions and all that stuff.
V: You're so beautiful, Devi.

December 27th, 2010
D: I'm hanging out by the hotel pool with Tessa. Wish u were here.
V: Ugh, I would love nothing more.
D: I'd love to see u in ur bathing suit with no shirt on ;)
V: What do you look like right now?

D: Blue bikini top with a black bikini bottom.

V: So sexy. I like two pieces waaaay more than one-pieces.

D: If you got it, flaunt it.

V: Lemme see a picture.

D: That's embarrassing.

V: For me? Please?

D: Fine (*sends a picture of herself by the pool*).

V: God, your body's amazing.

V: Wait, who's taking the picture?

D: Tessa.

D: Now you send me a nude. Now. Please.

D: Wait. Sorry. That was Tessa. She stole my phone.

V: Haha, you guys having fun down there?

D: Want me to kiss Tessa? How hot would that be?

V: That would be awesome.

D: Wait, that was Tessa again. U really want that?

V: I think that'd be pretty sexy.

D: But I'm not a lesbian...or bi.

V: No one thinks you're a lesbian if you kiss your friend once.

D: I only want to kiss you.

V: Whatever you want. I just want you to have fun.

V: I miss you, darling.

D: Here (*sends a picture of her kissing Tessa on the lips*).

D: Your wish is my command.

V: Goddamn. You're incredible.

December 28th, 2010

V: Does Tessa know about us now?

D: Of course not silly. Ur in my phone as Chace Crawford.

V: Not sure how I feel about that...

D: Relax.

V: Who does Tessa think Chace Crawford is?

D: Who cares? She has no idea it's u. I promise.

D: U know, I'm alone in my room.

V: Same.

D: What would you do to me if you were here?

V: I'd kiss your lips, then your ears, then bite your neck.

V: I'd have you close your eyes while I kissed different parts of your body.

V: I'd unhook your bra.

D: Wait, stop. I'm so horny right now. No more. Not without you here.

V: Haha fine.

D: I want to send you a picture.

D: I'm going into my bathroom. Brb.

V: Wow, baby. I'm so attracted to you.

D: All I have on is my pink bikini.

V: Send me one of you doing that duck face thing with your lips.

D: How's this (*sends picture in her bikini*)

V: Jesus, you get sexier every time I see you.

D: Want to see more?

V: Hell yeah I do.

D: (*sends a series of fully nude pictures of herself*).

V: You're the hottest girl alive. I'm absolutely obsessed with you.

V: Your body is unbelievable.

V: I might faint.

CHAPTER 3

DEVI RETURNED HOME LATER THAT week, and we started our second semesters. At this point, it became exceedingly difficult to take my eyes off of her in school. When Devi would see me in the hallway, staircase, or lounge, she'd wink, expose her shoulder, or even show me her cleavage. It had reached the point where weekly trips to our tree or five-minute theater bathroom hook-ups were no longer enough. I needed to see more of my coquettish vixen. I voiced this concern to Devi over text, and she agreed wholeheartedly. At the very least, we needed to find our new agora. There had to be another venue that could accommodate two hopeless teenagers.

Devi's excellent suggestion happened to be Carl Schurz Park. It was a tiny area adjacent to the East River and within walking distance from her apartment. A concrete boardwalk circumvented a dog park, playground, basketball court, and several grassy pathways that were mostly hidden from sight. It became our new after school habitat.

Devi and I would inconspicuously meet at 86th and York and then hold hands as we walked one block to the ornate park that was home to the mayor's famed Gracie Mansion. While on these frequent adventures, she and I barely spoke. I'd quickly ask Devi how her classes were going, and she despondently spoke of poor grades in her recent past but had an optimistic future of A's on the horizon. Then my elegant girlfriend would repeat my question, and I'd tell her about the most recent 96 I received on a paper or 94 on a quiz. I knew she felt insecure about her grades or even intellect, but I looked past that and tried to avoid difficult, deep conversations and compliment her whenever possible. Devi would frequently speak about complex topics to try to show me we were equals despite our age difference, so it wasn't out of the ordinary to hear her randomly pipe up about what Existentialism meant to her, for example. I always nodded and made sure to repeat the line:

"Wow, you're so smart. You should be taking 11th-grade classes."

More than anything, I felt penitent Devi had this need to impress me. I already liked her. However, her insecurity mounted the more we learned about one another. At the time, the less I spoke, the more she grew to like me. I understood part of her attraction to me stemmed from two fundamentally uncontrollable forces, the first being our age difference.

For plenty of high school girls, there is something particularly exhilarating about being able to secure an older boy. Very few ninth-graders in our area had success with upperclassmen, so it automatically made someone like Devi feel special. Secondly, my girlfriend and I had this ever-present secret neither of us wanted to reveal. And most are aware of the spark danger and mystery can add to a relationship. If Devi and I went public about our trysts and our friends and family were supportive, we'd instantly lose the felonious illusion of wickedness. Given our puritanical backgrounds, any kind of sacrilegious escapade immediately made us feel an impalpable sexiness we'd never been privy to before our relationship. However, the week before Valentine's Day, that vital spark permanently disappeared.

Devi and I were in Carl Schurz Park, sitting on a bench overlooking the East River. She was in her military green Moncler jacket, and I wore my navy J. Crew peacoat. We were engaged in a zealous kissing session that included occasional pauses to shiver and allow our respective teeth to clatter. There was nothing particularly unusual about this afternoon until we heard a shout from 50 feet down the concrete boardwalk.

"Devi, is that you?" The young voice cried.

"Damn. Damn. Damn," Devi frantically whispered to me.

"Who is that?"

"Devi?"

Her decibels rose above the frosty zephyrs until she was standing right beside my girlfriend and me.

"Hello kind sir. I'm Nitya."

"V, this is my sister."

Nitya stood before us. Her presence announced the end of the first stage of my relationship with Devi. Nitya had unknowingly extinguished a portion of our steadily burning blue flame. This delightfully appalled ingenue had the omnipotence to alter the future of a boy she'd never met before.

"Nice to meet you. I'm Vincent," I smiled as brightly as I could, given the weather.

"Nitya," Devi said. "What are you doing here?"

"I should be asking you that. I saw your tongue down this guy's throat."

Devi shouted at Nitya in another language.

"Nitya, do you want to have a seat?"

"No," Devi interrupted. "She's leaving."

"I sure would," her sister said. "I wasn't even spying on you guys. I needed to walk Fraulein Kareena."

I didn't understand what that meant until I saw an eight-pound dog strut by our black metal bench.

"Hi girl," I reached down, picked up the Papillon, and cradled it.

My mother had never liked dogs, and my father believed they were simply a sunk cost. Phyllis didn't appreciate the smell, clean-up, bathing, walking, dirtiness, and especially the shedding. Morgan, on the other hand, once gave Charleston a financial breakdown on a paper napkin that depicted why we'd never get a puppy. It displayed the annual costs of food, veterinarian care, toys, bathing, grooming, and emotional trauma following its inevitable euthanasia appointment in 12 years. Charleston was eight at the time while I was six. Having two of my favorite people teach me about the annoyances of dogs caused me to swear off the genus entirely.

However, at that moment, I knew becoming a dog person could go a long way. Hours of movies and TV shows had taught me all girls love puppies, and no one wants to hear logical arguments as to why they may be dirty, expensive creatures. You'll never change a dog person's mind.

I petted and cuddled Fraulein Kareena for a few minutes while the sisters argued. I was going to need an extensive bath and toothbrushing upon my return home, but for now, the Papillon and I were fast friends.

"Devi tells me you're her boyfriend."

"Yes, I guess I am."

"You like Fraulein Kareena?"

"How could I not?"

"She and my sister are my two favorite girls in the world. If they both like you, then I do too."

Nitya was 13 years old and somehow even skinnier than her older sister. Gangly, chestnut brown limbs accentuated Nitya's skeletal five-foot-six figure. She looked like her older sister, but had a fuller nose, longer forehead, smaller lips, and her black hair was parted perfectly down the middle. Unlike Devi, Nitya's face was personable and approachable. She had a prepubescent dorkiness and hadn't yet developed Devi's epicurean tastes. If I were a stranger, Devi would appear to be the lavish and vainglorious one, while Nitya was the down-to-earth, introverted type.

"So, where do you go to school, Nitya?"

"Verity. I'm a lot younger. That's why you've never seen me, probably."

"Oh, very cool," I said. "Do you like it?"

"How old *are* you? You look like you could be in college."

"17 and a half. Just 13 months older than your sister."

"You should shave your scruff."

"What else should I do?" I responded while continuing my love affair with Fraulein Kareena.

"Buy my sister flowers...wait, Devi. Go away."

"What? Why?" Devi asked.

"Vincent and I need to have a chat. We gotta like, get to know each other better."

"Just go away already, will you?" Devi began biting the tips of her hair.

"I asked you first."

"How much money do I have to give you to leave us alone?" Devi argued.

"Nothing. Leave Vincent and I alone for five minutes, and I won't tell Mama and Daddy about you two."

Devi nodded, stomped her foot, and perched herself on a bench 30 feet away. She took Fraulein Kareena and moped by herself. Devi's midnight black hair was still being used as a foul-tasting appetizer.

"How'd you and Devi meet?" Nitya continued.

"Acting Improv class."

"So, you're an actor who plays sports. You're like Troy Bolton."

"Yeah, I kind of thought the same thing myself. What do you like to do?"

"I watch a lot of TV shows, listen to music, hang out with my friends, read. I mostly, um, like to be on my own, though."

"To tell you the truth, I do too. Devi's one of the few friends I have. I think quality is more important than quantity."

"Agreed."

"What shows and music do you like?" I asked.

"I'm really like into *Pretty Little Liars* and *Gossip Girl* right now. *Gossip Girl* especially 'cause like, the girls at Verity are just like the girls in the show."

"I've never watched it, but Devi definitely talks about it."

"Yeah, she introduced me to it. Devi thinks I'm too young to watch some of the episodes, but I do anyway."

"I can see that. I'm sure a show like that can be a good teaching mechanism for a girl your age."

"Right?"

"What about music?"

"I'm really into Florence and the Machine right now. They have an album coming out later this year too. Wanna listen to some?"

"Sure, of course I do."

Nitya pulled her iPod out of her pocket, handed me an earbud, and pressed play on "Cosmic Love."

"This is amazing," I said. "I love the harp."

"Her voice is like, so awesome."

Devi raced back to us with Fraulein Kareena in tow.

"Are you done yet?"

"Oh, I forgot you were there," I said. "We're having a great time."

"Yeah, we're already besties," Nitya said.

After a half-hour together, Nitya wound up being a trustworthy ally to both Devi and me. She was a sweet and quiet girl who enjoyed seeing her older sister happy. After my first conversation with Nitya, I briefly compared what my first discussion with Devi was like. There was a chance my girlfriend's 13-year-old sister was easier to talk to and more similar to me. However, I quickly eviscerated that thought from my ever-roaming mind.

The new series of machinations permeating the forefront of my brain was what to do for Valentine's Day. I had never had a girlfriend on the famed holiday of love and had no one to seek out for advice. My father was my first option, but he was nothing but a failed romantic. Morgan Beattie was an uncouth oaf when it came to love. However, I'd learned from his mistakes. I didn't choose to purchase Sharper Image's newest back massager to procure Devi's love.

Instead, I followed the initial Beattie family blueprint for Mother's Days. I was to obtain the "Holy Quadrumvirate," or "The CFCG," as I astutely nicknamed the grouping. Devi would be receiving a card, flowers, chocolates, and a gift. There's no way I could possibly fail from a thoughtfulness perspective.

My first stop was the nearby Duane Reade, where I bought a comical, yet loving Hallmark card with two pink birds kissing. While there, I spotted Guylian chocolate truffles I'd seen Devi eat in the past, so I was already halfway through the quadrumvirate. After school on the day of, I bought a violet-colored orchid and brought it back to my apartment before I started to prepare for our dinner.

Several weeks prior, I made a reservation at The Water Club and felt that could suffice as my gift, given the hefty prix fixe pricing on

Valentine's Day. Upon telling my father about my February 14th reservation, he bleated and scolded me for spending all of his money.

"You're worse than your mother. Who the hell are you taking to The Water Club?"

"Just some girl I know."

"She splitting it?"

"No. Come on, Dad. I so rarely get to have fun and be social."

"I don't have any money. Don't you get that? Get a job."

"Won't happen again after this one night."

"Jesus. I doubt that. You need me to leave the apartment that night?"

"Don't be gross."

I'm not sure what Devi's conversation with her parents was like, or how she'd hide an orchid in her room after I handed it off, but if I could make our secrecy work, so could she.

We met at the luxurious, floating restaurant docked along the East River. I'd never been, and it was stunning to look across the water and see the shimmering lights of the Queensboro Bridge, Roosevelt Island, and Brooklyn. Naturally, Devi and I were the only couple under 30, but that made it more intimate. I felt I was genuinely maturing. We were amongst so many aging, married couples; it was hard not to picture what life would be like married to Devi.

We'd go to the same New England college, sleepover in each other's dorm rooms, and then I'd go to grad school and propose to her on the day of her college graduation. Devi and I would travel to Switzerland, Greece, South Africa, and Costa Rica before getting married in Kuala Lumpur. I'd work on Wall Street at my father's firm while she'd start a non-profit. We'd have no shortage of financial assistance from her family, especially after Devi had given birth to her parents' grandchildren. It would be a calm, predictable life, but given my girlfriend's fiery personality, we'd undoubtedly go through atypical ebbs and flows. I knew Devi and I would come out unscathed no matter what. I was sure of it.

We had only been together for five months or so, and I had no reason to think we'd ever break up. Devi was passionate, dramatic, and seemed to get more beautiful with each passing day. While we didn't engage in in-depth conversations, Devi was extroverted, fun, and incredibly stylish. My girlfriend and I never experienced the moments of insipidity that many couples before us had. I wouldn't allow us to end up like any of our unhappy parental role models. Devi and I would always put in the necessary toil to improve each other's lives.

"I hate the smell of clams," she said. "It's so gross."

"What are you going to get, darling?"

"I'm not hungry. I'll just have a salad, babes."

"It's prix fixe. You can get any of these things here."

"What do I do with this orchid?"

"Here..." I reached over and placed it underneath our table.

"I'm going to get the steak," I said. "But don't worry, I brought gum."

"Would you ever get a pet fish?" She asked.

"God, no. They just sit there and swim. You can't pet them or get close to them. They're a bad pet. It's a waste of money too."

"They're like four dollars...Well, whatever. I'd rather have a pet fish then eat one."

"You look really pretty tonight. Blue's a great color on you."

"I know. This dress is definitely slimming."

The waiter came by our table, immediately removed the wine list, and then took our orders.

"Are they gonna bring bread or what?" She asked.

"I'm sure they will shortly...it was great meeting Nitya the other day. She seems awesome."

"Yeah, she mentioned you too. Nitya said you were hot."

"That's funny..." I paused before continuing. "What are your plans for this summer?"

"Well, my family has a house in Southampton. It's south of the highway, so like very close to the beach. I can walk."

"That's cool. How often are you going to be out there, though?"

"Oh, don't stress babes. I'm taking two classes at Columbia University for college credit, so my father will drive me back and hang with me in the city on Tuesdays, Wednesdays, and Thursdays. Plus, I have my dance classes."

"What dance classes?"

"I haven't told you about that?"

"I have no idea what you're talking about."

"I've been taking classical dance since I was like a toddler."

"How did I not know this?"

"Yeah, it's no big deal."

"No, that sounds amazing. I'd love to see you perform."

"Well, I just practice after school or on the weekends with my friends. It's like really difficult work. Like, impossible. It's way harder than any sport *you* play."

After a few more minutes of chatting, the waiter brought over bread, followed by our appetizers.

"Devi, is anything wrong?"

"No, nothing at all. Why?"

"I don't know. It seems like there's something on your mind?"

"Well, like something little, but I'll tell you after dinner."

"Oh c'mon. You can't preface a story like that and then keep me in the dark for an hour."

"Why not? I can do like whatever I want."

"Sure, you *can*. But I'd prefer it if you expressed yourself. That's how we'll become even closer than we already are."

"Fine. But it's gonna sound weird now."

"Nothing sounds weird from your sexy lips."

"Okay babes. Here I go."

Devi took a deep breath, twisted her evil eye bracelet, and placed her hand over her mouth.

"I think I'm in love with you. Like, I don't think. I know I'm in love with you. Like, I really love you, Vincent."

"I love you too. That's so sweet of you to say."

"You do?"

"Of course I do."

"That's such a relief. I just get like nervous and insecure sometimes. I wasn't sure you loved me."

"I love you, Devi. See how easy that was? Always express yourself to me. We're rock solid together."

"Say it again."

"I love you, Devi."

"Again," she cackled.

CHAPTER 4

O VER THE NEXT FEW MONTHS, Devi and I sailed on aimlessly. We never hung out at each other's apartments, didn't tell any-one about our relationship, and had yet to round second base physically. I was mildly concerned with our stagnation, but Devi prom-ised she'd let me know when there were other options available. It was a minor drawback in an otherwise stable relationship.

My schedule became busier by March. I'd be spending a significant amount of time with college visits, ACT testing, and baseball, but I always found a chance to BBM my benignant girlfriend. Over spring break, Devi flew overseas to visit various extended family members, while my father drove me to Washington D.C. to visit GW and Georgetown.

Morgan and I had spent very little time together over the previous six months, so back-to-back three and a half hour drives would allow us to make up for lost time. On March 19th, we hopped in the now battered navy BMW and headed south on I-95.

"You lose your virginity yet?" My father opened the conversation.

"I don't know how to answer that."

"Grades good?"

"Getting A's in English, AP Gov, and AP Chem. Pre-Calculus is tougher. Probably sitting in the B range. Spanish 2 is easy."

"You go meet with the Calc teacher yet?"

"No, sir."

"What the hell do they got office hours for? Go meet with the guy. Problem solved."

"How's work?"

"It's a dog-eat-dog world, and I'm wearing milk-bone underwear."

"I don't know what that means."

"Work sucks. I don't make any money. By the time you graduate college, I'll be in the poorhouse."

"You think about Mom a lot?"

"Eh. Stuff happens. My parents died years ago. You just gotta move on. I'm focused on work."

"But, like, what's..."

"Don't say like."

"Sorry. What's the point of you working?"

"To put you kids through school."

"Does that bring you joy, though?"

"What are you, my therapist? You know, Freud said, 'the Irish are the only people impervious to psychoanalysis'."

"Freud didn't say that," I responded.

"Yeah, he did. Look it up."

"That's from *The Departed*, right? Yeah, definitely. Matt Damon said that."

"You're not as smart as you think you are."

My father turned on the CD he'd burned several weeks before Phyllis' death. It was one of only two CDs that were allowed to be played in his BMW. The other being, of course, James Blunt's *Back to Bedlam*. My father flipped through the first few tracks and then settled on "Peace Frog" by The Doors.

The music was eventually turned off by the time we arrived in Washington D.C. Since I had been taking AP Government, I was excited to see the famous landmarks and perhaps do a tour of the monuments, but my father had other ideas.

"Any way we can be in and out of DC by 4 pm? I'd prefer not to drive at night if it's supposed to rain."

"Dad, how are we gonna see two schools in four hours? I thought we were sleeping over."

"No, that's a waste of 200 bucks. I concocted another idea during the drive."

"I'm sure I won't like this."

"Probably...so in and out in four hours, then we sleep in our beds at home, then wake up at 8 am tomorrow and drive to Boston. We can see BU and Tufts, maybe hit Trinity on our way back to the city. We'll try to be home by 8 pm Sunday. It's perfect."

"That sounds terrible. For you, especially. You're going to drive like..."

"Don't say like."

"You're going to drive, what, 15 hours in a 36-hour span?"

"Crazy right? The things I do for my children."

"I suppose there's no point in arguing?"

"None whatsoever. In and out in four hours, bingo bango."

I was in a dour mood by the time we set foot on the Georgetown campus. My lassitude following 210 minutes of riding in a car and listening to '70s soft rock was palpable.

"I got another idea to speed things up. Let's skip the tours."

"Dad, this isn't some joke. This is where I'm going to spend the next four years of my life."

"I've done this before, and you haven't. Trust me. This whole process is all about feel. We'll walk around campus, look at the students, buildings, and maybe the surrounding off-campus areas. We'll grab a brochure and write your name in whatever book they have that denotes visitors."

"This isn't a bed-and-breakfast."

"Maybe we'll pop into admissions and introduce you to the director. Good-looking kid like you? She'll remember your face when she sees your application in the fall."

"What year do you think it is? That's not how any of this works."

"I went to Wharton. I know how the college process works. Trust me."

Over the next hour, my father escorted me around the pleasant Georgetown neighborhood, followed by the campus and, eventually, a five-minute walk along the Potomac River. The surrounding areas were pleasant, but the school itself had an austere feel. Georgetown's stone buildings and prominent crosses dissuaded me. I knew my mother would never want me to go to a devout Catholic/Jesuit school.

My father was the one who advised me to choose these schools in particular. He said I wouldn't be able to transition from Manhattan to a small, rural college, and that I needed city life to stimulate me. My father insisted I only choose schools that were an Amtrak ride away. Therefore, I settled on Boston and DC schools with perhaps a Trinity or Johns Hopkins application. I didn't want to follow in my father's footsteps at Penn, and Philadelphia didn't have any other schools that interested me.

By the time the weekend was over, I had realized each school had pros and cons, and it wouldn't really matter where I went. None of these schools would be heavenly, nor would they be hellacious. I assured myself I could have a middling experience at most east coast colleges. Therefore, I'd simply go to whichever one would create the brightest future for me career-wise. I elected not to apply anywhere early-decision and would delay my future until the final possible moment—May of my senior year.

In the meantime, I returned from spring break and alternated my free time between increasingly prosaic meetups with Devi, and Verity Prep baseball. The former was my own emotional problem that had nothing to do with Devi's chastity. As a 17-year-old, I listened to the boys in my grade talk about sex daily. Every free period, I heard about sexual positions, porn preferences, and 11th-grade girl rankings. I was always off to the side studying while eavesdropping, but the interminable conversations began to eat at me. I had this sempiternal itch that would seemingly never be scratched. However, as the docile and patient boyfriend to a ninth-grader, I kept my mouth shut. I just needed to be kind and considerate, and one day I'd be rewarded. I never wanted to pressure Devi. So instead of steamy sex scenes, I'd take her to see movies like *Rango* and *Rio* and *Kung Fu Panda 2*.

If there was a potential strike one for Devi and me, it was our lack of mutual interests, and taste in movies was one of many. She liked syrupy Bollywood romances, while I enjoyed Academy Award-nominated dramas and thrillers. However, I had always been taught the importance of compromise, so I found animated movies to be the best solution. They allowed us to spice up our routine, kiss in a new setting, and kept her occasional bouts of ADHD at bay. These middling animated films prevented my adorable girlfriend from pouty conniptions. While in the theater, Devi would cuddle against my chest, eat her popcorn, and cackle more than the average moviegoer. The animated movie became our go-to solution when the park hook-ups grew temporarily stale.

My primary focus then shifted to baseball. I was now on the varsity team with my only true friend, Austin. He was the team's number two pitcher, while I instantly supplanted the incumbent third baseman. The coach inserted me in my typical leadoff spot in the batting order from day one, and for the next two years, I never relinquished that position. I hit .380 with an on-base percentage of .448. And by the end of 11th grade, I was considered the best all-around player at the school.

Unfortunately, as was the case in my younger years, no one at Verity noticed or cared. During the average day, I learned to keep to myself. I was still the taciturn Vincent that had had a mostly successful tenure at Hollandsworth. I was probably known as the preeminent stoic in Verity's class of 2012. During free periods, I only spoke when questioned, and while I was a modest class participator, this was only because raising one's hand a few times each week inherently increased their GPA.

I overheard my peers talk about upcoming apartment parties, weekends in the Hamptons, or even what 12th-grade spring break would be like on the annual senior trip to Paradise Island in the Bahamas. I was certainly envious of the club rats and Moncler Girls, but I had come to accept my place in the school's social hierarchy. No one hated or bullied me, which I felt was a considerable win. I mean, how many other high schoolers can boast about that through three years in teenage society amongst the city's most malleable denizens?

Like many 11th graders, though, I had bouts of desolation. There were times when something would remind me of my mother, such as the smell of croissants from Corrado Bakery or truffles at La Maison du Chocolat. I'd breathe in those haunting aromas, and my eyes would instantly water. It reminded me of several madeleine cake passages from

Proust's *In Search of Lost Time*. However, in those instances, when I started to tear up, I'd take a few deep breaths and picture the omnipresent voice of my father repeating "man up" in my head. Then, I'd snap out of it.

Nevertheless, there were a few days when I'd race home after baseball practice, lock myself in my shower, and cry for an indeterminate amount of time. As a logical thinker, these inconsistent bouts were troublesome. I tried to rationalize them as remnants from the Phyllis Beattie era or pent-up anger over something my father or Devi or someone on the baseball team had said. Maybe I was simply nervous about my future. Some people don't conform to societal standards, I thought. I must just be one of them. No matter how much I wanted to be popular and hang out with Moncler Girls and basketball jocks, I had to come to grips with the fact I was awkward and had a different line of thinking. I'd never be the permanently well-liked, friendly guy who would brighten everyone's day. I was simply a wallflower attending a high school that seemed different from any other place, but in actuality, still housed a predilection for extroverts and an ordinary social milieu.

The summer arrived, and my father found me an unpaid summer internship at a boutique ghostwriting firm. The person he sat next to at Sabbaday Capital had a younger sister looking for assistance at her four-person company. My father offered my services without discussing it with me and happily accepted on my behalf. The job itself was quickly derivative. My first day, I arrived, made a coffee run, picked up my boss's laundry, walked the company dogs, watered the plants, and edited several chapters of non-fiction, self-help books. Every subsequent day followed the same formula. It was only three days a week, and I supposed it did get me out of the apartment.

Meanwhile, Devi traveled to Southampton every Thursday night with her father and returned to the city on Monday. The next three days, she'd take business and marketing courses at Columbia University for college credit, and I, being the self-proclaimed great boyfriend, would take the subway and bus to meet Devi on Columbia's campus for her lunch break. I worked Mondays, Wednesdays, and Fridays, and her classes were Tuesdays, Wednesdays, and Thursdays, so each weekday, when I wasn't working, I'd take the 86th Street bus to Broadway and the 1 train to 116th Street. Including the walk, it was a 30 to 40-minute commute, but it was worth it. The weekend BBMs weren't enough to appease our desires. We needed physical contact.

Upon seeing me on campus, Devi would leap into my arms and tackle me onto the green grass outside of Lewisohn Hall. She'd lay in my lap as we cuddled in the shade on the 90-degree summer days. Devi and I would kiss, listen to music, and discuss our weeks. And after our 20-minute conclave, we'd stop at Strokos Gourmet Deli and pick up fruits and salad for her and a chicken cutlet sandwich for me. My girlfriend and I would then find a cozy bench outside of John Jay Hall, and she'd lay in my lap. Most of our conversations were harmless and loving, but once or twice, we'd elevate to more profound topics.

"Feed me grapes, babes. I'm starving," Devi said one late-July afternoon.

"Anything for you."

Devi looked towards me as I admired her slender almond legs. I placed a purple grape in her mouth.

"I like it when you feed me. I feel like Cleopatra."

"You're more beautiful."

"Wait, I wanna like, feed you grapes too."

"Can't. I have gum in my mouth."

"Well, kiss me. I'll take the gum."

Devi sat up, and I leaned forward. Our tongues locked as she slipped the peppermint sphere into her cheek and grinned. My sultry girlfriend then proceeded to feed me the green grapes.

Ever since the waxing months of our relationship, she had found the swapping of gum to be a romantic gesture. Devi would request I spit my gum out into her hand or that she regurgitates her cinnamon flavor in between my teeth. Initially, I thought it was bizarre, but as our relationship progressed, I thought of it as an innocuous quirk. I clung to this oddity like a trophy. Devi had chosen me as the one person in the world whose pre-chewed gum she'd tolerate. It was an honor if anything.

"I love you, babes," she said.

"I love you too. It's always so much fun getting to visit my little gemsbok."

"I know okapi. I wish you could just come out to the Hamptons with me. It'd be so much fun."

"One day, we'll have our own house out there and endless alone time."

"That sounds, like absolutely flawless."

"Speaking of which, you think by the time school starts, you'll be ready to, um, you know...take the next step?"

"I don't know what you...oh...I'm not sure. I guess I'll know when I feel it."

"I'd never pressure you. I just want to be able to show you how much I love you, in addition to always telling you."

"Of course, babes. You're so sweet and patient...my main, um, hesitation is like, my religion. My family would never want me to have sex before marriage, and they wouldn't even want me kissing boys until like after college."

"Right, I remember."

"It's just like I'll see you shirtless in front of me, and I'll want you. Like, badly want you. Like, inside me...but then I hear like my aunts and uncles' voices and like, my grandparents and parents and sister and I can feel their disappointment. It instantly turns me off. Like, an emotional chastity belt or something."

"Jesus. That's some kind of cognitive dissonance."

"Yeah. Well, sometimes I wish we could just elope. I mean, we've been dating for like 10 months, and I already feel closer to you than anyone. You're my best friend in the world. I love you even more than my own parents."

"Devi, I love you so much."

She sat up, looked me in the eyes for a few seconds, and kissed me.

Devi and I would BBM every day, and our relationship continued to flourish even as we added distance to the complex algebraic equation. Every once in a while, she'd send me salacious late-night messages about what she wanted to do to me. It was arousing at first, but then I was forced to remind myself it may take months or even years before Devi would be ready to act on her thoughts. Despite that one perceptible foible in our relationship, there was a deep, pulsating love between us.

CHAPTER 5

M Y SENIOR YEAR BEGAN WITH constant studying for the ACTs, along with college applications, supplemental essays, and then the always uncomfortable parental meetings with the college counselor. My father didn't need anyone's advice on where his son should attend school, yet Verity required these meetings to make sure the counselor was fully aware of the parent-student goals.

"Yeah. We got it. Trinity, Johns Hopkins, Tufts, BU, GW, Georgetown. Fully on top of things."

"Well, we usually recommend students visit at least 12 schools and apply to eight," the counselor responded to my father.

"Vincent and I have it under control."

"I personally, and forgive me if I'm speaking out of turn, believe he needs at least two more safety schools."

"Safety schools by nature, aren't schools that Vincent will be going to. If he only gets into one bad school. He'll transfer. It ain't complicated."

"I believe all seniors should have a series of options."

"You know what my father once told me?"

"Dad, stop." I interrupted, knowing exactly where this was headed.

"Vincent, he needs to hear this."

"Well, I'm sure that's not true," I rolled my eyes.

"Perhaps, we can stay on the subject at hand," my counselor said.

"Now, let me finish," my father just had to get this point out. "My dad once said, 'the people who become college counselors are those who failed trying to reach their dream career.' No one wakes up as a teenager dreaming of advising on where kids should go to college. It's a joke."

"Jesus, Dad. Be quiet."

"If we could please get back to the matter at hand?" The counselor continued. "We've sent a lot of students to Sewanee: The University of the South and Trinity College in Ireland. A lot of happy Verity students at those schools."

"What on earth are you talking about? Vincent will only go to schools within a four-hour Amtrak ride of the city. He wants to attend a university in a city. It's like you haven't been listening to a word we've said."

"Dad, he's just trying to help. You're embarrassing me."

"He's wasting our time. That's what he's doing."

My father stood up, exited the room, and I followed with my tail between my legs. As we walked down the school's stairwell, I said:

"You know he has to call schools on my behalf, right? Now, he won't help me at all because of you."

"Oh, stop. Is that imbecile going to get you into Georgetown and Tufts? No way. It's all on you, bud."

"You don't have to be such a...a...blowhard all the time. Christ. This was an important meeting. Life-altering."

Several younger students walked by and stared at us.

"If things don't work out. I'll take matters into my own hands. I went to Wharton. I don't need some Sewanee College ignoramus telling my son where to apply."

"Even though it's his job? Gotcha. Sound argument."

"You're awfully belligerent today...ACTs. What does belligerent mean? Go."

"Um, argumentative or feisty? Speaking of which, I've gotta get to English."

The outré Ms. Ziegler taught my 12th grade English class. She was a 55-year-old, grey-haired woman who was known throughout Verity as a kooky oddball who played favorites. On the first day of class, Ms. Ziegler described how she owned two cows that lived on a farm outside

Paterson, New Jersey, and announced their names as Betsy Jade and Haroldy, which drew snickers from the class.

"Don't laugh. Those are my parents' names."

I remember that *I* could always tell when she was joking, but her bizarrely deadpan humor made the majority of students uncomfortable.

"Last week, I was hit by a bus," Ms. Ziegler announced.

The shocked class laughed awkwardly.

"Don't laugh. It was a traumatic experience."

"Where did the bus strike you, Ms. Ziegler?" I felt compelled to speak up. "I'm so sorry for your trouble."

"Thank you...uh...Vincent," she said as she read over her seating chart. "Well, it grazed my dress more than anything. I think I'm going to make it."

"Anyway, so I have my cattle," Ms. Ziegler continued. "I was hit by a bus. I have a stalker who sits outside my fire escape some evenings. Anyway, that's all you need to know about me. Now, my Shakespearean neophytes...oh...*neophyte*...write that down. You all will obtain vast, dare I say, Brobdingnagian vocabularies by the end of this course. That is the one entente I will make with you...the collective you."

Ms. Ziegler passed out our copies of *The Merchant of Venice* and immediately began to read from the text. That became our English class. A five-minute rant after the first bell rang, followed by our eccentric teacher reading Shakespearean comedies aloud for 30 minutes straight. Ms. Ziegler was an expert enunciator and would elongate the words: "oh", "ah" and "fie" for what had to be comedic effect. Occasionally, she even added her own "oohs" and "aahs" that altered the text's iambic pentameter. Ms. Ziegler was a punctilious reader and clearly loved her profession. While most believed her embellishments were abnormal and sorely out of place, I found her behavior to be infectious. During the middle of her daily productions, Ms. Ziegler would pause at the more exigent words of Shakespeare and ask the class their meaning.

"If a throstle sing, ooh, he falls straight a-capering..." She read. "... ooh throstle. Which one of my incandescent pupils knows throstle?"

"It's a bird," I answered. "A singing thrush."

"Aah, Vincentio. My vocabulary king. What an excellent answer. Perhaps you'll give us your rendition of a throstle's mating call?"

"Maybe next time."

"You know, Duke Vincentio, I'll hold you to that."

It was a delightful environment. Every two weeks, Ms. Ziegler would give us a pop quiz on Shakespearean vocabulary, and I'd look forward to seeing the words "Vocabulary King" written atop my paper once it was handed back. Several other members of the class immediately regretted Ms. Ziegler was their teacher, but she loved my ameliorating enthusiasm and generously graded my bi-monthly essays. It quickly became my favorite course, and Ms. Ziegler, my favorite Verity Prep teacher. Her unique class and passionate teaching style led to an easy A and a budding interest in early English literature. Though more importantly, her compendious style as it pertained to vocabulary made the ACT English section painless.

However, when the fateful day arrived, the life-altering standardized test delivered a toxic blow to my application process. While I did receive a perfect 36 on the English section, 12 on the Writing and an Ivy-League-level 35 on the Reading portion, my 29 on Math and 25 on Science placed me in a precarious position. I was a polarizing applicant whose senior year Calculus grade was slipping.

On a positive note, I was able to write a complex, but slightly pandering Common Application essay about my mother's drug overdose and paired it with a myriad of fascinating supplemental pieces. I was a bemusing applicant for any university, and by my 18th birthday, every essay, test, recommendation, and grade was submitted. It was now out of my hands.

On my birthday, Devi took me to Jean-Georges. She handed me a customized card with a picture of us kissing by the East River on the cover.

"I love you so much, babes," she said, holding my hands.

"I love you too."

"I'm so proud of you. You're all done with applications. You can finally kick back, relax, and wait."

"Well, there's that chance that I don't get in anywhere."

"Who cares, then we'll run away together and not be bound by anyone or anything."

"Good one."

"Um, actually, I have something I want to talk about...no actually, never mind. Not on your birthday."

"God, you know I hate when you do that. Why must every meaningful conversation have to wait for a romantic dinner?"

"I don't know. I, like, see you looking so handsome in a suit. I feel like we're grown-ups and can have grown-up conversations at these cool settings."

"So, what's on your mind?" I asked again.

"Hmph."

"Tell me, please."

"I don't want to."

"Darling?"

"Okay, but you're gonna be mad."

"I have no idea what it could be."

"I want us to go public," she squealed.

"I'm sorry. What?"

"Go public. Tell everyone. Tell my parents. Tell your dad. Tell everyone at school and teachers and stuff. I want everyone to know you're my boyfriend."

"I'm having trouble comprehending."

"We've been together for over 13 months. It's time now."

"I, uh...why?"

"'Cause I feel weird. Like, what do I do when guys approach me at school or like, at parties?"

"Say you're not interested?"

"I don't wanna."

"What about your extended family?"

"Well, maybe I won't tell everyone."

"Have you really thought this through?"

"Yes. Don't treat me like a child."

"So, what are the next steps then?"

"I'll make us Facebook official. We'll take pictures, and you'll meet my parents. I'll meet your dad. We'll hang out with each other's friends. We'll go to parties together and like, really be out there on the scene, you know? Everyone will know our names. Well, maybe I won't make us Facebook official yet...No. Actually, I won't."

"That was not a very compelling argument."

"So, what are you saying?"

"Let's talk about all of these things another time. I don't need any added stress right now. May we please enjoy my birthday?"

Devi rolled her eyes, crossed her arms, and chewed on the tips of her midnight black hair.

"I already told Tessa we've been going out for over a year," Devi announced in her callous tone. "She's thrilled."

"I wish you hadn't done that without talking to me. We need to communicate with each other. Make compromises."

"You're not making a compromise right now."

"Fair point. Here it is: at the start of 2012, so what's that? 56 days. Let's have this conversation again. I promise to be more open to your desires. I'm just...overly stressed right now."

The next week, I joined Devi for our Acting Improv class. Raven and Frankie had long since abandoned the course, and I was now the senior-most member. I referred to myself as President of Acting Improv on my college applications, which wasn't an outright lie, but not officially true. I did lead the class in stretches and vocal warmups, but that was the extent of my self-proclaimed presidency.

In this particular class, Devi stood next to a freshman boy and brought about her old vamp-like giggles that first seduced me over a year ago.

"You're so funny," she said to her unassuming co-thespian.

The anonymous freshman looked on with a mixture of dubiety and delight.

"Alright, everyone, break off into pairs," Ms. Cuzano said. "We're going to do one-on-one improv scenes."

This was common practice for the class, but typically Devi would either be my partner or Tessa's so that people wouldn't think we were together. Today, however, she chose her new freshman. She pranced around with her unnamed simpleton, glancing over at me every seven seconds to make sure I saw her inappropriate motions. Devi lowered her V-neck, touched his chest, and spent the next five minutes in a nitrous oxide-esque delirium. Her voice contained the subtly of a farm rooster at sunrise. Frankly, I was embarrassed I was dating someone so immature. However, I closed my eyes, meditated with my partner Tessa and avoided caviling about my sophomoric girlfriend.

The subsequent weekend, Devi and I met at Carl Schurz Park and silently kissed on a bench. The improv incident wasn't discussed, nor was her desire to make our relationship public. Everything returned to normal. Devi left the park that day with a tender: "I love you, babes." It was a necessary moment of relief.

On November 17th, though, I walked through the student lounge and found a different male freshman sitting on her lap. Devi spotted me, glared, and laughed uproariously with her high-pitched shrieking voice. I simply put my head down and walked away. It was an uncomfortable situation that continued to worsen each week.

One day, Tessa approached me in the student lounge during a mutual free period and said:

"I saw your girlfriend out at 1Oak this weekend. She was grinding on some older rich guy who bought her drinks."

"Jesus Christ. Did she kiss him?"

"No, definitely not. But I just thought I should tell you. I mean, Devi would kill me if she knew I was telling you this."

"Hmm, I bet she would."

After that brief tidbit, I texted Devi and asked her to meet me outside the Met at 3 pm. She responded with the curt "K." text all of humanity dreads. Her callow behavior had finally received the desired attention it so heartily craved.

After school, we sat on the steps of the Met and opened with a cordial kiss.

"So, what's going on with you lately?" I started.

"Whatever do you mean?"

"Stop it."

"What's this regarding?"

"Don't be immature."

"You're immature," she said.

"You wanted my attention. You've got it. Say your piece."

"I want to go public with you. It's literally that simple. I need someone who stands by me and is proud to be seen with me. I'm tired of hiding from like, my parents and friends and teachers and, like everyone."

"Fine. Deal."

"That's it? No argument."

"Nope. You're right. You handled it in the worst way possible, but you're right."

"Darn, I was like, low-key looking for a fight. I like when we fight. It makes me kind of...you know," Devi climbed on top of my lap and began nibbling my neck, unconcerned with the passing tourists.

"Okay. Okay." I said after a few minutes. "Down, girl."

She laughed, bit my earlobe, and lifted me to my feet. We began walking east towards our respective apartments.

"So, what's with this sudden desire to be seen?" I asked.

"Well, I was sitting in the lounge, like, the week before your birthday. It was a dull period, so I was mostly just like zoned out.

"Sure. Naturally."

"Anyway, I started listening to this couple in your grade talk. They're the hot ones. You know who I'm talking about. Like, the second hottest couple in the school."

"We're the first?"

"Duh."

"You mean, Oliver and Olivia?"

"Yeah. So, he's like sneezing and sniffling and stuff. He's, like, really sick. Olivia has a box of tissues and is helping him blow his nose."

"Seems unnecessary, but go on," I said.

"I hear Olivia say, 'I'm so sorry, baby. You're so sick. I'll take care of everything.' I thought that was like so sweet."

"Okay..."

"But then, Olivia stares at him, leans in to kiss him, and Oliver stops her. He says, 'no baby, I don't want to get you sick.' Then she says, 'I don't care. I want to be sick with you.' They made out for like 10 minutes straight with like his mucus dripping on her cheek. It was weirdly like the sweetest thing I'd ever seen, and I want us to be like that in public."

"That's just unsanitary. You don't want my mucus in your mouth."

"I don't know. At that moment, I guess I kinda did."

"You realize Oliver's just some vanilla guy and Olivia is Verity Prep royalty. A Moncler Girl. They'll never end up together."

"What's a Moncler Girl?"

"It's nothing...but anyway, go home, make us public on Facebook or whatever you wanted to do. I don't care. Whatever makes you happy."

"Thanks, babes. But I decided I don't want to post anything to Facebook 'cause like my extended family will see and freak out and disown me or something. I'm just gonna tell my parents and all my Verity friends. Well...maybe not my parents yet. But you tell your dad, k?"

"Sounds good. Love you."

The next few weeks were tense. I didn't tell anyone in my grade except for Austin, but no one would've cared. The real hassle was the scurrilous sophomores that were running around spreading rumors about Devi and me. It seemed every day, at least one 10th grader would brazenly approach me and say:

"I hear Devi gets naked and forces you to watch her pray while she touches herself."

"What the hell are you talking about?" I'd say.

Then a group of sophomore girls would come by and question me:

"Is it like true that Devi's bulimic? How many times have you seen her throw up? Does she force you to hold her hair back?"

"I hear she has fake Chanel."

"You guys aren't even like cute together. Do you want my number? We'd be way hotter. I'd let you do whatever you want to me, well not like whatever, but like within reason."

It became overwhelming for someone used to going unnoticed throughout the hallways. Devi, on the other hand, loved the attention. She'd say things like:

"You guys have no idea how great it is to be with an older guy. He's like so sensitive and understanding, but also like a beast in the bedroom. We're like so hot and passionate together. Vincent's like the perfect guy."

The incessant badgering somehow increased at our first event together as an official couple. Devi's friend was having a birthday boat party along the Hudson River on December 10th. The friend invited eight sophomores, and Devi begged him to allow her a plus one. Having a party on a boat in the winter was already a horrible idea, and the fact underclassmen would be surrounding me curbed my desire to attend. However, at that time, I was all for making Devi happy, so I put on my best smile and warmest peacoat and decided to make the best of the situation.

Before leaving the house, my father called out:

"Wear a rubber. Getting a girl pregnant in high school is the worst thing that'll ever happen to you."

I remember when I first told my father about Devi's existence, his first response was:

"Let's see a picture." Then after viewing the image: "Oh. Dark girl. Huh. She's got an exotic look about her. Not a Victoria's Secret model by any means, but I get it. Looks feminine enough for you."

He didn't ask me any questions about her, and I wasn't open to discussing our relationship, so it went swimmingly.

I arrived at the boat and kissed Devi, who was wearing her military green Moncler jacket with black jeans and thick heels. The adult chaperone took us out into the open water, and the rambunctious teenagers popped open a bottle of champagne before singing happy birthday.

"Picture time," Devi yelled.

My adorable girlfriend handed me her BlackBerry and had me take somewhere between 150 and 300 photos. It was Devi with the birthday boy; Devi with Tessa; Devi with each individual friend at a different angle; Devi with Tessa on the port side; Devi with the birthday boy on the stern side with the camera tilted horizontally; Devi with the birthday boy on the bow side with the camera titled vertically and the flash off and countless other combinations. It made me think of my 10th-grade math class and how many different permutations there were. Was it "8P7" or if order does matter, then is it a combination? Would it be "8C2"? Or were there a bunch of different combinations that needed to be added to achieve the answer, which had to be in the millions? I was appropriately miserable, but as always, anything for my girlfriend.

"Hey Devi, can we take a few now? Just the two of us?"

"Oh, V. I don't think we should."

"Why not?"

"Well, you know I can't post anything about you on Facebook. I can't have my extended family see me with a boy."

"But you just took like 600 pictures with a boy."

"But he's gay."

"Does your extended family know he's gay? That's a ridiculous argument."

"V, just stop. You're like not allowed on my Facebook. No pictures, no posts. Period, end of story."

"Seems fair."

"Love the sass babes. Cute look on you."

"This is fun."

Devi left to join her friends drinking at the bow. I took a seat on the starboard side and looked back at the notable midtown skyscrapers. I heard Devi's friends whispering what I believed were vituperative remarks about me. I didn't really mind, though. I was leaving for college in less than a year, so random sophomores finding insignificant physical or emotional blemishes on me was irrelevant.

"I have an announcement to make," Tessa shouted so the whole boat could hear.

I decided to walk over and listen because I'd always enjoyed her company.

"It may be the alcohol in me. It may be all you beautiful girls in your fancy clothes. I'm not sure. I've been thinking about this for a long time. It's been kind of eating away at me, and I want to let this out in front of my best friends."

Devi stared at me with her mouth agape. I'm not sure if she had any idea where her curly-haired classmate's speech was headed. It was blatantly obvious to me, but that's beside the point.

"I think I like girls...or I mean, I think...I might be a...lesbian."

The whole group gasped then looked at one another before eventually deciding this was tolerable. They all went in and hugged her.

Then a thought dawned on me. I tried to bash it back to where it came from, but the harrowing serpent ensnared my mind. I couldn't think about anything else. As I looked out over the water, I thought about the first time I met Tessa. She was effervescent and convivial—an innocuous eighth-grader with dreams of a career on Broadway. Then my mind drifted to that one night in Central Park that seemed an eternity ago. Tessa's bicycle and helmet leaned against the outer walls of the famed landmark. She wanted me to kiss her. Tessa wanted to see what it felt like. She could've been my Devi. If I had planted my lips upon hers, Tessa and I might still be dating to this day. Even if Tessa and I liked each other and dated for six months or so, it would've precluded me from dating Devi. Tessa never would've introduced us. Every single moment of the previous 15 months all occurred because I was too craven to kiss a pretty girl. Obviously, a relationship with Tessa could've had a sorry end from my perspective, though. One day, Tessa would've dropped the lesbian bomb on me, and my emotions would've splattered across the concrete sidewalks of the Upper East Side. However, that fascinating dynamic, that engrossing epic never had the opportunity to be written. I was thrilled to have been introduced to Devi, of course. She was my amazing girlfriend. I loved her dearly. I was a happy 18-year-old. Everything was great. There were no issues or anything. But it was an intriguing thought nonetheless. What would life have been like with Tessa? I wondered which girl my mother would've preferred? Then Devi walked over.

"Have a drink with me," she said, clearly intoxicated. "Come on babes."

"No, thanks. You know I don't drink."

"Well, you have to on special occasions, right? Did I tell you I'm going on winter break with all these people to Paris? 10 delicious days."

"I don't drink. And no. No, you didn't. Why didn't you tell me that? I thought we could spend a lot of time together? I could've come over to meet your parents."

"Bien sur. In due time. Have a widdle sippy. Pwease," Devi said.

"Come on. Stop. I can't believe you didn't tell me you're going to Paris. That's it. No more drinks for you."

Devi licked my cheek and whispered in my ear:

"I want you now. Take me below the deck. Ravage me? No, radish me? I don't...let's go quietly."

"I'm not allowing us to lose our respective virginities when you're intoxicated and on a boat with your geeky friends."

"They're not geeky. You're geeky. I want us to have sex. I like, want to tell everyone how perfect you are. I want everyone to know about your sexual prowgress."

"I'd love that. Maybe, on your birthday? You're turning 17 soon, gemsbok."

Devi licked my neck while her friends looked on from afar in horror.

"Let's have sex on the fifth-floor...shush Devi. We don't speak about the fifth-floor with Vincent."

"What are you talking about?"

Devi pulled me inside and led me to the bunk area while her friends giggled.

"I'm not asupposed to tell you. But my parents have like a second apartment in my building."

"What? How is this the first I'm hearing of this? We could've used that place a hundred times."

"It's like a studio on the fifth floor of my building. My extended family splits the rent since they all come to town all times."

"I don't know what to say."

"Kiss me."

Devi straddled me, ripped off her dress, and presented me with her nude body. I kissed her repeatedly until her moans became too loud and embarrassing.

"Don't stop. Sex with me now."

"You're drunk."

"Am not. I'll prove it."

Devi stood and danced topless in our private room below deck until I eventually helped her back into her dress. Before leaving the room, though, she whispered:

"Fifth-floor. My birthday. It's happening."

CHAPTER 6

I ARRIVED AT DEVI'S BUILDING at 11 pm on her 17th birthday. I had
the doorman call up to the penthouse as he'd done on numerous
occasions. I then entered the code: 698140, and Devi met me in the
foyer. She immediately grabbed my wrist and dragged me to a door I'd
never noticed before, which led to a dingy concrete staircase. My sexy
girlfriend then led me down one flight without saying a word. We exited
the stairwell, and she called the elevator from the floor beneath the
penthouse. My girlfriend and I rode down to the mystifying fifth-floor
and opened the third door on the right side of the hallway.

Apartment 5A was a small studio consisting of a kitchen, bathroom,
and a bed that took up three-fourths of the square footage. Everything
was decorated in eggshell white, and nothing appeared particularly
expensive. It was as if we were staying at a mid-tier hotel in a college
town.

"This is amazing. How come you never told me about this?"

Devi ignored my question as she double-locked and dead-bolted the
front door.

"Devi darling, don't you think we could've used this on like a million
occasions?"

She placed her index finger over her thick lower lip and ripped off
her "Pugs Not Drugs" teal pajama t-shirt.

"We could've been doing stuff like this months ago," I said.

Devi slapped me across the face as she unhooked her black bra and
pushed me onto the bed. My girlfriend then removed her sweatpants

and stood directly in front of me in nothing but her black Victoria's Secret thong. I then knew to shut my mouth.

I looked on stupefied; my eyes glued to her svelte figure. Devi picked up her iPod and handed it over, silently begging me to choose a song while she took off my shirt. 50 Cent's impossibly sensual "Just a Lil Bit" soon blasted from her device as she gyrated her hips on my lap.

I thought of Devi's childhood dance teacher and how she likely never expected her student to be using her gifts in this way. My girlfriend meticulously stripped off all of my clothes, pushed me back against the headboard, and climbed on top of me. Then, just before we were both about to lose our virginities. She stopped.

My girlfriend climbed off my body, laid on her back next to me, and started to cry.

"Are you okay, gemsbok? What's wrong? Talk to me."

My girlfriend was a bastion of virtue. Devi couldn't get her family's dogma out of her jumbled mind.

"I'm fine," she cried.

"Let me know how I can make you feel better."

"If...if...my friends ask," she sniveled. "Tell them I rocked your world."

"Anything you want, darling," I said, kissing her cheek.

We both stared at the ceiling in silence. Our naked, heterogeneous bodies laid completely still. I wondered what Devi was thinking about. There must've been a thundering tempest inside of her, but I had nothing to say. There was no way to place myself inside the mind of a possibly brainwashed teenager.

"It's...just...I see you naked, and me, like, naked, and then my grandfather or father or a god or something pops up. They start like shaming and cursing at me. They keep telling me to stop. But then I don't want to disappoint you or make you leave or anything." She was bawling now.

"Come on. You could never disappoint me. I just want you to be yourself and not force anything. We'll find a way for you to feel comfortable."

Devi nodded, wiped away her tears, and tied her hair in a ponytail. She put her bra back on, but then surprisingly spun around and started kissing my torso before working her way past my belly button.

"Devi, what are you doing?"

"Shush. I'm going to take care of you. You look so hot. I just can't, like, resist," Devi opened her mouth wide, but then paused again. "This doesn't count as sex. No one will be mad."

It was an unexpectedly fantastic and bizarre night. Devi was so fascinated by the experience she invited me over the next two nights to see if she could remove the emotional block obfuscating her mind.

The next day, Devi's parents didn't go to sleep until after midnight. My father had long since dozed off on the couch, so I left the apartment without him even noticing. My girlfriend and I began with the same routine of walking one flight down the stairwell and then riding the elevator three dozen floors to the scandalous Apartment 5A. Once inside, Devi triple-locked the doors and instantly removed my pants and boxers. She put on a new 50 Cent song and began with a titillating performance. When she was finished, Devi leaped on my shoulders and had me carry her to the bed.

After throwing her on the white duvet, I removed her pants and thong.

"Wait, stop."

I predicted a pause was coming.

"I need to tell you something."

"Of course. Anything."

"But babes, start kissing my boobs."

I obliged and between light moans she uttered:

"I've never had anything inside me before."

"Yeah, I know."

"No, you don't understand...fully."

"Okay. Enlighten me."

"I've never used a sex toy..."

"That's not that abnormal."

"Don't interrupt. I've never used a sex toy. I've never used a tampon, and I've never touched myself before I met you. Like, literally, nothing has ever been inside me before. I'm so nervous."

"You've never used a tampon?"

"No, only pads on the outside."

"Wow. That's actually impressive."

"Are you mad?"

"No way. Anything but mad. I think that's really sexy that you'd afford me this privilege."

"So, just touch, I guess. Like one finger and nothing else. We'll see where it goes."

I listened and started pleasuring her as gently as possible, my fingers dancing along her strict rectitude. Her proliferating moans reverberated throughout the diminutive studio. We never advanced past this point, but Devi invited me back the next night for one final attempt before her trip to Paris.

When I arrived, the same doorman was working and gave me a cockeyed grin as I asked him to ring the penthouse for the third consecutive night.

Upon arriving at the fifth-floor apartment on this December night, Devi desperately wanted us to have sex before her trip. She coveted a spiritual amalgamation that she could dream about every moment I was thousands of miles away. Devi wished we were the perfect sexually and romantically compatible couple she'd seen in hundreds of films. The characters' groans would overlap, and their kisses would elicit cries of joy. And yet, a few days in 5A wasn't enough to rid herself of 17 years of sexual frustration and purity.

We were nude and lying on the bed as I anxiously awaited Devi's next move. She ran her scrawny fingers along my thighs and up to my abs. My girlfriend was in deep thought as she contemplated her family, religion, innate desires, affection towards me, and exigency to understand the orgasmic feelings her friends had frequently discussed.

Eventually, as I laid there with my eyes closed, Devi's head fell against my chest. My girlfriend couldn't bring herself to engage with me physically. I felt a sprinkle of driblets roll down my rib cage. There was nothing I could say or do to alter her mindset. I simply petted the top of her head and whispered:

"It's alright. Everything's fine."

Devi could sense my disappointment, though. We strived to be the perfect couple, and she wanted to tell her envious friends how transformative her experiences were with the brooding senior boy. Devi needed everyone to know there was nothing aberrant her. She felt the rest of the sophomores would endlessly chastise her if they knew her truth.

"I'm gonna miss you so much," she said. "Take a bath with me. I want you to hold me."

I followed my exposed girlfriend into the tub and cuddled her beneath the scorching water.

"I love you."

"I love you too, babes."

With our heads propped up against the rim of the tub, we kissed until our fingers and toes pruned.

On December 22nd, Devi and her friends embarked on their metamorphic trip to the eighth arrondissement of Paris. I was skittish about a group of 16 and 17-year-olds traveling to France by themselves, but Devi assured me not to worry. The thought of her friends also placated me. These weren't the popular athletes and Moncler Girls. Devi and her friends fit comfortably into different subsections of the theater geek genus. They'd probably go to the Louvre, the Luxembourg Gardens, and shop on the Champs d'Elysees. This wasn't going to be like Verity's annual spring break trip to the Bahamas. It would be a docile experiment involving birds leaving the comforts of their nest for the first time.

I made sure to text Devi right before she took off, making sure to tell her I loved her in the event her plane went down in a fiery crash. My mother didn't invent this type of text, but she certainly convinced me to send them to my loved ones whenever possible. Upon landing at Charles de Gaulle, my energetic girlfriend texted me back.

D: Just landed babes. Miss u already.

V: Miss you too. How was your flight? What's on the agenda?

D: It was a little awkward.

D: I insisted on sitting in first class, but all my friends said it was too expensive and took coach. Now they're like peeved or something.

V: Why didn't you just fly coach and be with them?

D: I hate coach. It's like so gross. Everyone smells, and they're coughing and fat, and I hate it. I'm never flying coach for the rest of my life.

V: Hmmm...

D: Oh don't judge me. You've got like literally millions of weird things like that.

V: Me not liking cheese is a little different.

V: What are you up to now?

V: Are you mad at me?

D: Listen, I should probably set some ground rules.

V: What?

D: I can't be texting u every five minutes.

V: I never asked for that. Enjoy yourself.

D: I can't if I'm always stressed about texting u.

V: That's kinda mean. Just like text me once a day so I know you're alive and safe. That's not too much to ask.

D: I can't promise that. Leave me alone.

V: You can't allot 10 seconds of your 16 waking hours to send a text? Less than 1% of your day?

D: Ur needy. Bye.

December 25th, 2011

V: I love and miss you. How's the trip going? Haven't heard from you.

V: Devi?

V: Are you okay?

D: Yeah. Hey. What?

V: How was your night last night?

D: I don't want to get into it with u.

V: What do you mean?

D: You're just gonna like judge me.

V: What happened?

D: My friends and I are just having a good time. We've gone to night-clubs till like 4 am. I'm super hungover right now.

V: What? Why?

D: I'm just living life and being free. Lay off.

V: I'm just having Christmas with my dad and brother at home, thanks for asking.

D: Jerk.

V: They're doing well. They say 'hi'. We're going out for Chinese food tonight. Probably Shun Lee.

V: You there?

December 27th, 2011

V: I saw your latest Facebook picture...

V: I thought you couldn't have random guys in your photos?

V: Who are you huddling up next to at a nightclub in Paris and taking pictures with?

V: Devi?!

D: What? What do you want from me?

V: Why are you being so mean? What did I do to you? What happened?

D: I need space.

V: I've texted you twice in five days. I wouldn't consider that obsessive.

V: What's with the Facebook pictures with that guy? Were you drunk?

D: I don't remember.

V: What do you mean?

D: I don't remember what happened.

V: Jesus Christ. You know you're in a relationship, right? Where is this all coming from? You were so loving like a week ago.

D: Stop. I'm here with my friends. I want to live my life. Stop annoying me. You sound like my father.

December 30th, 2011

V: Gosh, I keep waiting for that apology text, and it hasn't come. It must've just been a WiFi issue. Love and miss you.

D: U again? I luv u, but you're smothering me. Let me be.

V: You're just making me really uncomfortable. I'm totally fine with you going on a vacation with friends. But your friends are single and you're not.

V: You can't be staying out to 4 am, getting drunk, grinding on random guys at the club, and not remembering what you did. That's not okay.

V: Answer me, please...

D: Maybe we should take a break while I'm here and go back to normal when I get home in a few days.

V: WHAT?!?!?!?

V: How can you even say that? We've been together for so long. I haven't even done anything wrong. Remember last week at the fifth-floor? What's with you all of a sudden?

D: I didn't say I was breaking up with you. Just a break. Bye.

V: Devi?

V: Devi, call me please. Let's talk this over.

V: I want to hear your voice.

January 1st, 2012

V: I saw you uploaded more pictures of you at nightclubs...

V: Grinding on guys, sitting on their laps, and hugging them...

V: Did you cheat on me?

D: STOP!

V: Did you hook up with another guy.

D: I'm not even going to dignify that with a response.

V: Too drunk to remember?

V: You haven't once asked me about my Christmas or Hanukkah or New Year's Eve. How selfish can you be?

D: Omg. I can't deal with u right now.

V: Did you kiss another guy yes or no?

D: I'll talk to you when I get back.

V: If you don't deny it right now, then we're over forever.

V: Devi?

V: You're going to give our beautiful relationship up for some club rats and popularity points with your nerdy friends?

D: LEAVE. ME. ALONE.

V: I'm breaking up with you. This is it. Delete my number from your phone. I can't take this anymore.

V: Don't bother trying to talk to me in school. I have nothing left to say to you. Goddamn it.

CHAPTER 7

O
N OUR FIRST DAY BACK from winter break, Devi approached me outside of the theater before Acting Improv. She grabbed my hand and led me to a place where we could talk.

"Babes," she said. "I love you so much. You're my everything. I didn't mean any of that stuff from Paris. You're not really breaking up with me, right?"

She couldn't alter my plaintive mood. I stood there in front of my now ex-girlfriend and couldn't build up the courage to hector or yell. My throat closed and outlawed me from uttering a single word. I glared at her cartoonish eyes. Devi's hair was unkempt; her fingernails lacked polish, and she was wearing a plain Hanes white t-shirt with magenta Juicy Couture sweatpants.

"Okapi," she whispered. "Come over to my apartment tonight. Let's talk this over...Or not...Or I could blow you as many times as you want. Deal?"

I couldn't look her in the eyes anymore. I stared at the floors, rubbed my eyelids, and entered into a months-long mournful lull. How could such a beautiful relationship end so swiftly and with so much vitriol?

"V? Kiss me. I want you to kiss me right now. I want to prove to you how much I love you. I like, should've paid more attention to you. I should've told you I was going to Paris. Or I should've gone on a trip with you instead. I should've texted you once a day. I made mistakes. I made literally lots of mistakes...just say something, please...Yell at me.

Tell me you hate me. Say anything. Open that pretty mouth of yours. Please V. For me?"

With my head still facing the ground, I trudged into the theater. I let Ms. Cuzano know that after three and a half years, I was dropping her club. I offered no reason, and when she tried to call me back into the room, I ignored her.

For the next few weeks, I didn't speak to anyone. I dropped out of all of my non-required clubs and electives and stuck to my five core courses. During my free periods, I'd exit Verity and enter Central Park. I'd wander around for half an hour watching various crowds of exultant children and adults play in the snow. Each person I encountered had parents or siblings or friends or significant others. Valentine's Day was approaching, and I'd be spending it alone in my room. There was no simple cure for the oldest and most prevalent disease in the world. I was encapsulated in isolation and elected to stop eating lunch during the week. I'd glance at a hot dog or hamburger and gag. If I saw Moncler Girls eating frozen yogurt, it instantly reminded me of Devi losing my credit card. If I heard 50 Cent playing, I thought of her gorgeous nude body rotating in front of me. If I saw any Middle Eastern or Southeast Asian girl, they reminded me of her. If I spotted two sisters, I thought of Devi and Nitya. If I heard a dog barking, I thought about Fraulein Kareena. If I walked down Madison Avenue, 20 different stores reminded me of Devi.

There would be times when I'd go two or three days without saying a word to anyone. I stopped participating in class and no longer picked out nice, clean matching clothes. Each morning, I'd pick the same grey zip-up hoodie, black jeans, grey and white Nikes with a red swoosh, and I would rotate between three or four t-shirts, but it was pointless. The only activity that kept me going was my workout routine. I knew if I stopped lifting weights, it would only damage me further, so my quad-weekly trips to the Y continued as if nothing happened. Those 45-minute sessions allowed me to zone out and listen to my newly created, aptly named playlist: "Heart-Wrenching Music."

1. "Born to Die" - Lana Del Rey
2. "The Ice is Getting Thinner" - Death Cab for Cutie
3. "Hurt" - Johnny Cash
4. "Blame Game" - Kanye West
5. "See You in My Nightmares" - Kanye West
6. "Fire and Rain" - James Taylor
7. "Goodbye My Lover" - James Blunt
8. "Fire on the Mountain" - The Marshall Tucker Band
9. "Collide" - Howie Day
10. "Wonderful" - Everclear
11. "Good Riddance" - Green Day
12. "Going Through Changes" - Eminem
13. "Space Bound" - Eminem
14. "Pinocchio Story" - Kanye West
15. "Marvin's Room" - Drake
16. "Don't Let It Bring You Down" - Annie Lennox
17. "I Miss You" - Blink 182
18. "Hero" - Enrique Iglesias
19. "How to Save a Life" - The Fray
20. "My Way" - Frank Sinatra

One February evening, on my way back from listening to my eclectic mix of ballads at the gym, my father stopped me in the living room and said:

"You okay big guy?"

"Fine."

"Don't be a sad sack. Is this 'cause you're not hanging around with that girl anymore."

My father was seated on our living room couch, eating his patented dinner of: a tortilla with scrambled eggs, bacon, peanuts, and Grape Nuts inside, with three Pilsner Urquells.

"I'm fine. I need to shower."

"Sit down."

"Stop bothering me."

"I said sit, boy."

I laid on the carpet and gave my father a modicum of my attention.

"I'm not going to have you moping around over some girl. You're a handsome guy. Get back out there."

"Just stop. You don't get it."

"My wife died you little bi—" he paused and composed himself.

"You didn't even like her."

"We were married for 20 years. Don't talk to me about who I did and didn't like. This is about you."

"I don't wanna talk."

"You look too skinny. If you don't start eating regular lunches, I'm going to force-feed you two dinners at night. That's non-negotiable."

"Yes, sir."

"Talk to people. Put yourself out there. Talk to friends. Meet people. You're a handsome kid. People would be lucky to spend time with you."

"Thanks."

"I mean, Jesus Christ. You're acting like your whole family was murdered. Lighten up. It's a high school breakup. You weren't going to get married."

I stood and walked to my bedroom.

"It's difficult taking advice from someone who only chooses to parent two or three times a year."

My father stood and marched over to me. I had this terrifying feeling he was going to hit me. Even though I was now an inch taller than him and more muscular, I wouldn't have been able to strike back at my father. Luckily, he simply put his arms around me.

"I'm sorry. I love you," he kissed me on the cheek. "Vincent, I just want you to be happy and healthy."

I hugged him back before proceeding to my nightly shower, which these days included a mandatory tear-filled few minutes.

The next day at school, I heeded my father's advice and was able to wolf down a lemon poppy seed muffin from Yura for lunch. In addition,

I decided I should talk to somebody my age, so I sought out Austin during a free period towards the end of the day.

"Hey Austin, do you want to go for a walk? Maybe grab a seat on a park bench?"

"Sure."

Austin and I left Verity and entered the park at 90th and 5th. We walked along the Bridle Path as snow sprinkled around us. He had lost a significant amount of weight since his first day of high school and was now comfortably under 200 pounds. While Austin still had his thick-rimmed glasses and wasn't particularly popular, he was a devoted listener, and I was glad to have him.

"I'm just having a difficult time getting up in the morning," I started.

"I mean, of course you are. You're dealing with trauma."

"But like, everything seemed so good for so long, and it all evaporated so quickly. Like, it's unheard of how quickly it all came crashing down. Like, I thought we were going to get married. I was going to spend the rest of my life with her."

"You say that now, but after you get out of this funk, you'll be able to look back and see things weren't so perfect."

I buttoned my navy peacoat and shivered as the brisk wind slapped across our faces.

"You may not remember this," he said, "but early on, you told me she was annoying. You said that you guys had nothing in common and her voice hurt your ears and Devi—"

"Can you not say her name, please. It hurts."

"Of course. The girl wasn't always perfect for you. She had flaws. You and I both know that."

"Like what?"

"Looks or personality?"

"Both," I said. "But personality first."

"In my opinion, granted I only spoken to her a few times, but she's self-centered. I mean, you are too, don't get me wrong, but she's a whole 'nother level. She's the type who would drone on and on about herself on a date and never actually ask the guy anything."

"I definitely do that, though."

"Come on. On dates, who did the conversation always revolve around? Think about it. I wasn't even there and know the answer."

"What else?"

"She's a brat, right? Any girl with that much money and expensive clothes has to be a brat. If you guys got married, what if you wanted to spend a weekend camping?"

"I don't think I'm that guy."

"Who knows? Maybe you want to throw a baseball around with your wife and kids. Maybe you want someone to go on a road trip and stay in cheap hotels. Maybe you'll want to sit in the nosebleeds at a double-A Reading game on a random weekend. That girl is someone who will never settle for anything less than the finer things. She's the definition of high-maintenance."

"Well, you didn't know her like I did."

"Dude, shut the hell up and let me make you feel better. Just listen."

"Fine. Fine. Go on."

"I've seen her in the lounge flirting with guys—both before and after your breakup. You don't want to live a life wondering when your girlfriend is gonna cheat on you. Having male friends is fine, but sitting on guys' laps and touching their biceps and stuff. That's too much, in my opinion."

"Where are you getting your experience from?"

"Movies, TV, real-life observation. *Freaks and Geeks, Saved by the Bell, That 70s Show, The OC*, whatever."

"When are *you* gonna get your first girlfriend?"

"Let's stay on topic here," he said.

"What about her looks?"

"She's a cute girl, I guess. But the more her looks improve, the worse her personality will get. You told me about her partying habits. She can't be tamed. She'll be the type to spend her 20s going to nightclubs and tossing around hundreds of dollars a week at salons. I bet if you actually sat her down and asked why she liked nightclubs and apartment parties so much, she'd say 'I don't know. I just do.'"

"Her cheeks are kind of chubby, and she has these almost indecipherable blue tints on her canine teeth."

"You're smarter than her too. You're more ambitious than her. And most importantly, you're more interesting and have more depth than she does. We'll find someone new for you either in the next few months or in your first week of college. Just keep working out and eat more, man. You're looking too thin."

"Thanks. I really appreciate this."

"You'd do the same for me."

"Seriously, if you ever need to talk about anything. Let me know."

"I'm good for now. Gonna be crazy going to a new school in the fall. Been stuck at the same place for 13 years. I can't even imagine what it'll be like."

"Anywhere is better than this soul-crushing place."

We exited the park and walked down Fifth Avenue past the Guggenheim.

"Are you going to PI?" he asked.

"Hadn't thought about it."

"You gotta go. It'll be good for you. Bikini-clad Moncler Girls as far as the eye can see," Austin said.

"Charleston went to Paradise Island two years ago. I'm sure my father would let me."

"Great. We'll room together. The next few months'll be great. Five days in the Bahamas, followed by our final baseball season. Classes are a joke second semester."

"College decision time will suck. I'll have to hear about less intelligent people going to better schools than me."

"You're never going to see 95% of them again after we graduate. Lighten up. Be a little more optimistic, man. It's gonna be a fun final ride."

CHAPTER 8

USTIN AND I EXITED OUR room at the Beach Tower section
of the Bahamian resort. I was wearing a new canary-colored
Vilebrequin bathing suit with black lobsters and paired this with
a pale blue t-shirt, green and purple Knockaround shades with amber
lenses, and an orange Edmonton Oilers Snapback hat. Austin wore a
similar outfit, which placed us in an unflattering light as we strolled
down to the beach. He and I were delusional misfits who believed in the
centuries-old fallacy that dressing like the popular people would make
us one. Austin and I were walking down a perilous road with a menda-
cious bravado that would undoubtedly lead to future misfortune.

We arrived at Atlantis Beach, took off our American Eagle flip-flops,
and waded through the scalding hot sand. There we saw an indecipherable idyll that would temporarily lift me from my sallow funk.

Our view was of a myriad of infallible 18-year-old girls in opalescent bikinis. And these weren't the trashy St. Petersburg or Myrtle Beach
spring breakers. PI in March consisted of only the cream of the crop.
Each private school clique was present. Verity had annexed their section
of the beach as had Cordelia, Dalton, Chapin, and Riverdale. At first, it
appeared to be a carbon copy of our student lounge, but in a chicer setting. However, unlike our typical school days, here we heard a cacophonous, tipsy voice yell over to us.

"Hey guys. Get over here."

Austin and I were highly intrigued by the sultry voice of one of
Verity's most enchanting Moncler Girls. Ainsley Kyle wasn't supposed to

talk to us. I mean, if she wanted to call me over to insult my outfit, I'd understand. Yet the sheer pleasantry that accompanied her typically sardonic voice was worrisome. Ainsley was wearing a leopard print bikini that barely covered her buxom chest. I couldn't tell the brand because I had spent so little time around beautiful young women in bikinis. She also had what I believed to be a subtle spray tan that may have been more obvious to a trained eye and impressively toned six-pack abs.

"Hey, what's going on?" I said as we stood over Ainsley and her friends. "Did you need something?"

"Oh, stop. Take your shirts off, sit down, and have a drink with us."

I noticed Ainsley had a Maitai while Olivia Corcoran and Kora Christensen were sipping piña coladas. Several more Moncler Girls were sunbathing a few feet behind them, while eight or so Verity guys were playing touch football.

The annual trip to Paradise Island wasn't a school-sponsored event, but it had been a long-running rite of passage for Manhattan private school seniors that all the high schools tolerated. Out of 100 soon-to-be graduating Verity students, 35 were able to convince their parents to send them chaperone-free to the covetous Caribbean. Since each New York City high school had different spring break dates, someone somewhere worked out the scheduling so there would be a balance of boys and girls from half a dozen schools attending during the same five-day period. By the end of March, six groups totaling 175 senior students flew down and wreaked havoc on the Beach Tower section of the Bahamian resort. Every year, we'd hear about who correctly took advantage of the 18-year-old drinking age, who spent a night in the local jail, who paid for a Nassau prostitute and who did the most cocaine. This was finally the class of 2012's turn to report back with both genuine and farcical tales to pass down to the classes of 2013 and beyond.

"Vincent, I'm gonna go grab us some drinks from the tiki bar."

I nodded, but remember being very curious as to what Austin's game plan was. He knew I didn't drink. I felt he'd probably get me a virgin piña colada. I trusted him.

"Well?" Kora said.

Her defining feature was her flowing curly blonde hair that covered her right eye. Kora was taller than me and was wearing a turquoise bikini that nearly matched her robin's egg blue irises.

"What?" I said.

"Take your shirt off. I hear you work out."

"I don't really feel comfortable in front of you."

"Listen, sweetheart; there are some fugly Riverdale slores that would like love to chat about sports and your recent breakup. They're like 50 feet down the beach."

"What?"

"Take your shirt off and drink with us or peace," Kora couldn't have been more serious.

I removed my garment, and the three buzzed Moncler Girls lowered their Roberto Cavalli, Fendi, and Dior sunglasses.

"Told you he's hot," Ainsley said.

"He's too pale, though," Kora responded.

"Don't you think he's like five pounds too skinny? The abs are nice, but I can kinda make out his ribs," Olivia also chimed in.

"This is kind of awkward for me."

"How's that?" Kora said.

"Well, I can hear everything you're saying."

"So? Why does that matter?"

"Well, it's just kind of mean. That's all."

"For the record, I called you hot," Ainsley chirped.

"Look, we could either say these things in front of you or behind your back. They're gonna be said either way," Kora announced.

"That's a fair point," I continued to be diffident.

"Oliver, get over here," Olivia called to her boyfriend.

Austin arrived with two drinks, and Oliver tackled his girlfriend and began aggressively making out with her.

"Austin, give it here," Kora held out her hand.

Austin gave the feisty Moncler Girl both of our drinks without a second thought. I instantly knew what was happening.

"What, are you gonna like spit in them?" Austin asked.

"Kora, don't embarrass the kid," Ainsley pointed at me. "Look, he's like a wounded baby deer. He's like Bambi. Don't hurt Bambi."

Kora took a sip from Austin's Manhattan and then from my piña colada.

"Vincent, drink this," Kora handed me the Manhattan.

"Rylie," Kora called over to the other group of Moncler Girls in the vicinity. "Get over here chica. Like now."

Rylie, currently tanning her back, hooked on her top and hobbled over to the rousing game known as "Peer Pressure the Sad Kid."

"Get off my back angel. I'm like basically blackout right now."

This trip didn't bode well for someone with Rylie's long red hair and freckles, but she was the skinniest of the bunch and had the most coveted backside in our grade.

"It'll be like one sec. Just chill."

Four girls were now lying face up in front of me, while Austin sat five feet off to the side. Olivia had thrown Oliver off of her so she could listen to this hotly contested conversation.

"Ryles," Ainsley asked. "Don't you think Vincent's hot? Like, the no alcohol and baseball combo should be like, a diet for girls."

"Totally get that. That dot not feather ex of his says he's like a total beast in bed."

"I could see that, Ryles. I like the quiet ones."

"Babe," Kora chimed in. "If you try to have a conversation with him for more than like 30 seconds, you'll want to blow your brains out. He's 'subtly' looked at my tits like seven times since we called him over."

"So, should I leave now?" I asked.

Kora brushed her blonde curls from her forehead and frowned.

"It's simple—you down this whole Manhattan. You can stay. If you can't handle a single drink, you don't belong with us. Your call."

"Incentivize me."

Kora fanned her face mockingly.

"My word."

"Boy's gotta little spunk," Rylie added.

"Ladies," Kora said. "Any of you want to hook up with him?"

"What?"

"'What' is a lousy catchphrase my friend," Kora said.

"I will," Ainsley said. "I'm like pretty drunk, anyways."

"Drink the Manhattan. Kiss my lovely brunette friend. How's that for incentive? She's got a great bod."

"I don't really wanna drink. It makes me uncomfortable to think about."

"Unbelievable," Kora said. "We're offering you a chance to change your life: red pill or blue pill man. Ainsley's body's off the hook. She's way hotter than your bug-eyed ex."

"Come on, man," Rylie added. "Kora, I guess he's not worth it. Sometimes you catch the little ones, and they need to be thrown back."

"Jesus Christ. I'll take the friggin' drink," I said.

I grabbed the Manhattan from Kora's hand and stared into Ainsley's sienna eyes as I tipped the plastic cup to my virtuous lips. It was bitter and gross and caused me to cough and wheeze as Austin looked on disapprovingly. However, as uncomfortable as it felt, I finished the drink in 30 seconds and was officially ready to move on from the dastardly Devi.

"Well, Ainsley," Kora said. "Your turn. Now you gotta do something gross."

Ainsley stood up, brushed her straight brown hair behind her ears, and walked over to me.

"Hi," she said; her breath smelled like a distillery.

"Hi."

"Wait, Ainz," Rylie piped up. "Don't kiss him. Wouldn't that be hilarious? There's no contract. He can't like sue you or anything. Why kiss him?"

"Well, I don't know. It could be fun," Ainsley said.

"Actually," Kora laughed. "Don't kiss him. Definitely don't. It's his first day here. Let the kid get some more experience first."

Ainsley rubbed my abs with her delicate fingers as my Vilebrequin suit began extending outward. Kora stood and grabbed Ainsley's hand.

"Come on, girl. You're drunk. You're not, like, thinking straight. We'll hit on some Dalton boys tonight at the white party."

"Okay. Whatever you say."

"Try again tomorrow, big guy," Rylie said as she waved goodbye to me.

Austin and I marched in the other direction and elected to sit by the resort pool for the next several hours.

"They're the worst," Austin consoled me. "Can't wait to graduate and move on from them. Sorry man."

"At first, I was pissed, but that was actually like really exhilarating. I haven't felt that alive in months."

"I don't want to tell you how to feel, but that's not how you're supposed to feel."

"They noticed me and acknowledged my presence for the first time. They mixed in compliments between the insults. I'm on their radar. I'd rather be talked about in that way than go unnoticed."

"You're ridiculous."

"One of the Moncler Girls said something about a white party. Can we go?"

"Let's do it. I will say...and maybe it's that everyone's tipsy, but no one is being their typical selves. It's weird."

Austin then put his iPod in as we both lay by Paradise Lagoon for several hours. I dozed off for a while and continued to replay that brief shimmering moment where I was the center of attention. Upon waking, though, our trip took an unfortunate turn. Austin and I were both horrifically sunburned.

We sprinted to the hotel convenience store and then to our room, where we lathered our faces in Aloe Vera. Then, following that depressing moment, we sat on our respective beds and watched several games of the First Round of March Madness.

"Let's go to the casino," he said.

"And do what? They don't have poker here, right?"

"No, but we'll place sports bets on these games and try blackjack and roulette."

"Fine, anything to get out of the sun...and then we'll put on our best whites, add another layer of Aloe and score an invite to that party."

We entered the rundown, colorless 18+ nightclub in Nassau, and were immediately surrounded by a coterie of Verity, Riverdale, Dalton, Cordelia, and Chapin students. It was only the Manhattan high schoolers occupying the club as no tourists or locals were allowed on this particular night. The only Bahamians were the DJ and employees of the mysterious nightclub. I briefly considered who was in charge of all these events and how this group ended up here, but then let that thought gracefully leave my mind as I stepped onto the dance floor.

Every popular person in our grade was there. I saw the Moncler Girls dancing in the middle of the mosh-pit with Frankie, Caleb, Dexter, and 25 others stationed around the room. The boys were wearing fine Italian linen shirts and white khakis or jeans; while the girls were clad in the tightest, most revealing white summer dresses sold on Madison Avenue. Austin and I stayed together the majority of the night as we jumped and fist-pumped to the DJ's hot 100 setlist. It was enjoyable for a while until the Aloe Vera began to mix in with the sweat on our faces.

I was drenched in a moist mixture of warm water and creamy lotion. Even after three trips to the bathroom to wash my face, the ugly but innocuous amalgam refused to depart from my cheeks and forehead. I was ready to leave, while Austin was drinking two mint mojitos by the bar, unconcerned with the acutely distressing grotesqueness that party-goers were forced to witness.

"I think I'm gonna take off," I said to him.

"Why? 'Cause of your face? Who cares? It's a party. Relax man. Have a drink."

"I'll just go back to the room, shower, and hopefully, the sunburn dies down by tomorrow."

"All good. I know I can't change your mind. See you later."

As I was leaving, the DJ paused his obnoxiously loud music and siren sounds to make an announcement.

"Alright y'all," he said in his thick Caribbean accent. "I need ladies up here for our annual booty-shaking contest. Who thinks they know how to twerk? Come on up. I need five of you."

I decided to stay and watch this competition unfold before departing. I became particularly intrigued as Rylie and Kora took the stage in near-matching short skirts and what amounted to bras on top. They were joined by a chunky Dalton senior and two Moncler Girls, whom I recognized as the respective queen bees of Chapin and Cordelia. I remembered several of these girls from my glorious Boxington days.

The DJ played "Dance" by Big Sean and the girls, four Caucasian and one Persian, each drunkenly twerked to the delight of the rowdy audience.

The Dalton girl opened the competition, and I instantly felt terrible for her. Here she was dancing next to four impossibly sexy 18-year-olds wearing their skimpiest whites. Several of the more buzzed males in the crowd booed her and insulted her weight, which made the Dalton girl run off the stage and into the bathroom.

Given my past struggles with weight, I felt empathetic. Even if the Dalton girl was plastered, she wouldn't forget that moment. I'll always remember how difficult it was to transform my body during my formative years. This poor girl had the temerity to show off her figure on stage and received repugnant taunts? I remember this sickening me for a few brief moments. However, when Rylie started to twerk, I instantly forgot about the size 10 Dalton girl. Rylie's body, particularly her lower half, was unrivaled. She had that covetous hourglass figure, and the meticulousness with which she shook her hips was both incredibly sexy and impressive. The future perennially blacked-out frat bros in the crowd shouted what they wanted to do to Rylie's body once she exited the stage. I was taken aback by the night's milieu, particularly the raunchiness of my male peers.

As the competition progressed, the subsequent three Moncler Girls gave eight and a half out of 10 performances, and their collective lasciviousness made me tremble. At that moment, I considered whether I'd rather date a Moncler Girl or any Hollywood actress and came to the conclusion I was more attracted to the former. There was something magnificent about how prim and haughty these young women could behave in the public eye and at school, yet they could transform into concupiscent sirens in the appropriate setting. The Moncler Girls' versatility and wealth combined with the fact that I saw them every day, and they remained wholeheartedly unattainable, made them the apogee of my desires.

I took a hotel shuttle back to my room following Rylie's win and went to bed within minutes. The next day was uneventful as I elected to stay inside while my sunburn continued to heal. I spent a few hours at the roulette and blackjack tables, where I lost 55 dollars of the stipend my father handed to me before I left. And then later in the day, I went to the gym, ate, and eventually watched March Madness. It was an anemic, but necessary day of relaxation in preparation for the trip's main event: the Wednesday night booze cruise.

Austin and I walked down the rickety dock and stepped onto the 50-person capacity boat. One of the three chaperones handed everyone who boarded a plain white Paradise Island t-shirt and a colored Crayola marker. Apparently, everyone was going to go around and write on their friends' shirts. The more intoxicated people became, the more inappropriate the messages. I thought this was a nice touch. After the final few attendees arrived, we embarked on our jaunt outside of our atoll and into the Caribbean.

The boat had two floors, with the top being propped up by four thin columns. We all remained on the bottom, which had plain white décor that included a few corny wooden wheels and circular life preservers hanging on the walls. The only true amenity was the large bar in the corner serving any type of moderately priced alcohol imaginable. One Bahamian local manned the bar, one steered the boat, and the last one was in charge of deejaying. The resident turntable operator played primarily EDM and had a propensity for blasting "Levels" by Avicii every 20 minutes.

Following a few moments of acclimation, the partygoers rotated between dancing, drinking at the bar, and writing on each other's shirts. Austin left my side to take tequila shots, so I just wandered around the deck waiting for an opportunity to present itself. I quietly observed the messages accumulating on my fellow seniors' shirts. A few examples were: "This guy sucks", "I've seen her fit two hairbrushes inside", "Look up to see this whale's blowhole", "If you can read this, you're not drunk enough", "Future 1st round pick", "Throw her overboard", "$20 for back-door action and $300 for GFE", "One night in Paris-dise", "Medusa reincarnated", "Stop staring at my tits, twerp" and a hundred others. And as expected, the drunker my peers became, the more swastikas, phalluses, breasts, and derogatory terms for various races, genders, and sexual orientations appeared on shirts. Unfortunately, no one wrote on mine. I was ignored for the first hour of the night, and my only noteworthy moment was when I did some fist pump dancing in the large throng of prideless seniors.

Eventually, I went to the bathroom and looked at myself in the mirror. My sunburn was gradually becoming an alluring tan, and I felt handsome for the first time in months. I glanced at my barren shirt and concocted a wondrous plan. Why don't I just write on my own shirt? Maybe a cute girl would see an appealing message and approach me? It was worth a shot. So, I wrote "Funniest kid ever" and "So smart and handsome" in sizeable green lettering before exiting the bathroom.

As I strutted back to the dance floor, the DJ cut the music.

"Everybody," the local shouted. "I need four brave dudes to climb on these poles and strip for us right now. We're flipping the script. Hurry up."

I instantly volunteered. I didn't want to be the staid loser in the corner for the rest of my life, so this was my next opportunity to make a name for myself. I thought about how I didn't need Devi to be happy anymore. I could find other ways. And pole dancing sober on a booze cruise was apparently one of them.

"We've got four strapping young men up here," the DJ said. "Ladies, get your dollar bills out."

There I was, a taciturn neurotic who had his first taste of alcohol two days prior, as the center of attention. My performance didn't have to be too embarrassing since I had spent years in a dance class as a tween. The DJ played my favorite song at the time, "N***** in Paris" by Kanye West and Jay-Z.

I spun around the pole a couple of times, and Austin was able to get a few Verity people to clap for me. I felt awkward being the center of attention, and my dance moves were average at best, so I took off my white shirt, followed by my undershirt. This was an easy and reasonable way to make sure the audience was on my side.

My interminable hours at the 92nd Street Y had finally paid off as several girls cheered and threw a few dollars at my feet. I smiled and continued to do my best to emulate my fellow competitors. When the song ended, a few of the more shallow and drunk teenagers came to me and rubbed my pectorals, while Austin gave me a high five.

"That was awesome, man," he said. "I never could've done that."

A petite brunette girl carrying two t-shirts walked up to me. She must not have heard the dress code called for promiscuity because this walnut brown-haired senior was wearing long black leggings with a light blue Theory cardigan and navy Toms.

"You dropped this," the meek brunette said.

"Perfect, thanks," I responded, but was too focused on a commotion at the bar to notice her.

"I liked your dance," she smiled radiantly.

I grabbed the shirts from the girl, walked past her, and followed Austin. I then spotted an unmemorable girl lying across the bar top with her shirt pulled up beyond her bellybutton.

"Vincent, get over here, man," Austin said. "They're doing body shots."

I didn't know what a body shot was, but I followed Austin and watched as a girl drank alcohol out of her friend's belly button. Then with an ice cube in her mouth, the girl transferred it to the teeth of her horizontal friend.

"You want to give it a try?" Austin asked.

"Not with this girl. But I guess I'm willing to drink more alcohol if it's out of a girl's stomach."

"That's the spirit. YOLO."

The nondescript senior hopped down from her spot, and the lively Bahamian bartender instructed another girl to lay across the sticky bar top. This newcomer was agog to try out the cultural fad. I recognized the tall, golden-beige skinned figure from the dance competition two nights ago. She was a blatant Moncler Girl, whom I had learned about through word-of-mouth over the previous four years.

My understanding was she was a queen bee-type with a multifarious mix of followers at her school—Cordelia. This young lady's arrant control over her intellectually and emotionally inferior peers was apparent. Through Facebook and daily gossip, I knew her name was Adara, and she was a future Yale 2016 graduate. Adara was the perfect combination of looks, wealth, and intelligence. The jealous Moncler Girls at Verity claimed she had a large nose and prominent collar bones, but to me, she looked like a real-life Princess Jasmine. Although, it's entirely possible the image materialized because Adara's shirt said, "Call me Princess Adara" on it.

I jostled my way to the front and prayed to be chosen as Adara's body shot partner by the omnipotent bartender.

"Who wants to take a body shot?" The bartender yelled as he poured a mysterious brown liquid in Adara's belly button.

Several other impuissant brutes jockeyed towards the bar while the local placed a lone ice cube in between Adara's blindingly white teeth.

"You," the bartender pointed at me. "Get up here."

In a life filled with hapless moments, this was an entirely luck-based occasion that favored me. I was initially hit with both instant elation and timorousness. However, before I had time to overthink, I was straddling one of the princesses of Manhattan on top of a booze cruise bar.

There was a proliferation of audience members as Adara leaned her chin forward and flashed her snow-white marvels in my direction. The rancorous males seemed to hiss as I inhaled the alcohol from her belly button. Then, as I'd seen prior to my bar top excursion, I leaned forward to grab the ice cube from Adara's lips. Once again, Austin led an altruistic cheer on my behalf as the plethora of Moncler Girls on the boat fell deathly silent.

I snatched the ice cube with my teeth as Adara's rum-flavored lips grazed against mine. The whole crowd cheered for me as the princess glanced around the area, wholly unsure of the wheels she'd set in motion.

"Another one?" The ultimate wingman and bartender asked.

Adara and I both nodded. The local then poured the mystery liquid in her sticky, tropical-flavored navel. After the ice cube was placed in position, I devoured the ounce of alcohol and seized the cold rectangle from between her exquisite teeth. Then, Adara and I locked lips once again, but this time it lasted for minutes, not seconds.

I brushed the light brown tendrils from her face and succeeded in finding the ideal spot on the aggressiveness scale. My kiss wasn't too wet nor dry, and there was an evident, nascent bond between us. Adara leaned forward, placed her hand on the back of my head, grabbed my frizzy hair, and pulled. Our classmates sang a paean as I eventually helped Adara down from the bar top.

"So...what's your name?" I said.

Adara chuckled and ran over to her friend in the corner as I hesitated and walked in the other direction. The princess' incantation had left me in a dumbfounded stupor. The coconut-flavored alcohol also aided in my temporary buzz, so I went to sit on a bench on the starboard side. However, after a few seconds, I was interrupted by an unfriendly face.

"What the hell are you doing?" Kora Christensen asked.

"What?"

"You're, like, so clueless. My destitute little Vincent."

"What are you talking about?"

"If Adara doesn't have your balls in her mouth by the end of the night, you're as hopeless as they say."

"I don't understand."

"She likes you, big guy," Kora continued after my dismayed stare. "Yeah, you. One of the main reasons is she doesn't know anything about you, so don't get too cocky."

"What should I do?"

"Kiss her. Don't let her out of your sight. Invite her back to your room. She probably thinks you're like some popular guy. Some well-kept secret. The fact that none of us ever talk about you is finally working to your advantage."

"How?"

"Walk over there and buy her a shot. Then chat about boring stuff and invite her back to your room. This is it, slugger—big moment. Don't be yourself. Be like...suave."

"Why are you helping me? Are you just gonna trick me again?"

Kora lifted me up and pushed me towards Adara and her friend.

The Cordelia queen bee was wearing these impossibly tiny turquoise shorts with her colored-in and tied-up white shirt. She had her hair in a ponytail and was coaxing her seated friend to dance as they hung by the port side.

"I thought you should've won that dance-off two nights ago," I interrupted.

"You've got some moves yourself," Adara said. "Oh...by the way, this is my friend Louisa."

I looked at the petite brunette in the blue cardigan.

"Oh, I'm so sorry," I said. "You're the one who gave me my shirts back. Thanks again."

Louisa smiled at me and rubbed her chin, which allowed me to instantly spot the navy Hermès Clic H bracelet that matched her Toms. I also now noticed the sunflower blonde highlights streaking down her back while her frightening indigo eyes stared at me.

"Can I buy you both a shot?" I asked.

"Louisa was just about to dance, but I'll take one."

Adara's friend whispered in her ear before vanishing into the mosh-pit. I then strutted to the bar and asked for two shots of tequila.

"Sorry, boss," the bartender said. "Only got enough left for one. You want a different drink?"

"No, we'll take one."

The local tilted his head to the side before pouring us the shot.

"Do you want the first half or the second?" I asked.

"Umm, first?"

Adara took a sip before I finished it and then led her to the port side of the boat, where we sat facing each other.

"So, how's your trip been so far?" I said.

"It's mostly amazing. I went jet-skiing, snorkeling, and even tried to surf. I love the warm weather."

"So, what's the negative? You said *mostly* amazing."

"Well, the food looks so good everywhere, but I don't want to mess with my Piet." I looked at her quizzically. "You know, my Paradise Island diet."

"You could eat as much as you'd like and still look sexy. I mean, you're stunningly beautiful."

Adara ignored the comment and looked out over the water.

"So, do you know where you're going to college?" I asked.

"Yale. Both my parents went there. It's the perfect school and not too far from Manhattan. Just a quick Acela."

"That's so exciting. What an unbelievable accomplishment."

Neither one of us spoke for a few seconds until Kora came over in what seemed to be an attempt to reignite the flame.

"You know, Vincent's like the funniest kid ever."

"I know," Adara laughed. "It says so on his shirt."

Kora walked away and winked at me.

"How come I've never seen you around?" Adara said.

"No clue. I go to a lot of apartment parties, I guess. Maybe hit Lavo once a month."

"That's cool. I more of a Cielo girl. But my favorite spots are in the Hamptons."

"Oh, where's your parents' house?"

"My house is Sagaponack. It's off Townline Road."

"Sweet. I know exactly where there is. South of the highway, right?"

"Duh."

Ainsley then stopped in front of us.

"You know," Ainsley said. "Vincent is like the smartest kid in our grade. I always try to partner with him on all my assignments."

"Did you write that on his shirt?" Adara asked.

Ainsley shook her head and skipped away.

"What's with your friends?" Adara asked.

"I don't know. Everyone at Verity always seems to have my back, I guess."

Adara peered out at the water again. She seemed to want to move beyond my inchoate conversation topics. However, I didn't know how to proffer up another opportunity to kiss. At that point, I was hoping Kora had one more trick up her sleeve, and just as that thought left my mind, a blackout drunk Dexter approached Adara and me.

"You two...are gonna hook up in...3...2...1..."

Adara and I began kissing once again. Dexter's on-the-nose tactic had been precisely the introduction I needed. My bond with the princess grew more intense by the second.

Louisa then came by and took pictures while several others followed her lead as Adara and I became the most discussed couple at the party. Even while kissing, we heard rumblings of:

"What's Adara doing with him?"

"Who's that guy?"

"Is that the awkward pole dancer with the abs?"

"He'll nut early. No doubt. I'll bet you my left ball."

Unfortunately, the final and loudest sound we heard was the guttural noises spouting from the docking boat. The DJ turned the music off and tied our magical ship to the Paradise Island shore. Adara and I continued to kiss, but I knew this was my life-altering moment. I broke away from our sultry smooch and rubbed the back of my hand across her spotless cheek.

"Let's go back to my room," I said in a smooth tone I wasn't aware I possessed.

"Sure."

Adara and I held hands the entire way back to the resort. We only let go when I spotted Austin and dourly whispered in his ear:

"Stay out of the room for the love of God. I'll text you when we're done."

As we entered the resort's elevators, I remained stupefied by the events that had transpired. Adara was arguably the most beautiful high schooler I'd ever seen. Devi paled in comparison to this queen bee that was about to enter my neatly organized hotel room.

"Well, Princess Adara...We've arrived."

She rolled her eyes, chuckled, and then began to kiss me as I guided her to my queen-sized mattress.

"Wait, I'm just gonna go to the bathroom quickly," she said.

I sat on the foot of my bed and took several deep breaths, thinking about how I should properly position myself on the mattress and what I should be expecting from her. I quickly found the one condom in my suitcase, and covertly placed it under the bed.

Adara exited the bathroom and joined me at the foot while we both looked straight ahead, waiting for the other to make a move.

"So...do you play any sports?"

"Oh, um, yeah. Field hockey and volleyball. I'm alright. It made my application more well-rounded."

"Nice. I've never watched field hockey before, but it sounds exhilarating."

"How about you?"

"I used to play basketball, but these days just baseball. I'm one of the Verity varsity captains."

"You're the varsity baseball captain, and no one ever talks about you? So bizarre. I swear to God I hang out with Verity girls all the time, and no one has ever mentioned the name Vincent."

"That is weird...so...uh...what do you like wanna major in?"

Adara closed her eyes and lowered her back onto my bed. I noticed she had a moderately-sized band-aid horizontally draped across her spine.

"Let's not talk about school," she said while rubbing her temples.

I turned towards her, leaned my elbow against the bed, and placed my head in my hand.

"You're really pretty," I said.

"I know."

I then removed Adara's shirt, chuckling once again at the "Call me Princess Adara" line that was displayed front and center. I kissed and lightly bit her neck and protuberant collarbones while she moaned softly. Next came the unhooking of the bra, of which I had little experience. I leaned her forward and made a three-second attempt before Adara took it off herself and threw it to the floor. I paused for a moment to take a mental picture of her stunning figure.

"God, you're the sexiest girl alive."

Adara rolled her eyes and remained flat on the bed as I removed her turquoise shorts and magenta G-string, continuing to kiss and lick each newly displayed part of her nude body. However, as I made my way back to her golden-beige face, I realized I was fully clothed, and Adara was completely naked. I didn't know if this was my fault for not purging myself of the linens that covered my body or if Adara should've been removing my clothes in unison. However, I quickly remedied this as Adara shimmied up the bed, so her head was on a pillow. I just couldn't stop staring at the princess's unmatched figure that would've been sculpted in marble to be remembered for thousands of years had she been born in the appropriate time period.

"So, should I get a condom?"

"Sure."

I found my clandestine spot underneath the bed and turned away from Adara as I attempted to put it on. My orange plaid J. Crew boxers were the only piece of apparel that remained, but after the Trojan was affixed, they came off too.

I turned around, and Adara smiled at me before motioning me back onto the bed.

"Hit the lights," she said.

I stood up, marched around the room, and twisted the two lamp switches before finally climbing atop Adara's mesmeric body, kissing her succulent lips and proceeding to thrust inside her.

CHAPTER 9

A FTER A SURPRISINGLY LENGTHY session, Adara pulled me up against the pillows and fell asleep in the nook between my right arm and chest. I laid awake, alternating between lusting after her tall, thin frame and staring at the ceiling. I had finally accomplished this seemingly Sisyphean task. A nude Adara Zamani was cuddled up next to me as we both proudly displayed our naked bodies containing an impressive paucity of fat. Through sheer bravery, smooth maneuvering, and remarkable foresight, I had extirpated the fiendish emotional Scylla whose nefarious intentions had previously gnawed at my formerly feeble mind.

Unfortunately, a knock at the door interrupted my triumphant tête. It also woke the graceful princess lying beside me. I angrily stood up, put my shorts on, and answered.

"What?"

"Oh, I didn't know if you were finished," Austin said. "I can only spend so long in the casino."

"Jesus Christ dude. Go away. This is a huge moment for me," I whispered.

Austin nodded and evaporated down the hall. But by the time I turned around, Adara was clad in her tiny turquoise shorts and magenta bra.

"Oh, you don't have to go."

"Sorry. My friends are wondering where I am...but let me give you my number," Adara picked up my BlackBerry and typed it in.

"I understand. No worries."

"Text me later. Let me know what you're up to."

"Will do."

Adara came over, kissed me one final time, and exited our Edenic room.

Before texting Austin to return, I decided to play some music. I remember the first song that displayed on my plugged-in iPod was Wiz Khalifa's "Real Estate".

I strutted around the room, wearing nothing but my J. Crew Nantucket Red pants, rapping to the braggadocios beat. There was a tenable belief that this girl, this song, and this night were the collective climactic moments that would permanently remove me from my lifelong social ineptitude.

The first action I took upon returning to my dull Manhattan apartment was friending Adara Zamani on Facebook. It was a peculiar situation because we were a spring break one-night stand. How often did those lead to steady relationships? I had no idea how Adara felt about me. I was hoping she could be more than just a fun anecdote to tell at parties five years later.

"Yeah, I actually lost my virginity to a Persian girl in the Bahamas on spring break."

Or could our March 21st rendezvous be a clairvoyant sign?

Adara accepted my request minutes later, and I wondered if I should finally text the potential girl of my dreams. Something was terrifying about sending that first message, though. The second I pressed one button, I could receive an immediate rejection or, worse, permanent disregard. Texting seemed too invasive and anxiety-inducing, but a simple Facebook friend request left our options open.

Within a few hours, Adara's friends and some of the Verity girls had put up all of the Paradise Island pictures. There were bikinis, boys taking shots, and everyone showing off their respective "PIets." However, there was one particular image that became the 21st-century version of Gustav Klimt's "The Kiss." Instantly after Adara's friend Louisa posted it, I was hit with a dozen friend requests from girls I'd never met before. They each wanted to learn everything they could about Adara's mystery hook up. Had the queen bee finally found her king, or was this Vincent Beattie just a jester? Even when I returned to Verity after spring break, I was hounded by upper and underclassmen alike. For several weeks, a slew of students who had heard the stories and gossip or had seen the Facebook pictures approached me during free periods.

"Dude, Adara and Devi? We're gonna have to start calling you 'the UN'."

"Was she nasty? Was she like a total freak?"

"You lost your virginity to her? I thought you and Devi did that?"

"Did you check to see if she had any bombs? Other than those tits, of course?"

"When are you guys going out again?"

It was exhausting to deal with and frankly, embarrassing. I thought I'd be lauded for my miraculous accomplishment, but instead, all the underclassmen's questions were lewd, obnoxious, and off-topic. The only one I actually paid attention to was, of course, "when are you guys going out again?" I had wondered this myself and spent the first two weeks post-spring break, hoping Adara would reach out to me. It was too daunting a task to text her. I spent several nights dreaming about her perfection and worrying that any further contact would lead to her being less than angelic in my eyes.

"Yo Vincent," Ainsley called me over to her table during a random free period in April. "Come here. Sit down."

Ainsley was seated with Rylie, Olivia, Kora, and two other Moncler Girls at one of the senior tables in the student lounge.

"Hey everyone."

"You're really blowing it with Adara," Rylie said.

"What did I do or uh, what should I do?"

"Apparently," Olivia said "Adara's getting harassed about this mystery guy daily. A bunch of Verity sophomores and juniors are like, friending her and then berating her with a million questions over Facebook."

"Yeah, she told me," Ainsley added, "that not a day has gone by where some skeevy boy or know-it-all girl doesn't stop her on the street or Facebook message her about you."

"Most importantly, though," Kora chimed in, "why in the hell haven't you texted her? Goddamn idiot. I swear to God."

I scratched my arm as my leg began to shake.

"I don't know what to do or say or handle anything. I desperately need advice."

"You're kind of pathetic," Rylie said.

"Seems like a one-hit-wonder. You're like the Daniel Powter's 'Bad Day' of boys," Olivia agreed.

"So, will you help me?"

"Will we help a guy so clearly wrong for a friend of ours?" Kora said. "Will we turn you into someone you're not? Um, no thanks, sweetie."

"Listen, Vincent. Just stay in your lane, mmkay?" Rylie said.

"Thanks, your advice is greatly appreciated."

"So snarky today, Vincent," Kora said.

"I'm just sick of this. I need advice. I have nothing but positive intentions, and nobody will help me. I'd treat Adara like a princess or queen, you know. I'd take her to prom. I don't know why you all have to be such jerks all the time."

I stood and walked to a different table.

"At least you and Adara had one night of fun," Kora shouted. "Nobody can ever take your one highlight away from you."

I put my headphones in and started to listen to music as I read Shakespeare's *Othello*. However, after just one page, a familiar face sat next to me.

"Bro, those sluts are just jealous of you," Caleb said. "You've got the limelight now. You and Adara are all everyone's been talking about."

"What do you want?"

"I'm simply spitting facts, bro. Do you want advice on how to talk to Adara? Hand me your phone...Now."

I took my headphones out of my ears and closed the book.

"How do I know you're not just messing with me?"

"That's not my thing. Look, I need some new guys to go out with on the weekends, and you could be one of those dudes. Just here to help. You tell me to pound sand, and I'll leave you alone right now."

Caleb's urbane nature made him difficult to refuse. I understood why so many girls liked him. He toed the line between abrasive and supportive, and I had nowhere else to turn.

"Here. Show me the message before you hit send," I said as I handed him my phone.

Caleb snatched the device, and I watched as his thumbs maneuvered around the keypad with the dexterity of a heart surgeon. After 10 seconds, he said:

"There. Sent."

"Wait, what? I told you not to send it."

"Bro, if I didn't send it, you would've talked yourself out of it. I'm an expert at this stuff."

"Jesus, man. What's it say?"

I grabbed my phone and read:

V: Hey Adara, it's Vincent from PI. I'm gonna be at this Dalton party downtown this weekend. You should swing by. It'll be great to see you again, princess. I'll text you the details if you're down.

"How'd you know to call her 'princess?'"

"Everyone knows she likes that. That's her thing bro."

"What's this party?"

"Friend of mine is having their 18th at this warehouse turned club in SoHo. Roll with."

"What if she doesn't respond?"

"She will."

I waited a few days for a reply, but it never came. That didn't stop me from letting go of my acrimonious feelings with some Jack and Cokes at this birthday party, though.

The club looked exactly as Caleb had described. All of the walls were grey, and it seemed quite rundown from the exterior. However, there were effulgent lights, an obnoxious strobe, a rowdy NYU DJ, and, most importantly, unlimited free alcohol. Apparently, the birthday girl's father convinced the club owner it was his daughter's 21st birthday. It sounded ridiculous and implausible, but I wasn't going to argue with Caleb, and I knew the right amount of money could solve nearly everything.

"Bro, what are you so down for?" Caleb said as I hung my head in the corner of the room.

"I thought this Adara thing was gonna work."

"So did I, but hey, we move on. I got maybe 300 smokeshows in my contacts. We'll find you a new girl."

"I don't want a new girl. I really liked her."

"No, you didn't. You like that she's hot, popular, and will smash five minutes after meeting."

"Don't talk about her like that. She's going to Yale, you know."

"Bro, she's a whore. And wait...before you interrupt, there's nothing wrong with that. I've slept with 88 women. 88. I'm the male version of whatever she is. I don't think it's a good thing. I'm not bragging about it. But it's fun. You guys had fun. Move on."

I was growing tired of his negativity, and the loud EDM forced us to shout back and forth.

"She and I had a lot in common. She's beautiful and smart and fun to be around. I'll see her again. Adara must've felt something too."

"She was drunk. Let's move on. Point to a girl here, and I'll wingman."

"I need a drink."

I went over to the open bar and drank two Jack and Cokes while I pondered my final few months at Verity. I had my last baseball season, college decisions next week, and prom next month. I felt irresolute about everything. Devi hated me. Adara hated me. The Moncler Girls hated me. My father simply tolerated me. I needed a fresh start. As I looked around the hectic room filled with rowdy second-semester seniors, I shook my head. Four months from now, I'd be in Washington D.C. or Boston or Baltimore. I'd be hundreds of miles from this drama and desolation. All of my childhood memories and high school stories would soon be irretrievable in the deep recesses of my mind.

A week later, college decisions started pouring into our apartment. My father was inexplicably intrigued. At first, I thought it was genuine interest but then reminded myself that couldn't be the case with Morgan Beattie. There had to be another reason. In the meantime, though, I was more focused on my own well-being and future to care about anyone or anything else.

"Another rejection today, Vincent. Johns Hopkins."

"Jesus Christ. What's left?"

"Tufts rejection was yesterday, so just Boston University and George Washington University."

"What the hell. I don't understand. Why am I not getting in anywhere?"

"Could be a million reasons. Slipping Calculus grade, bad supplemental essays, low Science score on your ACTs. Best not to dwell on it. You'll get in somewhere. Verity will make sure of that."

"It's just so frustrating. Why can't I ever get a win?"

My father walked to the kitchen and started making his tortilla with scrambled eggs and bacon while I poured myself a bowl of Rice Krispies for dinner.

"Don't give me the sad-sack routine. You've got a great life. Great future ahead of you. You're a handsome kid now. Buck up."

"Gee, thanks."

"I'm tired of you being so down all the time. Your life ain't that bad. I've got real problems. I'm making a third of what I used to. I'm almost 60. When you go off to college, all I got left is my job."

"You make way more money than the average American. That's not so bad."

My father placed his spatula on the counter and put his hand on my shoulder.

"Don't ever compare me or you to an average American." His voice rose. "That's how people wind up living in squalor. We Beatties have to hold ourselves to a higher standard. I should be in the top 1%, not the top 5%, and you should be at an Ivy League school, not some philistine safety school that any Joe Schmo from Kansas can get into."

"Okay. I got it, Dad."

"You're too smart to settle for mediocrity. I'm not spending the rest of my life telling people at work and cocktail parties my sons go to Northwestern and, er, um...GW."

"Well, what am I supposed to do now?"

My father went back to his pan and sprinkled salt over his food.

"Dad?"

He closed his eyes for a few seconds before saying:

"Sorry, I overreacted. It's just I don't want to spend $40,000 a year for 13 years of private school for my son to go to BU or wherever. I'll figure something out. I always do."

A few days later, the BU rejection was accompanied by the GW acceptance. However, I refused to tell anyone at school where I was spending my subsequent four years. It was too embarrassing. Anytime someone asked, I'd say:

"I'm waitlisted at a few places. I'll find out in late-May."

A few weeks later, Austin and I were sitting in the back row of the baseball bus on our way to a game against Fieldston. As the only seniors on the team, we did everything together, including: sit next to each other on the bus, lead the team's warm-ups, long toss and discuss the scouting report on our opposition. We weren't friendly with any of the execrable juniors and sophomores on the team, many of whom were among the first to message Adara asking her about my performance and our hours-long relationship. On the field, Austin and I were friendly and took charge, but off the field, we kept our distance from our insolent teammates. We were forced to halt infighting and reduce the juniors'

massive egos. I was silently apoplectic during many practices and bus rides. However, Austin was the calming force.

"Ever hear back from Adara?"

"Nope. Probably never will."

"I'm sorry big dog. You'll meet a ton of girls in college."

I reached down and began to put on my baseball socks and cleats.

"So, what else do you have going on," he asked. "I know you don't want to talk about colleges."

"Well, congrats again on Bucknell. That should be a great school for you. It's a beautiful campus and not too far from Manhattan."

"Thanks, but how's life, man?"

"Um, to be honest, my life is in shambles. Most people either hate me or are neutral towards me. Girls don't like me. I'm going to wind up at a disappointing school. The only highlights of my days are hanging out with you and playing baseball."

"Come on though. You have to look at life through an optimistic lens. If things suck now, guess what? They'll get better. Life isn't an endless series of valleys...or...downswings. There will be peaks, and there will be upswings."

"What are you guys talking about back there?" A junior yelled from a few rows up.

"None of your goddamn business," I shouted. "Little punk."

The back row was reserved solely for Austin and me. It was a rite of passage the juniors had to earn.

"I get your point," I said to Austin. "But like, how long can my rollercoaster remain on the ground? My mom, Devi, Adara, Tessa I guess, Raven I guess, Frankie, Caleb, my entire social life, my home life, I mean, what do I have? Oh, I forgot prom. I'm just gonna skip it."

"Stop living in the past man. By next September, what, 90% of your problems disappear permanently? You'll make friends. You'll meet a girl. You'll get a good education. You're set up for success."

"I guess so. In the meantime, it just sucks. Like, the Moncler Girls, for example. They're mean to me and everyone all the time, right?"

"Sure."

"Kora is going to Cornell. Rylie took my spot at Georgetown. Olivia is going to Duke. Ainsley is going to Columbia, and I hear two more of them got into Ivies."

"So what? That doesn't affect you in any way. 'Cept maybe the Rylie thing, but you don't know that anyway."

"Life's just so frustrating sometimes. I don't know man."

"Look, just hang in there. If you still hate your life by December of this year, then maybe it'll be time to panic, but not now. You're about to embark on a memorable journey."

"Okay. Okay. Fine...Who are you taking to prom by the way? Gotta tell me now since I won't be going."

"Some girl from Heschel who goes to my synagogue."

"You like her? Is she cute?"

"For something like this, her looks don't matter. I'll have a good time with her. She's a nice person. I don't care what the Moncler Girls or anyone else thinks of me."

The bus stopped at Fieldston, and our team exited ready to beat a fierce division-leading rival. Yet, we were trounced 11-3. Our team finished the season 13-4 before losing in the second round of the state tournament. I set a Verity Prep record with a 15-game hitting streak and won the team's MVP award while Austin went 6-2 with a 3.74 ERA and 1.19 WHIP.

The final few weeks of my high school career were as uneventful as any. I skipped prom. I never spoke to the Moncler Girls, nor did I go out with Caleb again. I didn't plan on keeping in touch with anyone other than Austin and muttered "good riddance" under my breath as I walked out of Alice Tully Hall on Graduation Day. At my post-graduation lunch with my father and Charleston, the former said:

"Your mother would be very proud of you."

I nodded at the sentiment but disagreed with him. My mother would've been disappointed. I started drinking alcohol. I dated a girl she wouldn't have liked. I neglected to come out of my doughy shell. I was no closer to finding my future career path. I constantly brooded and sulked throughout school, parties, and at home. Not only would my mother be disheartened by the sight of 2012 Vincent, but 2007 Vincent would dislike his future self as well. The combination of Austin's pep talk with my visceral reaction to my father's comment made me want to change before I stepped foot on the George Washington University campus. I needed to be kind, outgoing, pleasant, lively, inquisitive, bold, and malleable. In order to avoid a fate like my mother's, I knew I needed to take an introspective look and transition into an affable 18-year-old go-getter.

Book 4

CHAPTER 1

O N August 28ᵀᴴ, 2012, I begrudgingly opened the doors to
Thurston Hall and marched up two flights of stairs to room
333. I arrived before my unknown roommate and was thor-
oughly unimpressed by the dormitory. The closet-sized space barely
squeezed two twin XL mattresses and standard wooden desks, and an
execrable stench emanated from an indecipherable location. In addition, the room's blinds would allow incandescent sun rays to pierce
through my eyelids at 7 am. I did remind myself to remain optimistic,
though. I'd no longer be the petulant hermit who mopes, frowns, and
criticizes.

On the positive side, our room did have its own bathroom, which is
exceedingly rare for freshmen housing. And Thurston Hall was located
directly in the center of a wondrous and salient city. I also had an exciting course load consisting of Intros to Criminal Justice, Psychology, Film
Studies, and Nature and Well-Being. At a school like this, I felt as though
I could achieve a 4.0 GPA with these interesting, but basic courses.

My father and I unloaded my clothing, television, bedding, and toiletries from the decrepit BMW and exchanged an unmemorable farewell. I was now alone in my new home. And as someone who had never
attended camp or spent any significant time away from his parents, those
first few moments alone in Thurston Hall were calming. Austin was right.
Most of my Verity problems seemed trivial. So what if Devi potentially
cheated on me? Why do I care if Adara and Raven weren't interested in
me? Tessa's a lesbian? Good for her. This upcoming semester I wanted

to hear the clacking of polyurethane wheels against steel conduits as my emotional rollercoaster screamed skyward.

There was a knock at the door before Kai Ramirez entered. He was taller, tanner, and hairier than I. Kai had considerable scruff covering his broad chin and pudgy jawline. His black hair was combed flat, and his eyebrows were untweezed. My new roommate wore a tight shirt and wasn't quite a close friend to his local gymnasium, but rather a loose acquaintance. His khaki shorts gave way to his hirsute legs and Havaianas flip-flops. Kai approached me with his rakish demeanor and a considerable smile.

"Hi there, I'm Kai Ramirez."

"Vincent Beattie, a pleasure to meet you."

He looked around the room, as did his mother, who strolled in a few steps behind him. I shook her hand, and she proceeded to converse with her son in Spanish. My three years of classes allowed me to decrypt every fifth word.

"I was planning on taking this bed and desk, but I'm not married to them," I said.

"No, you were here first. No worries."

I didn't need him to like me, but I did my best to conceal my grandiloquent personality that had turned away plenty of potential friends in my past.

"Mom, you can go now."

"Come, kiss me. Don't be rude, hijo."

Kai left the room with his mother, said his final farewell, and reentered moments later.

"So," he began while making his bed. "Uh, do you like video games?"

"Yeah, I'm a huge fan."

"Oh cool. Same. What do you play?"

"Mostly sports games like *Madden*, *2K* and *NHL*. But recently, I've been diving into one-player games like *Red Dead* and *Skyrim*."

"I love *Skyrim*. It's my all-time favorite."

"I brought it. I was gonna make a new character." I said. "My TV and 360 are in the corner over there, and I have *Skyrim*, *Mass Effect 2,* and the new *Madden*."

"That's awesome."

"Yeah, feel free to play whenever you want."

"Cool, thanks." He said. "I'll have to supply the room with alcohol then. What do you like? Do you have a fake?"

We were simultaneously making our beds, mine with gold satin sheets and his violet cotton.

"I don't drink much and no fake. But I'm always happy to go out and meet new people."

"Okay. Cool. Good to know," Kai stopped making his bed. "I should let you know...it's not like a secret or anything. Everyone back home knows."

"Okay."

"I'm gay," Kai said.

"Cool. I mean, no worries. No problem here."

"Cool. Well, we're gonna have plenty of fun this year."

A few days later, I started my college education with Intro to Criminal Justice. I was undoubtedly anxious walking to the classroom and became more so when I entered the auditorium a minute or two early. 120 of the 200 seats had been filled. I'd never taken a class with more than 20 students, so this was particularly jarring. Then came the parlous moment where I had to choose my seat.

Throughout my Manhattan private school days, assigned seating was an arcane boon to someone like me. Not all of my classes allowed me this privilege, but I secretly cherished a teacher forcing another peer to sit next to me. The stress and unpleasantness instantly evaporated. However, now as a college student, with over a hundred nosy visages sizing up my every gesture, I was terrified.

The question of seat choice could be broken down into two parts. First was the eternal question of front row, back row, or somewhere in between. Many of my high school classes dealt with circular seating, so that ceased to be an issue. However, in a 200-person auditorium, this became crucial. The front row was presumably for the nerds and class participators; the 11:30 pm Saturday night library studiers. The back row was for the degenerates; the Division I scholarship athletes and the skate-boarding stoners. This wasn't unique to this college. This was canonical throughout the U.S. and perhaps the world. I would've anticipated being a middle row student, but then I needed to consider part two: could I meet a future best friend or girlfriend based solely upon seat choice?

This wasn't an 18-year-old's fallacy. Every day in colleges nationwide, this was and is how people meet their friends and significant others. Spending the entire walk to this classroom pondering where to sit may have seemed neurotic, but it was actually quite perspicacious.

After standing in the doorway for a few seconds, I noticed two attractive young ladies with empty seats beside them. One was seated in the sixth row out of seven, and the other was in the back. I walked in their direction and made my final deliberation based off of their shoes. The sixth-row girl was wearing a pair of cheap flip-flops, while her peer rocked off-white Birkenstocks.

Once again, my ugly partiality towards wealthier girls had taken over. It's an embarrassing foible I wished I could've hidden. But we, as humans, can't choose who we're attracted to and why. For some, they see redheaded or African-American girls as the apex of the species. Well, for me, hair color and ethnic background weren't how I discriminated. Unfortunately, the young women who oozed affluence were the true lionesses ruling the jungle within my hypothalamus.

Anyway, I plopped my ageless black North Face in the back row next to Birkenstocks. She glanced at me for half a second, smiled faintly, and continued doing something on her Mac. I looked around the room and noticed half the class with their computers perched on their desks; 80% of which weren't waiting patiently with a blank Microsoft Word document open. These ne'er-do-wells didn't seem prepared to gorge their minds and screens with an influx of Supreme Court cases; they were surfing Facebook or Tumblr and snickering aloud.

I used my keen peripherals to size up my potential friend. Birkenstocks was a petite girl with long blonde hair and a prominent birthmark on her left cheek. She wore a baggy salmon-colored long sleeve t-shirt and white jean shorts to match her shoes. Birkenstocks also had small pearl earrings and a New York City air about her.

The Criminal Justice professor arrived and passed around syllabi while discussing the course load. The main point that stuck out was she believed group work was an excellent foundation for success in her course. This meant me, Birkenstocks, and 200 others would need friends. Through my first few days of college, I was beginning to learn everyone was trying to meet new people. It wasn't like Verity Prep, where the majority of students had been there since kindergarten, and I was an odd man out.

Given these circumstances, combined with the fact Birkenstocks looked over at me three times during class, I had the confidence to talk with her after the professor's lecture ended.

"Hey, are you from New York?" I asked as I placed my spiral notebook in my North Face.

"Sorry, what?" Birkenstocks turned to me.

"Are you from New York City?"

"Oh, yeah I am. How'd you know?"

"Not sure. The way you dress maybe? I just had a hunch."

"So you must be too. What part?"

We both picked up our bags and exited the classroom, walking next to one another.

"I grew up on the Upper East Side and went to Verity. How 'bout you?"

"Oh, fancy guy. I couldn't tell by looking at you. Greenpoint, Brooklyn. I went to Fieldston."

"Wow, small world."

I had heard people say that phrase countless times in my life, and it always made me wince. However, in order to fit in and be well-liked, I had to become more normal. By that logic, I needed to utter the cliched lines of "Wow, small world" and "Happy Friday" as many times as possible.

"I know seriously. I love people from New York. Luckily, this place is filled with them."

"What dorm are you walking to?" I asked.

"Thurston."

"Oh, me too. I'm on the third floor."

"I'm on the second. How crazy is that?"

"So, why Criminal Justice? Are you just fulfilling a requirement, or is it something you're passionate about?"

"No, it's a strong passion of mine. I want to go to law school. I'm gonna study civil rights law and help the needy and disenfranchised. And maybe in 15 years, run for Congress so I can eliminate some of the bigoted hatred that is anathema to the Republican Party."

"Um...That's quite the future."

"Yeah, and my boyfriend is studying to be a zoning lawyer at Villanova. He's a sophomore."

"Gotcha. Nice."

"This might be a little sappy, but I believe the meaning of life is simply to improve as many lives as you can. Don't you agree?"

"Totally. How could I not?"

We walked through the Thurston Hall doors and parted ways in the stairwell. During our initial conversation, neither one of us remembered to ask for a name, so she was still just Birkenstocks to me. I liked her enough. She was an intelligent, pretty, quasi-New Yorker. Birkenstocks didn't have Adara, Raven, or Devi looks, but she was an impressive and driven girl. I'd happily take a new acquaintance and could see the benefits of having a female friend. It was something I'd never really had before.

On the second day of Criminal Justice, I arrived five minutes early and sat in the same seat. My notebook was neatly placed on the center of my desk with a trusty Ticonderoga lying gracefully beside it. Birkenstocks arrived shortly thereafter, and to my surprise, she made a beeline towards the empty seat on my right.

"You saved me a seat?" She smiled.

"Sure, if that's what you want to hear."

"So, I'm embarrassed, but I already forgot your name. Chip was it?"

"Nope, and you didn't forget. We just never got that far. I'm Vincent Beattie."

"Izzy Rutherford."

Her calloused hand offered a tough shake just before the professor entered the room and began the lecture with a lengthy discussion on *Marbury v. Madison* (1803). Izzy and I were the only two back row students actively taking notes. She even strummed up the courage to participate four times throughout the class. Izzy made it look so effortless. It gave me the courage to answer "*McCullough v. Maryland* (1819)" when the professor asked which 19th-century case gave the federal government certain implied powers.

"Why are you sitting way back here?" I whispered.

"I don't like the thought of 200 people staring at me from behind."

"Seems logical."

Izzy then crept closer to me and whispered as softly as possible.

"Speaking of staring at people from behind, why do you keep looking at that girl there?"

I blushed, shook my head, and returned to my notebook without responding. My covert keeks weren't as subtle as I thought. Since Izzy was unavailable, I broadened my search for my first college love interest. As it turns out, the girl in the cheap flip-flops I almost sat next to on day one, became my proximity crush.

I remember the sixth-row girl having short blonde hair that just barely grazed her shoulders. She fit squarely into my type as a petite and bubbly damsel. This sixth-row girl had sharp, brown eyebrows that juxtaposed the light hair atop her head. She had pallid grey eyes, thin lips, off-white teeth, and a miniature nose always adorned with an infinitesimal gold-colored nose ring. Through two classes, I could tell she wasn't from the east coast and didn't come from means. The sixth-row girl carried her books in a bulky, beige moccasin-like bag and alternated between the same pair of beat-up white Keds and cheap flip-flops. Her clothing was always baggy and hid her bony frame. On this day, for example, she wore a tan pencil skirt with a loose-fitting umber shirt.

The sixth-row girl was also perpetually strangled by a leather necklace with a silver peace sign and two brown cow's hide bracelets on her left wrist. She didn't have the hourglass shape some males appreciated, and her looks didn't compare to Devi or any Moncler Girls', yet, she was a new type of pretty. The diminutive blonde was cute and far from anything I was used to. Any time she turned around, I was drawn in by her natural beauty, fetching smile, upper back tattoo, and commendable attempt to pull off a nose ring.

"*Plessy v. Ferguson*," the sixth-row girl shouted as the professor called on her.

"Very good. And what's your name, miss?"

"Mary Huber."

"Thank you, Mary."

"Vincent, you're doing it again," Izzy whispered.

"What?"

"Staring at that girl."

"No, I'm not."

Izzy shrugged and turned away.

After class ended, my new friend and I walked towards Thurston Hall again. The campus was simply the radius of eight or 10 city blocks just west of the center of Washington D.C. It was a gelid smattering of grey sidewalks, streets, buildings, and skies. By the time autumn ended, the alleged campus would be devoid of any color. Yet, since I was then thinking with an optimistic mindset, I thought about how close the Washington Monument, National Mall, White House, and Lincoln Memorial were. Very few schools could boast innumerable landmarks at such close proximity. Plus, the street campus was similar enough to the sidewalks I was used to near Verity. Like everything else in life, it was a simple Libra Scale.

"You want to stop at Tonic? I hear they have awesome food, and I'm starving," Izzy asked.

"I haven't seen the menu, but I'm happy to sit with you."

"Come on. It's American food. Pancakes, waffles, cheeseburgers—"

"I don't eat cheese."

"What do you mean?"

"My statement was pretty straightforward."

"Whoa, snarky today. That's good. I love a little attitude and sarcasm."

"What's your favorite food?"

"We're not changing the subject that quickly. Why don't you eat cheese? Are you lactose intolerant?"

"Nope."

I held open the door to Tonic, and we both walked inside the casual eatery for lunch. The maitre'd sat us at a table in the back and handed us menus.

"Everyone I know likes cheese. You're from New York. What about pizza?"

"Well...here's where it gets weird..."

"It was already weird."

"Weirder. I don't eat cheese. I haven't eaten cheese in 14 years. But I eat pizza."

"So, you eat cheese."

"But that's it," I said.

"What about cheeseburgers?"

"Nope."

"Grilled cheese with tomato soup?"

"Nope."

"Cheese—"

"Before you keep going," I said. "Let me stop you...I don't eat cheese on anything other than pizza. That even includes artificial cheese like Goldfish, Doritos, and Cheetos. I won't even eat tomato and mozzarella with basil."

"Fine. So, what was the traumatic experience that led to this?"

"None. I can't remember anything specific."

"Well, people's taste buds change every seven years."

"I've heard every argument in the book."

"What if I snuck cheese in your food?"

"I'd probably never speak to you again."

"I can't tell if you're serious."

The waiter brought our waters, and I ordered an unsweetened iced tea, while Izzy asked for a black coffee with two Equal. After a few moments, the waiter returned with our drinks, and I watched Izzy instinctively pour the artificial sweetener into her mug without looking. When she placed the empty Equal packets on the table, I thought about my mother.

If my mother was still alive and zoomed in on my current day, she might've been proud. At least I was making an effort. Izzy was a pleasant companion with no romantic attraction. This was unequivocally a step in the right direction. Given the way I was raised, I didn't believe in an afterlife, nor did I think anyone was looking down on me, but I could still try to carry out my mother's legacy through my actions.

"May I please have a plain bacon burger. No cheese, lettuce, tomatoes, onions. Nothing on it. Fries on the side," I said to the waiter.

"Tater tots and the pigs in a blanket, please," Izzy said.

The waiter left our sight, and Izzy stared at me while shaking her head.

"No cheese huh? You're fascinating."

"It's not that crazy. Everyone has one food that they can't stand for some reason or another. What's yours?"

"I don't...well...it doesn't really count."

"Let's hear it."

"Artificial watermelon. I despise it. Jolly Ranchers, gummies, Nerds, Sour Patch, Pixy Sticks. I can't stand the smell or the taste...but I do eat watermelon."

"That's way weirder than mine," I chuckled.

"But let me guess, a weirdo like you must have more than one forbidden food, correct?"

"Maybe."

"How many are on that list? 10?"

"Probably 55."

"Are you serious?"

"You're loving this, aren't you?"

"A little bit. Yeah, I am."

"Let's change topics, though. I don't want to go off listing foods and getting some acrimonious reaction from you."

"Deal. But I do expect to hear that whole list one day."

"Fair enough; after you've decided you can tolerate my company for more than 15 minutes."

"So, what's with you and that Mary Huber?"

"Who?"

The waiter came by and dropped off her pigs in a blanket and tater tots.

"Yeah right. You're no actor."

"I did basically four years of Acting Improv in high school."

"Don't change the subject. You like that girl?"

"I don't even know her. She's just a classroom crush. Everybody has those. You walk in on the first day of high school and college courses and spot a girl you can fawn over the rest of the semester."

"God, you're strange. But in like a, let me watch this praying mantis eat, kind of strange."

"Hold on a second. That's not strange at all. Everybody does this. Very few choose to admit it to borderline strangers, but everyone has a mindset like this. Classes get boring. We all zone out occasionally. It's human nature."

"So, what are you gonna do?"

"Mary Huber is just my proximity crush. Whatever you want to call it. I just check out her outfits and smile at her if she turns around. It's nothing."

"You're a real piece of work, Vincent."

CHAPTER 2

MY FIRST WEEK WAS FOREVER behind me with a few positive trajectories. Kai and I were getting along swimmingly with discussions about our upbringings while playing Xbox games. Izzy and I were now inextricable both in and around Criminal Justice class, and my courses themselves were much easier than Verity's. Outside of classes and dorm room video games, I worked out at the gym four days a week, ate by myself in the cafeteria, and frequently took walks outside of campus to explore my new city. I had begun to develop certain whimsicalities I didn't used to possess. It took only a week for my Verity Prep plight to be squashed to the deep recesses of my mind.

In the subsequent Criminal Justice class, the professor made good on her promise of group activities. She described an assignment where everyone would split into groups of three and would be given a Supreme Court case at random. One member of the group would then write a concurrence on the decision; one would pen a dissent, and the third member had to read each side of the argument, make their decision and write about why they prefer one or the other.

"Hey, it's Mary, right?" Izzy nudged the girl directly in front of her.

"Yeah, how'd you know?"

"You participate a lot. You seem super smart."

"Thanks," Mary blushed as her vale-like dimples flashed.

"You wanna join our group. Vincent and I need a third."

"Sure."

"I'm Izzy by the way."

Mary was wearing black, low-top Chuck Taylors today with no socks and blue jean overalls above her white long-sleeve shirt. If I saw that on a mannequin, I probably would've called it hideous, but Mary's vivacious personality, country demeanor, and infallible face made any outfit work. I loved how her tiny gold nose ring shook when she was clearly enjoying herself.

Mary turned her desk backward to face us while a baseball cap was passed around the classroom with little slips of paper containing Supreme Court cases written on them. By the time the hat made its way to the back row, there were only five or six cases left. Izzy, with her eyes closed, grabbed *Terry v. Ohio* (1968).

"Mary, what dorm are you in?" Izzy asked.

"Oh, I'm actually up at the Mount Vernon Campus."

"Where's that?" I asked.

"It's the other, newer campus. A few hundred freshmen live there and take the shuttle to and from. It's like 15 minutes north of here. It's great for people not used to cities. It's all green grass and like, a real campus."

"That's neat. I should check it out," I said.

"There are plenty of classrooms there too. Maybe you'll have a course at Mount Vernon next semester."

Izzy looked over at me and smirked.

"Is there a place that would be convenient for you to meet, Mary?"

"No. I'll do whatever's best for you two. I don't want to inconvenience anyone."

"Why don't we all just meet in the Thurston Hall basement after our next class?" Izzy said.

"Perfect," Mary then picked up her moccasin bag and exited the room.

"There, happy?"

"What?"

"I'm expecting a thank you."

"Oh. Okay. Thank you, Izzy. That was so wonderfully kind of you."

"I'm a great wing woman. You should meet Blizzy."

"Who's that?"

"Blackout Izzy. She comes out on weekends when I'm blackout drunk. Best wing-woman there is."

"I might have to take you up on that."

Two days later, Izzy and I walked to the Thurston Hall basement and spotted Mary at a corner table. She had her leather bag and low-top Chuck Taylors on while wearing an ill-fitting grey, zip-up hoodie with nothing underneath.

"Hey Mary, how's it going?" I said.

"Good. I'm excited. I never really had group projects where I'm from."

"Where's that?"

"Elk City, Oklahoma. What about you guys?"

"I'm from Manhattan."

"And I'm from Brooklyn."

"Oh, did you two know each before this?"

"No," I said. "Just a weird coincidence."

"You ready to get started?" Izzy asked.

The three of us googled *Terry v. Ohio* and learned about the still prevalent case.

"So, who wants to argue what?" I asked.

"I'll take the dissent," Izzy said.

"Oh, I wanted to argue for Terry, too," Mary responded.

"Whatever, I'm cool with anything," Izzy added. "Terry is the correct side, but why don't I just take the closing section. Mary, you take the dissent, and Vincent, you can have the concurrence."

"Cool with me."

Mary and I spent the next hour furiously typing away as Izzy delved even further into Justice White's concurrence and Justice Douglas' dissent into this Fourth Amendment-focused case. Eventually, we reconvened and blurted out our thoughts with the blaring haughtiness of freshmen two weeks into an introductory college course.

The three of us sat at our corner table for several hours, debating each point of view, discussing our upbringings, and then going way off topic and somehow talking about princesses and tiaras. It was an arrant success. When we turned in our papers the subsequent day, each of us felt confident.

After class, Izzy and I walked back to Thurston on the wuthering autumnal afternoon. There was a certain blitheness we were both experiencing for the first time at college. The school days were shorter, homework was less cumbersome, and we didn't have to worry about vitriolic parents, intrusive teachers, catty cliques, or college applications. I was in an insouciant mood, and Izzy could smell it on me.

"I think Mary noticed you staring at her in the Thurston basement."

"What are you talking about? I wasn't."

"Every five minutes, while you were typing, you'd peek up. You were like a sketch artist drawing a portrait."

"Relax. It's not like that."

"I'll text her tonight for you."

"What?"

"Yeah. Simple. I'll just ask if she thinks you're cute."

"That's awkward."

"Not at all. Happens all the time. I'll be like, 'do you think Vincent is cute?' And she'll say yes or no."

"What if she says 'why do you ask?'"

"I'll say 'just curious'."

"What if she says 'did he say something about me?'"

"Come on, dude. Enough. You act like you've never spoken to a girl before. Don't be whiny. I'll take care of it."

"Thanks."

"Of course, Vincent. You're my boy."

I went back to my room and did homework for other classes, imperturbably awaiting the LED light on my BlackBerry to signify a message from Izzy. In the meantime, I was acutely focused on Freud, Pavlov, and Skinner. Since I'd been aware of the Oedipus Complex and Pavlov's dogs for years, nothing that professor said challenged me. And Nature and Well-Being was also a simplistic course. Our homework typically consisted of taking walks around the D.C. area and keeping a journal.

My final course, Intro to Film Studies, was the only one outside of Criminal Justice to offer any merit. While we were watching mostly what I considered "Classic Film Studies Movies," I had never seen the majority of them, so it was a worthwhile endeavor. The first week's syllabus displayed all the films we'd be watching throughout the semester:

> *Birth of a Nation* (1915)
> *The Cabinet of Dr. Caligari* (1920)
> *Stagecoach* (1939)
> *Citizen Kane* (1941)
> *Bicycle Thieves* (1948)
> *The Third Man* (1949)
> *Rashomon* (1950)
> *Sunset Boulevard* (1950)
> *The Searchers* (1956)
> *Breathless* (1960)
> *Belle Du Jour* (1967)
> *The Conformist* (1970)
> *McCabe and Mrs. Miller* (1971)
> *Cinema Paradiso* (1988)

After an hour or two of doing my Psychology and Film Studies homework, I received that fateful text.

I: She likes you!
V: What did she say? What did you say?
I: I said exactly what we talked about, and she said, "yeah, he's cute and seems almost too smart."
V: Haha, that's promising.

I: Text her now. Say I texted you. Ask her out for a casual date.
V: Where?
I: Go to the ice cream place all the freshmen go to: Cone E Island.
V: Cool. I will.
I: You're paying, right?
V: Yeah...why are you being so nice to me?
I: We're friends, dude. I have a boyfriend who lives hours away. I want to live vicariously through you.
V: I won't forget this. Thanks a million.

I delayed texting Mary because I didn't want to seem desperate. I'd finish my Film Studies paper on *Stagecoach* and then message her. My opuscule depicted why 'Doc Boone' should be considered the film's most compelling character. It was yet another strongly opinionated essay as I continued to evolve as a writer. In fact, two weeks later, I happened into a paid job thanks to my vociferous tone and eloquent style.

It was early October, and our professor introduced the class to a film blog run by one of his former students, David "Dutch" Traugott. We were told Dutch takes on two new bloggers every semester for a paid writing gig. The blog itself was a film review site called "Dutch's Angle." He did film reviews of both newly released movies and classics. Dutch's site had a lot of traffic and advertisers, so he was able to make a livable wage and paid contributors per article. I jumped at the opportunity, and as the calendar progressed to mid-October, I wrote a mixed review on the eventual Academy Award Best Picture Winner, *Argo* (2012). Dutch picked me to be one of his contributing writers, and I started earning $75 per review. During my first semester, I wrote approximately four a month.

However, on this September night, after my 'Doc Boone' paper was finished, I picked up my BlackBerry and messaged my agrestic-bred freshman crush.

V: Hey! It's Vincent from Criminal Justice.
M: Hey!

V: How are you? I loved the way your Terry v. Ohio paper turned out.

M: Thanks a lot! I really appreciate it.

V: Btw, I heard you spoke to Izzy about me.

M: Oh that lol.

V: Yeah, haha. Well, I do think you're really cute too. I'd love just to hang out casually. Get to know each other better.

M: I'd like that!

V: How's this Friday sound?

M: Stupendous! Where are we going?

V: Do you like ice cream?

M: I'm a human, aren't I? Lol.

V: Let's meet up at Cone E Island at 8 pm.

M: Sounds perfect. Can't wait :)

Before leaving for my date on Friday, I asked Kai for fashion advice. After much deliberation, we settled on dark blue skinny jeans, an off-white cashmere sweater, and my navy Sperrys with the white laces pre-tied in an "x."

While walking to 21ˢᵗ and I, Izzy sent me a good luck text. I was strangely confident that night, and it was a peculiar feeling not having any of the usual stresses tormenting me. The night would simply be delicious food and an atypical young woman.

Mary was standing on the steps outside of the parlor when I arrived. She was wearing a sleeveless, knee-length billowy dress. It was low-cut and had a small black and grey floral pattern that went well with her white Keds. Every time I saw Mary, though, I felt she looked cute. The dainty blonde girl had a connate ability to appear pretty with minimal effort.

Mary wrapped her arms around me and then held my hand as we walked inside the store. We were both instantly overwhelmed by the 50 different unique flavors this sublime ice cream shop had. I offered that she order first, and Mary obliged by choosing a waffle cone with mint chocolate chip and cake batter. I, on the other hand, quickly settled on chocolate peanut butter and Denali Moose Tracks in a cone. She and I both asked for rainbow sprinkles, and I happily paid.

We sat in the somewhat crowded upstairs section, licking our respective scoops and watching sprinkles tumble to the table.

"So, you're from Elk City, Oklahoma? What's that like?"

"Um, it's bittersweet like any place. My family owns a moderately-sized wheat farm, and we have at least 25 heads of cattle along with plenty of hens, roosters, sheep, and goats."

"Gosh, that's crazy. I've never met anyone with a background like that."

"It's kind of embarrassing, I know."

"No, not at all. It's distinctive. It makes you different from everyone else. It's a good thing."

"Thanks. I think..." She paused. "Wait, my ice cream is dripping down the cone. Give me a second."

Mary's pointy tongue licked the sticky green substance oozing down the narrowing cone.

"Don't laugh. This is serious," she said. "If I don't lick it quickly, the whole thing is ruined."

She flashed her Duchenne smile and pallid grey eyes to let me know she was kidding.

"How do you eat so neatly?" Mary asked. "They gave us so much, and it's melting too quickly. You're like a robot."

"Years of practice. It takes a lot of diligence. I'm constantly spinning and scanning the cone to see where the next drip will occur. There's a correct time to bite off a piece of the waffle. It's essentially a science at this point."

"You're funny."

Mary was more wholesome than any girl I'd ever met. There were no ulterior motives. She wasn't playing games. Mary was a genuinely benignant person. It was a type that one, unfortunately, doesn't find in east coast cities. She seemed like the kind of person who would be truly moved by a sunset, or flowers first blooming in the spring. Everything appeared so simple and naturally gleeful. From her eyes to her short blonde hair to her dark brown eyebrows, Mary's perpetually kind features were infectious.

"So," I continued. "What's bad about Oklahoma? You said it's bittersweet?"

"I mean, it's a little personal, but maybe I can trust you…So, it's lonely. I was an only child, and it's difficult when I had to go through like, typical high school problems. I didn't really have anyone to talk to. Plus, everyone lived pretty far away from one another. Like, Elk City's not a city like Washington D.C. is. And our farm isn't in like the center of town. We're a few miles out."

"Yeah, I wouldn't love that constant isolation either. That can't be easy."

"But, enough about my boring life. What about you. From the Big Apple? I don't have any kind of frame of reference at all."

"You've never been? Even as a tourist?"

"Well…promise you won't laugh?"

"Of course."

"Okay fine…Flying to D.C. last month was my first time east of the Mississippi."

"Wow, really? Jesus. I mean, I think that's cool. There's nothing embarrassing about that."

"Why do you say that?"

"I mean this in the best way possible, but…you're like an alien."

Mary gave me a quizzical look I should've anticipated, so I continued.

"You have this awesome opportunity to be an adult in what's essentially a whole new world. I mean, in my case, I was exploring different parts of the country and world as a five, six, and seven-year-old. I'd love to experience something new in adulthood. You get to see what a massive city is like and experience hundreds of different cultures you may have only read about."

"I'm not from outer space, Vincent. I'm from Oklahoma. But you make a decent point."

Her ice cream started to drip out of the bottom of the cone.

"Ah. Wait. Help."

"Hand me your cone. Quickly."

Mary gave me the leaking waffle monstrosity, and I quickly wrapped the bottom with a makeshift levee to plug the flooding.

"My hero," she said.

I took the final bite of my immaculately licked chocolate peanut butter dessert and wiped my fingers.

"All done."

"You need to teach me how to do that? I've never seen anyone eat ice cream more efficiently than you. It's like a gift."

"I'd rather have your gifts. Like, can you milk cows and goats or harvest crops? I have no clue what your childhood must've been like. That's so foreign to me. I'd be an alien on your farm. Did you have horses you rode?"

"Of course. I can do it all. You should see how efficiently I can milk a cow or shear a sheep. Unfortunately, they're not skills I'll use here, but they make good anecdotes, I guess."

Mary finished her cone and began licking her fingers individually. My mother would've been horrified at this, but Mary's actions were endearing. She didn't have the opportunities and privileges I grew up with, so it was silly to criticize her. Plus, she had a trait no one in my family possessed: unadulterated exuberance.

"Sorry. I must look like such a mess. My fingers are so sticky."

"No, don't apologize. You look really pretty."

Mary flashed her child-like smile.

"Thanks. You do too."

"You ready to leave?" I said. "Let's walk around a little. Burn off some of these calories."

"Are you calling me fat?"

"What? No. Not at all. I would never. You're perfectly trim."

"Bless your heart. I was joking. Loosen up."

We both laughed as we walked down the stairs and out the door of the ice cream parlor.

"Where are we fixing to go?" She asked.

"Well, it's a bit of a walk, but have you been to the Washington Monument yet? It's like a mile from here."

"A mile's nothing. I'm an outdoors kind of girl. I could out-walk you anywhere."

I laughed, grabbed her hand, and we started south towards Constitution Avenue. Mary and I were mostly silent as the waxing moon coruscated down on the already luminescent city blocks. The temperature was dropping, and the breeze picked up, so I offered Mary my sweater.

"But won't you be cold?" She said.

"My mother raised me to be chivalrous. I'd rather be cold than have you shaking."

Mary nodded, took my cashmere outerwear, and slipped it over her floral summer dress. I was now only wearing a white undershirt, but the kind gesture was worth it.

I was happy for the first time in a while and wished I could remain in the moment, but my perambulating mind had other ideas. The svelte Devi came slithering into the forefront of my mind. I imagined her laughing at me for being with a nice, simple girl like Mary. My inner id had taken the form of Devi and was explaining to me all of Mary's physical issues. Devi remarked on how Mary's face was flat, and her nose ring was classless and how Mary had a large tattoo on her upper back. The blonde's chin was pointy, and her style consisted of inexpensive garments from the Gap or H&M. She was carrying a cowhide satchel on a first date, and her hair also could've used additional brushing. Then the serpent reminded me I'd never end up with a poor, country girl like this. This was a temporary blip.

"Hey, Vincent, are you okay?" Mary rubbed my hand.

Thankfully, just hearing her honeyed voice eliminated all of those ornery thoughts. Devi crept back into the locked penthouse of my mind where she wouldn't be heard from for the rest of the night. Mary was exactly the type of person I needed in my life. Why did I care about her sartorial elegance? I just wanted to turn my brain off for the rest of the night.

"You know, I'm absolutely wonderful. Thank you for making this such a fun night."

Mary smiled vividly. The more she flashed her teeth at me, the more I appreciated them. Mary didn't have the whitest teeth, the deepest dimples, the most colorful eyes, or the least number of wrinkles, but her phosphorescent smile seeped with nostalgia. Through it, I was taken back to my childhood when my mother was alive and jocose, and my father was light-hearted and jokey. Mary's smile made me think of sandboxes and slides and swing sets. Her unmatched virtue and positivity could make even the vilest of demons croon.

"There it is! That's the monument. I've only ever seen it in pictures."

Mary let go of my hand and raced ahead. She paused at the base, tilted her head all the way back and beamed. I jogged to join in, and right when I stood beside her, Mary placed her hands on my cheeks and kissed me assiduously. I felt her gold nose ring tickle the light scruff above my lip. As soon as our tongues touched, I was infected by the short-haired blonde's inestimable jolliness.

Following that magical night, Mary and I began texting daily, and she'd sit on my left in each Criminal Justice class. While Izzy took significant pleasure in playing the role of Cupid in this modern-day romance, after that ice cream-filled evening, Mary became the apex of my priorities.

For our second date, Mary demanded I watch her Oklahoma Sooners take on the Kansas State Wildcats at the T.G.I. Friday's on 21st and I. As far as second dates go, I was pretty thrilled by her suggestion. I was equally intrigued when I arrived to find Mary sitting at the bar, watching the pre-game show in her number 12 Landry Jones jersey.

"Come here. I saved you a seat."

"That's quite the get-up."

"Weirdly enough, Sooners jerseys are the only thing my parents feel comfortable splurging on. I almost wore my AP jersey, but we're 2-0 since I started wearing Landry's 12."

"This is hilarious."

Mary kissed me on the cheek and ordered Red Bulls for each of us.

"How long have you been a Sooners fan?"

"Oh. Forever. Since my parents took me to the Palace on the Prairie when I was 4."

"Well, so why did you come here?"

Mary's grey eyes remained glued to the TV as she spoke. For the next three hours, my voice remained less important than that of the announcer, Gus Johnson.

"I had some stuff I needed to get away from."

"Spooky. What does that mean?"

"Nothing. I mean, really, I wanted a better school academically than Oklahoma, and I needed to see what the east coast and big city life was like."

"You could've gone to a school with a great football program on the east coast, right?"

"And have to maybe root against the Sooners? No way."

Our Red Bulls arrived, and we each ordered hamburgers and fries.

"What courses are you taking? Or...would you prefer if I don't talk while you're watching?"

"No, silly. I want to watch *and* talk to you. Your voice is soothing."

"I've always been told it's nasally."

"No, not at all. It's pleasant. And I like a little taste of everything, so I'm taking Intros to Macro Economics, Criminal Justice, Mandarin Chinese, and Marketing."

"That's great. I think that's exactly the way to look at our freshman years."

Mary cheered and hugged me as Oklahoma made their first field goal of the game. Unfortunately, Kansas State took the lead in the 2nd quarter, and Mary was visibly stressed. However, she never strayed from her textbook optimism.

"It's fine. Landry will drive us down and give us the lead before the half. No big deal."

Our food arrived, and Mary would occasionally yell at the TV with burger bits in her mouth, but I was definitely attracted to someone who could be so passionate. I wished I cared about anything as much as Mary did her Sooners. She did look pretty in her jersey too. I'd never seen a girl at Verity wear something like that just for fun.

"God damnit," she shouted.

The Sooners were losing 10-6 at halftime. At this point, Mary tilted her stool towards me.

"Sorry, you're my focus for the next 15 minutes. I don't want you to think I'm a total psycho. I'm kind of embarrassed about this side of me. Back home, this was totally normal, but here, I bet people think I'm a weirdo tomboy."

"Mary, don't worry about that. I think it's lovely. You're so fervent. It's fun to watch. Don't stress about being different around me. I like you exactly the way you are."

Mary smiled and quickly kissed me; her lively nature was only magnified with two Red Bulls in her system. The more the game progressed, though, the graver her tone became. Kansas State appeared likely to pull off the upset until a serendipitous Landry Jones touchdown pass brought Oklahoma within one possession with under five minutes to play. Mary was biting her thin lip and squeezing my hand as the clock waned. Her rabblement caused the onlooking locals to glare. However, I greatly enjoyed my preamble to a Sooner zealot.

Oklahoma lost the game, and Mary slammed her fists on the bar as the clock struck triple zeroes.

"I hate the goddamn Wildcats. Klein wasn't even good. This is such bull. Stoops should've ridden Whaley in the second half. This sucks."

"Sorry Mary. I was rootin' for ya. Shepard was really promising, at least."

"I guess. I'm gonna wear my AP jersey next week against Tech. It'll be fine. We'll still be ranked, and as long as we win the Red River Rivalry in three weeks, we'll be back on track."

"Feel a little better?"

"Yeah. I'm always cranky after a loss. But I shake it off quickly... thanks for watching with me. That was a lot of fun...even if you may be the Sooners' bad luck charm."

"Thanks," I chuckled.

Two weekends later, Mary and I were still enduring, and by October, we were officially boyfriend and girlfriend, and I was invited back to T.G.I. Friday's to watch Oklahoma beat Texas Tech. Then later in the month, we made our third trip to the family-style restaurant to watch them take on their bitter rival: Texas. It was billed to be a close, high-scoring game between two ranked teams, but the Sooners crushed the impuissant Longhorns. Mary, clad in her Oklahoma Adrian Peterson jersey, celebrated the trouncing by kissing me at the bar.

"I have an idea," she said as I paid the bill. "You should come up to the Mount Vernon Campus to see my dorm."

"I'd love that. Do I need to bring anything?"

"Yeah. Let's go back to your room first and pack your backpack. I want you to stay overnight."

"Really? You do? I mean, I'd love that."

"You're cute."

Mary pinched my cheek, grabbed my hand, and led me out of the bar.

"I get so jacked up after a big win. I just want to climb all over you."

Mary leaped onto my shoulders for a piggyback ride to Thurston. My vibrant girlfriend helped me pack my North Face before we said good-bye to Kai and hopped on the shuttle to the Mount Vernon Campus. We sat in the back row of the bus, and Mary continued to press her succulent lips against mine.

"You're so sexy," she mouthed.

The other passengers on the bus attempted not to look back at our ribaldry.

As the bus continued up Foxhall Road towards the secluded secondary campus, I glanced out the window and was ensorcelled by the resplendent trees circumventing the Mount Vernon buildings. The kaleidoscopic reds, yellows, and oranges slowly winnowed on the brisk mid-October day.

Mary bit my earlobe as the bus made its final stop by her dorm, Clark Hall. My new girlfriend yanked my arm as she led me off the bus. Mary then skipped towards the red brick building with me in tow.

"Wait, before we go inside," Mary announced. "I want to show you my favorite tree."

"Sounds great."

Mary led me downhill to the western area of campus, past the turf soccer field. While still carrying my backpack, I dodged a few branches and eventually spotted the immaculate tree of which Mary was speaking.

"Isn't she beautiful?" Mary ran her finger along her nose ring.

"It really is. It's so symmetrical and colorful. And it must be really old. Look how thick this trunk is."

"I come here to read and think and write in my journal. I'll even take little catnaps here. It's my favorite place on either campus, and no one knows about it."

"Mary, it's perfect."

"Come on. Lay here."

Mary and I sat in the shade, and she leaned her head on my shoulder. We were roosted in silence, miles away from the bustle of downtown Washington D.C. She was right about this section of campus. Mary's tree may have been the most docile place I'd ever sat. My adorable girlfriend and I remained there until the sun set off in the distance. After zoning out for a few moments, I turned to my left and found Mary fast asleep. We were so at ease that even *I* was able to turn off my brain, lean my head against her short blonde hair, and fall asleep amongst the foliage.

Mary woke up about an hour later, and her lips grazing my forearm caused my eyes to flutter open.

"Come on," she whispered. "Don't say a word. Follow me."

Mary kissed me on the lips, lifted me off the tree, and guided me back uphill towards Clark Hall. At that moment, her pulchritude was unmatched. I'd follow Mary and her mirthful smile anywhere.

The pride of Elk City swung open the doors to Clark Hall and pranced towards her single dorm room at the end of the corridor. Mary fiddled with her keys for a moment before eventually creaking open the wooden door to reveal a room as distinctive as she was.

The area was pristine with the perfectly-made twin XL bed on the right-hand side of the room and a desk with two succulents on the left. Mary had well-watered sunflowers on the window sill, and her walls were lined with the Oklahoma state flag, an Oklahoma Sooners pennant, a poster of a herd of bison, and a picture of a teenaged, overall-clad Mary riding a John Deere tractor. Mary's sheets, blankets, and pillowcase were all white, and she kept a crimson and cream dreamcatcher on her bed-post. I had seen nicer and more expensive rooms than this in my life, but Mary's 100 square-foot sanctum was decorated so impeccably for someone with her personality. I simply adored it.

She took off my backpack and placed it neatly by her desk. Then Mary bent down and removed my shoes and socks. Neither one of us said a word. At this point, I noticed she was lightly shivering, so I stood her up and hugged tightly. Mary then removed my shirt.

"Wow." She said as she looked at what was once the most embarrassing part of my body.

Mary then kissed and licked my torso before directing me to the bed. She sat with her legs dangling as she unbuttoned and unzipped my jeans. They fell to the floor as I climbed on top of her nimble body. At this point, I noticed she was fully clothed, and I was wearing nothing but my boxers, so I took off the jersey she was still wearing and viewed her athletic body for the first time.

"You're so unbelievably beautiful, Mary."

Her shivering had actually increased at this point. Perhaps, we were truly in love with each other, and this moment was just that powerful to her. I then sat Mary up and kissed her cute thin lips before working my way down to her neck and bra. I reached around to unclasp her white undergarment when all of a sudden, a loud whimper stopped my impetus. I immediately paused, backed away, and crawled to the foot of the bed.

Mary was now bawling. Her perennially joyful demeanor instantly shifted to that of an inconsolable girl with tears racing down her face. I sat stupefied at the foot of the bed, wearing only my boxers. A light mucus began dripping down her previously enchanting gold nose ring. The little makeup she was wearing was now melting off of her face. Mary fanned her eyes to stop the tears, but there was nothing she could do. Her breathing was scattered, and she eventually had no choice but to use her beloved Sooners jersey as a rag for her watery eyes and snot-covered nostrils. I simply sat cross-legged at the foot of the bed, waiting to see what was wrong, and for some sort of sign I should comfort her. The two of us remained in this plaintive moment for three or four minutes straight until eventually Mary whispered:

"I'm so sorry."

"No. No. Don't be sorry at all...can I hug you?"

Mary nodded as she wiped the tears from her cheeks. I shimmied towards her and wrapped my sinewy arms around her shaking frame and rubbed the back of her head as she cried into my chest.

"I...I...don't know what to say," Mary shuddered.

"It's fine. I'm here to listen if you'd like. Otherwise, I can hold you or leave. I'll do whatever you want."

"Can you pass me my sweatshirt? It's in my top drawer over there."

I hopped off her bed, dressed myself, and found the grey hoodie. Mary covered up and laid her face on the pillow. I decided to keep my distance and continued to sit at the foot of her bed. Mary then placed a pillow over her head, yelped into it and kicked her feet in the air.

"I really like you." She said, removing the pillow from her mouth. "You know that?"

"I feel the same way about you."

"So," she wiped the final tears from beneath her grey eyes. "I've never told anyone this story before."

"I'm here to listen. I'll do whatever you want. I just want you to be happy."

"Thank you, Vincent. You're a great guy. Truly. I just started to like you so much, so quickly."

"I won't interrupt. Say whatever you need to."

"So, during my freshman year of high school, I was on the school's varsity swim team. My family had a creek leading to a pond on our property so I'd spent my whole life swimming. It was something I loved to do, and I seemed to be really good at it," Mary took a deep breath. "I was the only freshman to make the varsity team. I practiced for hours after school. I was competitive and always wanted to be the best swimmer in the county. My coach was very attentive and would give me pointers on how I could increase my butterfly speed or better my freestyle technique...About once a month, our team had away meets in Oklahoma City or Tulsa. The older girls were pretty cliquey, and I was usually left by myself on the bus, so my coach would sit next to me. On our November trip to Tulsa, all the girls paired off to room with one another, but since we had an odd number, I had no roommate. My coach didn't want me to sleep in a room by myself at my age, so he and I shared a room. I was just so naïve at the time."

Mary sniffled and wiped her eyes with her jersey again. She took three more deep breaths before continuing.

"I stayed with my coach, and he was, um, inappropriate with me. I had never even kissed a boy at that point, and my encounter with him scarred me. I don't really want to talk about what happened in there, but I quit the swim team right when I got off the bus back home. I never swam competitively again and never told my parents or anyone why. I entered a deep depression after that, but couldn't tell anyone because the coach was so beloved that everyone would hate me for saying something. They'd call me a liar...so I carried on with my life and avoided boys for years. I thought finally by college I'd be ready to move on with my life, but then when you took my shirt off, it all started rushing back to me. My mind was in that hotel room with my coach. I just couldn't or can't, or I don't know."

"Mary, words can't express how sorry I am. I'm here for you no matter what. If you want to get help, I'm here. Tell me whatever you need, and I'll do it."

"Can you just come here and give me a hug?"

I ascended towards the pillows and embraced Mary as tightly as I could. Her rheumy eyes drenched the collar of my shirt.

"I just don't think I'm ready to do anything sexual right now. I'm so sorry for wasting your time."

"Mary, please don't say that. You're not wasting my time. I love your personality, and I'm here for you. Whatever you may need. I'm not going anywhere. I'm here for the long haul."

Mary kissed my cheek as her jubilant smile had briefly returned.

"I love you," my poor girlfriend said as she stared into my blue eyes.

"I love you too."

"Can you still sleepover tonight? I don't want to be alone."

"Of course, darling. Anything for you."

Mary kissed me on the lips and let out a loud, cathartic sigh.

CHAPTER 3

THE FINAL SEVEN WEEKS OF my semester were mundane as my girl-friend's understandable melancholy led both of us into a per-petually lugubrious state. Mary and I would still watch Sooners games, hang out at the Mount Vernon Campus and explore different historical areas of Washington D.C., but our relationship had lost its luster. I felt inadequate as a boyfriend because I had no way to heal her years of pent-up agony, and I could tell from Mary's smile she suffered from daily thoughts of uselessness. She wanted to please me and prove to me that she loved me, but Mary's crestfallen psyche never allowed her to go beyond clothed kisses. I'd tell her not to worry and that I didn't need us to be sexual to be happy, but my girlfriend still felt culpable.

Without mentioning specific details, I talked to Izzy about Mary. My Criminal Justice partner-in-crime explained the best thing for both of us was to sever ties. If, for whatever reason, Mary is unable to engage physically, I was hurting her healing process by remaining in a relation-ship. Throughout our walks back to Thurston, Izzy said I was part of the problem because my actions were making Mary feel worse. I was apparently and accidentally increasing her feelings of inadequacy and triggering Mary somehow. It was a moral dilemma no inexperienced 19-year-old could handle. I was undoubtedly in a precarious position and was actually glad to be going home for winter break. I needed some time to process the direction of my life.

Mary cried as I hopped in my cab on the way to Union Station. She delivered a forceful and passionate kiss before telling me she loved me and would call me every day over our near four-week break. I really did love her and, at the same time, hated that bastard swimming coach with every fiber of my being.

When I arrived back at my apartment in New York, my father was thrilled to see me. He gave me a long hug and took my bags from my shoulders.

"I just had Nara clean the place," he said. "She only comes once a week these days, but does as good a job as ever."

"You seem chipper."

"Why wouldn't I be. My own flesh and blood is home."

"Where's Charleston?"

"He's spending the holidays at his new girlfriend's house in Chicago. They met at Northwestern."

"Good for him."

"How's your lady friend? She didn't want to come up here?"

"She's fine."

"Get changed. Let's go out to dinner. I want to discuss some business with you."

"Oh, is that where this new attitude is coming from? I thought it was just loneliness."

"There's that snark I missed."

"Where are we going? How nice should I be dressed?"

"Just down the street to Genesis. I'm not made of money anymore."

My father and I put on our hats and gloves and walked five blocks to one of the many Irish pubs on Second Avenue. I was genuinely anxious to see what kind of surprise my father had for me. Living alone in the city for the first time in over two decades may have finally caused him to snap.

The hostess sat us at a booth in the back of the drab pub, and the waitress brought over two glasses of water.

"What can I get you two to drink?"

"Water's fine," I said.

"What do you have on tap?"

My father picked up the candle on the table and motioned it towards the drinks menu while squinting.

"Bud, Bud Light, Goose—"

"Goose IPA is good," my father said.

The waitress disappeared to the bar as I began looking at the menu, knowing I'd get a plain bacon burger regardless of the many tantalizing entrees.

"So, how did classes finish up?"

"They were super easy. I actually got all flat A's."

"I knew you could do it. That's awesome, Vincent."

"Yeah, I mean, they're all intro courses, so it's not that big a deal."

"And the girlfriend is good? What's her name? Mary, right?"

"Yeah, we're chugging along. Mary from Oklahoma."

"What do her parents do?"

"They're farmers, I guess. Wheat."

"Jesus."

"Nice, Dad."

"I mean, I'm glad that she's shooting higher than that for a future."

"There's nothing wrong with farming, Dad. It's honorable work."

"Someone's gotta do it, I guess. That's capitalism for ya."

The waitress came back over to the table and took our orders. My father asked for a turkey burger, and I, a plain bacon burger.

"So, what's this opportunity, Dad?"

"Oh that. Right. Well...don't say no right away."

"I'm all ears."

"So, on a scale of 1-10, how's college treating you?"

"I dunno. 4.8."

"Listen, you only go to college once, and you shouldn't be having a 4.8 time at what's supposed to be the best few years of your life."

"Jesus, Dad. Can you get out of work mode and just talk to me, please?"

"Fine. If you're not having a tremendous time, you should at least try transferring. Right?"

"Oh...I mean...maybe."

"Listen, people are going to ask you where you went to school for the rest of your life. Let me give you a little cocktail party preview.

'So, Vincent, where'd you go to college?' 'GW.' 'Oh, well that's really something.'"

"Uh-huh."

"You know what happens when people ask me? 'So, Morgan, where'd you go to college?' 'The Wharton School of Business.' 'Isn't that the best business school in the US? Didn't Warren Buffett and Donald Trump go there?' 'Why yes they did.'"

"Go on," I said.

"If you transfer to a better school, guys will respect you, and girls in our social environment will be more attracted to you. You'll have higher earning potential. It's a no-brainer. At the very least, I need you to try. Worst case scenario, you get in somewhere and turn it down, right?"

"I guess so."

"I just want to open doors for you that wouldn't be there otherwise. You and I both know your mother would want you to go to an Ivy League school."

"You're being borderline manipulative. You know that?"

"Doesn't mean I'm wrong. So, will you at least give it a shot?"

"Um. I don't know."

"Come on. We're Beatties. We're decisive. Yes or no? Give it to me straight, boy."

"Yes, sir...but where will I apply? How do I apply?"

The waitress dropped off our burgers and fries. The woman was unaware she was in the presence of a Sabbaday Capital legend. My father was a salesman at heart, as persuasive as they come.

"How would you like to tell people you go to Harvard?"

"I mean—"

"Rub it in the faces of all those Verity guys that called you a loser and Verity girls who wouldn't go out with you?"

"I wouldn't phrase it like that..."

"Good, because I just did, son."

"How can I get into Harvard?"

"Simple. There's this guy at Credit Suisse that I have a great working relationship with. He's been doing trades with me and Sabbaday for 15 years. We've also been playing fantasy sports for a decade. He graduated from Harvard undergrad with a 3.85 in '01. Really bright kid. He's a third-generation legacy there, and his cousin works in admissions."

"Okay."

"I've been talking about you and Charleston for years, so he's very aware of your existence. I told him you're stuck at GW because of a horsesh—sorry...bad college counselor. He sympathized. He's known me for a long time and would do anything to help me out. I've been sort of a mentor to this guy for years. His name's Edwin Duckworth. Great guy."

"Sounds pretty promising."

"Vincent. I think it's close to a mortal lock. All you gotta do is meet with this guy over break, then fill out the Common App, write a few supplemental essays and get two recommendations."

"Should I apply anywhere else?"

"No need. If you want to go to Harvard, I'll set this meeting up, and if you nail it, you're a lock. Duckie will take care of you. I promise."

"Why didn't we do this senior year?"

"'Cause you would've said 'no'. You'd want to get in on your own merits, and all that bs immature kids say. Twenty years from now, no one is going to ask how you got into Harvard, they'll only ask how you can help them."

"At the very least, it's worth a shot. I'm not gonna say no to opening more doors for myself."

I took a bite out of my burger and thought about myself as a Harvard graduate. My bellicose father was right. The Verity and Hollandsworth reunions would be a lot more enticing if I were a Harvard graduate.

"The application stuff is just a formality. Just make him like you and you're golden...to tell you the truth, I'm very excited for you. So few people get second chance opportunities like this."

"I don't really know how to feel right now. But...thank you. Just, thank you for thinking of me. This could be really good, Dad."

"I know Vincent. And look, it's not like it's not without merit. I mean, you have a 4.0 after your first semester. You're a great applicant. This is just one of the perks to our lifestyle."

The week after New Year's, I met with Edwin Duckworth at the New York Athletic Club. It was a Saturday afternoon, and Edwin didn't have much time because he had a squash lesson in 15 minutes. That was perfectly sufficient since I was still one to avoid long conversations with strangers whenever possible.

Edwin asked me about Hollandsworth, Verity, and GW and told a war story about my father helping him break into the industry some 14 years ago. Edwin then discussed his time within the secret "Tome and Marrow Club" at Harvard and told me he could get me in no problem. His final question was about what industry I wanted to work in, and finance seemed like the logical answer, so I went with that. I told Edwin I wanted to work with collateralized loan obligations at one of the big firms.

After 13 minutes and one scotch between us, the endeavor came to a close, and Edwin said:

"This went great. I'll see what I can do."

He went off to his squash lesson, and I walked back to our apartment. It was mostly stress-free, but I knew I had several more steps to go.

That night, my father congratulated me on a job well done and then told me to take the toughest freshmen courses GW had to offer to improve my standing as a transfer student. I obliged and spent the majority of the night adjusting my course load so it was more aesthetically pleasing for any director of admissions.

The other matter on my mind was the marvelous Mary Huber. My girlfriend was true to her word and called me every night over the break. They were brief three-minute conversations about our days, but I always looked forward to them. I had missed Mary's dulcet tones and was especially excited to see her exuberant face and genuine smile upon my return.

On my train ride back to D.C. in mid-January, I realized I couldn't tell her or anyone else I was transferring. Mary was already in a desolate mood, and the last idea that needed to creep into her fragile ethos was her one steady partner was going to maroon her. Besides, there was a chance I didn't get into Harvard. I'd hate to make Mary worry about something all for naught. Also, I wouldn't break up with her even if I was accepted. I loved Mary. Long-distance relationships work out plenty of times if the couples are truly infatuated. My misfortunate girlfriend and I didn't have to break-up just because I may be studying elsewhere. We were the strongest freshmen couple I knew.

CHAPTER 4

MARY BROKE UP WITH ME within our first week back at school. To say I was blindsided would be a severe understatement. Our starry relationship turned into a supernova I truly never saw approaching.

The semester had begun as expected with a heavier workload and Mary inviting me to come sleepover at her dorm on the Mount Vernon Campus on the weekend of January 26th. I was overjoyed to see her and spent the entire shuttle ride daydreaming about peering at her effervescent face for the first time in over a month. Mary wasn't the same jocose girl from our September ice cream date, but she and I had grown together, and I loved her now more than ever.

I hopped off the shuttle and sprinted to Clark Hall, where my seemingly weary girlfriend had a look of consternation hidden beneath her unflappable smile.

"Vincent, I missed you so much."

Mary leaped into my arms and kissed me with the power that can only be born from a lengthy absence.

"I missed you too."

Mary led me to her dorm room, removed my North Face from my shoulders, and cuddled next to me on her bed. My girlfriend then stood after a few moments, retreated to the closet, closed the door, and then re-entered wearing white, flannel pajamas. She then nuzzled her backside against my body and closed her eyes.

"Did you have a wonderful break, Vincent?"

"Yeah, it was great seeing my dad again. But I couldn't stop thinking about you. How was home after the recurrence of...you know?"

"It was...I don't know. I was apathetic to it all. I feel more comfortable away from there. As you can imagine."

"So, what are our plans for tonight?" I said while stroking her short hair from behind.

"Can you turn off the lights and tell me a story?"

"What do you mean? It's only 8:30."

"I'm tired," she shivered. "Just spoon with me and tell me a story until I fall asleep...please Vincent?"

I propped up her pillow, took off my sweatshirt, and cuddled between Mary and the dorm room wall. I kissed the back of her neck and said:

"Okay. And you want something true, or should I make it up?"

"Anything you'd like Vincent. I just want to hear your voice. Nothing soothes me more."

I paused for a second as my mind began concocting a mythical tale.

"Once upon a time, a girl named Mary washed ashore on a deserted island in the Mediterranean. She had taken a cruise ship from Istanbul to Sardinia that was sucked into an invisible whirlpool south of Sicily. The young maiden was the ship's sole survivor. Now alone on the island, Mary felt hopeless. There were no houses or people, and she was fearful of being alone. By the third day, Mary was starving, dehydrated, and forlorn. However, just as she was ready to give up, a black unicorn with a mane made of fire rose up from the sea and stood before her. 'Don't despair,' the deep-voiced gelding neighed..."

I paused as Mary was lightly cooing.

"Mary," I whispered. "Are you awake?"

She was fast asleep. My peaceful girlfriend missed out on the story's glorious climax and laid still as I stared at the ceiling.

The following morning, it was Mary who was checking to see if I was awake. My thoughtful girlfriend pressed her lips against my forehead and stood with her arms akimbo. Mary was still wearing her flannel pajamas.

"Vincent? Are you awake?"

"Good morning, beautiful."

"Vincent, we need to take some time apart."

"I'm sorry. What?" I rose to my feet and wiped my eyes. "What do you mean?"

"I thought about it all throughout winter break and decided that we're both better off without each other."

"What? No. Not at all. I love you, and you love me."

"I do, Vincent. With all my heart. But I can't be the girl you fell in love with. I need to be by myself. I need solitude."

"Mary, don't do this. I need you."

"Vincent, darling, this is about me trying to find closure. If you love me, you'll let me figure this out on my own. I need to meditate and travel and sleep and just do everything by myself from now on."

"That's not good for you."

"Vincent, I've been thinking about this for weeks, and we're both dragging each other down. I'll never be good enough for you. Not in my current state anyway."

"You're perfect just the way you are," tears welled up in my eyes.

"No, I'm not. I'm sad. I'm selfish. I'm lonely. I'm irritable and agitated. Around you, I have to pretend to be someone I'm not. I feel like I need to hide how I'm feeling to be your perfect girlfriend."

"No, you don't. Just be yourself. P-please Mary."

"Vincent, you have no idea how hard this was for me. But it needs to be done. I need some time alone...but maybe...maybe one day in the future, we can meet again. I'll never forget you."

I wiped the tears from my eyes, gave Mary a constricting hug, and left the room. Now that Criminal Justice ended and we lived on separate campuses, Mary and I wouldn't run into each other anymore. I also wasn't going to bother her if she so desperately needed space. I truly wanted what was best for her. Mary Huber was a sensational woman and could've been my wife in a different universe. Had it not been for a few innocuous butterfly wing flaps, Mary and I may have ended up married one day. Our relationship only lasted four months, but at times it was euphoric. There was never a moment of ennui around the miraculous Mary Huber. Sure, I could've fought for her. I could've tried to make her love me, but she deserved whatever she wanted. I was at my happiest whenever I could see her smile.

Aside from two texts exchanged over the next three months, Mary Huber and I never spoke again. It's one of my five greatest regrets in life. I'd like to think I'll check in with her in the future, but I know myself better than that.

I spent the following 10 weeks moping as I was wont to do. I was now taking six challenging courses and spent most of my nights alone in the Thurston basement learning about Geomorphology or Biomimicry. By mid-February, I had submitted all of my application materials to Harvard and was now anxiously awaiting a positive response. At this point, I was desperate to leave GW. It no longer had anything to do with the lack of academically stimulating courses or the school's solid but unspectacular reputation. The crux of the issue was simply my daily morale. It no longer vacillated from gleeful to lackadaisical. By March of 2013, my mood swung from clinically depressed to barely treading water. I no longer knew of a way to ameliorate my happiness when it decreased to unhealthy levels. I never did succumb to drugs like my poor mother, though. Instead, I chose to take cathartic field trips throughout Washington D.C. as my self-prescribed version of therapy.

For example, one Saturday morning in late-March, I dressed in jeans and a sweatshirt and left my dorm room. I had no direction nor destination. I simply walked down F Street and followed the street signs and stoplights. Whichever way the cars weren't driving was where I'd walk. This continued for about a mile until I stumbled into a subway station. I elected to ride in the first car that passed through and would exit whenever I felt like it. I was finally in control of my actions, and it was lustral.

By late morning, I exited the subway and happened to be in the Friendship Heights neighborhood. I had never been anywhere near there before and just wandered. It was the physical equivalent to free association. Eventually I saw a small park, laid on a bench, and fell asleep for half an hour.

Upon waking, I strolled down an unknown street until I saw a movie theater. I decided to see *Oz: The Great and Powerful*. It was an adequate film as I always found James Franco to be entertaining. However, after exiting, I decided there was no reason not to see a double-feature, so I walked into Tina Fey and Paul Rudd's *Admission* without paying.

Finally, after four hours of mediocre movie watching, I exited the building and made my way back to campus. It was one of my most indelible days of the second semester. I was able to unwind completely. I didn't need to talk to anyone or focus on any of my life's innumerable problems. As the semester progressed, every weekend, I'd walk around the D.C. metro area for hours at a time, never telling anyone where I was going or what I was doing. One Saturday, it was a trip to Georgetown; the next, it was a monuments tour; and then in April, I'd go to Nationals baseball games by myself. I'd do anything to avoid that possessed campus and decided I was leaving after my freshman year, whether I was accepted into Harvard or not.

On Saturday, April 20th, I returned to my dorm after an eight-hour jaunt around the city. Rather than opening the door to my dispirited room and collapsing onto my bed as per usual, this time, Kai and Izzy greeted me. The two of them were seated in chairs and facing the door in some sort of pathetic, two-person intervention.

"Vincent, can we talk?" Kai said.

"What's this about?" Without another chair in the room, I laid flat across the floor.

"Just trying to have a little chat," Izzy added. "Want to see where your head's at."

They pulled their chairs closer to me, as I looked straight upwards.

"Guys, I'm fine."

"No, you're not," My roommate said. "You're never around anymore. You don't talk to anyone. You're like a ghost."

"Don't be so melodramatic. I just got dumped. I'm taking six courses. I'm really stressed out. I gotta unwind somehow."

"Why are you taking six courses? Just drop one if you're stressed," Izzy said.

"I can't. I, uh, need to have a great transcript."

"Why," Kai said. "We're freshmen. You have like, years to figure out a career path and take tough courses."

I stood from my coffin-like position; deciding now was the appropriate time to tell them.

"You guys...I'm, uh..."

"Did you get Mary pregnant? Is that why you two broke up?" Izzy asked.

"Maybe you should just let me finish."

The room was perfectly still in anticipation of my momentous announcement.

"I'm, uh, transferring."

My curt comment temporarily benumbed my two friends. There was no correct way to tell someone this, nor was there a textbook reaction. It's a rare situation none of us had encountered before.

"How can you do this to me? We were going to room together next year. We were gonna live at one of the dorms near the Whole Foods. How long have you known about this?"

"Is this why Mary broke up with you after break? Because you told her this?"

"Guys, come on. Look at this from my point of view. This isn't the right school for me. I've been walking around sedated for the past few months. Yeah, Kai, we could've roomed together, but there are plenty of other guys you can room with. And, Izzy, Mary still has no idea I'm leaving. I haven't spoken to her in weeks."

"Where are you gonna go?" Izzy asked.

Kai stood up, took a deep breath, and left the room without saying a word.

"God, that's a little dramatic. He and I didn't even hang out that much."

"You should've told us, Vincent."

"I'm telling you now. What's the difference between telling you in January versus April?"

"I don't know. It just feels like you were lying all this time. Where are you going?"

"I haven't heard back yet."

"Oh, so you may not even be leaving?"

"No, I'm definitely leaving. I'd rather take a gap year and re-apply than come back here."

I sat in Kai's evacuated chair and turned to face Izzy.

"I'm sorry. You don't even know me that well, and you're getting dragged into this. I just, I don't know, I'm always like restless and pro-pulsive, I guess. I mean, I'm one of those people who can never just sit back and be happy. And it sucks. Trust me."

"You're just growing up, Vincent. This will all clear itself up in a few years. And look, wherever you wind up, we can still meet over the breaks."

"Thank you. I'd love that. I think you've got a really promising future. You're too good for this school too."

"I appreciate that, but I like it here. I have friends, and the courses are interesting to me. I like living in the city and being surrounded by politics. I mean, I got to stand outside the White House on the night Obama was re-elected. How many other college kids can say that?"

"We have different priorities, I guess."

"Wherever you wind up going, just don't be so closed-off. Can you do that for me?"

"You know I can't promise that. An okapi can't change its stripes."

"What?"

"Nothing. I just mean, I can't be perfidious to myself. I'm...an acquired taste. Plenty of people aren't going to like me, and I've come to grips with that. But I think I like who I am."

"I never doubted that," Izzy laughed. "Come here."
She stood and embraced me.
"Whatever happens, I'll miss ya, dude."
"Good luck with everything. I'm sure I'll see you again."

I arrived back in Manhattan in mid-May and was accepted into Harvard two weeks later. I texted my father, Charleston, Austin, Mary, and Izzy the news. I was actually distraught by how few people I had in my life. If other rising sophomores were going through this same situation, they may have had 40 or 300 people to tell. This imaginary person might receive congratulatory texts from complete strangers. Me? I wasn't even able to receive a hug from my own mother. Of the five people I did tell, Mary ignored me; Austin and Izzy sent heartfelt, two-sentence texts; and my somewhat insouciant family members surprisingly decided to call me.

Charleston's call was brief but meaningful. He seemed distraught we hadn't been in contact very frequently.

"Vincent. That's unbelievably fantastic news," Charleston said over the phone. "I'm so proud of you. We all are."

"Thanks, Charleston."

"It's really well-deserved. We all know how hard you work. I know Dad's friend helped you out, but that doesn't take away from the accomplishment."

I didn't love that mordacious comment, but the rest of the call was quite positive.

"Yeah, even though Dad had told me it could happen, I still couldn't believe it when I opened the envelope. I mean, I'm going to Harvard. How insane is that?"

"Seriously. Mom would be so proud of you. We should speak again soon."

"Thanks. And hey, when are you coming to the east coast?"

"Not for a while. Dad helped me get an internship at this Chicago hedge fund called Steep Rock."

"So, you're doing finance stuff then?"

"Yeah, seems that way...well anyway, sorry. I gotta go. My girlfriend's calling me. But congrats again and talk soon."

About five minutes later, once I had nestled my body into the soft couch cushions of Apartment 4D, my father called.

"Vincent. Congratulations. This is huge news for you and the whole family. Really, really fantastic."

"Thanks Dad."

"But listen. I don't want you to think you can coast from here on out. This is pedal to the metal time. You have to work harder and be smarter than as many people as you can. Sure, a 3.92 GPA at GW is fine, but Harvard's a different animal. Look, making friends and being social is all well and good, but how many people from college will you realistically speak to five years later?"

"This took a weird turn. I appreciate your congratulations."

"Stop it. Let's stay serious for a second. I want you in the library on some Friday and Saturday nights. Can't have another party animal son."

"What did Charleston do?"

"No, he's lollygagging. 3.12 GPA. I had to beg a guy to give him a summer internship in Chicago. Kid's living the frat life a little too hard, and I'm paying his fraternity dues. I swear you two suck me dry just like your mother."

"So, Dad, I got into Harvard..."

"Yeah, yeah. Don't give me the whole sad sack routine. I'm just making sure your head is in the right place before I drive you to Cambridge."

"Yeah, I got it Dad. Jesus Christ."

"Proud of you, son. Always a pleasure."

So, overall, my family and friends were quite pleased with my remarkable achievement. But I still had a few summer months before fall orientation, so I needed to find ways to fill my empty summer schedule.

For years, my summers had been uninspired, and this one was no different. I continued to work out four days a week, hung out and played video games with Austin once a week, grabbed Shake Shack, and chatted with Izzy each month and wrote reviews for Dutch's Angle. I wrote

12 throughout the summer with the below being a quick rundown of my review's ratings:

The Great Gatsby 8.9
Pain and Gain —7.8
Monsters University —7.7
Now You See Me —6.1
World War Z —6.1
The Purge —6.0
Man of Steel — 5.6
Lee Daniels' The Butler — 5.6
The Heat —5.0
This is the End 4.8
The Hangover Part III —4.4
Grown Ups 2 —1.5

Other than that, it was a monotonous summer leading up to what would surely be an all-time stressful school year. In the final days before the drive to Harvard, I replenished my wardrobe with J. Crew's newest fall line and splurged on a pair of royal blue, leather Yves Saint-Laurent sneakers with some of the money I'd earned from my writing gig. I then bought new sheets and blankets at Bed Bath & Beyond because I wanted a fresh start prior to my sophomore year. The last week of August, my father drove me up, helped unpack my clothes and bedding, and then left me to fend for myself as the Cambridge vultures were sure to gobble up my carcass.

CHAPTER 5

I WAS PLACED IN DUNSTER House, which didn't elicit any sort of reaction. I'm sure plenty of Harvard students, and frankly young adults everywhere, are frantic about housing, but I just needed four walls and a ceiling. Whether the room had 80 square feet or 130 was irrelevant. The one caveat I had was I desperately wanted to live in a single. I remember thinking I'd be content living the next 10 years of my life without a roommate to smirch my living quarters. I hated the whole concept of having to focus on the whereabouts of my roommate, and when I can and can't bring a female companion over; and when I can turn the lights off; and where my clothes and TV could go; it was all undesired tensity. Therefore, the moment I found out I was indeed living in a single dorm room, was among my three happiest of 2013.

I enrolled in five courses: Introductory Fiction Writing, Literary Arrivals, Principles of Economics, Acting and Authenticity, and Film Directing: From Script to Screen. It wasn't a particularly daunting schedule, but I was striving to begin my Harvard tenure with a GPA north of 3.5, if possible.

Unsurprisingly as it turns out, my coursework shouldn't have been my primary concern. Throughout my life, I had developed a predilection for routines and had always taken solace in knowing what I'd be doing at exact moments of the day. Now at Dunster, I had taken this to an entirely new level. To aid in my daily efficiency, I made several modest changes to improve the life I'd lived in D.C.

The first notable adjustment was my gym routine. Even by my sophomore year, I was still married to my quad-weekly workouts, but they had lost their patina over time. I believed a simple alteration was necessary. So, while my father was still on campus on day one, he drove me to a Medford Dick's Sporting Goods, and I purchased several weights with my own money. These included pairs of 25, 35, and 45-pound dumbbells, and an ab curler. In D.C., I had grown tired of the 33-minute walking commute to and from Thurston Hall and the Lerner Gym. Rather than wasting over two hours a week traveling, my Harvard plan involved me working out in my own dorm room. My father acquiesced and helped me carry the weights inside Dunster.

However, given my lack of online research, I neglected to discover Dunster, and actually all of the Harvard houses I could've lived in, each had workout spaces within their buildings. My father chastised me for wasting hundreds of dollars, but partially due to my stentorian stubbornness, I elected not to return the weights. In my eyes, I would've rather lifted in my sub-100 square foot single by myself while watching films on Netflix, than have to interact with strangers in the Dunster gym. Thus, my new routine was born.

Four mornings a week, I'd roll out of bed and lift, wearing nothing but my boxers. Over time, it also saved on laundry costs. Additionally, these weights could very well last for over a decade, and I wouldn't need a gym membership post-college. I was losing out on various leg lifts, bench press, and squatting, but we all have to make sacrifices for the sake of convenience. The only non-dorm related exercise I did was a Saturday and Sunday three-mile run down by the Charles River. After the first few weeks of my new regimen, I no longer felt a disinclination to lift.

To this end and somewhat regretfully, my conversations with other Harvard students were nearly non-existent. Now at an Ivy League college, I chose to sit in the front row or next to the professor in every course. I believed there was a direct correlation in GPA based upon where one sat and wasn't going to allow a benighted seat choice affect the most important classes of my life.

My sophomoric regression towards recluse affected me outside the classroom as well. I never surpassed small talk with other students in Dunster and didn't choose to initiate conversations before and after classes with my neighbors. Would I have wanted friends or a girlfriend? Sure. But I found solace in knowing I only needed to worry about myself.

On an average September or October day, for example, I'd work out in my dorm room while watching *A Man for All Seasons* (1966), *All the Kings Men* (1949), or *Eyes Wide Shut* (1999). I'd then shower in the shudder-inducing communal bathrooms and head to my daily classes. By the afternoon, I'd study or complete homework assignments in Widener Library, before gallivanting around Harvard Square looking for cheap, low-calorie dinner options. At nightfall, I'd retire to Dunster, play a game or two of the latest *Madden,* and then study for an hour or two before sleeping. Once a week, I'd travel to Davis Square or Boston Common to wander around, see a movie, or even just to explore the neighborhoods and doze off on a park bench. I also made sure to keep up with my Dutch's Angle blogging. All in all, it wasn't a thrilling routine by any means, but I didn't feel I had a lot of room for adaptation.

On Friday, November 8th, I elected to take the Northeast Regional back to Manhattan for a three-day break. The Wednesday before, I had spent my 20th birthday doing nothing noteworthy and felt particularly depressed by how few people had reached out to wish me well. I received calls from my father, brother, and Austin, along with a few meaning-less "Hbd" Facebook birthday posts on my wall, but overall, I was disap-pointed. I wasn't expecting a flood of caring messages, but every birth-day one needs to take stock of their life, and mine was stagnant. I was obtaining an Ivy League education, but nothing else in my life provided any excitement. I felt a return home and a celebratory birthday with my father might've been just the event I needed to kickstart my dull existence.

Upon arriving at 4D, I was blindsided by a pernicious purple orchid staring back at me. There was only one person I knew who would make that garish of a purchase for me. The card read:

"Dear Vincent, Wishing you the happiest of birthdays! Love always, Devi"

There also happened to be fire-engine red lipstick in the form of a kiss gracing the bone-white card. I didn't know why Devi was reaching out or what she wanted, but I remember it instantly annoying me. I had long since moved on and wanted to live a happy, drama-free life. The last thing I needed was this virulent plutocrat slithering her way back into my heart. I walked the orchid out to the fourth-floor hallway's garbage chute and dumped the whole pot and plant down with the rest of the building's trash.

However, throughout the next few hours and dinner with my father, I couldn't get Devi's tell-tale heart out of my head. I was visibly shaken as my father and I sat at J.G. Melon. We each ordered burgers and fries, and he was cordial and complimentary, but it didn't matter. There Devi was at the forefront of my mind. It had taken multiple years, two schools, and a failed relationship to rid myself of the pythoness' spell. I was exasperated, frenzied, and sickly, all at once. What was Devi's endgame here? I had deleted her from Facebook, BBM, and text, and that witch had figured out the one final way to contact me. I was sure Devi must've been single if she was reaching out like this. And with a purple orchid no less. I wondered what Devi looked like, though. She was now a high school senior, and I could've postulated she'd aged well. I just had to figure out some way to get her out of my mind. That one simple gesture from that vituperative little girl could alter not only my weekend in Manhattan but my entire semester.

After dinner, I adjourned to my shower as my father booed the Knicks from the other room. An ugly monsoon was forming in my fragile mind and picking up speed. After several months of avoiding interaction with people my age, this unforeseen interruption was leaving me unhinged.

I exited the shower, logged onto my computer, and clicked my ESPN bookmark. However, as I was attempting to unwind, I received an unwelcome Facebook message from my old pal Tessa.

T: Hey! Do you know when the early decision deadline is at GW?
V: Oh, hey. Yeah, it passed on November 1st. Sorry.
T: No worries. By the way, guess who I have sitting next to me?
V: Uh oh...
T: Hey Vincent, it's Devi. I figured u would come home for ur birthday. Did you like the orchid?
V: Threw it straight down the garbage chute.
D: Wow. Why? It wasn't free you know.
V: Look, I don't want anything to do with you. Please don't contact me.
D: I heard about Harvard. That's huge babes! You deserve it!
V: What do you want from me? I don't have anything left to give or say to you.
D: I'm just trying to be cordial.
V: Devi, I'm serious. I'm like one more message away from blocking Tessa.
D: Okay. Okay. I just miss you. That's all. I miss you so much. Don't you miss me a little?
V: Please don't do this.
D: Wait. Before you block Tessa, I have an offer for you.
V: Okay...
D: I'm not sure you heard, but my whole family moved out of the country when I turned 18.
V: I hadn't heard.
D: My father had a job opportunity, and they didn't feel it made sense to take me out of school when I was so close to graduating.
V: What's your point?
D: I live alone at the penthouse now. I remember how much you loved my apartment. I thought maybe you could come over tonight and take a look. Are you in the city?

V: I'm in the city.

D: It's just Tessa and me right now but she needs to leave soon and I get lonely.

D: And horny...

D: Vincent? Okapi? Would you like to come over? I miss your body, babes. I'm like craving you so badly.

V: How soon should I be there?

D: As fast as humanly possible...

A decade of social turbulence had severely affected my brain's ability to reason. Devi caught me at a moment of weakness, and I made a snap decision. But the execrable choices didn't end there and that night, unfortunately.

I put on skinny black jeans and an orange sweater Devi had bought me when we first became official. Next came the gel-based serum to eliminate the frizziness of my wavy, dark brown hair. And finally, I told my father I was leaving, although refused to tell him where out of sheer embarrassment.

During the walk over to the palatial York penthouse, I put in my headphones and played my favorite song at the time, "Power Trip" by J. Cole.

The walk to 79th and York was the most joyous moment I had had in the entirety of 2013. I thought about Devi's black hair, parted just left of center. Memories of her sandalwood and Argan Oil scent and her perfectly symmetrical face. Devi's svelte figure and supercilious fashion sense came rushing back to the forefront of my mind. Her salient military green Moncler jacket, navy Hermès Clic H Bracelet, gold Van Cleef earrings, and clover necklace all returned from the hidden penthouse in the deep recesses of my brain. Devi, my effervescent royal, wanted to see me. She was craving me. The exotic-looking minx was back in my life, and there was no hesitation I *needed* to see her. I missed her lithe body and had this licentious desire to see her nude once again.

I entered the elevator and surprised myself as my fingers remembered the door code: 698140.

"Vincent! Come to my bedroom this second," Devi's screechy voice yelled at the top of her lungs.

I raced down the never-ending corridor and burst through her bedroom door. Devi instantly leaped onto my torso, latched her arms and legs around me, and ferociously attacked. Her fire-engine red lipstick painted my face and neck, while my overly aggressive biting left fast-forming hickeys on her recently lotioned skin. Our carnal desires had completely taken over, and we didn't stop touching each other until we were interrupted by someone's throat clearing.

"Hey Vincent." It was Tessa.

"Oh. I didn't see you."

Tessa had apparently been sitting at Devi's desk chair alternating between watching us and texting on her phone.

"Tessa, how's life?"

"I'm fine. Don't let me bother you guys."

"Tessa," Devi's shrill voice hadn't improved. "You're leaving now, right? You like, got what you came here to see?"

Tessa, clad in a white undershirt and black leggings, strutted over to the bed and laid across the purple, magenta, and cornsilk duvet.

"I have an idea," she said.

At this point, I couldn't stop staring at Devi. She was still as fit as ever and now bustier. Devi's black hair was wavier that fall, and she was dressed in a more promiscuous manner than I was used to. My ex was wearing all black lingerie with garters, and an untied white and emerald kimono draped across her shoulders. I was more attracted to her that night than I'd ever been.

"Why don't we just have a three-way?" Tessa said with a smirk.

"Tessa, I love you, girl, but you need to leave now."

"Jk. Fine. I'll leave you two lovebirds alone."

Tessa picked up her accoutrements, blew Devi a kiss, and exited the penthouse. I then went to pounce on Devi, but she stopped me.

"Not yet babes. I've got a plan."

"What? Why? Now?"

"Let's get like, a really chic hotel room. One hundred percent on me."

"Why? Your apartment is way nicer than any hotel."

"I want my first time to be special. Like truly unique."

I laughed and shook my head. I was lost in a nebulous, dream-like oblivion and couldn't shake this lengthy lapse of interminable surprises.

"First time? You mean, you haven't?"

"No way. I was dead set on you being my first. No one could get in my way. Not even you."

"That's...really hot. I think."

"We're only halfway through my elaborate plan, babes."

"Well, what's the rest?"

"Shush. Come watch me get changed," my ex-girlfriend said. "But don't you dare touch your prize."

I followed Devi into her walk-in closet. At that point, she could've led me off a cliff. My ex had another outfit hanging, with a Bluetooth speaker right next to it. Devi pressed play as "Habits (Stay High)" by Tove Lo began to play. My ex was slowly removing her lingerie right in front of me as the Swedish seductress crooned.

The kimono fell to the floor. Devi's precise moves and hand gestures could only be emulated by someone with an impressive dance background. My ex was biting her lip, running her long fingers down her flat stomach, and then briefly flashed her brown nipples. I stood there, mystified. This was the same place where I had once hidden from her father years ago, and now all of our qualms had magically disappeared. It was a celestial series of moments, and I would've happily stayed in that dorm room-sized closet with Devi for the rest of my life.

"That's all for now," she said. "Now, I have to put on my shirt."

"No, please. No shirt."

"Babes, there's way more where this came from."

Devi then put on one of my old white button-downs she must've stolen, although I had no recollection of when that could've been. Then, she covered her silky, almond legs with baggy Adidas sweatpants.

"Keep watching," she said.

"You couldn't pay me to look away."

Devi kicked over a pair of black boots.

"Get on your knees and put these on me. Now."

I dropped down, kissed the tops of her feet, and placed them inside the shoes.

"Grab my jacket babes. It's by my door."

I found the fabled military green Moncler Jacket and returned to the closet.

"Oops," Devi said as she flashed her backside towards me.

"Wherever we're going," I said. "Let's leave right now."

Devi nodded, exited the closet, and cackled as I spanked her firm behind.

"By the way, look what I brought."

Devi revealed a box of condoms on the inside of her black Chanel purse.

I placed my hands on my ex-girlfriend's slender cheeks and kissed her.

Unfortunately, the next hour or so didn't go as Devi had planned. After leaving the house, we took a taxi to The Palace Hotel, but they didn't have any rooms available for that night. Initially, I was surprised the conniving Devi had concocted this intricate plan and yet hadn't booked a room, but then I remembered as of an hour prior, I'd hated her.

Next, we walked to the Plaza Hotel, but they were also booked for the night. It was 10:30 pm at this point, so she shouldn't have been shocked.

"Devi," I said as we dejectedly held hands down Fifth Avenue. "Let's just go to a cheaper place. There's a Marriott on the Upper East Side. I'm sure we could get a room there."

"No," she shouted at me. "The night has to be perfect. We're not going to some fleabag Marriott."

"Jeez, okay. Whatever you say."

Our final stop was a lengthy taxi ride to the Standard Hotel on 13th and Washington. At this point, I would've gone anywhere, but Devi was dead set on finding a perfect location. Upon arriving, we sped through the lobby towards the receptionist.

"No, you wait here," Devi said. "I'll take care of this."

I stopped 20 feet away from the front desk and listened acutely to Devi's whispered shrieks.

"You don't have a single room available?" Devi said to the woman behind the counter.

"No ma'am."

Devi looked reasonably disheveled at this point. She was wearing a men's collared shirt, sweatpants, and her lingerie could be seen if viewed under the right lighting.

"Listen, my boyfriend and I only need it for an hour or two. Isn't there some kind of deal we can work out?"

"No ma'am. I'm going to have to ask you to leave."

"Name a dollar amount and I will pay it."

"Ma'am, we're fully booked."

Devi trudged back towards me, scuffing her boots against the recently waxed lobby floor.

"You know what, we're going back to my place," my ex said. "All I need is you. I don't need some pathetic hotel room."

My ex and I found yet another taxi that she paid for, and we embarked almost 100 blocks back uptown. She leaned her recently Oribe-shampooed hair against my shoulder.

"Vincent, are you having a good time?"

"Of course I am Devi. Don't worry about me."

Devi then straddled me in the filthy taxi and ravaged my lips once again. My ex slowly grinded back and forth against my jeans while softly moaning for 20 seconds before hopping off and retreating back to her side of the cab.

"That was just a little taste for you. Wait until we do it without clothes."

The cab driver looked back at Devi through the rearview mirror.

Eventually, my ex-girlfriend and I burst through her penthouse door, and she demanded I carry her.

"Take me to my sister's room. The lighting's better in there."

I carried Devi where she directed and gently laid her on the queen-sized bed in the smaller but still gargantuan bedroom.

"What would you like now, Devi? I want to make sure you're as comfortable as possible."

"Don't. I don't want nice guy Vincent. Be aggressive and forceful, and take what's yours."

"Are you sure that's a good idea?"

Devi turned onto her stomach as I was still standing off the side of the bed. She somehow managed to unzip my jean zipper using nothing but her teeth.

"Now take off your shirt," Devi said.

I obliged.

"OMG. How have you gotten even hotter?"

"So have you."

"Shush. Don't speak anymore. I just want to admire you."

Devi ripped off my pants and boxers and reached for a condom from her purse. She fiddled with it for a few seconds before opening the wrapper.

"I missed this guy," she said. "Now, tear off my clothes."

In one fell swoop, I ripped open her button-down, took off her boots, and threw the Adidas sweatpants to the ground. Then I undid her garters and removed her sexy black lingerie so that we were now both fully nude and lying on her younger sister's bed.

"Are you ready?" I asked.

"Be gentle," she squeaked.

"Of course."

After a tricky 20 minutes, Devi exited her sister's bed and squirmed towards the bathroom.

"I'll meet you in the living room, babes."

I nodded, glanced at the garnet stain on the satin sheets, and made my way to the large, airy room at the center of the penthouse. I picked up my pants on my way out and sat shirtless and sweaty beneath a knitted blanket on the living room's olive sofa. I then thought about how

Devi had never been even an above-average girlfriend, and there was no denying our discordant personalities. A portion of me certainly felt an ignominious mortification. And yet, I also felt relief. Not just for me, but for Devi. Our equally obfuscating sexual histories were now steadying. After years of swaying atop white caps, through torrential downpours and tsunamic winds, Devi and I had finally found a tranquil water in which to float. As vital as that night was for me, it must've weighed eight times heavier on Devi's delicate shoulders.

"Hello, lovebird," Devi said as she entered the pitch-black living room.

My ex wore a clean pair of black lace underwear with nothing on top.

"Mind if I squeeze in here?" My ex said as she glided across the sofa and beneath the blanket.

I placed my arm around her as we stared upwards. The floor-to-ceiling windows were transparent as the drapes were drawn to reveal the mostly quiet Upper East Side.

"Vincent, I love you."

I kissed the top of her head.

"Didn't you hear what I said okapi? I love you."

"Devi please. We've had a spectacular night. Let's not dwell on the past."

"You don't love me?"

"I just need time to process all of this. Can we please talk about something else?"

Devi kissed my cheek.

"Put your hands on my boobs."

"Okay."

"Much better," Devi said. "You know, I've changed a lot since you last saw me."

"I can tell," I said as I ran my fingers along her chest.

"What do you think our future holds?"

"I don't have the slightest clue. A few hours ago, I hated you."

"I like, hated you for a long time too. Just so you know."

"Here's what I think. There are two endings to this story."

"Okay, I'm interested, babes."

"We're either going to get married or at some point, we'll never speak again."

Devi pushed my hands off of her and shifted her body a few inches to her left.

"Don't say that."

"I'm always honest with you."

"I never want to get married to anyone."

"Well, what makes you say that?"

"I just want to be free. I never want someone telling me what to do, you know?"

"You're looking at marriage from a pessimistic perspective. Marriage isn't about two people telling each other what to do all the time. To me, it's about two people striving to make their partner's life and their own as perfect as can be. Some days, that's doing mindless chores, caring for someone who's ill, or even just watching TV on the couch. Others, it's trying something not because you want to, but because your partner enjoys that thing, and you want to make them happy. Marriage is about finding your best friend and wanting to spend as much time with them as humanly possible. It's about having children, maturing, constantly improving while still maintaining an everlasting passion. I don't know. That's my two cents anyway."

"I want you to be my boyfriend again."

This statement actually caused me to stand up.

"You don't want to be tied down, remember? You said that 60 seconds ago?"

"It's different. I'm not married to my boyfriend. If it's not fun, it can be easily broken off."

"So, you just want security?"

"No, I just want you now and for as long as possible. Who knows when it'll end? Maybe I'll change my mind and want to get married one day, right? I'm still young."

"Can I say something without you getting mad?"

"I don't know."

"I'll never feel stronger about someone than I do about you."

I leaned down and kissed her thick lower lip.

"Why would that make me mad?" Whatever...Vincent Beattie, I'll love you until the day I die, and then whatever I'm reincarnated as, will love you until the day you die...now carry me to bed."

I lifted the 94-pound girl and carried her until she was laying neatly beneath the duvet.

"Massage my feet," Devi demanded.

I did as I was told as my elated ex drifted off to sleep. The evening ended with me kissing her on the forehead and contemplating our future while walking down the penthouse's mile-long hallway to the foyer.

CHAPTER 6

A WEEK LATER, DEVI AND I were in a committed, exclusive relationship. And once again, we agreed not to post about it or tell
anyone outside of our closest friends. Even though over 200
miles separated us, I was always more than happy to ride the Northeast
Regional to Penn Station and stay with my high school senior girlfriend
whenever she decreed. However, our second meet-up happened to be at
the Harvard campus on Saturday, November 23rd. This was the first and
only time Devi ever visited me in Cambridge.

I offered my piquant girlfriend my twin XL bed to sleep in for free,
but she declined. A dull evening of Dunster House copulation with fellow
horny millennials drunkenly mocking us from the hallway wasn't Devi's
idea of pleasure. Her new, devirginized self yearned for feral, rule-free
love-making as she continued to feel more comfortable with her figure
and abilities. Without allowing for objection, Devi sprung for a $300
room at the convenient, boutique Hotel Veritas along Harvard Square.
At 8:30 pm, Devi texted me to come to her second-floor room, and I
practically sprinted there to see what surprises my lovebird had for me.

Following a brief elevator ride, I banged on Devi's hotel room door
and was greeted by my five-foot-one-and-a-half-inch girlfriend wearing
nothing but a beige Burberry gabardine trench coat with just two buttons fastened.

The room was small and didn't possess a view of the campus or
river, but the fiery red quilt and headboard created the ideal, hedonistic
environment.

Devi motioned her index finger, and I tackled her onto the queen-sized bed. Without a moment's hesitation, our clothes and pillows were thrown to the floor, and her chihuahua-like yelps could've been heard from miles away.

Following a loud and sweaty sequence, Devi covered her body in her trench coat once again and insisted I buy her chocolate. And at that moment, I would've purchased an island and declared bankruptcy if she had asked me to.

Devi and I held hands as we strolled down the street in mildly inappropriate outfits consisting of inside out shirts, backward pants, and warm bodily sweat freezing in the sub-30-degree Massachusetts weather. I had decided on a trip to the local CVS near the T station, and Devi happily accepted, practically skipping along the stone streets. The lively beauty I had once loved was back. Although, only for a moment. Because as we passed a Harvard bookstore, Devi reached into her pocket and took out a cigarette and lighter.

"What are you doing, gemsbok?"

"It's so cold, and people say they're great after sex."

"You can't smoke around me. Why are you smoking at all? How big of an idiot must someone be to start smoking?"

"Stop."

"Seriously, if you're 60 and have been smoking for 40 years, I understand it's a near-impossible habit to quit, but how does a girl like you start smoking in the first place? Goddamn."

With the coffin nail between her index and middle fingers, Devi blew an obnoxious ball of smoke into the frigid air.

"I look like Marilyn Monroe, don't I?"

I shook my head.

"Don't ignore me. I flew all the way up here to see you."

"You flew here?"

"Yeah, first class. You expect me to ride on the Chinatown bus with the homeless people?"

"Christ."

We entered the fluorescent pharmacy and journeyed down separate aisles. I stared at my feet, wondering what other secrets the new Devi was hiding from me.

"Babes," she cried from across the store. "I remembered your favorite candy. Snickers Peanut Butter Squares. These ones with the yellow wrappers, right?"

I followed her shrieks while a stubborn frown adorned my pallid face.

"Yes, they are."

"Hey," Devi said in a grave whisper. "Quit acting like a brat."

She then gave me a slap across the face loud enough to alert the dozing cashier.

"Two choices," she said. "Change your attitude, start smiling those million-dollar teeth at me, and you can rock my world again back at the hotel. Or you can keep moping, go back to your dorm room, and jerk off into a sock to girls that look like me."

"Jesus Devi," I whispered as my cheek colored.

She did her best runway model strut towards the cashier, then turned around and winked at me as she must've known I couldn't keep my eyes off her.

Devi paid for our chocolates and a pack of gum before we began trotting back to the hotel. She puffed on another cancer stick and then flicked it towards the street. I will admit she looked very cool doing it, but that was no excuse.

"I'm chewing gum now, happy? Vincent?" She stopped walking. "Are you happy?"

"Elated."

"Good babes. I love you."

Devi then pushed me against a brick wall on Massachusetts Avenue and stuck her spiny, pungent tongue down my throat for fifteen seconds before we started walking again.

My partner and I arrived back in the hotel room, and she was naked the moment the door closed. Devi ripped the clothes off my body and shoved me onto the bed. Even though she was wholly inexperienced, Devi succeeded based upon this kinetic sexual energy exuding from every pore of her body. My girlfriend occasionally didn't know what she was doing, but her unmitigated confidence and aggression were always welcome. It also helped that my experiences were nearly as limited as hers. When I was in bed with Devi, her inscrutable beauty and ambrosial lips eliminated any concerns I had about us. I wholly recognized there was something particularly salacious about two people with a storied history, who once shared their respective first kisses, meeting in elegant bedrooms years later. I may not have been in love with this new Devi, but I was undoubtedly ensnared by her boa-like emotional gymnastics, hypnotized by the one girl who had never stopped loving me.

The next morning began with a similar sexiness excreting from Devi's every fiber. I was awakened by kisses along my hips and inner thighs, and this soon progressed to a refreshing shower with water cascading down my torso and onto the top of her head. It was an exceptional feeling to finally be so desired by not just an amorous girl, but one whose beauty increased each day.

Before taxiing back to Logan Airport, Devi asked to see my room, so I brought her inside the hallowed halls of Dunster House. We entered my drab dorm surrounded by empty white walls and furnished with a sole grey bungee chair from Bed Bath & Beyond. The first items Devi seemed to notice, though, were the dumbbells beneath my bed.

"Do you work out here?"

"Four days a week."

"What if I sit in this...um...chair and watch you lift?"

"You really want to do that?"

"Totes. Take off your shirt."

"Should I put something on the TV? I think you may get bored watching for 45 minutes."

"You have Netflix? Put on *Gossip Girl*. The pilot episode. I want to see if you like it."

"And you're just gonna sit there?"

Devi ran her fingers along my abs before nodding and taking a seat in the springy cushion-less seat. I then pressed play on the *Gossip Girl* pilot and began curling my 35-pound weights while my awestruck girlfriend watched.

"I don't know if there's a heaven, but this would be mine," Devi said.

Every few minutes, my girlfriend would squeak with joy as she stared at my muscles. I was extraordinarily uncomfortable by this sequence of events, but again, having a beautiful girl practically worship me eclipsed any oddness I felt.

As I moved onto ab exercises, Devi would point out the characters she liked and disliked.

"I used to think Nate was hot, but Vincent, your muscles are definitely bigger. And your face is cuter than Dan's."

I nodded as I breathed heavily.

"Who's hotter, Serena or me? Be completely honest."

"You are...Devi...you are...the hottest...girl in...the world."

"You're just saying that."

"I wouldn't...lie to you...baby," I stood and kissed her.

Following my workout, but before my shower, Devi and I had taken to my actual bed for the first time that weekend. Devi's staccatoed oohs and aahs drowned out the conversations of the impossibly attractive 20-something year-olds failing to pass themselves off as 17-year-olds on my 46-inch screen.

In the waning moments of our weekend together, Devi refused to join me for a shower in the Dunster communal bathroom and instead chose to ride with unkempt hair on a first-class Delta flight back to Manhattan.

Since I was only able to travel to New York every few weeks and Devi was reluctant to inconvenience herself with any more first-class flights to and from Logan Airport, our primary form of communication became video calls.

Through the end of November and beginning of December, our Skype conversations always revolved around three topics: discussions about the future, conversations that took sexual turns and arguing about our Friday and Saturday night schedules.

On the night of November 28th, we were engaged in an intellectual conversation about what our next few years would look like.

"I applied ED to Brown, you know."

Devi appeared on my computer screen, wearing a baggy white t-shirt and no makeup, while I was clad in an unzipped hunter green hoodie.

"Yeah, I'm really excited for you. When you get in, we'll be really close by."

"I didn't apply there for you. And I might not even go."

Devi chomped on a sandwich in front of her camera.

"What are you eating, lovebird?"

"Speculoos."

"What's that?"

"You've never seen me eat this? I buy it at LPQ. It's like a cinnamon butter cookie spread. It like goes great on a bunch of stuff."

"Huh. So why wouldn't you go to Brown?"

"I don't think I'm like ready to go to college. I kinda want to take a gap year."

"And do what?"

"I don't know. Whatever. Anything. I'll travel. Maybe visit my family. I just want to finally relax for once. I guess I could start a non-profit or something. Help teach underprivileged kids to dance. That could be fun."

"If you have a chance to go to an Ivy League school, you go."

"Well, not everyone has to follow the Vincent Beattie path."

"Are you feeling okay? You seem a little dour."

"I'm fine. It's just lonely here. I'm always so lonely, you know?"

"Of course. I wish I was there. We have such a great time in person."

"But not just that. Like, I miss my family, and I don't really like my friends anymore."

"Why not? Did you have a falling out?"

Devi rolled her eyes and finished munching on her Speculoos sandwich while I put the sweatshirt hood over my head to block out the Cambridge winter.

"Take your hood off, babes. I can't see your face."

"Fine, but tell me about your friends."

"They just seem like fake and hypocritical, you know?"

"Give me an example."

"Well, so you know how Instagram is getting huge these days?"

"No. What's that?"

"You're joking right?"

"I barely even use Facebook and still have a BlackBerry. You know this."

"Ew. Pathetic. I guess I tried to block that out. Well, it's this site where you post pictures, and people comment on them."

"Facebook already does that. I don't get it."

"Yeah, clearly. There's like filters, and you don't have to deal with like walls or birthday posts or annoying people. It's sleeker."

"Sure, whatever. So, what does this have to do with your friends?"

"Well...no, never mind. You'll just get mad."

"No. Don't just start a sentence like that and then move past it."

"Fine. So, I found the easiest way to get followers is to pay people to follow you. So, I started buying my Insta followers."

"What the hell? Why would you do that? Who cares if you have 100 followers or 300 followers?"

"I knew you wouldn't get it. Instagram is all about getting likes and people engaging with your pics. The more followers I have, the more likes I get."

"But so what? If you get two likes or 4,000 likes, who cares? They're all just irrelevant numbers."

"Shut the hell up. Let's change topics."

"Jeez. Sorry. Sore subject."

"Don't tell anyone I told you that. It's a secret."

"You never told me what happened to your friends."

"Do you ever think about death?" Devi's pixelated face asked.

"Not really. Every so often, I dream about my mom, but I don't think about my own death. Why?"

"We were doing a deep dive into existentialism in my AP Psych class and..."

"You're in AP Psych?"

"Why do you sound surprised? You still think I'm an idiot?"

"When have I ever said that? Of course not."

"Who's smarter, you or me?"

"Uh, we're both intelligent in different ways. I don't know much about dance, for example, and you don't know much about baseball."

"Who's smarter?"

"Devi. We're the same. Don't be insecure."

"Fine. Anyway, before you rudely interrupted, in AP Psych, we were learning about existentialism, and I decided to read Camus' *The Stranger* on my own."

"Cool, good for you. What'd you think?"

"Well, Meursault is so calm about dying. He never really panics. He embraces it, you know? It's not something we need to be afraid of, I think. There's something very chic about dying, don't you think?"

"No. Not remotely. It's the worst thing that can happen to humans."

"But we're finally at peace. All the hardships vanish into thin air."

"What hardships do you deal with?"

"Are you joking? What hardships do I deal with?"

"I mean, we both live pretty charmed lives. And, no one in your entire family has ever died during your lifetime. You told me that."

"How dare you," Devi rose out of her seat and started cursing before continuing. "I feel non-stop pressure from my whole family. I need to be this goody two shoes all the time. I'm expected to get perfect grades and be proper and focus on nothing but my religion and family life and schooling. I never get to have any fun. You know, when I found out my parents were leaving, I was so excited. I'd finally be free of them. But now, I've traded in freedom for 24/7 loneliness."

"Come on, Devi. I'm always here for you. You don't have to be lonely."

"Stop. You don't get it. You're being a jerk. You never understood me. Have a nice night, loser."

Devi hung up the video call, and we didn't speak again until December 2nd when she Skype'd me around eight at night.

"Hey sexy," Devi began our video call wearing her white and emerald kimono with nothing underneath.

"Jesus. Hello there."

"I want to dance for you."

"You don't want to talk about our previous conversation?"

"Will you stop. Don't be so serious. That's the trait I hate most about my parents. You're the only person I can feel comfortable exploring my body and letting loose...Don't speak again unless you're talking sexy."

"Fine."

"Pick any song for me to dance to."

"'Touch My Body' by Mariah Carey."

"Wow, no hesitation. I like that."

Devi tilted the camera to the right to make sure her good side was visible as I gawked through my computer's camera lens. My sizzling girlfriend gyrated her hips around her desk chair and let the silk kimono drop to the floor. Devi followed this by pressing her perky breasts together and making the pouty, duck lips she knew I loved. After another minute, she turned around, spanked herself and moaned loudly.

"Okapi, I want you so badly. I want your piece inside me right now. Tell me how hot I am."

"Devi, you're the sexiest goddamn girl in the world. I could watch you for hours."

"Tell me you think I'm skinny."

"You're so thin. You're hotter than any model."

"Yeah? Hotter than Chrissy Cavalier?"

"Who?"

Devi kept dancing as she asked perplexing questions to quell her insecurities.

"Tell me my boobs are nicer than Chrissy Cavalier's."

"Oh, that Verity girl? Yeah, yeah, your boobs are so much better. I wouldn't change a single part of your body. Everything's perfect."

"Yeah?"

"Yeah."

"I want you inside of me right now," Devi said.

We hung up a few minutes later, both incredibly ecstatic over our choice in partner. These sexual Skype calls became relatively frequent as one would expect for a modern-day long-distance couple. On nights like this, even weeknights, I was seconds away from just hopping on a bus back to Manhattan to enrapture her in person. However, before I could book a ticket, I'd remind myself I had classes the next day and piles of Econ and English homework. Devi always left me wanting more. She had a gift.

The third type of Skype call was my least favorite: the nighttime weekend schedule. Devi and I had different ideas of what it meant to be in a long-distance, exclusive relationship. I felt we could be wild and crazy in person, but it wasn't fair to go out clubbing until 2:30 am when we were 200 miles apart. At that time, Devi and I were a newly established couple, and my preference was we'd spend some Friday and Saturday nights Skyping when I wasn't visiting her York penthouse. However, Devi was a high-maintenance senior who was friends with other high-maintenance socialites who needed to be seen out on the town every weekend. On the night of December 7th, Devi Skyped me while getting dressed to go out with her peers.

"Lovebird, I'll be out super late, so don't wait up."

"Um, why do you need to stay out super late? You know it makes me uncomfortable. You're an 18-year-old living alone in a city with a ton of dangerous areas."

"Relax."

"And you're dressing like that?"

Devi wore a skin-tight Fendi black dress that just barely scraped her knees. At this moment, my girlfriend was doing her makeup in front of a mirror beside her laptop.

"Stop. Don't make me regret VCing with you."

"Maybe I should go out tonight? Maybe I'll put on a button-down and head into Boston."

"Don't even joke about that. Just stay in your room and play video games. I thought that's what you like to do, lovebird?"

"You don't see how you're being hypocritical?"

"It's totally different. You're a college guy surrounded by thousands of hot girls every day, and you have unlimited freedom. It's incredibly nerve-racking for me."

"You know I'd never touch another girl here."

"I know babes, but what if one night you saw someone you thought was super-hot and then—"

"Devi, you're not listening to me. I'd never, under any circumstances, touch another girl. You're the only one I want."

"Well, then why don't you tell me you love me?"

I put my sweatshirt hood on and stared at Devi's delicate, almond face. Once in a while, her glibness would distract me from her innate beauty, but then my girlfriend would tilt her head or stare straight into the camera, and I'd forget any unkind word she'd said.

"I'm just not ready to say that yet, Devi. I want to sometimes, but then I keep thinking about the way things ended the last time."

"Oh stop. We were both so immature then."

"I loved you then."

"Whatever. I can wait. Over winter break, when I'm blowing you, I'll make you say it."

"Um, I don't…uh…okay then."

"You didn't tell me I look pretty."

Devi stood and angled herself in front of the laptop camera.

"You're so unbelievably beautiful, Devi. You're my goddess. That dress looks perfect on you."

"Love ya."

"Where are you going tonight?"

"My friends and I are going to 1Oak."

"I thought you were mad at your friends. I thought you felt so lonely."

"Well, they sort of suck, but they're still my friends, I guess. Besides, what am I supposed to do, sit inside by myself all night?"

"We could Skype for the next two hours, or we could watch a movie together. Like, we'd start it at the exact same time and Skype while watching? Sorta like what they do in *When Harry Met Sally.*"

"It's not the same if I can't cuddle with you, and you're not massaging my feet."

"So, why are you going out? Like, what's the purpose?"

"You're so annoying sometimes, you know that?"

"That's mean."

"It's true though. Just get off my back and let me enjoy my final months before college."

"I thought you were considering a gap year?"

"There you go again. You need to learn to be quiet sometimes. Stop acting like you're so much smarter than me."

"Are you gonna drink tonight?"

"Duh. It's a Saturday."

"You know when you're in a long-distance relationship, you're supposed to occasionally take into account the other person's feelings. My girlfriend is going out drinking at a nightclub, no one knows she's in a relationship, and given how thin you are, an unconscious blackout is always in the cards."

"You think you're so cute with that thin comment?"

"I thought it was clever."

"You're infuriating sometimes. Bye."

Devi hung up our Skype conversation, which left me uneasy, but I was always found mild solace in my video games. At this point, I was sailing around the Caribbean Sea in the 18th Century with Edward Kenway and the *Jackdaw* in *Assassin's Creed: Black Flag*. I spent the next couple of hours getting lost in the meticulously animated cities of Nassau and Havana. I then traversed the southern Caribbean looking for booty and shooting heavy cannonballs at rival pirate ships. I also found the story-line quite compelling, particularly the fact Edward and his wife were in a long-distance relationship.

I paused the game after not having heard from Devi in a while. I had always asked her to text me once around midnight, so I knew she was alive and healthy, but she never obliged. On this particular evening, she ignored my 12:15 am, 1:38 am, and 2:12 am texts in addition to my 2:28 am call. Devi seemed to do whatever she pleased with a complete disregard for my feelings. Did I want her to have fun? Yes. But I didn't trust her.

In my opinion, the crux of the issue was a lack of discipline and accountability during her formative years. I learned this from stories Devi had told me about high school curfew. As a freshman, her parents supposedly required her to be home by 10:30 pm. However, most nights, she wouldn't burst through the front door until after 1 am. The hyper Devi would be greeted by two wide-awake disapproving, but devoted parents. There would be mutual castigating until Devi was grounded for a month. However, then came the apologies, and not from Devi. According to my girlfriend, every night after she was grounded, her parents would scurry down the hall, knock quietly on Devi's bedroom door and enter with tears welling. Her young parents apologized profusely for yelling and creating a household of invective. Then, they'd rescind the grounding and kiss their bombastic daughter goodnight. Apparently, this occurred over 50 times during her teenage years.

Back in my dorm, I was depurating myself of ill thoughts by slaughtering unsuspecting 18th-century pirates. The *Assassin's Creed* franchise created a therapeutic atmosphere for me to unleash my anger in a harmless way.

During this particular session, I was hunting for sharks when Devi finally texted me to get back on my laptop so she could video call me. It was an incoherent message, even for 2:40 am.

"Devi, thank god you're alright. I was so worried about you."

"I don't feel good."

"Jesus, you look like a mess. Are you drunk? How much did you drink?"

"I dunno...brb."

Devi exited her grandiose bedroom, and I heard projectile vomiting occurring in the nearby toilet.

"Goddamn it, Devi," I shouted loud enough for her to hear.

After about two minutes of my girlfriend presumably kneeling on her bathroom floor, she stumbled back into the frame. I had a tough time determining whether she needed a ruthless harangue or a docile wake-up call, so I broadsided her with a barrage of both.

"Devi, are you alright? I was so worried about you. You didn't answer any of my calls or texts. You could've been kidnapped or something."

"I did weed tonight V."

"Jesus Christ. And do I even want to know all the elixirs you tainted your liver with?"

"And a hookah bar."

"Devi, you can't do stuff like this when you're in a long-distance relationship. It's not healthy for you or me."

"Screw you."

"Do I need to hop on a bus home right now? You clearly aren't up to living on your own. Do I need to call your parents?"

"You're not my dad."

"Devi, I'm so disappointed in you. You didn't hook up with anyone, did you?"

"Who me?" Devi cackled.

"Gemsbok, I'm serious. This isn't fun for me. I'm not laughing."

"I wanna do coke next time."

"Devi, I can't talk to you like this."

I hung up on her, ignored the three follow-up calls, and went to bed, wondering if my girlfriend possessed the mutability necessary to be in a relationship.

CHAPTER 7

I CAME HOME FOR WINTER break on December 15th, and though I was
mad at Devi, she assuaged my anger through a few sensual Skype
stripteases. At this point, I felt seeing her in person for the first time
in a while would reignite our fading flame. Devi's 19th birthday was on
December 18th, and I had an incandescent, multi-step plan to show her
how important she was to me.

The first step was purchasing a lovely Tiffany's bracelet with "V" and
"D" carved into the genuine silver. It cost me an unhealthy portion of my
savings, but at this time in my life, Devi was the only person on whom
to spend money. Second, I had a bouquet of purple peonies sent to her
penthouse along with some champagne truffles, courtesy of La Maison
du Chocolat. In addition, I wrote her an insightful message spanning
three separate Hallmark cards with enough x's and o's to win a hundred
tic-tac-toe games. And then the final touch for our perfect evening was
dinner.

I could've made a reservation at The Water Club or Per Se or Le
Bernadin, but any schlub can let someone else cook. I figured I'd surprise Devi, who at this point had rarely seen me in a kitchen. I marched
to Fairway on the morning of the 18th with a myriad of vegetarian recipes
printed on a piece of paper. While in the store, I decided to make some
sort of quinoa curry, vegetable masala, and some shankarpali. I was
miles outside of my comfort zone, but I imagined Devi must be stressed
and homesick with her parents thousands of miles away. Spending hours

in the kitchen would all be worth it if it meant making her feel jovial once again.

Upon returning to 4D, I explained the situation to my father and asked if he could vacate the apartment from 5 pm to 9 pm, to which he shockingly agreed. I then spent two hours toiling in the kitchen before texting Devi.

V: Hey, I'm not going to be ready by 6. Can you meet me at my place?
D: Where are we going? I'll just meet you there.
V: It's a surprise. You're gonna love it.
D: Candle 79?
V: Just come over as soon as you can, lovebird. Xoxo. Happy birthday again!
D: Thanks babes. I've got a surprise for you too.
V: You don't have to do anything. It's your birthday.
D: Hehe, you'll love it.

Devi arrived wearing a purple sequin Gucci gown and holding a gift behind her back.

"Wait, why does it smell so bad in here? What's going on? Where's your tie?"

Devi placed her Moncler jacket on the table and sniffed around my empty apartment.

"What's going on?" she asked.

"Surprise."

"Surprise what?"

"Wait, what's behind your back?" I said.

"Tell me what's happening first."

"How about a kiss?"

"Fine."

Devi gave me a peck on the cheek before wandering into the kitchen.

"Oh no. Babes, you shouldn't have."

"Are you happy? I'm cooking for us tonight."

"Oh…"

Devi finally turned around and revealed the "gift" she had for me.

"It's a beta fish. I bought it just for you. Because—"

"Damn it, Devi. I don't want this thing. Why would I want a beta fish?"

"You don't remember our conversation from high school?"

"The one where I explicitly told you I'd never want a fish? Yeah, I remember that one."

"Pretty sneaky of me, right? Impressed by my memory, okapi?"

Devi sat at the circular four-seater kitchen table with an insolubly sly grin. My girlfriend did look magnificent. The deep plunging neckline and three-inch jet-black Ferragamos were extremely attractive.

"Whatever, we'll worry about that thing later. I got you some stuff too."

"Wait, stop. Get a bowl for Devi. She can't stay in this bag…that's her name. Devi. Like me. Clever right?"

"Oh, I got it. It's…something."

I rummaged through the kitchen cabinets and found a seldom-used bowl in which to place the beady-eyed fish.

"Gift time. What'd you get me?"

"Did you like the flowers and chocolates?"

"Of course, babes. But what'd you get me?"

I ran into my bedroom, picked up the iconic Tiffany's box and Hallmark card envelopes, and raced back to the kitchen.

"Here you go."

Devi's cartoonish eyes lit up at the sight of the robin's egg blue box.

"Wait, cards first."

"Yeah, no shot." Devi untied the Tiffany's ribbon to reveal her silver present. "Oh, Vincent. What is this?"

She ogled the bracelet, twisting and tilting it in her hand before constricting her wrist.

"Is it the right size and color and everything? I was so nervous trying to pick it out."

"It's nice. Thank you, V."

Devi stood up, hugged me, and placed the bracelet back inside its box.

"Let me see these cards...three of them? You must really love me, huh?"

"Hold on. I need to stir this monstrosity...dinner should be ready in just a minute."

Devi was entranced by my intoxicating prose emulsifying saccharine nostalgia with prurient details centered around her electrifying personality and savory figure. Her weepy eyes drenched my slovenly cursive.

"Vincent, darling, these are so beautiful. Do you really mean all this?"

"Of course, Devi."

She rose from her seat, embraced me, and then planted a long lipstick-infused kiss upon my suspecting lips. Devi then started to unbutton my white collared shirt.

"Wait until after dinner."

"Screw dinner. I want you now."

"I did work pretty hard on this, but I'll do anything you want. It's your birthday."

"Fine. Quick dinner and then I need to feel you ASAP."

"Deal."

"What's for dinner, anyway?"

"Curry, masala, and shankarpali. They're among your favorites, right?

"You got it. Don't be hard on yourself, though. There's no way they can compare to the curry and masala my family's chef used to make when I was growing up."

"Right."

Moments later, I set the table, lit two candles, and served the repellant dinner. Devi took one taste and said:

"Oh. Not great."

"Well, try the masala."

Devi lightly tongued the other dish, before adding:

"Yikes. This is even worse."

"Oh. Uh, I'm sorry."

"Don't worry about it. I'm gonna be in the living room. Meet me there in three minutes."

"Wait, that's it? You don't wanna talk or anything?"

Devi ignored me, and I could hear her swiftly undressing and positioning herself for a fabulous performance. I soon entered to find her naked body sprawled across the Beattie family couch my mother had purchased in France long ago. This sight made me completely forget about dinner.

The birthday tryst was more aggressive than usual as Devi demanded I slap, choke, and spank her. I cocked my head to the side at first but was willing to do anything to make her happy. An alluring yelp followed each subsequent thrust, and I was just so thankful to be spellbound in a relationship with such a flawless looking girl.

The primary issue with our romantic rendezvous was they actually made me dislike Harvard. Devi and I were so passionate, and our sexual chemistry seemed unmatched, so I hated the idea of the depression-inducing train back to South Station where I'd be locked in a frigid dorm room for weeks on end. The Skype sessions were solid, but being able to touch Devi's body and hear her off-kilter groans in person made an enormous difference. The thought of transferring to Columbia even crossed my mind, but I nixed that quickly. To distract myself from Devi's unmatched magnetism, I decided I needed to branch out when I returned to Harvard in January.

In the meantime, my winter break with Devi was short-lived. Her family begged for her to fly overseas on New Year's Eve, so Devi and I only saw each other once more before my second semester. I was glad she was with her family, though. I couldn't imagine being a high school senior thousands of miles from the people who cared about me most. It sounded like some kind of sick torture. Such lengthy times and distances between loved ones were bound to cause the occasional relationship chasms.

Devi Skyped me every few days from various countries, and our New Year's kiss was, unfortunately, only a virtual one. It was during the waning moments of 2013 I realized I'd never actually had a January

1ˢᵗ midnight kiss before. That's a harrowing realization for any high schooler, let alone a college sophomore. The good news was Devi was in line to be my first at the end of 2014. There was no other girl for me.

I rode the lonely Northeast Regional back to Boston in mid-January, no longer looking forward to my second semester. As my train entered the maw of South Station, I found it difficult to motivate myself to exit. I wanted to be in Manhattan and live in Devi's penthouse with her. She would've no longer needed to go out until 2:30 am without me. I felt I could've tended to my girlfriend's every need as she walked around that White House-sized penthouse in the nude. The two of us could've ordered delivery and watched *Shatranj Ke Khilari* on Friday night and then gone out dancing at Le Bain on Saturday. Devi and I could've traveled overseas to meet her extended family, or she could've come over to my apartment to hang out with my dad and me. We could've become one amoeba, shifting and adapting to every environmental challenge. This sounded like a pipedream, but by the time summer arrived, I felt all of our distance-related problems would've been solved.

I stepped off the train into the frozen tundra south of the Charles River and found a taxi to drive me deeper into the snowy wastelands north of Boston, each mile keeping me farther from Devi.

Back at Harvard, my second semester mirrored the first. I was inundated with heavy workloads from five different courses and then had to maintain my quad-weekly, in-room workouts while also writing for Dutch's Angle. The only true moments of relaxation I had were venturing through space as Commander Shepard in *Mass Effect 3* and the near-daily Skypes with the impeccable Devi Kapoor.

To not elevate my status as a recluse, I did visit my loving girlfriend once at the end of January and then for Valentine's Day a few weeks later. For these monthly visits, I'd take the train back to the city on a Friday night and wear my nicest suit and tie. Even if my outfit was ripped to shreds upon my penthouse arrival, it was worth it to see Devi gawking at me for a few seconds after I entered. My girlfriend certainly had a flair for the dramatic, and riding the Northeast Regional in my light grey Hugo Boss suit made me feel important.

The beginning moments of my two-night vacations to the York penthouse were always the most joyous. After spending weeks apart, Devi was always anxious to climb on top of me the second I entered 698140. We'd retire to Devi's or Nitya's bedrooms for hours at a time before showering together and scrubbing the sweat off each other's bodies. Then, my girlfriend and I would cuddle in the TV room and sift through an eclectic mix of movies on demand before deciding on whatever she wanted to watch. We were never able to make it through a film without pausing, though. Eventually, upon the movie's completion, Devi would demand a foot massage, and then we'd spend another hour or two in her bedroom before falling asleep.

Our in-person conversations were mostly light-hearted and shallow. I never delved into her personal life because Devi and I were so ebullient together. The last thing I wanted to do was bring up a sour subject and change the entire mood of the weekend. Over Skype, I'd denigrate Devi for smoking weed, drinking heavily, and staying out late, because there were no real consequences. While in person, I'd never castigate her because it would lead to pouting and her not wanting to touch me. It wasn't an ideal situation, but summer was right around the corner, and Devi and I had part of spring break to look forward to as well.

CHAPTER 8

EVI HAD A LENGTHIER SPRING break than I, but she was going
on her grade's Bahamas trip at the beginning, so we'd only have
an opportunity to hang out from March 19th through the 26th. It
wasn't ideal, but it also wasn't fair of me to always want Devi to hang out
with me. When my Circean girlfriend boarded her flight, I was undoubtedly anxious she was going to be encountering the same drunken trip
that left an ineffaceable memory on my still-developing mind. And
frankly, given her previous Parisian winter break several years prior, I
didn't feel I could trust her.

During the entirety of her trip, I managed to send Devi just two
texts. She ignored both of them, but I wasn't stressed. I had matured
since our high school relationship. I wasn't going to lambast my poor
girlfriend for enjoying her final months of high school.

Devi called me the day after she arrived in Manhattan and told me
to meet her at SPIN on 23rd Street later that evening. I was thrilled at the
prospect of spending a night out on the town after not seeing Devi at
all in the previous five weeks. I wore my black J. Crew skinny jeans and
black button-down, along with black and white Cole Haan sneakers to
the contrastive ping pong lounge.

Upon entering the dimly-lit underground area filled with ping
pong tables and neon decorations, I spotted Devi, along with Tessa and
another stranger. Would I have liked it if Devi told me Tessa was coming?
Yes. Although, I'm sure my girlfriend had a tenable reason for not telling

me. Besides, I hadn't seen my partner, who was dripping with vivacity as per usual, in so long that these micro problems didn't bother me.

Devi was wearing this striking fringe, sleeveless Alaia dress that fell two inches above her knees. Looking back on it, whether right or wrong, seeing Devi in-person after weeks apart always reaffirmed why I was dating her.

"Babes, I missed you so much," Devi began kissing every pore of my face before continuing. "Sorry, um, you know Tessa, and this is her girlfriend, Mya."

"Nice to meet you, Mya."

Mya was a tall, plus-sized African girl with a shaved head and her earlobes gauged. They were as unique a coupling as anyone on the Upper East Side.

"So, are we playing doubles? How does this place work?" I asked.

"Okapi, it's simple. The two of us will play on the same team against the two of them. And I ordered four French 75s."

"They didn't card you? And I don't like gin."

"I have a fake, silly. And who cares. Just drink it. Let's have fun. I'm so happy to see you."

"Vincent, you look dashing as ever," Tessa hugged me before picking up her paddle.

"So do you. It's so cool that you've found someone too."

"Thanks."

The four of us then started the fast-paced game.

"Devi, can I show you how to hold the paddle properly?"

"Stop, just let me have fun."

Devi would flail her uncoordinated limbs about as she missed three-fourths of the balls hit to her side of the table. Meanwhile, after winning a point, Tessa and Mya would give each other a gentle peck on the lips. And not to be outdone, Devi would graciously make out with me for five seconds following each of our points scored.

"Babes, I didn't know you were so good at this. You could go pro," Devi said. "I'm like so attracted to you right now."

"Thanks, but try to bend your knees. You're so upright, and you can't keep holding the paddle like that."

We continued playing for about half an hour before Devi announced:

"I'm bored. Let's stop and sit down."

Our group of four found an open table on the side of the lounge, and the three ladies continued sipping their drinks.

"V, get a drink. Come on."

"Yeah, Vincent," Tessa added. "Don't be a loser."

"I'm fine guys, really," I then looked at my tipsy girlfriend. "Devi, I think you've had enough."

"Relax, Vincent. Let your girlfriend drink. It's spring break."

"She's 95 pounds and has had two French 75s," I pulled Devi's third drink away from her.

"Tessi, can you come to the bathroom with me?"

Tessa and Devi left me alone at the table with the introverted Mya. I was still bad with strangers at this point, so we sat in silence until Devi and Tessa eventually returned and leaped back into our booth.

"Are you two okay? Devi, are you still conscious?"

Devi sniffled and then licked my earlobe.

"Down, girl," I said.

"Sorry, guys. I should take her home soon. She's all tuckered out."

"What are you talking about? I'm not tired at all. I could play more ping pong or go out dancing for hours. We could pull an all-nighter."

"Well, we're not going to do any of that."

Devi hiccupped.

"Can you excuse us again?" Devi said. "I need to use the bathroom."

"I'll come too," Mya said.

I was left alone at the table while the three of them talked about and did God knows what in the SPIN restroom. In the meantime, I checked my phone and saw a text from my father.

M: All good? Don't stay out too late.
V: You're so caring—like a John Hughes father.

M: Pissant.
V: Love you too.
M: Be safe son.
V: Yessir.

After 10 minutes, the triumvirate of ladies had yet to return, so I decided to pay the bill and wander off to the back of the lounge. Once there, I ran into Mya standing guard outside the women's restroom, but she moved aside after taking one look at my determined face.

I pried open the door to find Tessa standing outside of an open stall.

"Devi? Let me guess? My little gemsbok drank too much?"

"Get out of here," Tessa shouted as I approached the stall.

I then turned and saw Devi's face hanging lifelessly over the porcelain.

"Devi?"

"V? Go away."

When Devi turned around to utter this, I saw blood dribbling down her philtrum.

"Jesus Christ, Devi."

"Vincent, get out of here," Tessa said.

"Did you give her cocaine?"

"I don't know."

"Christ. What is wrong with everyone? This isn't safe. How can you all be so obtuse?"

I re-entered the stall, cleaned up Devi's face with toilet paper, and flushed the haunting sanguine vomit down the toilet.

"Tessa, how could you do this to the poor girl? I'm taking you to the hospital, Devi. Period. End of story."

I stormed out of the bathroom with Devi clinging to my shoulders. She was crying as we weaved through the crowd of onlookers.

"Don't look at me, V. I'm not pretty right now."

Devi shielded her face with her right arm as we made our way out of SPIN. My hospital suggestion wasn't some empty threat, either. I thought maybe a doctor could talk some sense into her. At least it was almost summertime.

During our cab ride to Lenox Hill Hospital, Devi passed out on my shoulder. Our yellow taxi juked passed several cars as we sped up Park Avenue and through the tunnel beneath the MetLife Building. Ashamedly, my ever-racing mind returned to the Tessa-time machine question. How different would my life have been if I had kissed that sprightly eighth grade thespian outside of Central Park all those years ago? Even though Tessa and I never would've lasted, perhaps it would've led me down a more wonted path. Tessa was known to fraternize with a cabal of girls I wasn't used to. Perhaps, after our inevitable breakup, Tessa would've introduced me to another aspiring actress who enjoyed watching old films and singing at karaoke bars. I mean, what college student would want to spend an evening over spring break riding with their high school girlfriend to the hospital? However, I still felt after a few months or years, my regal girlfriend would grow out of this childish phase.

Our cab arrived at 77th between Lex and Park, and I paid the fare.

"Carry me," a groggy Devi muttered.

"You can walk. Come on."

"Carry me, or I won't leave this cab."

I lifted Devi and threw her cadaverous frame over my right shoulder as we approached the hospital's receptionist.

"How can I help you?"

"My girlfriend is struggling with alcohol and drugs. I don't know if it's an overdose situation, but she needs help."

"Take a seat. Fill out this form."

Devi and I walked towards the waiting room to find chairs.

"Don't sit next to that guy," she whispered. "He's homeless and probably diseased."

We found a spot in the back corner, and I filled out Devi's paperwork as she alternated between antsy and languid. I definitely pitied her at this moment. Not just because a night of alcohol and hard drugs had enervated her, but because she was torpefied from an unusual child-hood. I could certainly relate to this, but Devi lacked the self-awareness to move beyond disheartening life events. She never seemed to marinate in her pain while I probably did too much.

A nurse brought Devi and me back to an open-area emergency ward where her vitals were taken. My girlfriend pouted throughout the ordeal and refused to look me or the nurse in the eyes. The man then handed Devi a cup for a urine sample before asking to speak with me outside of the room.

After Devi retired to the restroom and was out of earshot, the nurse said:

"What types of drugs do you think she's been taking?"

"I know for a fact you'll find alcohol and marijuana in her system. And maybe cocaine. And she's alluded to the fact she'll try ecstasy in the near future."

"I'm going to relay this information to the doctor, and she'll handle it in an appropriate manner."

"May I please speak to the doctor before she talks with Devi?"

"Of course. And you're her boyfriend?"

"Yes, and have been for a long time."

The nurse disappeared down the hallway, while Devi continued to stall in the restroom. I sat sullenly in a chair beside my girlfriend's temporary bed. Upon looking down, I actually found myself admiring my nighttime outfit. When I had something to be excited about, I could clean up well. It was just a shame this is where the night ended.

A tall, well-built blonde woman in a white lab coat then entered the area.

"Hi, I'm Doctor..." I missed her last name and felt uncomfortable asking her to repeat it.

"I'm Vincent. I'm Ms. Devi Kapoor's boyfriend."

"The nurse said you'd like to speak with me outside for a moment?" She whispered.

"Yes, please."

The sharp-featured doctor guided me out into the hallway and crossed her arms.

"So, what's going on with her? How can I help?"

"Well, a lot of things. For starters, she's been in the bathroom for like 15 minutes allegedly taking a urine test, but I guarantee she won't give you one drop."

"Okay, well, her vitals are a bit elevated, but nothing in her chart seems to be approaching dangerous levels. I'd like to take a look at her and have a conversation, though."

"Anyway, when we first met, she was carefree and bubbly and affectionate. Neither of us ever did drugs, as far as I knew. We were really happy. Unfortunately, Devi's parents moved out of the country after her 18th birthday, and she's living completely alone and unsupervised. Devi continues to act out and ignores my suggestions to avoid alcohol and drug consumption. Her coterie has become too wild this year, and I'm genuinely concerned."

"Well, I'm sorry to hear that. When I deem her up to it, Devi and I will have a conversation."

"And, if I may. Without her parents, Devi has no supervision and no parent to scold her when necessary. You're the doctor, but I think Devi would respond to a harsher experience. It's something very foreign to her."

"Let me have a look at the patient...Devi. I'm sorry, Vincent. This must be difficult for you."

The doctor and I walked back towards the occupied restroom and coaxed Devi to vacate. My girlfriend, with an empty cup in hand, proceeded to sit on the hospital bed while I plopped down in a chair in the corner of the room. The doctor then checked Devi's eyes, nose, ears, mouth, glands, and inner elbows before saying a word.

"Do you know why you're here, Devi?"

"I shouldn't be here. I'm fine now. I want to go home."

"Your boyfriend is very worried about you. He thinks you're going down a bad road."

"Well, he's wrong. Whatever he told you is a lie."

"You're spending your valuable time in a hospital bed, so I'm inclined to agree with your caring boyfriend here."

"But I shouldn't have come here in the first place. I wasn't even doing poorly."

"Was your nose bleeding earlier? Did you vomit?"

"Well, yeah. But it's no big deal. That stuff happens when you're out partying."

"Now Vincent, I wouldn't consider this an overdose. Your girlfriend's body had a strong reaction to the drug and alcohol combination, but it seems the actual amount of narcotic ingested was not noticeably problematic to her circulatory system."

"See V?"

"Now, that's not to say this isn't serious. You could've died tonight. Do you know how many times I've seen patients overdose on small amounts simply because they purchased them from an unknown vendor? Street drugs can be laced with all kinds of lethal additives. It's incredibly dangerous."

"You're not my mother."

"No, I'm not, but I'm concerned that this won't be the last time I see you. A young, pretty girl like you should have the world eating out of the palm of her hands. Please don't destroy your youth and wind up like the thousands of others that come through the front door here."

"Can I go home now? There's nothing wrong with me."

"You better be very careful about how you spend your nights moving forward. The last thing I want is to see a girl like you committed to an institution. You've got your boyfriend worried sick."

I shook the doctor's hand on her way out of the room and waited for the nurse to give further instructions. The good news was when the summer eventually rolled around, I felt I could monitor Devi more closely and make sure events like this didn't transpire.

"Close the curtain, babes. I'm actually kind of turned on right now. How would you like to rail me right here?"

Devi leaned back and placed her legs in the air in a V-shape.

"Let me take you home. I just want this night to end."

A scowl crept across my girlfriend's worn-out face. I wasn't exactly the boyfriend she wanted at this moment, but deep down, Devi must've understood she needed me as much as I needed her.

After another hour at the hospital, my darling gemsbok climbed on my back and rode me out towards Park Avenue, where we hailed a taxi and headed towards her apartment. While in the cab, I made sure to text my father so he knew why I was staying out so late.

Upon arriving upstairs, Devi had me carry her to her bedroom and watch her change out of her expensive, but stained, dress. Even at that moment, there was no denying my unwell girlfriend's pulchritude.

"Will you tuck me in, babes?"

"Sure."

Devi burrowed underneath her duvet and silently motioned me over to her backside.

"Are you mad at me?" She said sweetly.

"I don't know."

"You can't stay mad at me, V. Right?"

"Right…um, why don't you ever wear the Tiffany's bracelet?"

Devi removed her bra and requested I turn off the bedroom lights.

"Can you lie next to me and hold my boobs until I fall asleep? I need you."

"Anything for you."

My post-spring break life at Harvard was as dull as ever. Now, I only had myself to blame for the sempiternal tedium, but my daily routine had allowed me to achieve a 3.38 GPA in my first semester. There was no need for me to branch out in the final weeks of the school year. Maybe when my junior year began, I'd finally hatch from my steel shell, but until then, I always had Devi.

Our final six weeks between the end of spring break and the beginning of my summer were certainly rockier. Devi no longer wowed me with weekly Skype stripteases; her kindness towards me had become exceedingly rare, and my two final trips back to the York penthouse were disappointing. My number one qualm at that time was her passion for me had clearly waned. I visited her the weekends of April 11ᵗʰ and May 2ⁿᵈ, and neither sojourn included any sexual situations.

During the first visit, Devi explained she was on her period and wasn't feeling up to having sex or doing anything physical. I was understanding and felt content merely watching movies, massaging her feet, and delivering her Speculoos sandwiches with the crusts cut off. When I suggested we see *Terms of Endearment,* Devi declined, grabbed the remote, and played *Vicky Christina Barcelona* with no argument from me. She then demanded I tell her Penelope Cruz was her doppelgänger, and I obliged simply because her happiness was of paramount importance. Devi would still pause the movie once or twice for some clothed dry-humping, but it wasn't the same. Then again, she was my angel. As long as she was smiling, I was happy.

On May 1ˢᵗ, the day before I was planning to visit her in the city once again, Devi Skyped me and relayed what I considered to be unfortunate news.

"Hey babes?" Devi said through her laptop's lens. "I, uh, have something to tell you."

"Okay. What's going on?"

"Can you take your hood off, please?"

"Yeah, sorry. What's up?"

"I declined Brown."

"What? Why would you do that? That's ridiculous."

"No, it isn't. I'm not ready to go to college."

"Well, so you're deferring a year?"

"No, I just declined."

"Devi, I can't sugarcoat how idiotic of an idea that is."

I noticed she wasn't wearing any makeup. This had become much more frequent as our relationship progressed.

"It is not."

"Yes, it is."

"No, it isn't."

"Christ, Devi. You know how many people would kill for an Ivy League education? You're so lucky to have had this honor bestowed upon you."

"Honor bestowed upon me? They're not giving me a tiara or anything. It's only college, and I'm not ready."

After zoning out for a few seconds, I realized Devi might be fabricating the truth here. My girlfriend certainly had the skills required to dupe me, and the motive. If she did actually get in, for the rest of our lives, Devi now had intangible proof she was considered smart by an elite school.

"Well, princess, what will you be doing for the next year? Where will you live?"

"I'll live here, and I haven't figured out what I'm going to do. Stop stressing me out."

"Your parents aren't going to sell that penthouse?"

"It's our home."

"Gotcha. Well, let the records show I think this is a huge mistake. What did your parents say? They don't seem to visit you very often."

"Let's not discuss this any further. Topic change please."

"Fine, gemsbok. What would you like to talk about?"

Devi stood from behind her desk chair and began to stretch. I always adulated her unique grace, both silently and audibly.

"My dad is buying me a car, you know."

"I'm sorry, what? Why?"

"Well, like, a few reasons. He feels bad that he can't be here. He feels bad I'm not going to college next year, and he wants me to explore the country."

"Jesus."

"Don't say Jesus. You should be happy for me."

"Will you come and visit me next year?"

"Only if you're good."

"Maybe we can go on a road trip this summer?"

Devi sat back in her chair as a bead of sweat ran past her perfectly tweezed brow.

"Should I get a BMW, Jag, or Merc?"

"I don't know what any of that means?"

"The cars: BMW, Jag, or Merc?"

"Is that actually how you speak? You feel the need to abbreviate Jaguar and Mercedes? That's a little pathetic."

"Don't be mean. Why are you in a bad mood? Be happy."

"I can't just turn it on and off. I mean, I thought you and I would go to school like 45 minutes away from each other next year. It's an amazing school. I'm sure it would've made all of your loved ones proud."

I knew it was too late, but a smidge of inveigling couldn't hurt.

"If you're going to keep bringing up Brown and insulting me, then don't bother coming over tomorrow."

"No, babes. I didn't mean it. I want you to do whatever makes you happy. I was just offering my advice, but I'll never bring it up again. I'm so sorry if I was callous."

"Thank you. You're allowed to come over then. You know, Providence is really gross anyway. I can't imagine living anywhere outside of New York."

"Right."

"So, anyway, before you got all catty, what car should I get? If I want to be speeding down the highway, like over 100, what's the best car and color?"

"I haven't the slightest idea."

"I think a Merc. In like a deep purple."

"Here, Devi, I think I need to get going. I have a lot of homework to do. But I can't wait to see you tomorrow."

"Wait, don't hang up yet. I have good news."

I glanced around my room, zipped up my hoodie, and ran my hands through my frizzy hair.

"Yes, gemsbok?"

"Babes?" Devi said in the sweetest voice she possessed.

"What?"

"Will you go to prom with me?"

"Oh, shoot. I completely forgot. Of course, I will. I meant to ask you months ago."

"Thanks, V. And I don't want you to feel awkward being the only college guy there."

"Right, well, I don't care what those people think of me...what night is it?"

"May 17th. Saturday."

"Oh. Damnit."

"What? What could you possibly have that's more important?"

I stood and walked across the room to my bedside table.

"V?"

"My older brother's graduation is on the 17th and 18th. My dad booked the flights already."

"So?"

Devi twirled a pair of headphones around her fingers.

"Well, I mean, it's his graduation. It's a huge deal."

"And my prom isn't?"

"Would you like to come to my brother's graduation? I don't want to leave you alone."

"Miss my one and only prom? Not gonna happen."

"Well, what do you suggest I do?"

"Go ahead. Go to your brother's thing. I'm sure I can find a hundred eligible guys to take me in your place."

"What do you mean by that?"

"I don't know. I just think I deserve to be treated as your priority. So many guys would kill to take me to prom, you know."

"You're not making this easy on me."

"Go to your brother's graduation. Don't let me stop you."

It was unusually cold for the first week of May, and I was beginning to both shiver and sweat. I knew Devi wasn't one to vacillate, so now was decision time.

"I'd love to go to prom with you, Devi. Count me in. I'll call my brother and dad tomorrow and let them know."

"Thank you. You made the right choice."

This Skype wasn't an ideal way to preface my final sophomore year visit to the York penthouse, but seeing and touching Devi in-person typically solved any problems we were having. Therefore, the next evening after classes ended, I boarded my Amtrak at South Station and arrived at my girlfriend's apartment around 9 pm.

"V, you're late," she said as I burst through the elevator door.

"I brought you a little fun gift I found during my travels."

"Oh? Gift? Come to my bedroom. Now, I'm excited."

Devi, clad in her oversized "Pugs Not Drugs" t-shirt, skipped through the endless hallway and then belly-flopped onto her bed while I calmly strolled behind her.

"Here you go."

Devi snatched the bag from my hands and opened a medium-sized box containing an adorable onesie pajama outfit. It was hot pink with little chocolate chip cookies on it, and the onesie had the words "Tough Cookie" scattered from the shoulders to the bottoms of the feet.

"Cute, right?" I said.

"I, uh..."

"I figure you never wear the Tiffany's bracelet, so maybe a cheaper, thoughtful gift might work."

"It's hideous and childish...but, um, let me try it on. Thanks."

Devi brought the outfit into her closet and closed the door behind her.

"I can't watch?"

"Not today."

Devi returned wearing the garish garment containing a lengthy zipper that could journey from the pelvis to the collarbones.

"You actually look kind of sexy."

"You think? In this thing?"

"Yeah, I mean, you always look sexy, but this is like a new kind of hot."

"Why though?"

"I don't know. I can't explain it."

"Come with me to the TV room. I want a foot massage."

I placed my North Face on Devi's bedroom floor and followed her to the den.

For some reason, during my 24-hour stay at Devi's apartment, not once did she remove the onesie.

Our relationship's intimacy, spark, and spontaneity had clearly weakened for some unknown reason. It could've been due to her recurring family and religious obligations. Perhaps, Devi was stressed about her future. I certainly could've done something wrong. I don't think I was blameless. I didn't want to ask her about it because Devi had a propensity for getting defensive, so I just kept my mouth shut.

By the end of the weekend, we binge-watched *Gossip Girl* Season 1 and never left the apartment. I gave Devi five extensive foot massages; despite disliking the feel of her crusty dancer's feet. Other than that, it was another frustrating stay at the penthouse. She had become too comfortable around me, and after years of turmoil and tribulation, maybe she'd grown tired of me. I understood how my personality could be exhausting sometimes. I wished my mother was still around. She would've been able to sift through mine and Devi's issues and sort out the crux of the problem. At this point, I realized that without physical contact, Devi and I had little in common. I knew that in 11th grade and had buried that thought down for many months. Maybe it was the new drugs clouding her mind? I was entirely out of my element and felt that communicating about our concerns would only exacerbate them.

The final conversation Devi and I had before I left the apartment for the weekend was especially bizarre. It made me apprehensive enough to be concerned about my girlfriend's very well-being.

While packing my North Face in the foyer, Devi, still in her hot pink Tough Cookie onesie, leaned against the living room doorway and said:

"I have a fun idea for prom. But you have to agree to it now before I tell you."

"Well, I'm not doing that."

"You can't get mad."

"I can't promise that."

"Towards the end of prom night, I want you to roofie me."

"I'm sorry, what?"

"You heard me, V. I want you to roofie me."

"Devi, that's not a joke. That's really serious. I can't do that to you."

"I think it'll be so hot if you just like take advantage of me. You'll just take charge and be aggressive and fulfill all your fantasies. I won't be able to get in the way or stop you or anything."

"Devi, I'm always one to make you happy, but there's a zero percent chance I'm comfortable doing that."

"Don't be such a pussy, V."

"Christ, will you dial it back a notch. Where does one even get roofies?"

"You figure it out."

"No, nevermind. It's not happening. Period. End of story."

"You're no fun anymore."

"It was great seeing you, Devi, and I can't wait for prom night."

I gave her a quick kiss on the forehead before calling the elevator.

"I can't believe you won't do this one little thing for me. I love you, Vincent Beattie. Please."

"Bye Devi."

I exited the building, rode in a taxi to Penn Station and boarded my Northeast Regional. It was during this ride I made the unfortunate and lugubrious call to Charleston about the graduation dilemma. I was extremely apologetic, and my brother seemed to understand this decision really ate at me. It was either be the jerk brother or the jerk boyfriend. The deciding factor was two brothers inherently had near unconditional love, whereas Devi and I were more frangible.

I FINISHED MY FINAL PAPER at Harvard and returned home for the summer in the middle of May. I spent the next day and a half shopping for a new tie, pocket square, socks, and shoes for the upcoming Saturday night. It was undoubtedly awkward prepping for prom as a 20-year-old. Running into old teachers and younger students at the event would be cringeworthy as well. Yet, this is what Devi wanted, and at this time in my life, her increasingly rare smile made me cheerier than anything.

I arrived at Devi's penthouse at 6 pm on Saturday the 17th wearing a black suit with a long cobalt blue tie and fuchsia and blue pocket square. I added some gel-based serum to my hair, which was typically saved for special occasions, and I draped myself in Chanel Allure Homme Sport. The final bauble on my person was the corsage I had bought, which was constructed of baby white roses, the type my mother would've liked.

"I'm back here, babes."

I removed my Brooks Brothers wingtips and wandered back to the familiar bedroom. However, on this occasion, I heard Devi's inharmonious voice followed by that of an older man. This caused me to speedwalk the rest of the way before I stumbled upon Devi and a person likely in his forties.

"V, this is my hairdresser from Valli Gregory. They make house calls for the right price. And my makeup artist is also in the bathroom right now."

"Nice to meet you. And Devi, you look magnificent."

She was wearing a low-cut zebra print Roberto Cavalli dress with a slit and blue undertones that happened to go perfectly with my tie. Devi turned her desk chair to view my outfit.

"I knew it. I knew you would wear that tie. That's exactly why I picked this dress. I had a backup just in case, but I was so sure you'd wear blue."

"Cool. But yeah, Devi, I mean, wow. You look...you're the prettiest girl I've ever seen. My god."

"See, I told you," the flamboyant Israeli man muttered to a beaming Devi.

"So, what's the plan?" I asked her.

"Wait, don't sit down."

"Why not?"

"You'll wrinkle your suit. It needs to look perfect for pictures."

"Okay, whatever."

"But yeah, so like, we'll finish with hair and makeup, and then I want us to go upstairs to the roof, and Ali here can take a million pictures of me overlooking the East River. No one else in my grade is going to do that."

"Uh-huh."

"And then we'll order an Uber Black to prom. It's at some rooftop club that faces the Empire State Building. It's so luxurious, babes."

I nodded, then leaned against her bedroom wall, put in my headphones, and closed my eyes. I had become quite fond of Lana Del Rey's *Born to Die* album at that time, but at this moment, her more fitting "Young and Beautiful" began to play.

I actually happened to doze off while standing. My breathtaking, model-like girlfriend chose to wake me with a firm slap across my ashen cheeks.

"We're going to the roof now. I need you looking your best."

Devi held my hand and dragged me through the ample corridors until we reached the fateful hidden staircase that had once been used as a prop in our furtive, sexual explorations. Devi impressively scaled the one flight in her three-inch ebony Louboutins while I lingered two steps behind. Ali's face was one of a man lost in a hall of mirrors. His emotions were a clear amalgamation of uncertainty, confusion, and inexperience. However, I'm sure Devi was paying him an obscene amount, so he likely would've hopped on one leg while rubbing his stomach and barking if asked.

Devi opened the door to the roof and allowed the gleaming sun to blind us instantly.

"Ali, over here. Follow me. I'm going to give you my camera. Just take like a zillion pics."

I followed Devi towards the building's northeast edge. The roof to this York palace was surprisingly vacant of both people and deck furniture. On a sunny, clement day such as this, I would've expected a plethora of sunbathers prepping for their summers in the Hamptons. However, the entire rooftop was blank and grey. I supposed additives were unnecessary, considering the true boon of this setting was its backdrop. To the east was the mirage-like river I'd glanced at on countless occasions throughout my life. From afar, it was one of New York City's truest beauties, especially with today's scintillating sunbeams. However, if I was to walk through Carl Schurz Park to the edge of the water, there would be grime, garbage, bodily fluids, and copious amounts of bacteria affecting the ever-capricious pH levels.

"V, what are you doing. Go stand over there. We're going to start with just me."

I didn't argue. It was her night, after all. I walked over by the southeast edge, closed my eyes, and allowed the unseen carcinogens to seep through my skin.

"V, watch me. Now."

I turned, nodded at my loving girlfriend, and put on the best smile I had left in me. It was distressing to watch Ali fumble with the professional Nikon camera while Devi struck over a hundred unique poses, some of which included near unnoticeable facial alterations. My girlfriend knew what she was doing. She had a gift.

"Gemsbok, do you want me in any of these?"

"Just stand over there. We'll take one together right before we leave. Now shush."

The dress looked phenomenal on her. Devi was a fashion aesthete with taste and looks any high school girl would kill to have. I felt so proud to be with her at that moment. The zebra pattern dress was in my top five favorite Devi looks of all-time.

Eventually, Ali took two couple pictures before Devi and I marched back to the penthouse, collected our essentials, and departed in an Uber Black. Unfortunately, as we made our way up 86th Street, Devi pulled out her phone's camera and looked at herself.

"Babes, the wind on the roof messed up my hair. Oh my gosh. This can't be happening. I'm the unluckiest person in the world."

"Devi, darling, it looks exactly the same as when I walked in."

"Driver, take us to 80th and Madison and wait there for me. It'll only be a few minutes, and I'll give you a huge tip. I promise."

"We're gonna be late. Don't do this."

"Good. I can make an entrance."

"It's prom. You don't need a grandiose introduction. You'll never speak to 95% of these people after graduation."

Devi ignored me and started texting as the Uber turned right on 79th and Park and made its way to Valli Gregory Salon.

"It's up here on the left, driver. Just double-park. I'll literally be two seconds. V, wait here."

Devi sprinted out of the car and raced up the stairs to the salon as I waited behind.

"You watch the Mets?" The driver said.

"Yeah, they suck."

"You know who I love to watch pitch? Mejia. He's the next Mariano, I think."

"Mmhmm...I should go check on my girlfriend. You'll still be here?"

"Ain't going nowhere."

I left the car carrying Devi's corsage, made my way up the stairs to the salon, and spotted my girlfriend immediately. She was smiling without a care in the world as another Israeli man poked and prodded at her head. I walked over and interrupted her nonchalant chat.

"Devi? We have to go. And we need to exchange our boutonnière and corsage."

"I said I'll be two seconds. Go wait in the car."

"Okay fine."

"Here's the boutonnière I got you. I can't put it on 'cause I don't wanna damage my nails, but it'll look great on you."

"Cool."

"Just leave my corsage with the receptionist. I'll grab it on my way out."

I dejectedly trudged to the front desk and handed the woman the chilly plastic container.

"Also, miss, could you please put on my boutonnière?"

"Oh honey, of course. But don't you want your girlfriend to do that?"

"Ideally, yes."

The nice lady delicately attached the white flower to my lapel before adding a much appreciated:

"You look really handsome tonight."

I thanked her, made my way back to the Uber and Devi wasn't right behind me, but eventually did enter the car maybe 12 minutes later.

Shortly after that extremely necessary pit stop, we arrived at the venue, walked up the stairs, and opened the doors to a rooftop dance floor overlooking the Empire State Building.

"V, I'll be right back. I wanna go find my friends."

"Whatever you want."

I perched myself by one of the ledges and gazed out at the colossal steel structures surrounding us. I found the Art Deco edifices to be both wildly impressive and possibly unsafe. Aren't we relying too much on a bunch of Great Depression-era construction workers who lacked modern-day technology and dexterity?

Following that brief tête, I went over to find my twirling girlfriend.

"Devi, may I have the next dance?"

My girlfriend nodded and continued meticulously motioning her arms and torso in that buoyant zebra-patterned dress.

Elton John's "Your Song" was the next to play, and I skipped over to Devi and held her hand.

"Come on. Let's dance." I said.

"I don't like the slow ones. Too boring."

"Or romantic, but whatever."

"Yeah. I need to use the bathroom."

I stood off to the side, not engaging with any of the high school seniors. I thought about what Charleston and my father were up to at that very moment.

Then J. Cole's "Power Trip" suddenly blasted from the speakers. While we had never discussed it formally, this had become our song at one point. My wingtips clicked across the wood floor as I went to find Devi, and thankfully, this J. Cole tune had some meaning to her as well because she ran out of the bathroom and kissed me.

"Now this I can dance to," she said. "Come closer to me."

The rest of the seniors were also more interested in this modern hip-hop classic than an Elton John ballad, so the middle of the rooftop became quite crowded.

"Babes, I want you now," she whispered. "Put your fingers on my thigh, like where the slit is."

"Devi," I murmured back. "There's a hundred people watching."

"I know. It's so hot. Give me your hand."

I placed my hand on Devi's inner thigh as our bodies clenched together.

"Touch me, V."

I moved my hand further up her svelte limb and began to rub it along her body, which was surprisingly devoid of underwear. Devi moaned softly and bit her lip as my fingers traveled inside of her. The dance floor was tightly packed, but someone must've seen us.

Right when "Power Trip" ended, Devi removed my fingers from her body and ran back to the bathroom. At this point, I decided to take a seat by the bar that was serving every type of virgin drink imaginable. Knowing Verity Prep students, I'm sure there were flasks hidden in the bathrooms, and people had pre-gamed this event. The most popular club rats and Moncler Girls would never go to prom stone-cold sober.

After about 10 minutes, Devi left the bathroom and flounced around the room, searching for me. My high-strung girlfriend appeared off-kilter as she approached.

"V, I'm ready to leave."

"Why? We haven't even been here an hour."

"It's just time. I'm not having fun anymore."

"Are you feeling okay? Are you ill? Devi, I'm worried about you."

I gave her a tender embrace, but she pushed me away. My hand then grazed Devi's warm cheek.

"Devi, if you'd like to leave, I'd be happy to. Do you want to go to your place or mine? It might be fun to go to mine since we rarely do. My dad's obviously out of town."

"The Hamptons."

"Now? Well, we need to pack bags, right? Where would we stay?"

"No. I'm staying in the Hamptons overnight with my friends. There's a huge after-party, and everyone's leaving now."

"Oh, that sounds great. I have nothing going on tomorrow. I'll go."

"No. You can't. It's seniors only."

"What? What do you mean?"

"I'm leaving now. I'll talk to you in a couple of days."

I pulled Devi off to the side by the roof's ledge.

"Devi, what's wrong with you? How can you be so cold? What did I do?"

"Nothing. Stop. It's not about you. Just let me go."

"Devi, we're in a relationship. We need to communicate."

"Stop smothering me. I want to be with my friends. You'll just make everyone uncomfortable."

"You know, you don't treat me very nicely."

"Relax. You're a real drama queen. You know that?"

"Hopefully, you're not like this all summer. I'm really looking forward to spending time with you."

"I'm leaving now. Bye."

"Thanks for inviting me. How about a kiss goodnight?"

"No. I'm mad at you," Devi turned and walked towards the door.

"I missed my brother's graduation for this? Friggin' Christ."

I had a bad night's sleep, tossing and turning for hours until eventually waking at 8 am. I had no plans for the day except for a 92nd Street Y workout, so I decided to get that out of the way immediately.

I lifted at the free weights section of the 3rd Floor while playing some hardcore trap music, such as "Surface" by Aero Chord and "Krishna" by Dropgun. It was an angrier workout than usual, but I knew by the end of it, I'd feel more at ease. These quad-weekly sessions had kept me sane for years.

As I finished my third set of pull-ups, I received a call from Devi.

"Hold on one sec."

I exited the weight room and paced in the hallway.

"V? V? You there V?" Devi's voice was shaking.

"Are you okay, gemsbok?"

"Babes, I did something terrible, but you have to promise not to get mad."

"What? What are you talking about?"

"Promise?"

"No, I can't promise that. What happened?"

"I'm telling you this because I love you."

"Oh God."

"I, uh, I'm so nervous. I'm like literally crying right now."

"Devi, you didn't?"

"V, I'm...so, so...sorry. I kissed this guy last night."

"You what?"

"It was just a kiss. It only lasted like five minutes. I was drunk and had a little X. I wasn't even—"

"You goddamn slut," I screamed. "What the hell is the matter with you?"

"V, it meant nothing. I've been so mean to you, and I don't know why. Everything's going to be different from now on. I've learned my lesson."

"Are you joking? I don't want anything to do with you. Disloyal cunt."

"I know. I know. I'm such an idiot."

"You're not an idiot. You're a...a...strumpet. A goddamn filthy whore."

Devi was now bawling over the phone. She couldn't utter a coherent word.

"I can't believe I ever loved you. You're just like, a really terrible, black-hearted person."

"S-s-stop. It was a small make-out with some guy I b-b-barely knew."

"I don't care who it was. Without loyalty and trust, there's nothing there. You betrayed everything we ever stood for. So many beautiful moments forever tarnished."

"I'll make it up to you. V?"

Three different gym-goers peaked out of the weight room to see if I was okay. I shooed them away as obscenities continued to pour from my previously virtuous lips.

"You can't. Not only have I completely lost my faith in you, but how can I trust another person ever again? I loved you so much, and this is what I get? Goddamn slut. I never even looked at a girl at Harvard. I was yours and only yours. Christ."

"I, I, c-c-can come home today. I'll blow you as many times as you want. I promise. Everything will be fine. It'll all be like normal again."

"I'm such an idiot. How could I have ever loved a girl like you?"

"V, please. Give me one more chance."

"Devi Kapoor, I never want to speak to you again. You're the worst thing that ever happened to me, and I don't care whether you live or die."

"Okapi, you can't say that."

"Lose my number. You're getting blocked from all my profiles tonight. You're the goddamn devil."

I hung up my phone, ran into the men's locker room, and cried for 20 minutes straight. Even as the crusty older men strolled by me in the nude, I couldn't stop weeping. All I could picture was my beautiful princess locking lips with some complete stranger, while I slept alone in a tiny apartment as my brother graduated. Devi Kapoor forever altered my life for the worse.

While sobbing uncontrollably in that nauseating locker room, I thought about that awful phrase: "tis better to have loved and lost than never to have loved at all," which I believed to have been Tennyson. At that moment, I would've gladly removed all of my Devi memories, good and bad, simply never to have to think about her again. The agony I felt after hanging up that phone was far greater than any pain I felt following my mother's death.

Over the next few weeks, Devi called and texted me hundreds of times and even sent me another orchid with an apology note. Unfortunately, the calamitous events over not just the previous few months, but the past few years needed to be buried permanently. I never answered any of her messages and believed that my friend, then girlfriend, then ex-girlfriend, then girlfriend, then ex-girlfriend would eventually become nothing more than a turbid whitecap in the vast ocean of my mind.

Book 5

Three Years Later

CHAPTER 1

COMPARED TO THE UNIFORMITY OF the previous few years, 2017 was a monumental one filled with several perdurable moments that permanently garroted my childhood. Even as those around me cemented themselves in their unassuming lives, I was undergoing imperative undulations, reaching both the most desirous pinnacles and desolate nadirs.

My father, whether content or not, was still taking the 6 train every day. This was followed by the same elevator ride and bowl of Grape Nuts and Wheaties at the same desk chair at Sabbaday Capital. The once-promising Morgan Beattie would then return home on the 6, eat his tortillas filled with bacon, scrambled eggs, Planters peanuts and Grape Nuts, and then turn on any of nine different New York sports teams; making sure to boo at the television. In my formative years, I dithered between despising the selfish man and admiring his keen work ethic and peculiar sense of humor. By 2017, I mostly pitied him. Morgan Beattie was a man who shocked all of Hamden, Connecticut, by departing the dilapidated town, attending Wharton, and working on Wall Street. Unfortunately, once his descent appeared complete, he stopped trying. Rather than reach the unimaginable heights his fellow Penn graduates did, Morgan seemed most comfortable with relative mediocrity and a modest alcohol problem that permeated every townhouse or apartment to which he came home at night.

After I graduated from Harvard, Morgan Beattie told me he was planning to move to rural Idaho by the end of 2020 and purchase a modest wood cabin. He'd then adopt an older dog, and the two of them would try their hand at hunting, fishing, kayaking, and avoiding the terrifyingly haunted concrete forest situated less than 100 miles from his birthplace.

My relationship with Charleston Beattie wasn't much better. After college, he stayed in Chicago, moved in with his longtime girlfriend, and took an entry-level position at the hedge fund group, Steep Rock. Charleston and I called each other every season or so to check-in, and he'd return home for the December holidays, but we never felt the bond many brothers grow to enjoy. Charleston and I were two cordial acquaintances who both saw the merits in brotherhood, but our two childhoods, shrouded in malaise, had permanently birthed an interminable, wordless, and actionless argument.

Izzy Rutherford and the rest of my GW and Harvard compatriots had long since vanished from my daily life. Aside from the occasional song or meal that reminded me of a college friend, I rarely thought about any of them by 2017.

Lastly, there was the always reliable Austin Weinberg. He graduated from Bucknell and was immediately hired at Deloitte, doing an admirable job in their blockchain department. Outside of his career, Austin continued his athletic pursuits by playing on a weekly fast-pitch softball team in the North Meadow of Central Park. He split his time between pitching and playing right field, while his former varsity Co-Captain was patrolling the infield behind him at shortstop.

On June 25th, less than halfway through the season, me, Austin, and the entire Antelopes team had just won both games of our double-header against the rival Silverbacks. Following a team meeting on the mound, Austin and I separated from the group and made our way to our respective apartments. We walked side-by-side, discussing the critical plays of the game until we split at 84th and 3rd. He was returning to his one-bedroom on 69th and 3rd, and I was celebrating our win with a protein smoothie from the Upper East Side staple, Juice Generation.

The store's interior was square-shaped and quite puny. Juice Generation's capacity was no more than 10, and there wasn't a seating area; merely a long wooden panel beside the entryway where people could stand, drink from their plastic cups and people-watch out the storefront window.

I was the only person in line that afternoon and ordered my usual Peanut Butter Split, but with mangoes instead of vomit-inducing bananas. After I was handed my receipt, I drifted to the other side of the shop to await my 16-ounce beverage. It wasn't until that moment I noticed a petite brunette girl with sunflower blonde highlights standing in the corner of the store by the refrigerator.

I remember the first abstract opinion I had was this young lady was quite trendy. She wore an invigorating, frilly vanilla Zimmermann romper with plain white canvas sneakers, a white Hermès Clic H bracelet, Van Cleef clover necklace, bubblegum belt, and matching pink lenses on her simplistic Ray-Ban Clubmasters. The woman also had a fashionable, white sunhat that hid her facial features from anyone not standing steps away. Her final piece was a classic Louis Vuitton rolling suitcase that stood erect by her side. As intoxicating as her perfectly-assembled outfit was, I was equally impressed by the considerable amount of delectable power this mystery girl exuded simply from her posture. I looked like a mess of sweat and grime compared to this stately and vintage 20-something-year-old beauty.

"One Hi-Fibe with extra kale and cucumber, no apple?" The worker bellowed.

Then, instinctively, with a headphone in my right ear, I muttered something a little too loudly.

"Gross."

"That's me," the woman called out.

The zesty dynamo rolled her suitcase towards the counter, lowered her sunglasses, and glared at the contumelious, backward-hat wearing ne'er-do-well. In that instant, though, it hit me and may have struck her as well. I'd met this Moncler Girl at some moment in my past.

"Hey, don't I know you?" I said while taking the headphone out of my ear.

The pink-lensed girl snatched her disgusting, green smoothie from the Juice Gen worker and then wheeled her bag in front of me.

"Do you now?" She removed the sun hat, which revealed her voluminous blonde-speckled strands that cascaded down her shoulder blades.

"Did you go to an all-girls school around here?" I spoke with an intrinsic confidence that only reared its beautiful head following a baseball victory.

"Yeah, so what? And what's with calling my smoothie gross?"

"I went to Hollandsworth and Verity Prep. Graduated high school in 2012."

"Oh," she took her sunglasses off and bit the edge of one of the temples. "I was the same year. Weird."

"Did you go to Boxington Dance like a million years ago?"

"I did. But wait, now I see it too. Take off your hat. It looks ridiculous on you."

I obliged and ran my dominant hand through my coarse brown locks.

"Peanut Butter Split with mangoes instead of bananas?" The smoothie worker announced.

"Gross," the girl flashed a defiant, pearly smile.

I walked a few steps towards the counter, took the plastic cup and straw, and positioned myself in front of the Moncler Girl.

"I think I've seen you more recently than Boxington," she said.

I removed the paper wrapped around the biodegradable straw, placed the conduit in my mouth, and attempted to puncture the firm hole at the top of the cup. After two or three tries, I succeeded.

"Wait, you do that too?"

"Do what?"

"Let me guess: you don't want to touch the straw with your grimy fingers because then they'll contaminate the drink?"

"Yeah," I said. "I just always do this instinctively at this point."

"Look, I get it. I always carry a mini-Purell squirter in my purse. Being a germaphobe is a gift and a curse."

The girl's frightening indigo eyes stared directly into grey-blue ones.

"I've got it," she said. "We met in Paradise Island years ago."

"Uh-oh. Did I do anything wrong? That was when I first started drinking."

"No, no. Well sort of. Maybe. You were with my best friend at the time...Adara Zamani."

I couldn't help but chuckle at the absurdity of this coincidence.

"God, this city. I swear I run into people from my past every week on the Upper East Side. Doesn't anyone ever leave this 20-block radius?"

"I'm Louisa Laurent," she chuckled. "I'm usually super strong with name recollection. Don't tell me."

I sipped my peanut butter drink while subtly glancing at her toned, sun-kissed legs.

"You're Vincent something right? What's the last name."

"Beattie. That's really good, Louisa. Wow...Jesus, I must look like a sweaty mess."

"No, not at all. I love the baseball look. Don't all girls?"

"Um, I don't know. Where were you coming from?"

"Oh, just a weekend in the Hamptons. My parents have a house in Sagaponack."

"That's awesome. I love it out there," I fidgeted with my baseball glove. "So, what are you up to these days? Where'd you go to school? Where do you work?"

"Yeah, I went to Princeton, and I'm working on a political campaign right now. How about you?"

"Princeton, that's so cool. Congrats...I went to Harvard, and I've been working at this indie film company in Manhattan for around a year."

"Harvard? Wow, very impressive."

We paused for a moment, awkwardly determining either where the conversation should go next or which one of us should exit the store first.

"Hey, uh," I hesitated. "We should grab drinks some night this week. I'd love to get to know you better."

"I'd like that. Let me give you my number."

I dug into the back pocket of my grey baseball pants and handed my BlackBerry Priv to Louisa, who had a quizzical look on her face.

"Is this a BlackBerry?"

"Yeah. I get made fun of a lot these days, but I don't see any reason to cut bait. I'm a very loyal person, and when I trust a brand, I never see a reason to give it up."

"Huh, I can actually respect that. I have two phones: an old BlackBerry Bold for my job and then my iPhone for personal."

"So, you half get it."

"Great seeing you again," Louisa smiled and then glided out of Juice Gen with her Louis Vuitton in tow.

CHAPTER 2

O N Wednesday, the 28ᵀᴴ, Louisa agreed to meet me at Amber on 80th and 3rd for drinks and sushi after work. While walking to the restaurant, a red-hot magma was bubbling inside of me as I felt this could've been the first step along the road to my hopefully promising future. Louisa Laurent had a stately, gregarious demeanor combined with statuesque looks that made her a more than suitable partner. After three years of morose moping, two failed first dates, and one kiss total, I had finally discovered an infallible young woman, who I needed to find a way to impress as opposed to the more common inverse.

I arrived 10 minutes early and was directed to a table in the back area of Amber. This restaurant was neither formal nor casual, and the food was neither mouth-watering nor putrid. However, it was an ideal spot for when one was unsure about the predilections of their date. The walls contained a mixture of bamboo and Japanese rock collections, while plants and trees circumvented the Kigumi white oak tables. As I took my seat facing the empty booth, I was content with my choice. I felt the worst idea for a first date was to pick an overly fancy place and have the woman feel uncomfortable, underdressed, or unsure about our collective intentions.

To my surprise, Louisa arrived several minutes early. She was wearing an exquisite alabaster off-the-shoulder top with ultra-skinny charcoal jeans and black pumps. Her hair was parted down the middle, and the walnut wisps trickled past her shoulders and made way for the blonde highlighted strands at the bottom. Upon spotting our table, Louisa wrapped one arm around me and rubbed her tawny cheek against mine, while making a "mwah" sound without her maroon-matted lipstick barely grazing my face. Louisa scooted past our table and sat at the booth.

"Gosh, this place reminds me of high school," the refined belle said.

"Oh, I'm sorry. We can go somewhere else if you want?"

"No, no. Relax. Who doesn't love a little nostalgia?"

The waiter delivered menus and waters to the table as Louisa flaunted navy Ferragamo reading glasses.

"So, what do you usually get here?" She asked.

"Well, I typically like to incorporate both some kind of dumpling dish and then sushi."

"What's your opinion on food sharing then?" Louisa removed her glasses and bit the right temple.

"I would say very pro, but it depends on what you order."

"Are you a picky eater?"

"Not really," I said. "I just know the foods I like. I'm a decisive eater."

"Sounds picky to me," she chuckled. "Here's what we'll do," Louisa's glasses returned to her nose.

"Are you ready to order?" The waiter interrupted.

"One moment, sir," Louisa then turned to me. "So, you get the gyoza dumplings, and I'll get shrimp for starters, cool?"

"Yes."

"Then, I'll get the tuna avocado and eel cucumber rolls, and you can get the king crab and spicy lobster avo," she glanced at my irresolute facial expression. "And we can just split a bottle of Chardonnay unless you want to do champagne? I've always been a champagne girl."

"Oof. Maybe I am a picky eater then."

"Where did I lose you?"

"Immediately. I wouldn't eat tuna avocado, eel cucumber, king crab or spicy lobster avo and I've been maintaining an abstemious diet as of late."

"Okay, I like a good counter. I consider myself a problem-solver. I'll make this work."

I laughed at the genuine ferocity Louisa exhibited with each sentence and hand gesture.

"What fish do you eat?" she asked. "I have a feeling this is going to be an embarrassing answer."

"Shrimp."

Louisa took out her phone and started scrolling through something.

"Keep going. I'm listening."

"I'm finished."

"You're joking? You're hopeless," she laughed. "What if I force-fed you some sushi with your eyes closed?"

"I probably wouldn't want to see you again."

"Gotcha. So, if this starts going poorly, you just gave me a way out… So, what do you want to eat? I'll work around your, um, decisiveness."

"I'll eat any shrimp, chicken, pork, or beef dish on the menu."

"Why'd we come here if you hate all fish? You're quite the enigma."

"God, you're gonna make fun of me for this too. I really dislike cheese, so I lean towards Asian restaurants when I can."

"You better have a lot of great qualities 'cause this diet thing is bordering on a strike one."

The waiter returned, and Louisa ordered various dumpling dishes and shrimp tempura rolls for the two of us and a glass of champagne for herself.

"So, what's your job like?" She asked. "How did you get in the entertainment industry? That's so fascinating to me."

"Thank you. Yeah, I'd spent a few years writing for a film review blog and taking film studies classes. Then after graduating from Harvard, I applied to all the most well-known indie companies in Manhattan. Gilbert Blaine Productions was the first to interview me, and that's where I've been for the past year."

"What types of things do you do day-to-day?"

"Well, I just got promoted from assistant to development coordinator within the past month, so my primary job is reading and analyzing incoming scripts, particularly a lot of the bad spec stuff. I'll then talk to talent agents and coordinators and help with the casting process for our movies."

"That sounds quite gripping. I love any job where you're not doing the same thing every day for 40 years. Do you ever work out of the office or on sets?"

"Not yet, but I will starting this summer. We're shooting our next project in Vancouver, so I'll probably be there for a week in August. Plus, I want to start meeting with talent agency coordinators and casting directors in person."

"This is all so cool to me. It's like a whole world that no one knows anything about."

"Well, I'm talking too much. You said you do something vaguely political, right? I want to hear all about that."

"Well, this could be strike one, unfortunately. A lot of people are uncomfortable with what I do. Like I've lost friends over it."

"Well, I judge people based on their personalities. I'd never avoid spending time with someone just because they work on something I don't agree with."

Louisa smiled and took her first sip of the newly arrived glass of Veuve-Clicquot.

"My father is a second-term congressman in the first district of New York."

"That's awesome. And you work for him? What's wrong with that?"

"Yeah, I think it's really cool, and he's the best, but he's a Republican and the chair of the House's subcommittee on counterterrorism. And, I mean, if you google Congressman Davis Laurent, you'll see a bunch of stuff about his beliefs in regards to enhanced interrogation tactics and defense of black sites."

"Whatever. I don't worry about any of that, Louisa; I want to learn about you."

She breathed a sigh of relief, immediately followed by her face lighting up at the sight of a dozen dumplings being placed upon our table.

"Well, so, what do you do in your day-to-day?" I asked.

"Oh, yeah. I got sidetracked. I'm the chief campaign researcher for my father's 2018 re-election campaign, so my primary goal is to learn about the NY-1 constituents and their hopes and goals."

"Wow, I mean, that's a huge deal. You're so young, and you already have such enormous responsibilities?"

"Yeah, I love what I do. I want to run for office in the near future too. That's my ultimate dream."

"I'd vote for you in a heartbeat. From a voter's point of view, you come off as very intelligent and passionate, and you're not icy or belligerent at all. You're always smiling, and you come from a great background. You're also really pretty and have a great sense of style."

"You're sweet."

"Only to people who deserve it...but anyway you, uh, have this certain...regality."

"Thank you," Louisa blushed as she masticated on a shrimp dumpling.

"So, how was the Hamptons, by the way? You know it may be my favorite place in the world. I haven't been out there in years, though."

"I love it so much. It's my dad's district, you know. So, my parents are always splitting time between Sagaponack, Manhattan, and D.C."

"God, I'd love that life."

"It's amazing. The Hamptons house is right on the ocean. My mom and I are always going sailing, and then I'm trying to improve my dressage. My horse, Calliope, is stabled there. And to be honest, I like her more than most humans."

"You have an awesome life, Louisa. Great job, great education, traveling between the two best places in the U.S., and you sail and do dressage. It's all so impressive."

"Come on," she chuckled. "Tell me more about yourself. I get uncomfortable with compliments."

"I don't know. I mean, I spend most of my time either at my job, playing baseball or doing other movie or sports stuff."

"Cool, so what are your favorite movies?"

"That's such a tricky question for me. You know, one of my claims to fame is by the time I was 22, I'd seen every Academy Award Best Picture Winner."

"Oh, wow. So, you're *really* passionate. Tell me a few of your favorites."

"*Gone with the Wind, Casablanca, Marty, The Bridge on the River Kwai, Lawrence of Arabia, One Flew Over the Cuckoo's Nest, Ordinary People, American Beauty, Silence of the Lambs, The Departed* and then probably *Birdman* or *The Artist* so far this decade."

"Wait, really? *Ordinary People* is one of my all-time favorites. It's such a powerful portrayal of family drama, death and mother-son relationships," Her frightening indigo eyes gazed longingly. "I'd watch it again with you any time."

Louisa and I finished our dinners as we shifted from the more cordial small-talk into profound topics such as my mother's untimely death and the disturbing hate mail her family receives on a semi-regular basis. By the time the waiter arrived with the dessert menu, I was already smitten.

"Are you a chocolate fan?" I asked.

"I know it's cliché, but Vince, I could eat chocolate for every meal. It's my one foible."

"Hmm."

"What? Don't tell me you don't like chocolate. Please."

"No, I love chocolate. It's also my favorite thing in the world. It's just, no one ever calls me 'Vince'."

"How's that possible? Your name is Vincent, and no one calls you by the most common nickname? That's bizarre."

"Yeah, huh, I guess it is."

"I like it. Now anytime you hear the name Vince, maybe you'll think of me?"

"I wouldn't mind that...where's your favorite chocolate place around here?"

"I have two if that isn't cheating."

"Go for it."

"Ladurée. I'd die for their seasonal Beurre Cacahuete macaroons. And then truffles from La Maison du Chocolat."

"Maison du Chocolat was my mom's favorite too."

"Well, then she had great taste."

"Yeah, she would've liked you."

"You know what my favorite Maison du Chocolat memory is?"

"No, but I can't wait to hear it."

The waiter came by, we declined dessert, and I asked for the check. Louisa reached into her purse, but I declined her assistance before the gracious girl's story began.

"So, I one hundred percent believe Manhattan is the best place in the world to Trick-o-Treat on Halloween."

"Totally."

"'Cause growing up, my bff's apartment building had 36 floors. So, each year, my friends and I would start at the top and collect chocolate from apartments A through K all the way down every floor. We'd have like 10-pound bags to bring back to my place. But then after eating maybe 20 Reese's cups, my father would offer to take us to Maison du Chocolat for 'some real chocolate' as he called it. My friends and I would munch on their Fine Champagne Truffles until we just passed out on the floor, and my father would have to carry me home."

"Wow, yeah. Definitely makes me miss childhood."

"After you pay the check, you want to go for a walk around here?"

"Absolutely."

"Maybe we can walk down to Carl Schurz Park?"

I hesitated for a moment before nodding.

"You have something against CSP?"

"No, nothing. Just more memories, that's all."

Louisa, looking magnificent in her alabaster off-the-shoulder top, led us out of Amber and up Third Avenue before making a right on 84th. Her Manolo pumps clacked against the sidewalk as she subtly slipped her left hand into my right and grinned.

We walked in silence for the majority of the eight blocks, admiring the ideal 75-degree weather with a few light zephyrs that would breeze through the brown and blonde tendrils neatly coiffed behind Louisa's ears. I remember then honing in on her high cheekbones and thin jawline. After being mostly involuntarily abstinent for so long, I was enthralled by Louisa's beauty. Her sharp facial features, distinctively colored hair, elegant fashion sense, and impossibly fit body quickly penetrated my malleable mind and formed a new afflatus of whom I stood in awe.

We eventually arrived at Carl Schurz Park and sat on a black bench along the concrete boardwalk overlooking the East River.

"Vince, where do you see yourself in five years?"

"So formal all of a sudden."

"I don't know. I'm always curious."

"No worries. I get it. I hope I'll be a film producer based out of Manhattan, but occasionally traveling to sets across the country. I guess I'd like to be newly married by then with a child on the way and then two more arriving in the next five to seven years. Other than that, I'd like to have a house in Southampton and spend parts of the summer in the south of France with holiday ski trips to Switzerland or Italy. Family would be the most important thing to me, with my finances and career a close second. How about you?"

"You have thought of this, haven't you? You know, I'm really happy you asked me out. I wasn't sure what to expect—some random baseball guy in Juice Gen, who I barely remembered. But I don't know, we seem compatible. I've had a great time."

Louisa then leaned over, gently placed her thumb underneath my chin, and pressed her maroon matted lips against my lightly chapped ones.

CHAPTER 3

S EVERAL DAYS LATER, AFTER A few thoughtful and complimentary
texts were exchanged, Louisa and I agreed to meet again. On this
occasion, she chose the restaurant, her all-time favorite eatery,
Sant Ambroeus on 78th and Madison.

I arrived early, wearing mahogany wingtips, blue suit pants, and a
white button-down with the sleeves rolled just shy of my elbows. However,
to my surprise, Louisa was earlier than I and looked dashing as ever. My
date, the girl with the frightening indigo eyes, wore a black sleeveless,
Vince Camuto tie-waist crepe jumpsuit and black Manolos. Her navy
Hermès Clic H bracelet and Van Cleef clover necklace were both visible, as was a gold Cartier ring wrapped snugly around her right middle
finger. Louisa's rosy orange matte lipstick naturally drew me in towards
her booth, which was ideally situated in the back-left corner. I viewed it
as the type of seat placement a patron would need to know the manager
personally to procure it on a weekend.

The evening began with Louisa giving me her patented cheek-to-
cheek faux kiss while we exchanged outfit compliments. Then the waiter
came by, brought our waters, and I ordered a glass of champagne for my
date. We proceeded to chat about our tangential previous few years and
opaque futures while a mutually subliminal seduction permeated the air
around our table. The waiter soon returned to take our orders.

"I'll have the tagliatelle alla bolognese with no cheese," I said.

"May I please have the spaghetti al pomodoro e basilico and no
cheese on mine either."

I could tell Louisa had taken an Italian class or visited the country at some point, given the way the consonants rolled off her trigonal tongue.

"Louisa, you can get cheese. Don't not get it on account of me."

"If it makes you uneasy, then I don't want it. The least I can do is respect your poor taste buds."

"Well, you don't have to do that, but thank you."

"Of course, and this way, we can split our meals, right? *Lady and the Tramp* style?" she winked.

As our second date progressed, I realized how easy it was to have a conversation with her. It became immediately apparent Louisa was wiser than any other woman I'd dated. We discussed Renaissance art, 1970s music, pre-21st century film, her potential political platform, and brainstormed an embryonic, apocryphal project I could bring to my boss at work one day. Louisa quoted 19th-century literary aphorisms and divulged her exegesis of Jung's Electra Complex and how it manifested in her family. I was spellbound as each subsequent word capered off her orange-matted lips.

After our meals were devoured, I paid the bill, and we chose to amble aimlessly up Madison Avenue, walking hand-in-hand.

"Insomnia or 16 Handles?" She broke the silence.

"What? Now?"

"Yeah, I was thinking we could grab some dessert and bring it back to my place. My parents are at the Hamptons house."

"I'd love that. Let's do Insomnia tonight, but they're both awesome."

Louisa and I continued strolling to 82nd and 2nd and ordered a six-pack of warm cookies: two double chocolate chunk, two double chocolate mint, and two peanut butter chip.

"Do you live nearby?" I asked as we headed south down 2nd.

"70th and 5th."

"Are you sure you want to walk that far in heels?"

"Of course. How else am I supposed to get toned calves and allow myself to eat these?"

Louisa leaned over and kissed my cheek. After a moderate walk to Madison, we made a left turn on 80th. As my feet roiled inside their leather prison, I could only imagine how my date's poor heels and toes must've felt.

"We're almost there," she said.

"Oh, it's fine. It's lovely outside."

As we walked past 79th Street, I was stricken with unexpected goose-bumps and a prick down my spine, which caused me to stop on the side-walk and let go of Louisa's hand.

"What was that? Are you feeling okay?"

I dazedly looked around and quickly spotted the sources of my dis-content. The combination of the former Beattie family's favorite Italian restaurant, Serafina, with the odor of day-old truffles from La Maison du Chocolat had wafted through my nostrils and caused a subliminal response.

"Yeah, whoa. I, wow."

"What is it? Are you feeling faint?"

"No, no. It's nothing. It's…just, my mom."

"What do you mean?"

"These were her favorite places to eat. I walk down this block, inhale the weird mixture of stenches, and it reminds me of her. It's the strang-est thing."

"Oh gosh. I'm so sorry."

"No, you have nothing to be sorry about. This just shook me for a second."

"What can I do to help?"

"Nothing. I'm fine. Just a weird thing."

Louisa wrapped her arms around me.

"I'm here for you. If you still want to come over, I'd love to have you, but if you need to go, I totally understand."

"Louisa, I'm really happy we've met."

"So am I. I like how you have this sensitive side. You seem like a really sweet person."

My date and I exchanged a brief kiss before walking the final 10 blocks to her pre-war apartment and riding the elevator to the 11th floor.

Louisa turned the key to 11H, and we entered her family's opulent home that more closely resembled the Versailles phylum than that of my family's 92nd Street two-bedroom. The ceilings were 20-feet high; there was a chandelier in the middle of the living room; the floor-to-ceiling windows overlooked Central Park; there were genuine gold mirrors and picture frames; the drapes were made of handwoven silk, and several of the paintings were pieces that seemed recognizable at first glance.

"Come on, follow me to the kitchen," my vivacious companion said.

We walked from the foyer through the living room to the den and, finally, the kitchen. Louisa hopped onto the marble countertop and motioned for me to join her.

"I want the mint cookie first. How about you?"

"Louisa, this place is amazing. I, uh—"

"Yeah, I love it here. I hope it'll be mine one day. My dad told me my great, great-grandfather moved to Manhattan in the latter half of the 1800s. He was supposedly some big businessman in Louisiana and made a fortune there doing a variety of dubious things, but wanted to raise his children in the more cultured, less barbaric New York City. His son, my great-grandfather, was the one who bought this place in the early 1900s. He was into politics in the city before my grandfather worked on Wall Street. I don't know. It's boring stuff."

"No, it's fascinating to me. I love history. Like, is that a Caravaggio in the living room?"

"Wow, great eye. My favorite is the van Dyck in the den. No one painted portraits like him. He's the greatest."

"Yeah, I remember one of his specifically from the Met. It's crazy to me that a family can own this much Baroque artwork."

"I'm so glad you like the place. I rarely have people over 'cause it's embarrassing to be still living with my parents at 24."

"Well, you know I still live with my dad. It's just the fiscally responsible thing to do. I'm incredibly thankful that I have a certain amount of privilege, and I'm not going to take it for granted."

"Right, well look, you and I could talk for hours, but let me put some music on. Maybe we can unwind."

"What's the right mood? I still can't figure you out, you know. You could play anything from Kygo to Chet Baker to Kanye to Sinatra. I have no clue."

Louisa laughed, connected her phone to a Bluetooth speaker, and played Rachmaninoff's Piano Concerto #2.

"Oh, I know this one. Are you just trying to impress me, or do you actually listen to Rachmaninoff for fun?"

"Can't it be both?"

Louisa jumped back on the counter and kissed me as the piano played in the background.

"Prepare yourself for a crazy mix," she said. "Rachmaninoff then Shostakovich's Waltz and then alternating between The Weeknd, A$AP Rocky, and Avicii."

"I'm ready for anything," I laughed. "If that's your list, I wouldn't be surprised if, like, the Super Mario theme song pops on."

Louisa started to kiss me, moving her orange matted lips around my forehead, hair, and ears before abrading my neck's skin with her teeth.

"Would you care to come to my bedroom?"

"I'd love that."

Louisa leaped off the countertop and picked up her Bluetooth speaker.

"Meet me in the bedroom in four minutes," she said. "Just follow the music, and you'll find me."

Louisa, now humming while carrying her Bluetooth speaker, vanished into a distant room. I took out my phone, checked the baseball scores, inhaled for several seconds, and eventually garnered the cogent fortitude to face my future.

As I wandered from room to room, admiring the invaluable paintings and sculptures, I heard Britney Spears' "Everytime" pulsating from a previously unseen room. I shook my head, chuckled, and marched forward until I reached the unmarked, vanilla door.

Upon entering, I discovered Louisa wearing a gold and silver Venetian mask, her Manolo heels, and nothing else.

"Louisa, I…uh…just so sexy."

"I thought you might like it."

Louisa eventually pushed me onto her California King-sized bed with a navy duvet and climbed on top. I attempted to remove her mask, but she swatted my hand away and continued to kiss me. My provocative date then pulled out a condom from her off-white bedside table as The Weeknd's "Often" played.

I woke up the next morning lying beside the flawless Moncler Girl whose frightening indigo eyes were transfixed upon my lips. It was that morning, when I was half-asleep, and Louisa had exited the room to put on makeup and lipstick before climbing back beneath the navy duvet, that we agreed to become a couple. After our exhilarating first few dates, this conversation was a forgone conclusion. Despite years of social ineptitude and lack of human contact, I was now completely ecstatic and ready to soar again in my newfound Elysian life.

Not wanting to leave each other's company just yet, Louisa and I walked to EJ's on 73rd and 3rd and had a hearty breakfast of flapjacks and orange juice while discussing what our collective jovial futures had in store. For example, the following day, Louisa was being driven out to the Hamptons to both work and spend time with her parents. I, on the other hand, had a softball game and was looking forward to telling Austin about this unimaginable development.

My breakfast date with Louisa ended with sidewalk displays of affection and a friendly promise to text my dashing girlfriend whenever I was thinking about her.

CHAPTER 4

TWO DAYS LATER, ON THE night of Independence Day, Louisa called to wish me a happy holiday. At the time of her 8:05 pm phone call, I was sitting by myself on my couch watching *The Verdict.*

"Hey Vince, I miss you," Louisa said over the phone.

"I miss you too. Where are you?"

"I'm at the beach with my parents and a bunch of constituents. It's so beautiful here." A firework went off as she spoke. "And loud. Wow."

"That's so cool. I wish I were out there with you right now."

"Oh, that's one of the reasons I called. I want you to take off a week from work at some point this summer. I know it's forward, but I want you to stay at my place and meet my parents."

"Really? I mean, great. But are you sure?"

"Vince, I don't make mistakes. I'm 100 percent sure about you. I've been telling my parents all about your schooling and how we got reacquainted and your job. They're so excited for us. My friends are too."

"Well, then I'd love to come out. I told you it's my favorite place in the world. I can't wait to see what your house looks like. Sagaponack is super trendy."

"I love it here. I'll make an itinerary, and we'll hit all the great brunch, dinner, and clubby spots."

A series of fireworks exploded over the phone.

"What are you up to tonight?" She asked.

"I'm...wait...hold on...I'm getting another call from a number I don't recognize. Gimme a second."

I removed my BlackBerry from my right ear and saw a foreign area code I didn't know off the top of my head.

"Hello?" I answered quizzically.

"Is this Vincent Beattie?" an accented voice said sternly on the other end.

"Yes sir."

"I'm, uh," the man's voice trembled. "My daughter Devi Kapoor is dead."

"What?" My face turned bloodless, and the room's temperature rose by 15 degrees. "I didn't catch that."

"Yes, it's, well, it's an unimaginable tragedy. There are no words."

"I'm so incredibly sorry for your loss and for your family's loss. I'm, I'm speechless. I don't uh," my voice trailed off.

"I don't want to go into detail as to what happened, but she took her own life."

"Jesus Christ."

I turned my BlackBerry on speakerphone and placed it in my sweatpants pocket. Tears trickled down my cheeks, and mucus dripped as my breathing became erratic.

"Vincent," the father continued, "we're holding a small service on Saturday the 8th. I'm sure she would've liked you to join."

"Of course I'll be there," I took several deep breaths, calmed myself and wiped the driblets onto my shirt sleeve.

"Nitya will send you the details via Facebook Messenger."

I hung up and started to tremble again before realizing Louisa must've still been on hold.

"Louisa? Are you still on?"

"What? Oh hey. I forgot you were there. These fireworks are quite hypnotic."

"Right."

"Are you okay? You sound different. Who was on the other line?"

I took yet another deep breath, as it was the only way I knew how to console myself.

"My, uh, I don't..."

"Vince, you're scaring me. What's happening?"

"My ex-girlfriend, uh, of, um, what was it like 21 months if you add it all together? She just killed herself."

"Oh my gosh. Are you serious? That's so awful. Do you want me to come home? I'll take the car home right now if you need me."

"She was 21."

"I'm coming home right now. I'm walking out of," another loud boom interrupted her. "Goddamn it. I can't hear a thing with these idiotic fireworks."

"No, no. You don't need to come back. Hold on, let me pour myself a glass of water."

I trudged into the kitchen, filled an Orioles souvenir cup from the tap, and took a long quaff.

"Vince, let me know what you need, and I'll do it. Anything. This is so tragic. I'm so sorry. Where's your dad?"

"He's out with some date, I think."

"Well, you should call him and tell him or better yet, give me his number and I'll call him."

"Louisa," I took another sip from my cup. "I'm gonna be fine. I had the wind knocked out of me for a moment, but it'll all be okay. No need to come back."

"When's the service? I can go if you need moral support. I just want to help you."

"I know. Thank you so much for your kindness. I really appreciate it. You're amazing. Just give me a few days to process this. I'm going to the service on Saturday by myself."

"Are you sure? Gosh, I don't know what to do in this situation. You just take as much time as you need."

"Yeah, it's something I have to do alone. I'll call you after the service. I promise."

"Text me tomorrow to let me know you're okay."

"Of course. Louisa," I paused. "Happy 4th of July."

Devi Kapoor's service took place at a modest funeral home in Queens. The building was a far cry from the aesthetically pleasing palace I had come to associate with my ex. I wore a black suit and tie, and much to my chagrin, Devi was presented in an open casket. She was wearing yellow with large bouquets surrounding her skeletal body. All of the Hindu attendees were wearing yellows, greens, and blues, which I guessed were meant to celebrate Devi's life and not mourn her death. I then noticed a few other Verity students, wearing their most expensive jewelry and carrying designer bags. With each subsequent Gucci and Prada logo I witnessed, my contempt for my high school peers grew. I elected not to approach any of the people whom I once knew and disliked. I did see Devi's sister and felt it necessary to speak with her.

"Nitya, I'm so sorry for your loss."

"Thank you," the college-bound sister responded.

"I don't know what to say. I mean, it's just so tragic."

"I have something to show you."

Nitya took out her iPhone and handed it to me, as a zoomed-in image appeared.

"This is Devi's suicide note."

"Christ."

"You know what, let me just send it to you. You're probably gonna want to read it alone."

I nodded, gave Nitya a hug, and then watched as she quickly typed away on her phone.

"Nitya, I don't know who else to ask this, but I have to know."

"You want to know how she did it?"

"I'm so sorry. It's just been eating away at me over the past few days. I know how rude this is."

"It's fine. I get it. My parents keep telling me we all grieve in different ways," she wiped her eye and continued. "Devi had a cleaning lady come to the apartment once a week. The woman found Devi on her bedroom floor," Nitya started to cry. "I'm sorry...I was, um, so, apparently, she'd been lying there undiscovered for nearly four days. It was an extreme drug overdose. She took a whole bottle of something and left this note by her body."

"That's so awful. I can't tell you how sorry I am."

I gave Nitya one last hug and then retreated to a corner of the room to read the picture of the handwritten suicide note that had been texted to me.

To Everyone I've Disappointed:

By the time you read this I'll either be gone forever or like reincarnated into either a chihuahua Egyptian cat or gemsbok depending on who you ask. I don't really know how to start or end this. I guess I should talk about like reasons. First to my aunts and uncles and grandparents and cousins you never got to know the real me. You put all this pressure on me to be like a matriarch or heir or whatever and never asked what I wanted to do. You wanted me to be a quiet princess who married whichever boy you chose for me. I'd either end up depressed in a loveless marriage or disappointing you all. Not just disappointing but you probably would've disowned me right? That's what my parents said anyway. Speaking of my parents Mom and Dad you guys just left me when I needed you. If you knew me at all you'd know that I hate being alone! We also never did anything fun together. Everything was about work or rules and stuff. The way you guys treated me made me hate you. Um Nitya I'm so sorry for letting you down. I've never been a strong enough big sister and I'm sorry to just leave you. You were my favorite person in the world and I'll always love you. And then there's Vincent Beattie...Some of you may not know who he is, but he was my white American boyfriend and the person I hated most. Vincent I hope you read this. You're a mentally unstable narcissistic unlovable cruel selfish impossible to please lonely miserable loser. You forever tarnished my opinion of guys and were never there for me the way I needed you to be. I hope you join me in the afterlife sooner rather than later.

Here you won't be an okapi but rather a parasite or something like that. If we never met I'd still be alive. I think. But I guess you won and got your wish. You always seem to win don't you? And to all my so-called friends who used me and said I was a brat or spoiled or a retard I'll be haunting you from beyond. You know I will...More than anything I'm just so tired. So tired of all the fake people and being forced to live someone else's idea of a life. And I was never able to just relax and be at peace. Maybe now I can finally just chill and not worry about disappointing everyone.

No Regrets,

The Great Devi Kapoor xoxoxo

To this day, I still have the note saved on my phone, and while I didn't cry while reading it for the first time, I did feel a bone-chilling numbness circulating throughout my fragile body. After reading it, I thought about the first time I met Devi. I remembered the strawberry-watermelon lollipop I've still kept after all these years. I also hadn't forgotten the bizarre game of Park Bench we played where she wound up kicking me onto the stage floor with everyone watching. Then there was our first kiss in the theater bathroom foyer and the ensuing hook-ups in Central Park by the 97th Street transverse. There was the key to her family's fifth-floor studio and the meet-ups at the Columbia quad. We shared so many wonderful meals together, and I particularly enjoyed the peculiar but appreciated teeth-brushing or gum-chewing post-cheesy or meaty ones. I just couldn't comprehend what had happened. I was paralyzed at the thought of a 21-month period of my life being erased completely. I now had a multitude of stories no one would ever believe. I was the only living person who experienced them. It was the strangest, most overwhelming feeling...and then the service started.

Devi's mother, father, and sister each took a turn speaking before the group of 25 or so attendees. Her parents spoke first, while Nitya attempted to follow, but couldn't get through her improvised eulogy. It was unequivocally the most devastating spectacle I'd ever witnessed.

The whole day just felt wrong. Devi Kapoor didn't need to die. There was a time where I could've presented an argument that she was the most perfect person on Earth, and even though that debate would become less winnable over the years, she still had a myriad of positive attributes.

As the service was coming to a close and gallons of tears had been shed throughout the room, Devi's father asked if anyone else would like to speak about his eldest before we closed.

Without thinking, I raised my hand and rose to the front of the room. Even though Devi probably wouldn't have wanted me to speak given her heinous note, for my own selfish reasons, I needed to remove the colossal chains that had been weighing down my limbic system for years. My eulogy sounded something like this:

Hi Everyone,

I know most of you don't know who I am, but I'd like to say a few words about my beloved gemsbok. Look, I don't really know what to say. There's nothing anyone can say at a time like this, and it doesn't help that this is my first eulogy. Anyway, I just read your disconcerting note, Devi. And as I'm now looking at your devastated family and friends, I realize how unbelievably trivial any disagreement we had was. I have nothing negative to say about you. You were the love of my life in a time I so desperately needed one. Devi, as the years have passed, I've realized how well we fit together. Even if we were polar opposites, we were two perfect puzzle pieces. You were always the bubbly and affection-ate and passionate and resplendent and so often just breathtak-ing person. While I disagreed with a lot of your decisions in life and the way things ended between us...which I'm sorry to say, I'll never get over...you still have such a steady presence in my mind and heart. Hold on, I'm sorry. I didn't think I'd get this emotional. One second...O-okay...Um, my, uh favorite memories of you were the simplest ones. Just cuddling up next to you in a park or couch or bed...oops...sorry. Whatever, so, we'd look into each other's eyes and talk about how strong and everlasting our love was. Two soulmates lucky to have met so early in life. For as long as I live, I'll never forget your voluminous black hair and that unique scent you always emitted. Then there was your, um, interesting voice and the way it felt when you looked at me, especially after it had been a long time since we'd seen one another...God, I don't know why I can't stop crying. Hold on...Um...Okay...I-I just wish I could've stopped you from all this extracurricular stuff. Devi Kapoor, without the drugs, the alcohol, the insecurities, and especially the cheating, was the perfect girl for me...Gemsbok, your carefree attitude and the sheer joy you always exuded was intoxicating. Goddamn it. This just really sucks. I know we all feel that way. I mean, I'm sure I could've stopped this somehow. I don't know. If only I were around more. If only we weren't always separated by hundreds of miles. I'm making a fool of myself right now, but let me just say, I love you so much both now and for the rest of my life. My biggest regret will always be that two people who loved each other as much as we did, couldn't find a way to make our love work. It will eat away at me for the rest of my life. It's my greatest failure and maybe yours too. God, I just can't believe you're gone. So many people loved you so much. I just wish I could rewind the clock and start from the beginning. If we just had one reset, it would all work out. I'm sure of it. Two soulmates who fall in love, get married, have kids, and grow old together. I don't believe in an afterlife or any of that nonsense, but I know your legacy will live on through me and the hundreds of others you impacted.

Goodbye Gemsbok.

CHAPTER 5

FOLLOWING THE FUNERAL, I TOOK the subway to 96th and Lex and walked towards Central Park. I felt one final stop by Devi's fabled tree from half a dozen years ago would be a fitting end to the day. I solemnly drifted along the Bridle Path where she and I had once skipped, held hands, and had gleeful piggyback rides.

I veered off towards the 97th Street transverse and found our trunk with the dangling willows that concealed us from the public eye. I laid beneath the tree and meditated for a few moments before deciding to erect a permanent image on my deceased ex's behalf. Using a sharp rock beneath the tree, I carved a heart deep into the bark of our once prurient clubhouse. Then, I sliced a "V" and "D" in its center. This wasn't a symmetrical masterpiece, but rather a jagged rendering of a troubled relationship that needed to be remembered. I closed my eyes, placed my hand inside the heart, and exited the leafy stronghold.

On my walk back to the apartment, I made a somber call to Louisa that concluded with an invitation to her Hamptons house the next day. She had convinced me to take off a week from work and mourn as far away from my own personal Thrushcross Grange as possible.

The following day around noon, I boarded the Hampton Jitney carrying a duffle bag filled to the brim with pasteled evening wear and bathing suits. I was fortunate enough to have the back row of the bus to myself and instantly placed my headphones in my ears to avoid any pedestrian conversation. The first song I picked was one I listened to when Devi and I started dating years ago: "Thinkin' 'Bout You" by Frank Ocean.

During the early part of that bus ride, I realized the sheer magnitude of regret that was spuming inside of me. I wasn't sure where it all started, but the first thought that came to mind was never finding a true common ground with Missy on the sailboat all those years ago. I could've been a more engaging conversationalist. There's a chance she would've really grown to like me if only I'd made an attempt. And I don't know, I should've thrown out that back massager before we delivered it to my ailing mother. I knew it would drive her into a wrathful frenzy, but I just sat back and allowed my father and brother to overrule me. Also, what if I had gone to White Plains more frequently? I could've demanded my father drive me or maybe just taken the train by myself. My mother could've used more face-time with her younger son. Well, and then, what about Raven? What's the worst that could've happened if I'd asked her out? She would've said no. Then what? Maybe a few guys in school make fun of me. Then what? How about therapy? There is no doubt in my mind that would've been beneficial for me. If I had truly pushed my father, he'd have no choice but to pay. I had so much to get off my chest and had no one to listen. I hate to blame my parents, though. During my childhood, was my father icy? Absolutely. Was my mother strict? No doubt. Did they both have their vices? One hundred percent. And Charleston's true foible was his outward ambivalence that trickled down to his younger brother. Those three weren't the issue, though. Then there was Adara. That night in the Bahamas was among my best ever. I fully embraced the jollification of teenage life. I was one of the popular kids if only for a night. I met a girl who was as perfect as anyone, an infallible princess who found me charming, witty, and suave. Yet, I cowered and complained and never took a risk after that magical evening. I was just such an idiot. And a coward. What if I had contacted Adara after our return from Paradise Island? What if we began dating? I never would've broken up with a girl like that. We'd probably still be together to this day. I never would've responded to Devi's pleading birthday message, and she'd still be alive. That eternally youthful girl would've grown old as a human being instead of whatever ridiculous reincarnation she was expecting. How could Devi not be happy as a beautiful, young girl living in a twenty-million-dollar penthouse on York by herself? That would be a dream come true for me. What about GW then? What if I had stayed there and not transferred? Izzy and I could've become best friends over the years. She tolerated my quirks and burgeoning germaphobia. More importantly, though was Mary Huber. Even after the breakup, I could've stayed in touch. I'm sure we would've gotten back together eventually. Mary was such a kind and different young woman than what I was used to. Being with her long-term could've delivered a life similar to Charleston's. Mary and I would've graduated college and moved out to the Midwest; maybe a suburb outside of St. Louis? It would've been close enough to drive in and catch a Cardinals game, but far enough so the always prevalent city smog didn't destroy the lungs of our three children. Mary and I would've been rid of the old and brooding East Coast, from the haunting D.C. landmarks to the sickly, incoherent, and deadly neighborhoods east of Central Park. I wouldn't have become a farmer, but maybe a small-town lawyer who worked short hours and coached his children's flag football, baseball, and basketball teams. Mary would've been a doctor or real estate agent. And I'd love to have both boys and girls, ideally. Three total. Me, Mary and the kids would've gone bowling once a week. We would've had ping pong and pool tables in the house, with maybe a pop-a-shot. The five of us would've spent our annual vacations at Disney World. I would've done absolutely anything to make her happy. That goddamn swimming coach. But you know what? Maybe I need to rewind the clock back to that singular, gut-wrenching, and traumatic moment when I could've kissed Tessa outside of Central Park. She was sexually curious back then, and I was desperate for human affection. That appeared to have been the butterfly effect moment that would've undoubtedly led to Devi still being alive today. Although there were other solutions, I guess. I never really considered spending a year abroad. That may have done wonders for me. I'd take a gap year after high school and reapply to colleges as a worldly 19-year-old. Maybe I would've flown to Paris and taken the TGV down past Avignon and Marseille. I'd meet a trilingual French woman on the beaches of Saint-Tropez. Or actually, maybe continue south to Sardinia and happen to meet a Swiss girl on vacation with her college classmates. This girl could've fallen in love with me and convinced me to stay in Europe and sail the Mediterranean with her. She would've inherited a sailboat after her mother's death, and this girl had always dreamed of traveling the world with one special person. All of the crude oil money her family had mustered wasn't enough to satisfy her artsy, romantic, and adventurous desires. We'd be each other's missing pieces. Or maybe not. I guess there's just something about post-college life that rots everyone's brains. That 22 to 25-year-old range is the deadliest, most influential of every human's life. We all make massive, life-altering decisions in such small spans of time. In half a decade, I built up a life's worth of happiness and depression. Love, toil, truth, adventure, regret, so much regret, and change. Change was a crucial part of life I'd never fully accepted. My life was shifting interminably, and I needed to adapt on countless occasions. Maybe that's what my father had come to grips with? Perhaps during the three to four years of a quarter-life crisis, he realized he feared change. Rather than continue striving to reach the top of his industry, he subconsciously just quit. Not his job, but quit trying to grow. His mind said enough change and turmoil. Monotony was a better life sentence. There was no more need for disappointment for Morgan Beattie. The world was fine just the way it was. He built a life many would dream of and then just plateaued. My father could never be a true role model because I'd never see myself stagnating for long periods of time. I never really had a role model.

My phone rang. It was Austin.

"Hey man. I'm so sorry again about you know...everything."

"It's fine," I said. "I'm not really bothered by it."

"That's good. But feel free to talk to me. I'm here for you. What are you up to now?"

"Going out to Louisa's house in Sagaponack. On the Jitney now."

"Oh, cool. I mean, that should be great. A solid way to take your mind off of things. Nice of her to have you."

"Yeah, it is."

"How long you there?"

"Open-ended, I guess. Seven days maybe. Little vacation."

"Wow, I'm envious," he paused. "Well, not envious, but you know what I mean."

"I've dealt with death before. I'll deal with death again. I can't talk for much longer on the Jitney. They'll get pissed at me."

"Gotcha. Well, just wanted to say sorry again. Must be really tough. I'm here no matter what. Just a phone call, text, or FaceTime away. You know that."

"Thank you. I really appreciate it."

"Have fun with Louisa. She sounds great."

I hung up and realized Austin was right. Louisa was a terrific person in so many ways. She was intelligent, well-rounded, brazen, convivial, fashionable, worldly, refined, well-mannered, caring, kind, nurturing, and impossibly alluring. From her silky brunette hair with blonde highlights that never seemed to encounter a split end, down to her talented feet willing to walk miles in heels just to impress those around her. Louisa's frightening indigo eyes, high cheekbones, unusual lipstick combinations, sun-kissed skin, statuesque frame, thin thighs, and perpetual radiance just made her an unbelievable partner on paper. I'd never met a young woman with such a bright future and concrete direction. Her decisiveness was ostensibly unmatched.

And yet...why would our relationship work out? Nothing tends to progress in my favor. I've encountered a plethora of failures by 23 and a half and have dealt with unforeseen toxicity at numerous turns. Something is bound to go horribly wrong with Louisa. With my felicitous track record, one of us was likely headed for an early death. Maybe a drug, alcohol, or gambling addiction, maybe mental health issues or some dreadful, indeterminate event not even I could dream up. Frankly, though, and it takes a certain amount of self-awareness to admit this, the girls were never the problem. I was always the issue. I could've done more. More of what I'm not sure, but just more. I needed to be better for Missy, Raven, Tessa, Devi, Adara, and Mary. I was struggling with the onerous task of creating harmonious relationships when I was an undoubtedly unusual and maybe unlikeable person.

Then the Hampton Jitney pulled over in Southampton, and I looked out my window to see the always timely Louisa leaning up against a baby blue Porsche 911. My newest and maybe undeniably best girlfriend was the most striking woman in Southampton. She was wearing a chic, white crop top with white Lululemon leggings, pink flip-flops, her pink-lensed Clubmasters, and an obnoxiously large white sun hat. Louisa, also clad in her Hermès Clic H bracelet and Van Cleef clover necklace, was a Moncler Girl through and through.

I stepped off the bus with my suitcase in hand and found myself craving her touch. We shared a palpable magnetism many do early in relationships, but ours seemed to be especially deadly and impregnable.

"Hey, handsome," Louisa lowered her sunglasses.

I put down my bag, wrapped my arms around her, and squeezed as tightly as possible for several minutes.

"Thank you."

"Don't thank me. Ever. Being there for you during tough times is the bare minimum. And I expect the same from you," she smiled.

I opened the car door, placed my bag inside, and took a seat in the currently roofless Porsche.

"I think we could both use a long drive," she said.

Louisa leaned over and delivered a saliva-filled tongue kiss before starting the car's ignition and pulling onto Route 27. As she sped east towards Sagaponack, I felt safe. My face turned left to scrutinize my girlfriend's perky, sunflower blonde highlights. And as she stared back at me with her frightening indigo irises, my mind wandered to the Boxington dance classes of old. Something struck me. Louisa and I had definitely danced together as 13-year-olds. I don't have a vivid memory of it, but there was fox-trotting. We may not have spoken to one another then, and I may have been intermittently cloddish, but my hands had touched her white gloves over a decade ago. And now, as two supercilious yet benevolent fledgling members of New York high society, Louisa Laurent and I were driving 20 miles over the speed limit past Bridgehampton. We headed towards an ambrosial future filled with nothing tactile, but rather inexplicable and imperceptible saccharine nectars and trite amatory thoughts that could quench our insatiable appetites for at least a little while, and after that, who knows?

ABOUT THE AUTHOR

WIL GLAVIN WAS BORN in Philadelphia, raised in Manhattan, and graduated Tufts University in 2016, where he majored in English with a concentration in fiction writing and journalism. During his time at Tufts, he wrote nine short stories, 40 articles published in the *Tufts Daily*, two feature-length screenplays, and his piece, "Allie," was awarded the runner-up prize in Tufts' most coveted fiction competition: "The Morse Hamilton Fiction Prize." He has spent his past four years working a variety of roles at Sony Pictures, ICM Partners, and Marvel Entertainment.

Outside of work, he spends his time watching classic Hollywood films, playing both real and fantasy sports, traveling, playing poker, reading, and working on his second novel. He currently lives in New York City, but will likely be moving to Los Angeles later this year. You can visit him on LinkedIn or Instagram at @wilglavin.